THE YEAR OF THE GADFLY

BOOKS BY JENNIFER MILLER

Inheriting the Holy Land

The Year of the Gadfly

For Ben

You may feel irritated at being suddenly awakened when you are caught napping; and you may think that if you were to strike me dead as you easily might, then you would sleep on for the remainder of your lives, unless God in his care of you gives you another gadfly.

— Plato's Apology

I

PIEZOPHILES

These pressure-loving microbes live in the ocean depths under extreme hydrostatic pressure. They exist not in spite of the ocean's crushing weight, but *because* of it. Without this pressure to fight against, they would perish.

— *Marvelous Species: Investigating Earth's Mysterious Biology*

Iris

AUGUST 2012

THE DAYS WERE already growing shorter, prodding us toward summer's end, when my mother and I left Boston for the sequestered town of Nye. She hummed to the radio and I sat strapped into the passenger seat, like a convict being shuttled between prisons. In the last six months my Beacon Hill neighborhood had shrunk to the size of a single room: Dr. Patrick's office, with its greasy magazines and hieroglyphic water stains. The vast landscape that opened before us now wasn't any more comforting. The mountainous peaks resembled teeth. The road stretched between them like a black tongue. And here we were, in our small vehicle, speeding toward that awful mouth.

From the maps and photographs I had uncovered at the Boston Public Library, I knew that Nye would be a nest of gloomy woods sunk into one of these mountains. The mountain had no name, which troubled me. Even the word "Nye" sounded like a negation, an absence, a place conflicted about its own existence.

My mother (Ivy League MRS recipient and full-time philanthropy board member) was unimpressed by this detail. In fact, she was chipper as a *Today Show* host. "Isn't it exciting, Iris! Starting high school on a new foot?"

"You want to replace my biological foot with a prosthetic one?"

"Don't give me that cliché nonsense."

You mean anti-cliché nonsense, I thought, and switched the station to NPR. I tried to let the familiar voices soothe me, but every mile

3

brought us closer to the hunching mountains, those hills overlapping like the folds of a thick curtain, hiding Nye from sight.

The official reason for my family's move was professional. My father (savvy businessman, befuddled parent) was opening a second Berkshires resort for tourists who liked to experience nature while they had their leg hair singed off with lasers and their eyelashes dyed. The unofficial reason we were leaving Boston, however, was Dr. Patrick. I'd started seeing him six months before, after my mother found me arguing emphatically with the wall. Well, all *she* saw was the wall, but I was having a conference with my spiritual mentor, Edward R. Murrow. (And, yes, I knew he'd been dead for forty-seven years, but why should a person limit her interlocutors to the living?) And because there was no "What to Do When Your Daughter Talks to Dead Journalists" chapter in the myriad self-help books my mom had been reading, she shipped me straight off to the good doctor.

After rooting around inside my head for a while, Dr. Patrick decided I was in the "gray area for developing depression and anxiety." ("Gray area" was a cliché, I complained to Murrow. If Patrick was going to worry his patients with ominous diagnoses, he could at least do so with less tired nouns and verbs.) Of course, the announcement of my encroaching mental collapse sent my parents into nuclear-winter mode. It wasn't healthy, they fretted, for a fourteen-year-old to spend her time writing rough drafts of her Pulitzer Prize acceptance speech, or to show a greater interest in nationally renowned media personalities than in boys, or to make imaginary friends instead of real ones. I'd had a "very difficult year" (hardly breaking news to this reporter), and I needed a chance to heal. So off we went to my very own Magic Mountain.

I'd been watching the trees flash by for hours now, hypnotized by the endless thicket of forest, when our car rounded a bend and hurled us toward a wall of rock. I gripped the seat, bracing for the crash, but the road skirted the rock face by inches and swept us into the mountains. Their shadows engulfed our car like nets and hauled us in. Soon we were ascending a series of slopes, each steeper and more densely wooded than the one before it. Whoever built these roads had confused a highway with a roller coaster, and my stomach twisted with the wrenching turns and precipitous climbs. The leaves shivered, reminding me of my best friend, Dalia, bare-armed and shaking in the late-fall wind. I don't remember why she'd run outside on that particular occasion, only that her father was forced to carry her back into the house.

"Roll up the window, sweetie," my mother said, and the picture of Dalia dissolved in a blur. I stared in the side mirror, watching as the trees swallowed the road. The seat belt held me like a straitjacket.

In the late afternoon we turned onto Church Street. After our long ascent toward Nye, we were suddenly plunging downward as though into the pit of a canyon. Tall, turreted Victorians rose to the left and right, narrow and sharp as spikes. They reminded me of oversize dollhouses in various stages of decay and abandonment. My mother kept her foot on the brake, the car sliding around each turn. And just when I swore we were going to fall into some sinkhole and never be heard from again, we stopped. There before us were three stories of creamy, upper-middle-class, Colonial largesse, complete with wraparound porch and swing. This home belonged to my father's friend Elliott Morgan, and we'd be living here while the house my parents had bought underwent renovations. Mr. Morgan was in my father's final club at Harvard (i.e., mated to him for life), and as he was currently in London researching a book on long-winded British writers, he'd offered us his family manse. A small team of movers who'd come ahead with my father scurried back and forth through the open front door.

I unfastened myself and went to inspect an enormous oak tree standing sentry at the yard's edge. The tree was gnarled with branches that rose above my head in endless chutes and ladders. I felt an urge to shimmy up the trunk and burrow into the leaves. Instead, I went looking for my bedroom. I was to live in the space previously occupied by the Morgans' only child, Lily, now grown and departed from the Commonwealth. "It makes perfect sense," my mother said when she first announced the decision. Perfect sense to sleep in another girl's bed, study at her desk, pee in her toilet? Or maybe we were doppelgangers, since I was a flower (Iris) and she was a flower (Lily). Of course, Lilies were no competition for Irises. Iris was the goddess of dawn and helped the Dionysian masses wake up hangover free. Lilies, on the other hand, reeked of death. Even in new bloom, their sweetness smelled rotten.

I'd never met Lily, but I knew (excellent eavesdropper being part of my growing reporter's skill set) that she had suffered some awful tragedy as a teenager. The parents Dupont refused to provide specifics when I questioned them, worried as they were about my fragile emotional state. "It's in the past," my mother said.

Anyway, I knew Lily's room when I found it. From the carpet to the flowered wallpaper to the matching bedspread, it was colored like a powder puff. I eyed the pink dust ruffle that skipped across the bed frame and the lacy pink pillows. Not only did Lily appear to have a princess complex, but her room looked like it hadn't been touched in years. Most parents turned childhood bedrooms into home offices when their kids left for college, unless a child died young. But Lily was alive and well, my parents said—a health worker in Africa.

I walked by the boxes the movers had left on the carpet and checked out the view. Church Street rose slick and black uphill, sweet for sledding as long as I minded the oak tree at the bottom. Beside the window sat a desk with a monstrous computer and a corded telephone. They seemed like relics from a distant past.

"Iris!" my father's voice boomed from the first floor. "Iris, are you in the house?"

I opened Lily's closet. Had the movers already unpacked the navy blue and maroon uniforms from my new school? No—these were Lily's old clothes, still on their hangers after a decade. Bizarre people, these Morgans. I pushed her uniforms back to make room for mine.

Nye has two school choices for families concerned with academic rigor and social prestige: Mariana Academy and Blessed Sacrament. And because Mariana has been scandal central in recent years (the New England parental grapevine travels at broadband speed), I was sure I'd be packed off to Blessed Sacrament faster than you can say

Jesus Christ Superstar. Luckily, Mr. Morgan stepped in from across the pond to make a pitch for Mariana's academic superiority. As the school's former headmaster, he refused to hear of me going anywhere else.

The absence of dictatorial nuns was a bonus, but Mariana's uniform wasn't much better than the one at BS. Sartorial brainwashing, I told my mother, and she countered by producing a *New York Times* Sunday Styles article about the "hot private school trend" of accessorizing. I explained that a so-called trend in a major national newspaper these days consisted of no more than three people (usually the reporter's friends) doing the same thing at the same time. And in any case I had my own kind of accessories: a smartphone with digital recorder, a reporter's notebook, and ballpoints.

"Iris! Sweetie, are you all right?" My mother had joined my father in the search effort.

I started opening boxes. I found a picture of my junior high newspaper staff and then a photograph of Dalia. She stood in the snow, her lips red as though stained with cherry juice.

"We were calling you, Iris!" I turned to see my parents in the doorway. My mother looked at me with concern. My father looked at my mother with concern. And I wished the door were closed so I wouldn't have to look at either of them.

"I heard you *loud and clear*," I said, infusing the cliché with ample sarcasm. My mother didn't notice, though, because she was looking at the picture of Dalia in my hands. I put the picture down, and my mother glanced up, her eyes damp. My father put his hand on her back and led her away. When they left, I found my Edward R. Murrow poster and hung it on Lily's wall. The poster showed Murrow beside a British taxi, the suave tilt of his fedora casting a shadow over his left eye, an unlit cigarette propped between two gloved fingers. Moments after the photo was taken, he would have zoomed off to report the action of the day. But for this one moment he stood frozen, his shrewd face ready to greet me whenever I walked into the room.

• • •

The next morning, I woke up inside the cotton-candy cyclone of Lily's pink sheets. Sun streamed through the window, illuminating just how little unpacking I'd accomplished the previous night. The problem was Lily's stuff. Glossy magazines lined the shelves along with stacks of CDs including the likes of Pink Floyd, the Ramones, and some heavy metal–type album hand-labeled *Sacrificial Lamb*. I wondered if Lily was schizo, because frilly room + hipster culture + metalhead = Total Confusion. There was only one empty shelf in the whole room: directly across from the bed and bearing a single book, its cover facing out like a bookstore staff pick.

I climbed out of bed and pulled the book down. The dark blue cover bore an ornate faded script: *Marvelous Species: Investigating Earth's Mysterious Biology.* I gently opened the flap, and the book released a puff of dust. Coughing, I turned to the title page and read the inscription: *To Lily, marvel of my life. Justin.*

A boyfriend, I thought, swallowing a pebble of bitterness. But there was no reason to feel competitive. Just because I was living in Lily's room didn't mean I had to be her equal in all things. Not to mention the fact that my journalistic ambitions gave me little time for boys.

I replaced the book and moved on to Lily's dresser. Was I supposed to pretend my underwear wasn't sharing a drawer with somebody else's? I fingered a plain cotton bra (34A) and a pair of cotton undies (size Small). I was smaller than her, but my breasts were a lot larger — so there! Only then I felt guilty; Murrow would not approve of petty snooping.

Later that day, my parents drove me to school for the pre-frosh ice cream social. The buildings on Mariana's campus were 150 years old, according to my new-student packet, and they loomed before us like a nineteenth-century castle upon the English moors. The majestic green fields and Gothic edifices (stone arches, ribbed vaults, and what looked like a couple of flying buttresses) were beautiful, but I felt a pang of paranoia. The place screamed asylum more than school.

We passed through the iron gates and parked outside Charles Prisom Hall. This was a fortress in its own right, and I imagined a dungeon below it, naughty students shackled to the walls. According to my packet, Prisom Hall included the main office, a refectory, and classrooms. But instead of bustling life, stillness prevailed: if I yelled, the walls would not only swallow my voice, but steal it from me.

Beside Prisom Hall sat Mariana Quarters, home to the library, Admissions, the Diversity Center, and the Development Suite. (What in God's name were they "developing," and why did the activity require multiple rooms? It was enough to make a reporter shudder.) The final building was Henry Prisom Gymnasium, its synthetic tennis bubble a glaring aesthetic anachronism. These three structures, as well as the adjacent lower/middle school campus, were connected by a maze of slate walkways that bisected and intersected at the buildings like rivulets. According to my campus map the walkways stretched even farther, beyond the soccer goalposts, past the archery range, and into the woods that lined the school's eastern rim. Eventually they pooled together, dead-ending at a single dormitory.

"Known colloquially as the Outpost," the student packet read, "this former dorm houses the occasional visiting sports team. Our students relish scaring their opponents with ghost stories about the Outpost's historied halls." Talk about overselling a place. But the immediate buildings objected. *We are* all *historied,* their stone façades seemed to say, *and who are you to dispute it?*

Suddenly a girl rushed by me, so close she brushed my sleeve, and jumped into an embrace with her friend, who was coming from the opposite direction. Their thin arms and long hair entangled, and laughter spilled from their mouths. Dalia and I used to laugh so hard we worried that our stomachs would explode. My nose twitched, the precursor of tears. *Keep it together, Dupont,* I thought, and put on Edward Murrow's *See It Now* stare, an expression that said, *Back off.*

My parents were returning to the car. "See you in an hour!" my mother called. My father waved too, but he looked relieved, as though the car were suddenly lighter without my emotional burdens. The two girls had skipped off. I was stranded. What would Ed Murrow do, I wondered, and turning around, spotted a pale, skinny man not ten feet away. He had a sharp, devilish chin and a burst of flame-colored hair, and though he resembled an awkward schoolboy all the way down to the hands stuffed in khaki pockets, his expression of displeasure and intelligence suggested a serious adult. He scanned the crowd, shaking his head. He was upset. Here was a potential friend, I thought, someone who felt as out of place as I did. I shuffled a few feet closer. "Are you all right?" I asked.

The man snapped his head in my direction. "Excuse me?" His voice was inexplicably indignant.

I steeled myself against his scowl (now clearly directed at *me*) and reminded myself that it was a reporter's prerogative to address total strangers. "I didn't mean to pry," I said.

"Oh, but you did. The empirical evidence of prying is quite clear."

The man fixed his blue eyes on me, and I had the feeling that they were zooming in like camera lenses. I shrunk into myself. The way he stared at me, his unblinking eyes sliding over my face like some kind of retinal scanner, reminded me too much of Dr. Patrick. I shuddered at the thought of this stranger navigating my cerebral topography. I wanted to run away, vaporize if possible, but I couldn't move.

Then the man blinked. Now he was an ordinary person with a bored expression. "Shouldn't you be off chatting with your friends?" He nodded toward the ice cream tent. I detected more than a little disdain in his voice, as though to have friends among this crowd was the worst of all options.

I considered responding that I didn't have any friends here, but I didn't want to provoke him. "Sorry to bother you," I mumbled, and hurried away without looking back.

The line in the ice cream tent was long, which was good, because it gave me something to do. I wondered what kind of ice cream Edward Murrow liked but decided he probably wasn't a dessert person. I wondered about Lily Morgan's pre-frosh social. As the headmaster's daughter, she must have had people flocking to her, if only to ingratiate themselves with her father. I imagined Lily as a girl whose life was a string of parties, dances, and dates. And at least one person had been genuinely in love with her. *Lily, marvel of my life.*

At the front of the ice cream queue, the scooper—an older student who looked like he'd rather be spending his last days of summer freedom playing violent video games—handed over my cone and nodded for me to scram. I peeled away from the line and was again stranded alone. I edged through the tent until I found an empty spot from which to scan the crowd. The groups of students seemed to break apart and reconstitute in new configurations every few seconds. It was dizzying to watch. There was just a single person who wasn't moving: the red-haired stranger. His gaze zigzagged through the crowd, but when he found me, his eyes slammed into mine. He shook his head like I'd disappointed him—like I owed him something. This made no sense, but I felt rattled anyway.

When a student moved in between the stranger and me, I ducked into the crowd and tunneled through, moving away from his skinny body and red hair. Then I turned and fled. I spent the rest of the hour in the girls' bathroom, eating my ice cream in slow bites, waiting for my parents' return.

Ever since my mom caught me talking to Murrow, I'd been forced to confer with him on the sly. I stopped speaking to him aloud each night before bed and instead directed silent thoughts and questions his way. Maybe talking to an apparition was abnormal, but I didn't care. I'd read enough biographies and broadcast transcripts to fill in Murrow's side of the conversation, and if I was ever in doubt, I had only to follow one dictate: tell the truth, no matter how much it hurts. With this knowledge, I'd imagine Murrow in the room with me, the two of us speaking frankly about school, or the despicable state of the broadcast media (always a favorite topic), or my journalistic ambitions. It was a stark contrast to my conversations with other adults. Back in Boston, you could put a teacher or a parent within three feet of me, and within seconds I'd be drowning in pep talks and sympathetic smiles.

The night before I started school, I was in need of an intelligent exchange, something to distract me from the strange man at the ice cream social. I could still feel his gaze worming through my head, yanking at my secrets and fears like loose threads. I was hoping he worked in the creepy Development Suite and I'd have to see him approximately never.

It was easy to conjure Murrow. I thought about him for a minute and then there he was, standing on Lily's pink carpet in a Savile Row suit and his signature red suspenders. The glowing eye of his cigarette pierced the dark. It winked at me like it knew something I didn't.

"Thank God a person doesn't have to smoke three packs a day to be considered a real journalist anymore," I said. "It's a disgusting habit." Sometimes I called on Murrow for commiseration and ended up getting persnickety with him instead.

Murrow exhaled a cloud of cancerous smog.

"You lost a lung—or did you forget that little tidbit of your biography?"

Murrow pulled on the cigarette and said nothing.

"And you weren't even sixty when you died, which makes you pretty selfish. Think about how much more you could have done for journalism, and political integrity, and—"

"Iris." Murrow's face hovered in the dark, close enough for me to smell his cigarette breath. "I know you're unhappy about being here. But think of Nye as a challenge. Have you ever known me to rest on my laurels?"

Even Edward R. Murrow sometimes spoke in clichés, which only proves how ubiquitous and insidious they are.

"What kind of challenge?" I sat up in bed.

"Well, I suppose"—and here Murrow spewed a stream of reeking effluvia from his lips as he considered his answer—"that your new home presents a challenge to do more than merely survive."

I looked at him, puzzled.

"I know you plan to join your school newspaper," he said. "But think beyond participation. Your goal should be revolution."

"You should be careful with that kind of commie talk."

Murrow chuckled. "Good night, Iris," he said, his figure growing hazy. "And Iris?" Murrow sounded thoroughly pleased with himself. "Good luck."

The room was silent. The darkness pulsed with tiny crackling dots. My eyes finally heavy, I drifted off to sleep, wondering why I really could smell Camels in the air.

The next morning, my dad dropped me off at school on his way to the hotel, and I walked through the long, vaulted corridors of Prisom Hall, my trusty briefcase at my side. Uniformed figures were everywhere, like in a room of mirrors, endlessly reflecting pleats and plaids. Comedians joke about members of other races looking identical, but they hadn't seen anything like this.

Inside my wood-paneled locker sat a sheet of paper with a newspaper-like masthead.

THE DEVIL'S ADVOCATE
"Carrying the Torch of Prisom's Party since 1923"
New-Student Edition

The rest of the page was blank. Then I noticed a small index card.

Dear Ms. Dupont. Welcome to your very first day at Mariana Academy! We are certain you will find this school to be everything you expected. Breathe deep.

I breathed.

You are smelling the rarefied scent of privilege being taken for granted. Your copy of *The Devil's Advocate* is blank as a symbol of your own clean slate at Mariana. For the sake of this community (and for your personal safety), we implore you: don't give us any muck to rake.

Sincerely,
The Editors

I looked around. A tall, dark-haired boy stood a few lockers down, organizing his books. "Excuse me," I said, following the length of his gangly body until I located his face. (The face, it should be noted, wasn't unattractive.) "Do you know what this is?" I held out the blank newspaper.

"New students get those." He resumed putting away books.

"But what's Prisom's Party?" Whoever they were, I didn't like the fact that they knew which locker I'd been assigned before I did. Meanwhile, the boy didn't turn his head, and I couldn't tell if he was rude or just shy. "I'm Iris," I said.

"Peter," he mumbled, still focused on his books. "Just don't cheat or lie and you'll be fine."

Was the presumption at Mariana that I would? The indignity!

I walked into biology, and like a smack in the face, there stood the austere man from the ice cream social, his orange hair a volcanic eruption atop his pale forehead. He lorded over the teacher's desk, his eyes following me to my seat.

The man cleared his throat, kneaded his hands together, and ran his fingers through his frantic hair. He looked angry, as though we'd already done something egregious.

"I'm Dr. Kaplan," he said, his voice grainy. "I hold a PhD in microbiology from UCLA. For the purposes of this class, however, you can call me *Mr.* Kaplan. I know there are English faculty who insist on the title 'Dr.,' but as far as I'm concerned, such an appellation is bullshit unless you can save somebody's life, which I most probably cannot."

Mr. Kaplan paused, then nodded slowly. "I raise the topic of bullshit—because I will not tolerate it in this room."

The double mention of bullshit made a couple of kids snicker.

"That's exactly what I'm talking about," Mr. Kaplan said, staring down the offending students. "I know you're used to being coddled like toddlers or lap dogs, but in this classroom we are going to treat one another like adults. Do you understand?"

The students nodded uncertainly, but my own head felt paralyzed on my neck.

"What about you?" Mr. Kaplan's eyes whirred into my face like drill bits.

"I understand," I peeped.

Mr. Kaplan nodded and began pacing back and forth in front of his lab table. At the end of the room he paused and turned, fixing those laser eyes on us. "In addition to studying microbiology, I am also an entomologist. Currently, I am working at the University of Massachusetts, examining insect colonies that have been bamboozled by patterns of climate change. And though we all know how much your headmaster likes to have a couple PhDs on hand, I assure you that I am *not* a trophy teacher. I am here to give you something you have not had thus far in your studies: namely, an education in science."

My classmates stared at their desks.

"I am familiar with this school and its reputation." Mr. Kaplan paced with his hands clasped behind his back. His cuticles were swollen and raw. "I know you all work hard, but I am doubtful as to whether you *think* hard. You do what you are told. You strive to succeed within the parameters your parents and teachers have outlined. But do any of you truly know what success means?"

For me, success meant a cover story for the *New York Times Magazine* or an editorial position at the *New Yorker* or a Pulitzer Prize. So what did Mr. Kaplan know that I didn't?

"For the next few weeks," he continued, "I will be replacing the usual biology curriculum with a unit on my academic specialty — extremophiles, the extreme-loving microbes from which all life originates. I am sure you've never considered it before, but at this very moment microbes are swarming in your intestines and crawling on your skin. Microbes were the first life on earth, and they transformed it from a planet with a serious identity crisis to the comparatively stable hunk of rock we know today. Three and a half billion years ago, the earth was a crucible of cell-sizzling radiation, oscillating temperatures, and environment-altering earthquakes. The atmosphere was mostly methane, carbon dioxide, and water vapor. Miraculously, a couple billion years later, microbes learned to photosynthesize. It is thanks to microbes that you and I inhabit a lovely green planet where the atmosphere doesn't burn our skin off and the ground only occasionally cracks open beneath our feet. And the relatives of those very first microbes haven't changed. Some of them live in boiling water. Others can be frozen and resuscitated. Still others sustain pressures that would crush a Mack truck, let alone your own nubile bodies." Mr. Kaplan paused and looked from face to quivering face. "If you think this sounds extreme, you have a self-centered view of the situation. Put any of these extreme-loving organisms in your normal environment and they would die. Just as you would expire instantaneously in their habitats. Any questions?"

The room was silent. Mr. Kaplan stood there looking at us like he was prepared to wait all day. After an uncomfortable moment he started talking again. If anyone in the room believed human beings originated from mud pies, he said, we could pack our things and head over to Blessed Sacrament. "There is going to be no religion in this classroom. As far as this course is concerned, the only religion is science, and the only commandments are the laws of physics. In this classroom we are going to use our minds, not our hearts. Our brains, not our beliefs." He snarled "beliefs" like it was a dirty word.

"You!" He pointed to a girl with curly brown hair in the second row. "What's your name?"

"Marcie Ross."

"Ms. Ross, where did you come from?"

"Uh . . ." Marcie looked both ways as though she intended to cross a busy intersection. "My mother's womb?"

"You weren't listening, Marcie." Mr. Kaplan wagged his finger. "You!" He pointed at a meaty, big-nosed kid. "What's your name?"

"Christopher Barnes."

"Mr. Barnes, where did you come from?"

Christopher sat back in the chair and cocked a half smile. "God."

"You are hilarious, Mr. Barnes. Unfortunately, you weren't listening either. I said no bullshit. And so you'll pay attention next time, you are going to memorize the periodic table, down to each atomic mass, and be ready to recite it in front of the class tomorrow morning."

Christopher's smile vanished.

"Here's a copy of the table." Mr. Kaplan pulled a paper from his bag and handed it to Christopher. "You've already wasted thirty seconds of precious study time."

Mr. Kaplan looked around the room as though challenging any more smart alecks. But even the smart alecks had shrunk into their holes.

"The reason I'm asking where you came from," Mr. Kaplan said, "is not simply because it forms the basis of our curriculum this year. I am asking you this question because it impacts everything you will do *for the rest of your lives!* Your biological ancestors were extremophiles, and I am here to help you return to your extremophile roots — meta-phorically speaking, of course. Embracing extremity will bring out the characteristics that make you unique and independent — *different* from everybody else."

Mr. Kaplan scribbled the word "difference" in large, messy letters on the chalkboard and then turned back to face us. "We are going to have a class slogan this semester: 'Difference is the essence of extremity.' Say it with me. 'Difference is the essence of extremity.'" He swept his hands through the air like an orchestra conductor, and we repeated the phrase in chorus. "Again!" Mr. Kaplan proclaimed, and our voices rose and fell together. *Difference is the essence of extremity!*

When the room was silent again, Mr. Kaplan looked at us, his brow knitted, his eyes compressed to small points. He scanned the rows, shaking his head. "You!" He thrust his finger at a girl in the third row. The very force of his hand seemed to fling her against the chair. "Why did you just say 'Difference is the essence of extremity'?"

"Because you told us to."

Mr. Kaplan nodded. "And do you agree with this slogan?"

The girl shrugged. "I don't know. I guess I'd have to think about it."

"Now, this is curious," Mr. Kaplan said. "Why would you recite a slogan if you weren't certain you agreed with its message?"

"Because you're the teacher," the girl answered, shrinking against the chair. "If we don't do what you say, then we'll get in trouble. Or get a bad grade."

Mr. Kaplan nodded. "Do you know what I'm seeing at this particular moment?" It was unclear whether this question was rhetorical, but everyone seemed to make the same calculation: talking = possible beheading. "I'm seeing twenty young people who are utterly afraid to think for themselves. I see that you are willing to repeat what you are told, without taking any time to think through what you are saying."

"My name is Sarah Peters," the girl beside me announced with a haughty cock of her head. "And you tricked us! You didn't give us time to think about the slogan before you asked us to say it."

"Thank you for speaking up, Ms. Peters. But I did not trick you. I proved a point. You all need to take some risks, even though there may be repercussions—like a bad grade or being forced to memorize the periodic table."

I was surprised to see Christopher Barnes actually smile at this remark, as though his chore had suddenly become a mark of distinction.

"If all you needed from this class was a textbook and an exam, there'd be no reason for me to be here. But you need so much more. I am here to teach you biology, of course, but I am also teaching you how to think about biology."

I perked up. *Yes,* I thought. *He's right.* But the kid next to me, a boy with sandy hair and freckles, didn't seem so convinced. He put his hand up slowly, like he was afraid Mr. Kaplan might bite it off at the wrist.

"But what you were saying about extremophiles . . . Are you telling us we're extremists?" he asked. "Like Al Qaeda?"

Mr. Kaplan grabbed a piece of chalk and started attacking the board. "'Extremophile,'" he said, "comes from the Latin *extremus,* meaning extreme, and the Greek *philia,* meaning love."

He stared at us as though he'd just imparted the meaning of life, but the class stared back with various expressions of terror and dismay. Except me. What I'd just witnessed from Mr. Kaplan was the most amazing pedagogical display I'd ever seen.

"What's your name?" Mr. Kaplan said, snapping his eyes at my face.

"I'm Iris." I swallowed. "Iris Dupont."

"And why are you smiling, Ms. Dupont?"

When he used my last name, shivers scurried up my arms, as though his invocation of Ms. Dupont had transformed me into a different person. I was the focal point of the room. I realized I could shrug and look away, uniting with my fellow classmates and giving myself a fighting chance of social solvency at this school, or I could speak my mind, thereby aligning myself with Mr. Kaplan and irreparably destroying my reputation before I even had the chance to build one. I looked over at Christopher Barnes, who was furiously reading the periodic table. Then I looked at Mr. Kaplan.

What would Ed Murrow do? But of course I knew the answer. "I want to be an extremist—I mean an extremophile."

I felt nineteen pairs of eyes roll in their sockets, and behind me somebody whispered a snide remark about my briefcase.

"And how will you achieve this extreme status, Ms. Dupont?"

I hadn't expected a follow-up, and my palms started to sweat.

"I open this question up to everyone," Mr. Kaplan said.

At first I thought he was simply saving me from my misery, but then I realized he really did want the others to jump in. He waited, and the silence was even more excruciating than before. Was he faltering? If so, he recovered immediately.

"No one has any suggestions? No advice about how we can display our unique minds? No methods for showing your extremity—your distinction from the group?" Mr. Kaplan shook his head. "It seems," he said, beginning to pace, his shoes squeaking against the linoleum, "that rousing you from your collective stupor is going to require an anathematic approach. A test of your courage. A display of your difference." He halted and turned to face us, his eyes glowing, crazed.

Maybe he was bizarre, but I didn't care. Murrow was the only other person I'd heard speak about individuality and courage in this way. In Boston, I had sometimes lain awake, listening to his old broadcasts, absorbing his words, their sounds and images nutrition for my mind. Most people no longer spoke like Murrow or lived by his standards. But once in a while, you came across somebody who surprised you. Like Mr. Kaplan. Or Dalia. Tears rose behind my eyes for no good reason, and I forced my face into the *See It Now* stare.

The rest of class was all business. Mr. Kaplan explained the syllabus. Class participation, including daily exercises in the Socratic method, made up nearly half our grade. In addition to tests, there were interactive experiments and long-term projects. Mr. Kaplan was a young PhD, obviously brilliant, so maybe that was how he'd received approval for this unusual curriculum. But if he was a prodigy, why was he teaching high school?

I was mulling this over when a scream ripped through the room. We jumped out of our chairs and rushed out the open door. The hallway was empty save one startled girl gasping outside the bathroom door. Mr. Kaplan pushed by and walked into the girls' bathroom without hesitation. We followed, only to stop short. Looking down on us from the mirror above the sinks was a horrific face with four eye sockets and a sinister, smiling mouth.

The face was nothing more than a rough sketch, but it was drawn in red dripping paint. I thought I could hear the creature's deep cackle echo across the tiles. Mr. Kaplan's face, so assured just a moment before, was white. Everyone started talking at once. But I just stood there, looking at the ugly image, unable to shake the feeling that it was laughing at me. Its eyes were locked on mine, just as Mr. Kaplan's eyes had been at the ice cream social. I glanced at him to check his reaction, but he was no longer there. He'd slipped away as though fleeing the scene of a crime.

The following week, I put on a business suit and went to see Ms. Mallory, the college counselor. All Mariana sophomores must choose an academic major to impress the colleges, but waiting a year made little sense for my own four-year plan. Before I'd snapped open my briefcase, however, Ms. Mallory eyed my suit with disapproval and said, "Iris, I'm afraid we don't offer a journalism major here. Besides which, all the local papers are closing. Wouldn't you be better off going into PR?"

Defecting to the Dark Side was more like it.

"In any case, Iris, it's only the second week of school. Get acclimated. Have some fun."

"Ms. Mallory," I said. "At twenty-one, Edward R. Murrow was elected president of the National Student Federation of America. He believed students should care more about current events than 'fraternities, football, and fun.'"

Ms. Mallory looked nonplused. "Are you talking about that terrific George Clooney film? That's what I mean, Iris. Go to the movies with your girlfriends. Gossip about movie stars. Be young!"

I could see Joseph Pulitzer having a postmortem conniption fit. But I'm a professional, so I thanked Ms. Mallory for the advice, picked up my briefcase, and walked out.

As I changed back into my school uniform in the third-floor handicapped stall, I thought about Murrow facing off against McCarthy, and decided not to let the newspaper naysayers deter me. There were far too many reasons to preserve the print media: the sharp, sweet newsprint smell and the sound of crinkling paper; the experience of reading words printed on a page. I love blogs and web news, of course: the constant stream of new information, the democratic nature of everybody having a say. But there's something comforting about words that stay put. Words that, a day later, will be exactly where you left them. Unlike the news, the news*paper* is consistent. Even if you go to bed reeling, it's okay, because by sunrise the paper's there waiting for you.

Journalism major aside, I'd already decided to take up the cause of newspaper preservation at Mariana. *Think revolution*, Murrow had said. And that's what I was doing. The *Oracle* had no online presence, no multimedia interface, no investigative team. If I was going to implement these things before I graduated, I'd have to be named editor-in-chief ASAP.

Unfortunately, my prospects didn't look good. Murrow had been president of his high school, a star member of the debate team, and a basketball phenom. But at the *Oracle*'s first staff meeting of the year, I was given the position of staff writer's assistant. (Having the word "assistant" on my resume is like saying, "I suck; don't hire me." Right now, even *I* wouldn't hire me.) Worse, I quickly learned that Mariana's paper is little more than an instrument of the state, an outlet for rah-rah instead of reality. In most schools this would be expected, but Mariana is supposedly run by its students. There are no proctors in the rooms during tests and no teacher monitors in the refectory. The handbook has an entire chapter dedicated to the student-elected Community Council and how it runs all clubs and helps adjudicate disciplinary infractions. Given all this, I'd have expected the paper to be the indispensable opposition. Instead, the *Oracle*'s editor-in-chief, Katie Milford, doubles as the Community Council's senior class delegate. (God forbid that one of the Watergate Seven had been E-I-C of the *Washington Post*!)

At the first meeting, Katie gave the news team an uninspiring spiel and then assigned stories on the refectory's vegan dessert bar and the lobby's new smart monitors. The only topic of controversy, which Katie and the senior staff haggled over for half an hour, concerned whether America was now a "postracial" society, and if so, couldn't the paper quit using PC qualifiers like "African American"? At the meeting's end, new reporters finally received their assignments. In addition to me, there was Russell Murphy, who only wanted to cover sports (he pitched an article on whether the electronic tennis team should be eligible for athletic funding), and Sophie Richie, who only wanted to cover fashion (she pitched a retooled version of the Sunday Styles piece on accessories!). I'd written up a beat note the first week of school and pitched pieces on Mariana's egregiously consumptive carbon footprint, the economics of the school uniform ("From Cotton

Bale to Collared Shirt"), and a Best Teachers package, with service-oriented sidebars on how to pick the best classes.

Katie shot down every one of my ideas. "I'd like to start you off with an obit," she said. "Mrs. Kringle, the school secretary, is close to kicking the bucket, and we have to plan for her demise."

I cringed. "Why not write a story on Mrs. Kringle's life? Wouldn't that be — "

"Obit," Katie said, and turned away with a dangerous whip of her ponytail.

I left the meeting aching with indignation. *Aren't my pitches good?* I thought to Murrow. *What did I do wrong?* But Murrow was a realist. *These are the trials all reporters face,* he thought back. *Get used to disappointment.*

He was right. And I had other problems to worry about, namely Mr. Kaplan. Even though I'd boldly committed social seppuku in front of our class, Mr. Kaplan spent the week ignoring me. Over the weekend I'd given serious thought to the situation: analyzing my body language and whether I appeared standoffish or overly inviting; wondering if I smiled too much or too little. Perhaps this was my first experience of a man playing hard to get, not in a romantic sense, but in the game of mental tag we were engaged in.

My mind frequently jumped back to our first interaction at the ice cream social. Sometimes I wondered if Dr. Patrick was right and I really was becoming hyper-anxious. Or maybe Mr. Kaplan had a strange ophthalmologic condition that caused him to give people the Sauron Eye. My classmates had obviously made up their minds about him. They joked about his enormous hair and his tie that was constantly askew. They mimicked his cold glare and wild gesticulations. But they did these things, I could tell, because they were afraid of him. I hadn't been at Mariana long, but it was clear to me that no teacher had dared be a smart-ass to any of *them* before. No teacher had Mr. Kaplan's fierce energy or snapped around the classroom like a live wire. And for all of these reasons, I believed Mr. Kaplan and I shared something profound. The way he looked at me that first day had been like a challenge: *Could there be a link between us? Are you perceptive enough to uncover it?* There could, and I was.

Luckily, I had a guide—Lily's book, *Marvelous Species: Investigating Earth's Mysterious Biology.* It was uncanny that the universe had handed me a veritable textbook on Mr. Kaplan's academic specialty, a tome that resembled the kind of encyclopedia God might have used to create the world. Not that Mr. Jonah Atheist Kaplan would buy this scenario. Still, I could just imagine the Almighty sitting around thinking, "I'd like to make something slimy and poisonous with three antennae and seven eyes. I think I'll consult *Marvelous Species.*" And bingo—there it was on page 783, complete with assembly instructions in English, Swedish, and Japanese.

The book contained chapters on extreme-loving organisms, adventuring scientists, and philosophical musings on the natural world. Though I was already bombarded with schoolwork, I carved out a mandatory reading period each night to study it. It was like running my own independent study, and I hoped that somehow it would lead me to uncover a link between Mr. Kaplan and me.

Jonah

SEPTEMBER 2012

A T THE END of my second week teaching biology, Headmaster Pasternak gave me an assignment: keep the freshmen out of College Night. This event is a Mariana Academy tradition and a downright Jacobin one. Back when I was a student, we used to call it the Night of Terror. And for good reason. For two hours, students are forced to hear representatives from the nation's most prestigious universities explain why their 3.9 GPA, near-perfect SAT score, and accomplishments as viola virtuoso, editor-in-chief, star thespian, and/or math whiz don't give them a fighting chance at Harvard.

Still, Mariana provides its pupils with reason to hope. The school has one of the nation's highest Ivy League acceptance rates, so it's not surprising that our students rev their stress levels like particle colliders. I'd only been teaching freshman biology for two weeks and already my students were biting their nails down to the stubs and, if their eyebrows were any indication, suffering from trichotillomania. My twin brother and I spent our adolescence inside this academic crucible — I was Mariana class of '02 — so I shouldn't have been surprised when, on the night in question, a slew of freshmen did try to march through the auditorium doors. I simply shook my head and sent them packing.

Meanwhile, the blazered panel from Harvard, Yale, and Princeton were taking their assigned chairs on the stage. (The delegate from Tufts sat at the end of the table, which by her expression might have been Siberia.) I turned to see Iris Dupont moving briskly toward me, her long brown hair swinging behind her tiny body, her breasts bouncing, a wide smile on her little mouth. Iris walked through life like she was leading a marching band. She had a picture of Edward Murrow taped to the front of her binder, and she often sat through an entire class with a pencil tucked behind her ear. Of all my students she was the most eager, the most enthusiastic, and, unfortunately, the most exasperating. If there was one member of this adolescent elite who wasn't going to sit back and passively accept the spoils of her trust fund, it was she. I recognized in her my own teenage intensity. But on the very first day she'd foiled the unity of opposition I tried to foster within the class. I had intended to create an alliance against the despot (me) that would eventually mature into respect as my subjects (the students) worked harder and harder to meet my demanding standards. But Iris bounded across the picket line and disrupted my planned student unity before it coalesced. I needed to regain the upper hand and return Iris to her place in the proletariat. But I had to tread carefully. That girl had ambition like the young Clark Kent had strength, and like Kent, she didn't yet know how to harness her power.

Iris walked straight toward me, and for a moment I was sure she was about to salute. I prepared to bar her way, but then her parents strode up, seemingly out of nowhere, clearing her a path through the doors. The Duponts presented as a nondescript pair in their well-tailored suits, but their simple looks were deceiving. I knew from frequent mentions at the last faculty meeting that these two were Superparents: parental mutants whose excess of money and social clout made them myopically bent on their child's protection and success.

As Mr. Dupont walked by, he looked me over like he was appraising a watch. As Iris passed, she smiled, but I returned the uncompromising frown that was quickly making me notorious among the student body.

On the auditorium stage Headmaster Pasternak had stepped up to the lectern, his body rickety but implacable, like a battered fence that refuses to fall down. He'd been my junior-year English teacher, and even then he was a crusty old man who didn't teach so much as creak. I remember him churning through the hallways, scattering students to their classrooms with all the force of a manual lawnmower. He was appointed assistant headmaster after I graduated, and when Elliott Morgan, the previous HM, retired, Pasternak took over the post.

"I am delighted to see such a strong turnout for tonight's event," Pasternak intoned.

As if a single junior or junior parent would pass on the opportunity to soak up even a droplet of sweat perspired from the foreheads of these panelists. And Pasternak knew it. He'd done everything in his power to cement Mariana's place as the paragon of New England prep schools, including a new College-Based Education Initiative geared to giving Mariana students the upper hand in a college admissions system that had spun out of control. Not only would students declare academic majors, but standard courses like biology would also have specializations, such as microbiology. When Pasternak learned that I was involved with the UMass entomology project (the man has spies scouring half the educational institutions in the Northeast), he offered me a position and a hefty salary for my trouble.

My UMass grant was pitifully small and the work didn't even start until spring, so I welcomed the money. But there was another reason I agreed to come. As a student I'd never been given a fair shot at this school, and I liked the idea of returning with total immunity. So here I was, exonerated from my boyhood improprieties and energized as I hadn't been in ages. If the classroom was a cell, then I was its nucleus. The feeling thrilled me.

"As we all know," Pasternak announced, raising his arms as though he stood before the waters of the Red Sea, "Mariana is committed to helping Jimmy Cardozi battle his leukemia through the Jimmy Get Well campaign."

Cardozi was a scholarship kid whose parents couldn't pay his medical bills. The school had set up a lockbox in the lobby for donations, and two student clubs had formed to raise money — the Leukemia Sux Society and Students Against Fatal Diseases. Noble efforts, but I worried that the kids didn't understand their mission. As far as I knew, not a single member of either club had visited Jimmy Cardozi in the hospital. And the fundraising had become competitive, with both groups announcing their contribution totals at every assembly. They'd even begun hanging up negative ad campaigns accusing each other of pocketing contribution money. Pasternak had ordered the clubs to quit their adversarial practices, but the battle just transitioned from the school hallways to the Internet. Pasternak couldn't be happy about this, but he was taking an "out of sight, out of mind" approach to the matter. It seemed to be his current modus operandi. He'd said nothing about the bathroom vandalism (the demonic image had appeared on half the school's mirrors by midday), and after nobody came forward to snitch, he had the janitor clean off the paint.

"Our school is an emblem of selflessness and generosity," Pasternak bellowed to the juniors, their parents, and the lone freshman, Iris Dupont. "And the reason, as you all know, is our Community Code: *Brotherhood, Truth, and Equality for All.*"

Perhaps, but from what my colleagues in the science department had told me, the pressure to succeed academically and socially was so intense that kids also kept covert spreadsheets of each other's SAT scores and conducted shady business deals to obtain coveted refectory real estate. And, as in my own student days, we still had an underclass of kids who were taunted, shunned, and generally denied desirable positions on teams and clubs because they were socially awkward or refused to conform. Every school has such an underclass, but not every school claimed to champion equality and brotherhood the way Mariana did.

And not every high-profile prep school had porn addicts on its staff. Rumor had it that my predecessor, Mr. Franks, was fired for masturbating to anime porn on his office computer. Apparently, over the summer, somebody sent Headmaster Pasternak photos of him *in medias res.* I doubted the veracity of these rumors. Still, I'd already swapped out my desk chair for one in the supply room and wiped down my keyboard with disinfectant.

When Pasternak stepped down, the college reps began introducing themselves. I was supposed to stick around for the meet and greet afterward, but I needed to listen to these scarecrows like I needed a shot of sulfuric acid in the eye. I slipped into the hallway. As I passed the back stairwell, I paused. At the bottom of these stairs was a black door, and behind it the Trench. The Trench once housed the office of the Academic League, a *Jeopardy*-like quiz bowl team that had defined my student life at Mariana. Along with my brother, Justin, our friend Hazel Greenburg, and the rest of the AL team, I'd spent all my time there. The Trench had been closed for a long time, and though I was curious to revisit my old habitat, I was also wary of opening locked doors. Besides, all the people who had once made that place home were gone.

I fished my gloves, hat, and scarf out of my satchel. At 5 p.m. the daylight sagged with defeat. Justin called this hour the gloaming. He had the romantic's tendency to commemorate a melancholy moment and especially loved dredging up words no one had spoken since the fourteenth century. Nye in winter was the perfect place for such despondency. Our freshman year, he'd suggested that our town welcome sign read, *Nye, Massachusetts, Population 9,000 — Open for Suicide, October thru May.* Prescient words these, though I didn't know it then.

I stuffed my scarf into my jacket and tucked my coat sleeves into my gloves. The wind-chill in Nye is like a pack of hornets zeroing in on your neck, a smart missile programmed to find even the smallest patch of exposed skin. My protective layers finally in place, I pushed into the cold, but after a few steps something compelled me to turn back. In the door's glass window I glimpsed the inquisitive eyes of Iris Dupont ducking out of sight.

On the first day of school, she'd announced her intention to become an extremophile. I hoped to teach her that extremity was already in her DNA — that it was the legacy of life's earliest forms. How was it, I wondered as I climbed into the car and turned on the heat full blast, that humans had adapted to conform, long after such conformity was necessary or even advantageous? I stomped my feet to warm them. My students needed to learn new survival traits — how to speak up, break out—but instead of eons, they had only a handful of semesters in which to educate themselves.

I pulled out of the faculty lot and onto the road. I would give my students a test, I decided, an exam that demanded their individuation. It would be painful for them. But tests of survival usually are.

Iris

O N KATIE MILFORD'S orders, I started reporting Marthella Kringle's obit. All the major papers have pre-mortem obituaries on file for the world's most famous and infamous personalities, which is morbid but necessary in a time crunch. As for the *Oracle* — no intelligent person would ever turn to Mariana's rag for breaking news. Nor could they; the paper appeared only every few months.

I went to see Mrs. Kringle in the school office, where she answers phones, and sat down with my notepad and recorder in hand. She wore a high-necked black dress and tights that resembled Ace bandages. Her old-woman bosom rested on her lap like a sack of potatoes. She yawned and her onionskin face crackled.

"Iris Dupont," she intoned the second I planted my butt in the chair, "formerly of Boston, currently residing at 95 Church, childhood home of Lillian Morgan, daughter to the former headmaster."

I gaped, but Mrs. Kringle looked unfazed. "I know the name, address, and class schedule of every student at this school, Ms. Dupont. It is my particular talent. I also know that you are here to extract my life story for an article to be published on the occasion of my eventual expiration, but I will tell you right now, my life is private, besides which I do not trust reporters. Especially novices."

She glared at me over her wire-rimmed glasses. They were pushed so far down her nose, I was afraid they'd fall off. *Murrow,* I begged silently, *how do you cajole an unwilling source?*

"However," Mrs. Kringle continued, "since you are new here, I will take pity on you and relate a few details." And before I could stop her, she'd launched into a history lesson.

"In the mid-nineteenth century," she said, her voice sounding like a rubber band pulled to the point of snapping, "when Charles Prisom was young, an awful stutter subjected him to horrific ridicule at his New Hampshire boarding school. In his letters Prisom recounted an experience of spectacular cruelty in which a couple of nasty boys decided to fix his stutter for good. One night, they burst into his room, held him down upon the bed, and tied a string around his tongue. Then they began to pull. This experiment succeeded in rupturing the central muscle of Prisom's tongue, and for months he couldn't speak at all. When the muscle finally healed, he was left with a pronounced lisp, but the stutter"—Mrs. Kringle nodded emphatically—"was gone."

"There are letters?" I asked.

Mrs. Kringle eyed me through her glasses, thick as double-paned windows. "I believe Elliott Morgan is in possession of some. He has quite a collection of local artifacts." Mrs. Kringle leaned toward me with a conspiratorial air. She smelled of lemons. "Who knows what you might find, poking around that house." Then she sat back, business-like. "You'll find the other letters at the Nye Historical Society." She scratched her cheek, and I was terrified her nail would rip through the skin.

"After that dreadful experience," she continued, "Prisom vowed to create a school where no child would ever be subjected to such terror. When he was just twenty-two, his beloved mother, Mariana Prisom, passed away, but her financial legacy enabled him to found an all-boys boarding school in her name. Mariana Academy. The school's motto was 'Brotherhood, Truth, and Equality for All.' He used the remainder of his mother's legacy to fund the tuition of underprivileged students. This was in 1885. And I will tell you that at that time such a project was unheard of."

"Did you know Charles Prisom?" I asked.

"Miss Dupont!" Mrs. Kringle's eyelids shot up like window shades. "How old do you think I am?"

I shrank back in my chair. "Not a day over twenty-five."

Mrs. Kringle smiled, the corners of her frown lifting as though by some mechanical apparatus inside of her mouth.

"So what happened to Charles Prisom?"

She shook her head like I was an especially foolish person. "He died, of course."

"I meant before that . . ."

She sighed. "In 1907, his son Henry assumed leadership of the school. And then . . ." Mrs. Kringle's eyes grew bleary as she gazed into the middle distance. "Well, 1921 was not a good year. It was the beginning of the end."

"What do you mean?" I perked up.

Mrs. Kringle leaned forward over her breasts, coming close enough that I could see the profusion of wrinkles etched into the skin around her mouth. "This school is nothing like it once was, what with all the grade grubbing and backbiting and lip locking. And of course, that Prisom's Party is driving us all halfway to Halifax! It all goes back to those nasty upheavals and the school's closing."

Prisom's Party had left the blank newspaper in my locker, but I still had no idea who or what they were. "What nasty upheavals?" I asked. "Why did the school close?"

My need to know yanked me forward, but Mrs. Kringle looked up as though just noticing me. "Miss Dupont!" she exclaimed. "You are late for science."

Specifically, I was late for my first science exam, an event that Mr. Kaplan promised would "put the fear of gravity" into all of us "self-assured, overachieving novitiates." When handing out assignments, my other teachers loved detailing their bullet points with bullet points, but Mr. Kaplan had provided no guidelines whatsoever. "Human nature will guide you," was all he said.

I hurried from Mrs. Kringle's office to the science lab and found a note on the door instructing our class to convene outside the theater. This was odd, but sure enough, Mr. Kaplan was waiting for us before the doors, stiff as a Buckingham Palace guard. Beside him stood a woman in a white lab coat. She wore her brown hair in a low, sleek ponytail and had the airbrushed face of an actress in a pharmaceutical commercial.

"This is Dr. Van Laark," Mr. Kaplan said when the class had finally assembled. "She's a professor of educational psychology at the University of Massachusetts and a colleague of mine from graduate school. As it turns out, her research dovetails quite nicely with my educational project for you all, in particular the discussion we were having on the first day of class about difference. Remember our slogan? 'Difference is the essence of extremity.'"

The class nodded unhappily. Mr. Kaplan smiled. "Dr. Van Laark's work concerns behavioral demonstrations of obedience among emerging adults. I told her there was no collection of intellectually buzzing brains better suited to helping her research and the advancement of science than you all."

Dr. Van Laark nodded, her bright eyes flitting from face to face. "I'm not at liberty to provide specifics about my experiment in advance," she said. "Except that you will find it a mentally challenging and rewarding experience." She handed out release forms. "These signify your consent. All information collected is strictly confidential."

"And if we don't want to participate?" said Stephen Fry, whose lips were always chapped and flaking.

"Then you can use this double period as a study hall," Mr. Kaplan said. "There's no penalty for sitting out, but I'd encourage everyone to participate."

"And our test?" a bunch of people asked at once.

"This is your test."

"But we didn't study for *this!*" Marcie Ross protested.

"Oh, but you did." Mr. Kaplan nodded slowly. "Just remember our slogan—'Difference is the essence of extremity'—and you'll do fine."

"You will be participating in pairs of two," Dr. Van Laark said before anyone could interject again.

"Safety in numbers," Mr. Kaplan mumbled. I tried to catch his eye, but he wouldn't look at me.

"As the release form specifies, you are not to observe any part of the experiment until it is your turn. You are also not to talk about it until everyone has participated."

My pen wavered over the signature line. *Murrow,* I thought, *something isn't right.* Then a shadow fell over me, and I looked up to see Mr. Kaplan. I scribbled my name and thrust the paper at him. "Very good," he said, and for a moment there was that challenge: *I know you, but do you know me?*

"First up," Mr. Kaplan said, shuffling through the release forms, "are Stacey Markson and Jeremy Binder."

They stood up and followed the adults into the theater. For a few minutes people speculated about what was happening inside. Stephen Fry pressed his ear to the door and announced that he heard nothing, so I pulled out *Marvelous Species.* I'd been carrying the book around school. It was heavy, but I didn't mind. I liked to have it available in case I ran into Mr. Kaplan between classes. That way, I could surreptitiously slip the book into his line of sight. On the days I had biology, I made sure to be reading it when Mr. Kaplan came to class. He usually arrived early to set up, which meant that if I got there first, we'd be the only two people in the room for a good three or four minutes. The advantages of this were twofold. First, it allowed Mr. Kaplan to see how serious I was about his class. Second, it let him catch me absorbed in what was clearly nonrequired reading. This, I hoped, would pique his curiosity. Sure, I could wag the book in his face and say, *See what* I'm *reading, Mr. Kaplan!* But that was crass. Much more subtle for him to see me perusing the yellowed pages and wonder, *What's that girl up to? She's not like the others.*

The theater doors finally opened, and I instantly raised *Marvelous*

Species in front of my face. When I didn't hear Mr. Kaplan's voice, however, I put the book down. Stacey and Jeremy had just come out, and they looked horribly upset.

"Jesus," Chris Coon whispered. "What's going on in there?"

"They probably answered all the questions wrong," said David Morone, looking up from *Heart of Darkness*. "I bet a hot professor chick like Van Laark gets off on making her subjects feel dumb."

Mr. Kaplan appeared. He scanned our faces, saw me sitting on the ground like all the others, which is to say reading absolutely *nothing*, and called for the next two students. "A word of advice," he added. "Difference is the essence of extremity." A bunch of people groaned, but Mr. Kaplan just smiled and shut the theater door.

I resumed my reading, but Mr. Kaplan's slogan kept doing a little tap dance in my head. I searched for the phrase on my phone and, sure enough, the third hit directed me to a page titled "Famous Sayings of Molecular Philosophy," where I read:

> "Difference is the essence of extremity" was coined by Dr. Lucinda Starburst, shortly before her death in 1994.

Lucinda Starburst, I thought. How could such an odd name sound so familiar?

> Dr. Starburst's pioneering role in the field of molecular philosophy has had far-reaching implications throughout the scientific world. Before she died, she oversaw the founding of a new publication, the *Journal of Extreme Studies,* published by the University of Massachusetts.

I saved this page and ran a search for UMass and the *Journal of Extreme Studies*. Up popped a black-and-white photo of none other than Dr. Van Laark. First on her list of academic papers was an article titled "Eichmann and the Extremity of Obedience." The Eichmann reference brought to mind Murrow's description of Buchenwald in 1945, the "rows of bodies stacked up like cordwood." I felt queasy and had to close my eyes. *What's Dr. Van Laark doing with us?* I thought. *What's*

Mr. Kaplan doing with us? And why do I recognize the name Lucinda Starburst?

At that moment Kelly McGuinty rushed from the theater. Harrison Cox emerged after her, head hung, looking like a pebble that somebody had kicked in frustration. My stomach began a slow, funnel-like churn. Maybe I could peek in the back door of the theater or, if that was locked, sneak into the sound booth. *But you've signed the release form,* Murrow whispered. *You've given your word.*

"Sarah Peters and Iris Dupont." Mr. Kaplan's voice cut through the hall.

Sarah stood up and rolled her eyes. "Bringing your briefcase?" She laughed and headed through the doors.

Home to one-acts and plays, Mariana's theater is called the Black Box. It's utterly unlike the auditorium (used for assemblies and musicals), upon whose polished stage you'd expect to see a soprano with serious décolletage belting out high Cs. The Black Box has no formal stage; the design students build new sets for each production, and the school's website boasts pictures of student actors soliloquizing from suspended catwalks and in boats floating on water. Right now, though, the room was chilly and dark. It was difficult to orient myself because the four walls were mirror images of one another. I felt trapped, and yet something about the Black Box felt vast, as though the tangle of black wires and lights above me expanded into infinity.

Dr. Van Laark's lab coat was startlingly bright in the darkness. She stood beside a machine that resembled a sound mixing board but had fewer buttons. Next to each button was a number, starting with 20 and increasing by intervals to 200. On the side of the machine, a label read: *Control Panel. Property of UMass. Unauthorized Use Prohibited.* Dr. Van Laark led us around a divider in the center of the room. On the opposite side was a second strange machine. This one resembled a stereo. Two wires protruded from the front. On the end of these wires were wrist cuffs. The funnel in my stomach was picking up speed, like the beginning of a small-scale tornado. I looked at Mr. Kaplan, but his face was blank.

"Thank you again for participating, girls," Dr. Van Laark said, her lips curving into a fruit slice of a smile. "In a moment, you will select slips of paper with a designation—interviewer or subject. The subject will sit here and wear the cuffs. The interviewer will sit in front of the control panel and read questions from a list. For every question the subject gets wrong, the interviewer will press a button, giving a slight shock. It's no more than a slight buzz and totally harmless. All right?"

"And then what?" Sarah asked. "What are you trying to prove?"

The little tornado in my stomach gained speed, but Mr. Kaplan's dispassionate expression reassured me. "Just a little shock?" I asked.

"Totally harmless," Dr. Van Laark repeated.

Sarah and I flashed competing glances at each other; neither of us wanted to be the subject. But then I thought about the kids who'd come before us and emerged looking so upset—all four of them, come to think of it, not just the two subjects. Maybe they were *instructed* to act upset. Maybe all of this was some kind of psychology trick in which the people outside of the Black Box were really the experiment subjects. *What do you think, Murrow,* I wondered. *Is that the catch?*

"Sarah," Dr. Van Laark was saying, "why don't you select first."

Sarah plucked a strip of paper from Dr. Van Laark's palm. "Interviewer," she announced, like she'd won a prize.

There was only one other option, but I picked up my paper anyway.

"Have fun, Subject," Sarah scoffed, as Mr. Kaplan led her around the divider.

"Iris," Dr. Van Laark said, "please take a seat."

I looked at the wrist cuffs, my heart beating fast. Dr. Van Laark opened a laptop, and Mr. Kaplan and Sarah appeared on its screen.

"Now, Sarah," he was saying. "You should press a higher-numbered button for every question Iris gets wrong. These deliver increasingly stronger volts."

I looked in horror at Dr. Van Laark and was about to protest when she put her finger to her lips. Then she leaned down, so close that I could smell her perfume. It was deep and sweet, like a rare, intoxicating flower. "The machines are fake," she whispered. "You won't even wear the cuffs, but for each question you get wrong, you must give an increasingly strong reaction. Twenty volts should be a relatively minor yelp. The higher we go, the more intense. Here's a sheet with suggested responses. Understand?" She placed the instructions before me.

So that's the catch, I thought. *The interviewer thinks she's in control, when really* she's *the subject.* Mr. Kaplan glanced at the video camera that was recording the scene on his side of the divider, and I swear he was looking right at me, his expression full of intimate understanding. For the first time since coming to Nye, I felt confident, even powerful.

Mr. Kaplan handed Sarah a stack of note cards. She flipped the first one over and asked me a question about piezophiles, microorganisms able to withstand extreme pressure. I answered correctly. She asked a second question about piezophiles. Also right. I'd studied a lot over the weekend. I got the third question wrong, but it required a mathematical equation, and I didn't have a pen. "Administer twenty volts," Mr. Kaplan said. Sarah pressed the button and it buzzed.

"Kind of tickles," I said, reading from Dr. Van Laark's response sheet. On the monitor, Sarah chuckled.

I answered the next two questions, about halophiles, right. Then I goofed a second time.

"Administer forty volts," Mr. Kaplan said. Sarah pushed the button and I gave the instructed yelp. Sarah smiled, but she looked uncomfortable.

Dr. Van Laark nodded at me. "Just like that," she whispered. "You're doing great."

I answered the next question incorrectly, too. It didn't matter, but I didn't like being wrong twice in a row. Meanwhile, Mr. Kaplan was asking Sarah to administer sixty volts. When she buzzed, I groaned, louder this time. Too loud.

"She's okay?" Sarah asked.

"Please continue," Mr. Kaplan said, his voice emotionless.

The next two questions related to extremophiles I'd never even heard of, so of course I answered wrong. Sarah buzzed. I moaned. She buzzed again, and I moaned louder. Both times she shut her eyes as she pressed the button, like she didn't want to see what her own finger was doing.

And it was then — around eighty volts — that I stopped caring about getting the questions right. A girl my own age, who was sitting less than ten feet away, believed she was giving me high doses of electric shock! *Jesus Christ, Murrow,* I thought. I must have whispered it out loud because Dr. Van Laark put her finger to her lips.

For the next few questions I moaned and cried out as I was supposed to, increasingly sickened every time I watched Sarah push a button. My heart was snapping in my chest, quick as a metronome, and I realized we were nearing 120 volts, the standard voltage of an outlet, and enough to kill a person. I kept looking at Dr. Van Laark for direction, wondering how Sarah could possibly keep going, but Dr. Van Laark's smile was jelled in place.

At 140 volts, Sarah stopped again to ask Mr. Kaplan whether I was okay. Again he assured her the shocks were harmless. She pressed the button, and in that moment a sickening sound grew in my belly, pushed its way up my throat, and flew from my mouth. *How could you?* I screamed inside my head. *You hear me! I can see it in your eyes. You hear me in pain! How can you keep hurting me like this?*

I wasn't wearing the wrist cuffs, but I was sweating like I really was strapped down. If I'd picked the role of interviewer I'd have stopped shocking Sarah at the first sign of trouble. No matter what Mr. Kaplan or Dr. Van Laark said. I would have known, instinctively, to stop. *What's wrong with her, Murrow?* I pleaded. *How is this possible?*

We were up to 180 volts and I answered the next question wrong.

"Please administer two hundred volts," Mr. Kaplan said.

Sarah bit her lip, her face pained. "I really don't — "

"The experiment requires that you continue."

"Iris?" Sarah called out into the dark. "Iris, are you okay?"

Dr. Van Laark put her finger to her lips and shook her head.

"Iris?" Sarah's voice echoed girlish and small in the black room.

Mr. Kaplan leaned down next to Sarah and whispered with chilling solemnity, "The experiment requires that you continue."

According to my instruction sheet, I was supposed to give a loud cry and say, "Please stop." But that wasn't an adequate response for 200 volts. Not even close. Didn't Sarah realize how dangerous it was to shock someone with 200 volts of electricity? *There's no way she'll agree to it,* I thought. *No way she'll—*

She pressed the button.

"Oh, God!" I screamed. "Oh, Sarah. No more!"

Dr. Van Laark looked at me, startled by my outburst, and started scribbling furiously on her clipboard. I didn't care. I wanted Sarah to hear the sound that 200 volts made when it ran through the body of a 110-pound girl. I wanted my pain to echo inside her head until it sank into the very tissue of her brain. "No more!" I cried. "Please stop, please!"

"Mr. Kaplan?" Sarah whimpered. "I don't want to do this anymore. I don't think she's okay, Mr. Kaplan. We have to stop."

Dr. Van Laark motioned for me to follow her around the divider. Sarah stood beside Mr. Kaplan, wiping tears from her face. "You're okay!" she exclaimed when she saw me, but I couldn't look at her.

"How could you?" I hissed between my teeth. "I never would have done that to you."

"But Mr. Kaplan said you were . . . It was part of the . . . It's not my fault!"

I looked at Mr. Kaplan, waiting for him to upbraid Sarah for what she'd done. "Ms. Dupont," he said. "Don't judge Ms. Peters."

"What?"

"You are both culpable for what has just taken place. You knew Ms. Peters wasn't actually hurting you and yet you allowed her to continue, Ms. Dupont. You participated in the manipulation, and you did so with enthusiasm."

I was stunned. I wanted to sink into the darkness of the Black Box.

"The point I'd like to emphasize," Mr. Kaplan continued, "is that either one of you could have stopped the experiment at any moment. But you didn't. You think it's extreme to administer two hundred volts, but unfortunately it's quite normal. Few people in either of your experimental roles ever stop. In this case, walking away is the extreme thing to do."

I looked around for Dr. Van Laark, expecting an explanation, but she'd hidden herself behind the divider, almost like she was embarrassed for Sarah and me.

"'Difference is the essence of extremity' is not just a trite motto," Mr. Kaplan said. "It is a challenge to live up to."

He dismissed us and prepared for the next two students. My body was clammy with sweat. *What have I done, Murrow?* I asked, walking out of the Black Box into the blinding lobby.

"What's the matter?" Chris Coon called out as I hurried away from the theater.

"She probably failed Van Laark's test," David Morone snickered. "Just like everybody else."

It was only after we'd all participated in Dr. Van Laark's study that Mr. Kaplan explained its origin and purpose. The experiment, he told us the next day in class, was based on the work of Yale psychologist Stanley Milgram, who'd conducted a similar shock experiment in 1961, the same year an Israeli court sentenced Adolf Eichmann to death for helping to murder six million Jews. At his trial, Eichmann claimed that he was just "following orders." The Israelis didn't buy this (obviously), but Milgram was curious. What about all those clerks and administrators who had run the concentration camps? How was it, he wondered, that ordinary people came to commit acts of evil?

"Difference is the essence of extremity," Mr. Kaplan announced for the zillionth time as we slumped, dejected, in our seats. "To be extreme, you must assert yourself. No matter how much pressure you feel to obey. Because, I assure you, that pressure is everywhere. Remember our lesson on pressure-loving organisms." Mr. Kaplan assaulted the board with his chalk, dust flying everywhere. "In Milgram's original experiment, over fifty percent of the participants believed they were administering fatal-caliber shocks. Now imagine if those participants had been raised in environments where, from an early age, they'd been taught to question and resist. Do you think Milgram would have gotten the same results?"

When Mr. Kaplan asked this question, his eyes caught mine, as though he'd directed it to me alone. I looked down at my desk, a cold-water chill rushing through my body.

For the next few days, I worried incessantly about Mr. Kaplan. I couldn't stand the thought that he viewed me as a zombie, the kind of person who would have failed Milgram's experiment. But how could I convince him otherwise? Murrow advised patience. At lunch the next week, he reminded me that I was lucky to have Mr. Kaplan as a mentor. *He could save you from a lifetime of mistakes. Who knows what would have become of me without Ida Lou.* This was true. Murrow had been a business major before his mentor, Ida Lou Anderson, turned him on to speech and helped him become the world's most lauded journalist. Without Mr. Kaplan, I might have been heading for a lifetime of delusion. My classmates considered him a sadistic asshole, but I knew he was trying to help us — to protect us.

Still, I felt sick over what I'd done to Sarah Peters in the Black Box.

Human nature has its dark side, Murrow said as I pushed peas around my plate. *If you want an optimist, I'm not the best guy to be talking to.*

I smashed a couple of peas flat. The person I needed to talk to, of course, was Dalia. Back in Boston, we sat together at lunch every day, discussing our post–junior high plans. Dalia wanted to be a famous novelist. "Crazy people make the best *arteests!*" she liked to say. "You're not crazy," I'd tell her, but I knew she didn't believe me.

I never expected to have a friend like Dalia at Mariana, but I also didn't anticipate the school's draconian enforcement of community bonding. To avoid self-segregation, students are assigned to lunch tables composed of various ages, races, and social groups. An upperclassman presides over us, leading exercises in table togetherness. On days like this one, feeling as unsociable as I did, I only wanted to read the *New York Times* with my mashed potatoes, but on the first day of school, my table leader had pointed at me in front of the entire table. "No news for you!" he'd proclaimed with an imperial air.

So now I just sat beside my chattering tablemates, staring at my plate, waiting for the end-of-lunch bell to ring. Every few minutes I glanced at the large clock that eyed us from above the refectory doors. The clock was enormous, like the trophy kill of a Cyclops hunter. It seemed to me the minute hand was barely moving. Only then, at ten to one, something happened.

"Attention, please! Attention!" The announcement boomed down from the PA system. "Attention!" The voice was jovial and energetic, like it was about to explain how to locate the emergency exits. It continued, "The following is an assessment of the Mariana community's collective conscience." There was a loud static crackle, and then: "Under the spreading chestnut tree, I sold you and you sold me. There they lie and here lie we, under the spreading chestnut tree."

This was a different voice from the previous one. Female, with pitch-perfect diction. "Under the spreading chestnut tree, I sold you and you sold me. There they lie and here lie we, under the spreading chestnut tree."

Nobody spoke. And then all of a sudden a couple of table leaders at the far side of the refectory stood up. "Under the spreading chestnut tree . . ." Their voices were hesitant at first, but they seemed to draw strength from one another, and soon their words rebounded across the room. "Under the spreading chestnut tree!" More students followed their leaders and stood up beside their plates until nearly half the room had joined in. "Under the spreading chestnut tree, I sold you and you sold me. There they lie and here lie we . . ."

The chant picked up intensity and speed as the voice from the loudspeaker championed it on. And then the table leaders left their chairs and began to walk, still reciting, coalescing around a table in the center of the room. I jumped down from my bench and hurried through the throng, pushing my way toward that middle table. I managed to stake out a spot between two students who were standing on a bench. Peering between their legs, I saw that the entire table was up except for one student: a fair-haired boy cowering in the middle of the bench. He looked around anxiously, a red flush spreading up his neck and across his face. Meanwhile, his tablemates pummeled him with their words, speaking each phrase like a curse, their faces twisted with disgust.

"What are you doing? What did I do?" The boy's panic was sweaty and thick. "Stop it! Stop it!"

"Under the spreading chestnut tree, I sold you and you sold me. There they lie and here lie we, under the spreading chestnut tree. Under the spreading chestnut tree, I sold you and you sold me. There they lie and here lie we, under the spreading chestnut tree!" The voices chanted in lockstep with the intercom, and the words flew down over the poor, frightened student. He gave up protesting or trying to make sense of the situation and covered his head with his arms. It occurred to me that most students in the refectory couldn't see the boy; they were shouting because the ones in front of them were shouting. *Murrow*, I thought anxiously, *I have to help him!* But I was stuck in the crush and couldn't move.

"UNDER THE SPREADING CHESTNUT TREE, I SOLD YOU AND YOU SOLD ME. THERE THEY LIE AND HERE LIE WE, UNDER THE SPREADING CHESTNUT TREE."

And then suddenly there was a tremendous record-like scratch, and the intercom voice went silent. The room fell silent too. The boy at the table kept his head buried, his shoulders quivering.

"Today's flash mob was brought to you by Prisom's Party," the original intercom voice declared. "Our diagnostic assessment of the school's collective conscience has determined that you will harass a blameless student simply because the Community Council asks you to. The instructional email many of you received this morning did not come from the Council. It came from us. Prisom's Party declares the collective conscience poor."

At that exact moment, the bell rang to signal the end of lunch. Everybody started talking at once and pushing toward the refectory doors. Meanwhile, the embattled boy had raised his head and was looking around dazed, as though he'd woken from a nightmare.

Holy breaking news! I thought, and rushed off to find Katie Milford.

II

INTRATERRESTRIALS

These extremophiles thrive in darkness, feeding on poisonous methane and sulfur gases. The renowned molecular philosopher Lucinda Starburst has written that "intraterrestrials grow strong on substances utterly destructive to human life, and yet they shape our lives at the most fundamental level. They force us to reexamine what it means to create and destroy, to benefit and harm."

— *Marvelous Species: Investigating Earth's Mysterious Biology*

Jonah

UNTIL I STARTED teaching, I never knew how much faculty and students have in common. For one thing, we're as territorial as our charges. The science teachers, for example, keep mainly to the department office. It's where we grade papers, take coffee breaks, and complain about making so much less than our public school counterparts.

I store my lunch in the departmental mini-fridge, a dirty box packed with miscellaneous containers of Chinese food (circa who knows when), mushy fruit, Red Bulls, and half-eaten yogurts. That—and a whole lot of loose paper—is what you get when seven science nerds share a tiny office. But I like to eat in less cluttered accommodations. The teachers' lounge is spacious and newly renovated, albeit in a manner meant to preserve Mariana's "aesthetic integrity." That just means it has Gothic windows, heavy furniture, and dim lighting. The second week of school, somebody stuck a sign on the door that said, *Ye Olde Teachers' Lounge*. (Probably a science teacher; we're the only department with a sense of humor. At a recent science department trivia night, we decided to dub ourselves the Left Brains—the Bloods of the prep school faculty set. Pasternak put a stop to the game, because he didn't want the students to think we were encouraging cliques.)

Anyway, I walked into Ye Olde Lounge (reeking of ye olde coffee) and found half the English department settled around the oak table talking shop. I chose a high-backed leather chair and sat down with my tuna sandwich to listen in unobserved. As a student of animal behavior once told me, the trick to studying creatures in their natural habitat is to let them forget you're there.

If you were ever a fruit fly on the science department wall during one of our staff meetings, you'd hear an in-depth discussion of SimCity High, the online multiplayer video game where social cliques maneuver for power like feuding countries and Queen Bees can be dethroned and put on trial for rogue activity. We never talk pedagogy. But the English teachers are obsessed with all brands of academic quackery.

"You clearly haven't read *Blake's Apocalypse!*" a gruff voice spat as I removed the foil from my tuna. This was Mark Haloran, seventy-four years old and arthritic. A person could easily date this group of pseudo-scholars by their hair (gray), their foreheads (veiny), and their attitudes (self-righteous). At least two were PhDs who'd slunk back to these minor leagues after they failed to receive tenure.

"I can't take any more Harold Bloom today," said Diana Trop, English department head. "Listen, I have invented a new procedure to help students with textual analysis. It's called the Motif Number System. You give your class a list of motifs, say from *Catcher in the Rye,* numbered in order of importance. Innocence is one, experience two, herd mentality three, et cetera. And every time a motif appears in the book, the class writes the corresponding number in the margin. You repeat for each book. So in the *Odyssey,* Odysseus's guile is ranked one, the guest/host relationship two, and—"

"I was never very good with numbers," Haloran muttered.

I wasn't at all sure about the Motif Number System. Undoubtedly there'd be some kid attempting to turn it into real math. *Mr. Kaplan! I just proved that the square root of Odysseus's guile is equal to Holden Caulfield's hat. I totally deserve extra credit!*

The fact is, English class was always abhorrent to me. I've never forgiven my high school Epic Literature and Film seminar for destroying my love of *Star Wars.* I still can't watch those movies without thinking about the myth of the hero, the etymology of Yoda's name (the Sanskrit for warrior is *yoddha*), and, worst of all, how Obi-Wan Kenobi is a

stand-in for Jesus. Have you ever noticed the ubiquity of Jesus in literature discussions? Think about it. A character is compassionate? He's
like Jesus. He's got long hair? Jesus. He builds something out of wood?
Definitely Jesus.

My brother loved excavating texts, and at times he seemed to want
to physically merge with the pages and ink. I once caught him with his
nose shoved into a copy of *War and Peace*. I accused him of jerking
off to it, but Justin wasn't amused. Books deserved to be honored and
cherished, he said. I replied that a book was inanimate and thus deserved nothing. But if he persisted in believing a lot of spiritual hoopla,
at least he should consider the importance of the book in question. In
the grand scheme of things, Tolstoy wasn't exactly the Talmud.

Looking back, I realize that this brief exchange over book sniffing
encapsulated our entire relationship. Physically, Justin may have been
larger and stronger than me, but emotionally, he was a weakling. He was
obsessed with ideas — and, worse, with ideals. He not only believed in
true love and pined after lost causes, but he let us all know exactly what
he was feeling. Still, as much as I hated him for his vulnerability, I loved
him for that vulnerability, too. He was my brother — my twin. What else
could I feel for him but a combination of hatred and love?

Our friend Hazel once told me that these emotions were the antipo-
des of our existence. She loved to recite this Catullus poem: *I hate and
I love. Why does this happen to me? I don't have a clue, but it hurts like
hell.* Justin was my twin. When he hurt, I hurt. And he hurt all the time.
His instability threatened my carefully calibrated emotional equilib-
rium. I had to fix him for my own sake. Besides, the idea that I could
help him made me feel strong. It compensated for the seventy-pound,
six-inch discrepancy between us. So I set about teaching Justin that
cynicism was an invaluable buffer between a person's heart and the
outside world. Again and again I told him to forget the books, the ideals. And when telling didn't work, I went further. I took extreme measures to show Justin that we lived in a world of hard evidence, of fact. If
only he'd listened.

• • •

I finished my sandwich and headed to chemistry before the bell. Ever since yesterday's flash mob, the halls had echoed with menace. It was only 1 p.m. and already the afternoon had descended into a minor key. The English teachers in the lounge were willfully ignoring the ominous feeling that pervaded, consumed as they were by their Harold Bloom, and I envied their selfish persistence.

"Jonah!"

I'd just entered the main stairwell and looked up to see the exophthalmic orbs that were Pasternak's eyes. He was rippling the tips of his fingers — index, middle, ring, pinkie — at nervous speed. He looked like a fly preening. "Can you come up here?" his voice boomed down from on high. An interrogation was at hand.

When I finally reached Pasternak's landing, he glanced around. Down, up, left, right. We were alone in the cold, cylindrical space. It resembled a belfry, but instead of bells overhead there was only a dirty skylight.

"If you'd been in the refectory yesterday . . . I arrived just before the mob ended." Pasternak looked at me like he expected me to say something about this. Like I knew something about it. "You've read *Nineteen Eighty-four,* right?" He scratched his thinning hair with a jaundiced finger. "Of course you have. It's been on the eighth-grade English curriculum for two decades."

What did he want me to say? Yes, kids played pranks, but there were more than a few who yearned to be the heroes of their own epic story, who turned their books into bibles and worshiped them with religious zeal.

"Jonah —" Pasternak pursed his lips, looked past me down the stairs. "Do you know how that recording made its way onto the intercom?"

Why was he asking me this question? I shook my head.

"You don't?" His bug eyes seemed to pop inches from his face. He nodded absently. "Well, do you know how Prisom's Party managed to hack into the Community Council's email?"

"Are you insinuating something about my involvement in all this?"

As obsequious as Pasternak had been since my arrival, it was difficult to shake the old indignities. Sometimes he still seemed to consider me a kind of antimatter in the school, unpredictable and destructive.

"Insinuating? Jonah, I'm asking for you to—"

"I'm sorry," I interrupted. "But I have students to teach." And I left him there in the stairwell.

Iris

I COULDN'T GET A meeting with Katie Milford for a full twenty-four hours after the flash mob, and when I finally snagged five minutes with her, she rejected my proposed investigation of the event outright.

"Do I need to break down for you what happened, Iris?" she said, shoving a stack of edited news copy off a chair and pointing at me to sit down.

"No," I mumbled, and sat.

"For starters," Katie said, pacing in front of my chair, "Prisom's Party hacked into the Community Council's email account and sent out instructions for a flash mob. They then asked the student body to verbally attack a weak underclassman, Marvin Breckinridge, whose sister Mary happened to be a huge liar but who himself never hurt anybody. And, finally, this action 'proved' that the school is full of mindless robots. Now you're telling me you want to smear this iniquity across the front page? Do you know what will happen then, Iris? Colleges will hear about it, and the school will lose esteem in the eyes of the admissions officers. And then people like me — the seniors, who've been working insanely hard for years — will be screwed."

Katie's face flushed red and sweat prickled along her forehead. I knew I should keep my mouth shut, but questions spouted geyser-like from my mouth. "What is the deal with Prisom's Party? Who are they? What do they want?"

At first I thought I'd gone too far and Katie was going to order me out, but she sank back against her desk and sighed. Prisom's Party, she explained, was an underground society that sporadically played "arcane, pseudo-intellectual pranks" on the student body and published the *Devil's Advocate,* which exposed dirt on various community members and even led to student expulsions. "Not that I read it," she added. "Prisom's Party bills itself as student vigilantes fighting for the underdog. But they're really a student SAVAK, and the *Devil's Advocate* is crackpot journalism. In my humble opinion."

"But their stories check out? I mean, if kids were expelled . . ."

"Sometimes their stories check out. Although I already told you they invented a load of crap about Marvin Breckinridge. But let me ask you something, Iris. Did *you* scream and yell at Marvin?" Katie leaned toward me, her nostrils flaring. "Were you duped just like everyone else?"

I shook my head.

"Well then, you also have a vested interest in keeping this event out of the public eye," she said. I began to object, but Katie only accelerated. "Back in the day, under less disciplined leadership, this paper would print every titillating detail it could dredge up. And here's what happened. Admissions officers and internship gatekeepers stopped focusing on our academic records and our extracurricular achievements. They were distracted by all the scandals. So if you persist in this mindless idealism about exposing the truth, at best, your hard work will be taken less seriously; at worst, you'll be guilty by association. Is that what you want?"

"Of course not," I said, but I was already repackaging, scouring the cutting-room floor of my brain for useful scraps. And as Katie argued on, her lips opening and closing over the black hole of her mouth, I began to fashion a new approach. The story I needed to tell wasn't the flash mob. To focus on that alone would be to bury the lede in the world's largest crater. The real scoop was Prisom's Party itself. But to research it, I needed investigative free rein. And I would get that by selling Katie on a fluff piece about the life of Charles Prisom — "The Man, the Myth, the Legend," or some such bullshit — which would provide me with an excuse to examine the *Oracle* archives, to open Mariana's locked doors, to finally converse with the school's historied halls and see what I could make them confess.

I made my case to Katie and held my breath. She scowled at me, but then, as though Murrow had blown some magic Camel smoke over the proceedings, she nodded her assent.

The *Oracle* archives are located in the school basement, which everybody calls the Trench. People talk about the place like it's a nuclear bunker or a secret government facility — the kind of place where very bad things happen. According to one rumor, a psychopathic drama teacher ran a sex cult out of a Trench classroom in the 1970s, seducing ingénues from the spring musical and making them perform sadomasochistic theater warm-up exercises. I'd heard talk of secret societies and suicides. All kinds of stories about why the Trench was closed to unauthorized students.

When Katie unlocked the Trench door the following Saturday afternoon, cold, stale air blew up from what appeared to be a black cavern. "Light's at the bottom," she said. "Don't trip."

We headed into the chilly darkness, a rotten-egg smell wafting up from below. I was trying so hard not to stumble that I didn't realize we'd reached the bottom until I bumped into her. "Watch it," she snapped, and I vowed that as editor I'd never snipe at my subordinates.

Katie asked me to help find the light, so I felt along the wall until my hand brushed something squirmy and skittering. I yelped and Katie chided me. Finally the lights came on. I was standing at the end of a long hallway lined with rusty lockers and stacks of chairs. Holding my arms against my chest for warmth, I followed Katie below the crackling light fixtures, past classrooms with small windows, all of them dark. It was utterly quiet save the sound of our footfalls. Every few steps I felt a brush against my neck, and I'd whirl around to see nothing but the lonely hallway behind me. It had to be a draft, I decided, though where the draft was coming from, I couldn't tell. There were no windows, no doors to the outside. Katie turned a corner up ahead and disappeared from view. I rushed to catch up.

I located her in a small room with four gray file cabinets. Inside were old editions of the *Oracle* grouped by year.

"Make your Xeroxes in the school office," she instructed. "The Trench door locks on its own, so you can have my key."

Then I was alone in the room, listening to Katie's shoes squeaking down the hall. I stepped out into the hallway, feeling uneasy. As an only child, I'd been alone often enough. Alone in my house. Alone in classrooms. Even alone in the woods. But the aloneness I felt in the Trench was different, like I was inside a submarine at the bottom of the ocean. The Trench felt like a time warp. When I emerged, I might have missed the next big terror attack or environmental disaster and everyone I knew might be dead.

But these were mental digressions. *Start thinking like a journalist,* I commanded myself. *You're not stuck in a science fiction novel, you're in the school basement.* Clearly, because the gray-tiled floor was littered with scraps of paper and gum wrappers and soda bottles collecting dust: normal teenage stuff. A gray parka with a fake-fur hood hung on a line of coat hooks. I wondered who it belonged to and whether someone had been called out at home for losing it. It was an ugly coat, made even more so when I thought of it sitting down here for so many years. It had been abandoned, and abandoned things always seem to be worth less.

I picked up a gnawed pencil at my feet and poked the fur hood. At that moment, a loud clang erupted above me and a burst of hot air hit me in the face. My heart practically flew out of my mouth before I realized it was only a heating vent. But I didn't feel any better. Standing in the middle of the hallway surrounded by all those darkened classrooms, I had the feeling that I wasn't alone in the basement. That someone or something was hidden inside, watching me. I hurried back to the archive room and shut the door.

A quick scan of the file cabinets revealed that the years 1921 through

1940 were missing. I wondered if that could have something to do with Mrs. Kringle's "nasty upheavals." Then I pulled out the first paper ever published at Mariana, dating to March 1900. I couldn't believe that something this old was just sitting in a file cabinet in the school basement and that no one had bothered to preserve it. Now small flecks of its crumbling pages sloughed off like dead skin and fell onto the carpet. I pulled out a few more early issues and carefully carried them out of the basement, making sure to shut the black door behind me. I was in the school office Xeroxing for maybe half an hour. Then I went to return the papers.

Walking through the Trench a second time was less scary. I was just thinking how childish I'd been when I noticed that something was different about the archive room. Taped to the center file cabinet was a piece of white paper. My first thought was that Katie had left me a message, but then I remembered she'd given me her key. I pulled the paper down and opened it.

GIRLS WHO KNOW WHAT'S GOOD FOR THEM LEAVE HISTORY ALONE.

"Katie?" I called into the hallway. There was no answer. I looked furiously from left to right. The stairs leading out of the basement seemed very far away. The hall was silent and dim. The lights overhead snapped and buzzed. If someone was hiding down here, he could be anywhere. *Okay,* I thought, *you're going to walk, not run, down the hallway, up the stairs, and then out the door. You will not be afraid.* I put one foot in front of the other, listening for anything that might be creeping up behind me. I was halfway down the hall when the vents clanged on. I burst into a run, skipped up the stairs two at a time, and slammed the black door.

Seconds later I was on the front steps of Prisom Hall, shivering and watching for my mom's car across the fields. The school grounds felt desolate and remote, an uninhabited planet. I pinned my eyes on the road. As long as I could see it, I could reach it and be free. I waited and waited for my mother, wondering who else had access to the Trench.

• • •

Later that night I went looking for Charles Prisom's letters. I'd only peeked into Elliott Morgan's study, but now I stepped into the attic nook where the sloped ceiling and porthole-shaped window was like a ship's cabin. I switched on the desk lamp and started opening drawers. Not snooping, I told myself, but research.

I picked through old invoices and bills before stumbling on a drawer that interrupted my search altogether. Inside were files on all things Lily. I found her birth certificate (she was born on September 3, 1983, at St. Luke's Hospital in Springfield, Mass., which made her currently twenty-nine years old) and her school records. She'd attended Mariana from pre-K through tenth grade, after which point I couldn't find a single paper concerning her career there. What could possibly have happened to her in 2000? Had Lily gotten pregnant and been shipped off to a home for teenage mothers, or come down with a rare disease? Had she run away from home?

I kept reading. She resurfaced eventually, perhaps after having her illicit child or getting cured of her ailment, or being dragged back to Nye by the police. In 2001 she went to Emory, and after four years of college she stayed on for a master's in public health. In the same file cabinet I found a photo album of Lily's birthday pictures, aged one to sixteen. There was something odd about these pictures, but it wasn't until I brought them over to Mr. Morgan's desk lamp that I began to understand what. Lily's skin was the shade of raw milk, her hands translucent as rice paper, her hair the color of day-old whipped cream. In the light of sixteen birthday candles, her eyes flickered a disturbing ultraviolet.

Looking at her, I shivered, as though her whiteness were infectious, and suddenly I saw Dalia standing half-naked in the snow, shaking violently, her arms stretched toward the night sky, imploring the wintry mix of black and white. "Help me, Iris!" she called as her father picked her up and put her, kicking and screaming, in their station wagon. "You have to help me! Why won't you help me! I don't want to go!" But what could I do? They had to take her to the hospital; it was the only way to protect her. I watched, the tears streaming down both our faces. "You're not my friend! You're not my friend! You're not my—" But then Dalia's mother slid in beside her and slammed the car door.

I closed Lily's photo album, wiped my face dry, and opened a browser on my phone. *Albinism,* I read, *is a genetic condition characterized by loss of pigmentation in the skin, hair, and eyes, due to the lack of melanin. Albinism is frequently a condition of the eyes as well, resulting in nystagmus: extreme nearsightedness and light sensitivity that causes the pupils to move quickly back and forth.*

I felt bad for judging Lily; how cruel of her parents to name her after a white flower. How awful it must have been to look so vampiric, what with her bone-white skin and violet eyes. Now that I thought about it, I couldn't recall a single picture of Lily in the house. No photos of her smiling with friends. No images of her playing sports or performing in a school play. But then I remembered the inscription on the *Marvelous Species* title page: *To Lily, marvel of my life. Justin.*

I closed my eyes and saw the bouquet of white lilies on Dalia's coffin. *One true friend,* I thought, *is all a person needs.*

Lily

O N   A   F O G G Y   morning early in her sophomore year, Lily Morgan sat shotgun in Dipthi's Volvo, watching the flat, dull world creep by. Lily was sixteen, and despite the fact that special driving glasses were available for individuals with moderate ocular albinism, her mother refused to even consider them. Maureen Morgan was Nye County's premier event planner and a contingency whiz, ready with multiple solutions for inclement weather, culinary disasters, and hyperventilating brides. (Could it be, Lily wondered, that her mother was forever compensating for the one contingency that had bested her?) Thus, Lily neither played outdoor sports nor went on summer camping trips. Driving was most definitely verboten, so Lily imposed upon Dipthi to chauffeur her to and from school.

On this particular morning, Dipthi was complaining about the recent Students for Social Justice "campaign" (a.k.a. bake sale), where the boy manning the table had refused to sell Lily a cupcake. "Can you believe he accused your father of representing the school's *hegemonic infrastructure*?" Dipthi spat out, tapping her fingers against the steering wheel. "I mean, hyperbole much?"

Lily shrugged.

"And when I demanded my money back, that SSJ kid had the nerve to call me 'sister' and tell me I was from the Third World. I mean, Jesus Christ, I was born in Boston. Really, Lily, you should have slapped that douche in the face."

Dipthi was a violin prodigy who loved to stand center stage in every situation. But Lily couldn't afford to draw negative attention to herself. Though she had studied teenage normalcy with the same commitment that Dipthi had applied to Bach, she still felt like a clumsy beginner. No matter how she behaved, people refused to see past her white blond hair and unearthly skin.

At school, the girls parted ways, and Lily headed off to first-period history. Half the class was already clustered there, furiously studying for a suspected pop quiz. Mr. Armstrong was notorious for asking questions about material covered in footnotes and docking points for grammatical mistakes. According to school legend, an erroneous "that" instead of "which" had stripped one senior of her valedictorianship.

Lily circled the tightly locked group, seeking a way in. It was a familiar situation. Throughout junior high she floated on the periphery of the various cliques, and they tolerated her presence like a harmless parasite — a tooth amoeba that nibbled on whatever the toothbrush missed, or maybe a dust mite that made you sneeze constantly but didn't cause any real damage. When she approached the popular girls at recess, their circle would automatically constrict like a cell warding off a virus. Once in a while Lily was able to permeate — to get a shoulder, or even a comment, through. But other days, when she approached, the cell would split, an instantaneous mitosis, and the girls would scatter. By high school, Lily no longer pursued these popular contingents, but exclusion, she'd learned, came in numerous forms.

The study group had relaxed its perimeter, and Lily was just about to slip in when a creaking noise startled her. Justin Kaplan hovered close by on crutches, his eyes glued to her like a fly to tape. Beside him stood the voluptuous, heavily freckled Hazel Greenburg, otherwise known as Queen of the Geeks. Hazel was in the class above Lily, and though the two girls had once been friendly, they hadn't spoken since middle school. Hazel raised her eyes at Lily as though in provocation, then abruptly strode off down the hall.

Justin didn't move. He just stood there, staring. "Hi," he said, finally. "I wanted to —"

But at that moment the bell rang. Lily hurried into the classroom.

There was no quiz after all, but Lily felt little relief. According to a recent magazine article she'd read, people of similar attractiveness, intelligence, and social rank were romantically compatible. In light of this, of course Justin would be fixated on her. She was an albino freak and he — she glanced at the cement-like boot on his foot — well, he was a freak too. Justin was a Trench kid who spent his waking moments memorizing endless amounts of obscure knowledge and training to regurgitate said knowledge in nanosecond bursts at monthly competitions. He took failure worse than anyone she knew. Rumor had it that he was wearing the plastic boot because he'd slammed his foot against the gym wall after losing the last Academic League tournament. Some people said it was a fracture, others a full-on break.

At this moment, Justin was charging full speed through a series of questions about Andrew Jackson, as if he was attempting to claim his own academic manifest destiny. His opponent in the conversation was his twin brother, Jonah, the epitome of trouble. He'd most recently infuriated the English department by handing in an essay titled "Gatsby's Green Light of Greed: How Mariana Academy Destroyed the American Dream." He goaded his classmates, argued with the faculty, and was frequently ejected from class. He was also brilliant, seeming to sail through school on a wave of easy A's. But Jonah was also scrawny, pimply, and pale. People called him Prepubes. As in, *Think Prepubes got his wet dream yet?* Or, *Prepubes is so skinny he can suck his own dick.*

In any case, whoever put the Kaplan twins in the same history class was seriously deranged, because the two boys fought like sworn enemies. It baffled everybody how the Academic League managed to achieve even a modicum of success with both of them vying for champion status. Right now in Mr. Armstrong's class, they were duking it out over Jackson's legacy.

"You want to talk about *morale?*" Justin was saying. He vibrated with energy, as if he was about to spring from the chair. If only his cast wasn't weighing him down like a rock. "What about *morals*? Jackson suspended habeas corpus in New Orleans! The man was a despot!"

Jonah barely blinked as he began to tick off a series of arguments about Jackson's excellent mix of pragmatism and idealism. In response, Justin rattled off his own catalogue of events and legislative acts. His eyes pulsed with rabid intensity, and spittle glistened on his lips. But his brother just sat back, dismissively spinning his pen, dismantling each of Justin's arguments. By the end of class, Justin wore the pained look of a lab animal with a needle in its stomach.

The class packed up and Justin hoisted himself out of the chair. He fit the crutches under his arms and creaked toward the door, reaching it just as the next class started to enter. Instead of letting him through, the incoming students poured around his precariously balanced body. He waited for the last stragglers to come in before he finally wobbled into the hall.

Later that afternoon, Lily sat on a picnic table watching the varsity boys' soccer team run laps. When the sweating pack passed by, she could smell the cleat-turned grass and almost feel the heat radiating from their faces. She saw them eye the cheerleaders as they ran by, and wondered what they were thinking. Were they imagining their naked girlfriends? The girls they wished were their naked girlfriends? Or was it only body parts flashing before their eyes: cheerleader breasts and thighs bouncing up and down. How many of them were having sex, Lily wondered. How many of them had received oral sex or given it? She remembered some of them talking in the hall a few weeks back.

"It smelled like tuna fish," one of the players said.

His friend pretended to gag. "Dude, I don't do *that*."

"Bet your mom likes it," the first one said.

"Hey, headmaster's daughter," another one said as he walked by, "how about a tuna sandwich?" And he stuck his tongue into the V of his index and middle fingers.

Lily had once stuck her finger down her underwear and brought it to her nose. The smell was pungent and heady, but nothing like tuna. Lily wondered if all women smelled like her, but she had nobody to ask. When she and Dipthi changed for gym, they shielded even their bras from view.

The varsity team started passing soccer balls. Alexi Oppenheimer juggled a ball from knee to knee. He was too far away to see clearly, but Lily easily summoned the image of his face: his long, thick lashes and shaggy hair. Sometimes she imagined Alexi kissing her—kissing her down there. But she wasn't going to imagine that anymore. Because if guys thought it was so disgusting, then to want such a thing must be abnormal. Lily shifted on the picnic table. She felt wet. She closed her eyes. When she opened them again, Justin Kaplan was standing in front of her.

She flushed. What if there was a wet spot on the table?

Justin's back was hunched, all his weight supported by his one healthy foot. He stood close enough to her that she could see a string of small pimples along the side of his chin. They were a shade redder than his hair. His face was a near-perfect oval with a straight nose and full lips.

She shifted uncomfortably. Justin was always there, always watching from a distance, seeming to invade her space simply by looking at her. She wished he would quit trading Secret Santas so he could fill her locker with candy, wished he would stop sending her carnations on Valentine's Day. Everyone at Mariana knew that Justin had been infatuated with Lily since elementary school. At junior high dances, popular students played a game they called Fix Up the Freaks. Packs of glossy-lipped girls would encourage Justin to ask Lily to dance, and he was only too willing to comply.

"Tough argument in history," she said now, trying not to look at his injured foot.

Justin smiled—a rarity—and his simple face was suddenly a complicated landscape. Lily looked down at the picnic table and picked at a sliver of wood. Then she noticed an object on the ground. Lying under the bench was the largest dragonfly she'd ever seen. Its greenish body must have been three inches long, with a comparable wingspan. It was dead.

Justin saw it too. Suddenly he was kneeling down and collecting the dragonfly into his palm with a tenderness that turned her stomach. He stroked the creature's back, then looked up at her. Justin's eyes, she noticed, were a shade of blue nearly as pale as her own.

"Lily, I was wondering if you'd like to go out with me sometime."

Her mouth opened, but nothing came out. One second of silence elapsed. Then two. Then three. She couldn't say yes. Not to a Trench kid, not to Justin—a kid cradling a dead insect in his palm. But what would happen if she said no? Last week after getting back his Latin exam, Justin had flung his binder against the wall so hard he broke it. She'd seen him rip up tests with less than satisfactory grades, storm out of classrooms in frustration. And of course there was the broken foot.

"So . . . here's my number and email." Balancing one of the crutches in his armpit, Justin fished in his pocket and pulled out a piece of paper. She took the measly offering. "See you tomorrow, Lily," he said. Then he hobbled away as if he doubted tomorrow would come.

Iris

I<small>N</small> E<small>LLIOTT</small> M<small>ORGAN</small>'<small>S</small> study, I found a school invoice signed by Charles Prisom, a newspaper clipping about the school's ground-breaking, and an old refectory menu. Otherwise, there was nothing of investigative interest. *I'm stuck, Murrow,* I thought as I returned to my room from the attic nook. *There's the Historical Society, sure, but I need human sources—people who might know how Charles Prisom is linked to Prisom's Party.*

I sat down on Lily's bed and pulled open *Marvelous Species: Investigating Earth's Mysterious Biology.* Since I felt stuck regarding the Prisom case, I decided to focus on Mr. Kaplan instead. I'd discovered something unusual at the back of the book—a handwritten appendix. One that Lily had added herself.

Titled *Art Studio Life,* the section catalogued the behaviors of the Studio Girls, a group of four friends in Lily's class. Within pages labeled *Habitat, Dress, Interests, Media,* and *Misc* were descriptions of each girl, the conversations they'd had, the clothes they wore. It must have taken Lily months of observation to collect so much detailed information. It was almost like she was writing a dissertation on this particular group, or some kind of travel guide to their social milieu. Whatever her motives, she'd done her research. The magazines and music on her shelves corresponded to the lists she'd made. On the last few pages of the index were photographs of bizarre paintings and sculptures. One showed a freestanding globelike object, about the size of a large beach ball, whose surface was covered with a mishmash of obscenity — insects, oversize male genitalia, a breast with a spider crouched over the nipple. Another photograph showed the portrait of a girl with thick black bangs and raccoon-ringed eyes. The girl's irises were white instead of black. She looked possessed.

"What kind of girl collects information on other people like they're scientific specimens?" I said aloud, but quietly, so my parents wouldn't hear me through the door. I conjured Murrow into the room, and there he was on the edge of the bed, his suit jacket folded over his lap, smoke curling from his smoldering cigarette.

"Oh, I don't know," he said. "Biographers, detectives, investigative journalists."

Murrow was right. Wasn't this the very reason I was studying *Marvelous Species* so meticulously — in order to glean even the smallest morsels of information about Mr. Kaplan's academic passion? The problem was, the more information I learned about Mr. Kaplan, the more troubled I felt.

After the flash mob, he tried to get our biology class talking about the incident. "How many of you participated in the mob?" Mr. Kaplan asked us a few days later, and of course not a single person raised a hand. "How many of you tried to help Marvin?" He waited, but nobody moved. "Were any of you thinking about Dr. Van Laark's experiment when the mob was taking place?" A couple of people nodded. "And knowing what you did about obedience to authority, why didn't you *do* anything?"

"Because we were in a room full of screaming students," Marcie Ross ventured. "We *couldn't* do anything."

"Yeah," Chris Coon complained. "I mean, if you weren't in the center of the room, you didn't even know what was happening."

"What does this have to do with biology?" Sarah Peters muttered. "This isn't supposed to be a psych class."

The room fell dead quiet.

"That's right, Sarah," Mr. Kaplan said slowly. "And I will be the first to admit that I am stretching the boundaries of a basic biology curriculum. Discussing the flash mob will teach you nothing about photosynthesis or cell reproduction. But I told you on the first day of school that if you are going to understand extremophile life, you must understand the basic nature of extremity. You must know it, appreciate it, *strive* for it!"

Mr. Kaplan was growing progressively more animated, the color rising in his face. Sarah, I realized, was so taken aback that she couldn't even look Mr. Kaplan in the eye.

"If we were only talking about photosynthesis, you'd all secretly be wondering, *What's the point? What does plant life have to do with me?* Even as you swallowed pages of information, even as you studied so hard for your precious four-point-oh, you'd still be wondering, *WHY?* So forgive me if we take a few precious class periods to discuss something that's relevant to your lives right now!"

I'd left class that day feeling uneasy. After researching the phenomenon of flash mobs online, I discovered that their creator—a journalist!—was inspired by Stanley Milgram's work at Yale. This could have been a coincidence, but more likely it suggested a connection between Mr. Kaplan and Prisom's Party. What if the flash mob had been Mr. Kaplan's doing—another attempt to force the issue about blind obedience? This time, though, there'd been a victim: a helpless boy. I didn't know what to think, but the dread I'd felt on my drive to Nye had returned, beating a slow and steady rhythm in my chest.

I had to figure out what was going on, and *Marvelous Species* wasn't going to answer these pressing questions. I needed to observe Mr. Kaplan in the same manner that Lily had watched the Studio Girls. Only with a teacher that wasn't so easy. Certainly I couldn't walk up to him and ask if he was connected to a group of student renegades.

"You need to cultivate your sources," Murrow said. "Get to know them. I can guarantee you'll learn much more through casual banter than through any formal interview."

"But that's like fooling people. And you're for the truth above all."

"I'm for speaking truth to power, Iris. And to do that you need to be pragmatic. The truth is finicky. It ducks and hides. You must *lure* it out." Murrow scratched an itch behind his ear. He coughed and his lungs sounded muddy. Then he stood up and put on his jacket. "You can't keep carrying that thing around" — he gestured to *Marvelous Species* — "just hoping Mr. Kaplan will notice it. Especially when you now have a specific reason to show him the book."

"And that reason would be?"

"Dr. Lucinda Starburst."

Then Murrow vanished, his cigarette still smoldering.

I opened *Marvelous Species* to the index, and sure enough, there she was, listed under "Starburst, Lucinda," with a dozen references. Two of these mentions came from a chapter titled "Intraterrestrials," and the latter was accompanied by a quote: *Difference is the essence of extremity.*

It turned out that I'd initially come across Dr. Starburst's name in chapter one — read it and forgotten it. But the unusual appellation had lodged in my head anyway. Now the words "Lucinda Starburst" exploded in my mind's eye like firecrackers. I'd been acting so precious, waiting for Mr. Kaplan to notice Lily's book and say something. But now I was going to treat *Marvelous Species* like an investigative instrument. I'd be a truth surgeon, and the book would be my scalpel. I needed only to open Mr. Kaplan up a little bit, and before long, he'd be sharing all kinds of information with me: about Milgram's shock experiment, and flash mobs, and, eventually, Prisom's Party.

A few days later, I requested a meeting with Mr. Kaplan in the library after school. He wasn't there when I arrived, so I sat down in one of the reading chairs, my eyes trained on the door. All that week I'd had the uncanny feeling that someone was watching me. Just two days before, I'd been in the computer lab, typing a paper on *Wuthering Heights,* when suddenly the text started spinning out of control, letters and numbers spewing from beneath my cursor. My paper had been hijacked! I kept hitting Delete, but the text wouldn't stop. "What's going on!" I hissed at the screen.

The kid at the terminal next to mine leaned over to inspect. "Looks like a virus," he said. "Your computer's been hacked."

I was about to shut the computer down when the cursor spit out the last few words. "CEASE AND DESIST OR WE'LL —" I was so freaked out that I cut the power before the sentence finished.

The library door clicked, but it was only the librarian running an errand. Now I was all alone. Outside the windows, the playing fields sprawled away from the school before finally colliding with the woods. Above the barren branches, a flock of black birds swept across the sky. I could hear the pulse of my heart, and after a while it began to sound like those very birds, each beat like a flap of dark wings. I imagined a black bird nesting in my chest, its wings unfurling inside of me. I suddenly missed Dalia so much it was like a punch in the gut.

"Sorry I'm late." Mr. Kaplan hurried in, and I snapped on a smile. Mr. Kaplan stood over my chair. In class, he was militaristic, but outside, he was nervous, like the dorky kid who never knows what to do with his hands. Mr. Kaplan gazed out the window.

"It's bleak up here," I said.

Mr. Kaplan didn't respond. I wished he would stop hovering and sit down.

"I'm happy I didn't grow up here," I continued. "I spent my formative years in Boston. Which is much more cosmopolitan, you know? Do you like Nye? It must be pretty different from UCLA. Where'd you grow up?"

"Iris." Mr. Kaplan eyed me. "Was there something you wanted to discuss?"

"I wanted to show you this." I held up *Marvelous Species*. "I discovered another reference to Lucinda Starburst, and I was wondering if—"

But Mr. Kaplan cut me off. "Where did you get that?"

"From my house."

Mr. Kaplan took the book and sat down. He stared at the cover, transfixed. It was clear that my previous attempts to make him notice the book had failed.

"Are you okay? . . . Mr. Kaplan?"

"What?" he snapped. "Yes."

His chest heaved once, and I thought I detected dampness around his eyes. *Murrow,* I thought, *the book isn't supposed to upset him!*

"You said you brought this from home?"

"Yes, but it's a temporary situation. I mean, it's my house but not really my home."

"Whose house is it?"

"Elliott Morgan's. He used to be headmaster here. He's friends with my dad. I'm sleeping in his daughter's room. She must have really loved this book. She had it set up on her bookshelf like a shrine."

Mr. Kaplan was digging his index finger into the cuticle bed of his thumb, and I couldn't tell if he was paying attention.

"Aren't you even going to look inside?" I asked.

Mr. Kaplan's nail punctured the skin, and blood welled up on his thumb.

"Mr. Kaplan, you're—"

He opened the book but stopped at the title page and ran his hand over the paper, as if his fingers were capable of erasing the text. Then he noticed his bloody thumb and shut the book. "I have to get going." He put *Marvelous Species* on the table. "Can we finish our discussion later?"

I nodded, but he was already hurrying away, sucking on his thumb. I lifted the book cover and turned to the title page.

To Lily, marvel of my life. Justin.

An angry smear of blood ran across these words now, the stain already turning brown.

That night I was sitting on my bed with *Marvelous Species* when my mother came in. She'd been on the phone all afternoon with members of her many charities, and she was dressed in black heels and pearls, as if she'd actually been out visiting boardrooms and foundations. Given that she'd been conducting this business from the dining room table, she was wearing way too much perfume.

"So." My mother folded her hands in her lap. "What are your plans for Friday?" I held up the book. "Oh, come on." She faked a smile. "There must be something more fun than that. Why don't you call a girlfriend and go for coffee in town. I'll drive you."

"Thanks for the offer," I said, "but I'm really okay."

"Iris?"

I looked up. Now my mother looked different. Her face was set — determined — and her lips were drawn tightly together.

"I know it's hard being the new kid, but you're not even trying to make friends."

"I went to the ice cream social."

"Iris, you should go out."

"Okay." I looked back at *Marvelous Species*.

My mother glanced at the chapter I was reading. "What in God's name are extremophiles? Don't tell me you've become a fan of science fiction."

"It's for Mr. Kaplan's class." This wasn't exactly true, but it was close enough.

My mother shook her head. "Why are so you interested in science all of a sudden?"

"Unlike some people" — I glanced up — "Mr. Kaplan takes me seriously."

"Garrison Pasternak says Jonah Kaplan was nearly kicked out of school when he was a student. Did you know that?"

"Mr. Kaplan went to Mariana?"

"And now he's brainwashing my daughter." My mother picked my phone up from the bed. "Call a friend."

"No thanks."

"Take the phone."

I didn't move. I was thinking about Mr. Kaplan's omission and how it felt more like a lie. I asked him where he was from, so why didn't he acknowledge growing up here?

"Take the phone, Iris."

I took it. My mother smiled, but it was the expression of a 1950s housewife on the verge of a homicidal rampage.

"Now then, who are you going to call?"

"Nobody." Was I overreacting about Mr. Kaplan? But why had he handled Lily's book like a hunk of enriched uranium? I needed to think his reaction through. I needed my mother gone.

"This is not up for discussion," she continued. "You are not going to sit around and read about extremo-whatevers all weekend. Now pick somebody and call her."

"Who, Mom? Who do you suggest?"

"For God's sake, Iris. Out of the hundred people in your class, there must be at least one girl you're friendly enough with to invite to the movies." She started rattling off people whose parents she knew from the school board. Then she grabbed the phone from me and started searching through my address book. She was getting more agitated by the second. I asked for the phone back, but she ignored me. She suggested Lauren Nevins, who was my lab partner, and Amanda Petroff from my literature study group. I was starting to panic.

"Katie Milford?" my mom said. "You've mentioned Katie lots of times."

"Mom, please," I whimpered. "Please don't. She's editor of the—"

"All right, all right." But she held the phone out of my reach as she scrolled through the address book, mumbling names to herself. And then she stopped. "Dalia Zalowski." She looked up at me. "Oh, Iris . . ."

I looked away.

"I thought we talked about this, sweetie. Remember what Dr. Patrick said. You need to erase it."

"Give it back!" I reached out my arm. Tears had begun to drip from my eyes and sink into Lily's pink comforter.

"Iris, are you listening to me?"

I looked up as if I hadn't actually heard. But I had. The black bird I'd felt inside my chest earlier that day began rustling its wings. I shook my head, crying. It wasn't my fault that I didn't have anyone to call, that Dalia's phone was disconnected and put in some box in her room with everything else she wasn't ever going to need again. Dalia's number was the only thing I had from my old life. I'd already given up the main thing—the thing that mattered—so why couldn't I just keep the number?

Frantic, I lunged for the phone and grabbed it, and before I knew what I was doing, the phone was hurtling toward the wall. It smashed and clattered to the floor. My mother looked like she'd just witnessed a car crash.

"I don't know what to do, Iris." She was crying now. "I'm trying to help you."

"I don't want your help," I yelled. "I want you to leave me alone!"

My father appeared in the doorway. He looked from my mother, balanced on the corner of the bed, to me, curled up against the headboard. When he noticed the phone, he gave me an exhausted look. He walked over to the bed and helped my mother up. "I'm trying to help her," she sobbed into my father's armpit. "Nothing's working."

When they were gone, I felt a strange sense of calm, like my brain was an empty shell. On the floor across the room, the phone's cracked screen glowed white. I turned around to see Murrow's picture on the wall. He'd lost people, too. Jan Masaryk, George Polk, and worst of all Laurence Duggan, who'd been Murrow's first real friend in New York City. The government went after Duggan, accusing him of spying for Russia. Duggan couldn't take the intimidation, so he jumped out the window of his Manhattan office. He fell sixteen stories and landed on the sidewalk. The impact knocked off one of his shoes.

The night after Duggan's death, Murrow went on the air and told the nation about the injustice that had killed his friend. He talked and people listened. But nobody was listening to me. "You had a whole country of people who cared what you thought!" I shouted at Murrow's poster. "But I don't have anyone. Not one! Just like my mother said. So what am I supposed to do?" I waited, heaving. "Answer me!" But the room was silent.

Like Duggan, Dalia had ripped herself out of the world. The cut was sudden and messy, and she'd taken part of me with her. This hole, I realized, had filled up with shadows, with dark, beating wings. I climbed under Lily's covers and curled up with *Marvelous Species*. Somewhere inside, I reasoned, there must be a creature as misunderstood as I was.

Jonah

IN NYE ALL climatory bets are off, so I wasn't surprised to wake
up one day in early October and discover a hefty fall of snow. It was
the kind of morning that made you want a woman in your bed, another
sleep-warmed body to pull close for just five more minutes. Of late, I'd
taken to reminding myself that over 450 species of bdelloids in swampy
waters and damp mosses never had sex and didn't seem to mind. My
six months of celibacy was nothing extraordinary. But comparing myself to leechlike creatures wasn't exactly a mood booster.

Even worse, I knew exactly who I wanted in my bed. I'd been in
Nye for two months and still had no sighting of Hazel Greenburg, the
woman whose girlhood iteration I had loved, and who, before she
stopped speaking to me, had been my closest friend. My mother had
spotted her in Nye months ago, and yet I had not run into her at the
bookstore or the bar or the pharmacy. She was unlisted and, despite
my efforts, untraceable.

I stumbled into the bathroom. Without turning on the lights, I
shook a couple of extra-strength Excedrin from the bottle (headache
remedy and daily caffeine dosage all in one!). As I brushed my teeth, I
ran a hand through the red mess of my hair. A little greasy but not too
bad.

Back into the dark bedroom, I put on the week's final pre-ironed
shirt and pants. I was out of clean socks, so I pulled yesterday's from

the hamper. I slid on my beat-up brown loafers, then remembered the snow and pulled on a pair of boots instead. I grabbed a banana from the kitchen and my satchel from the doorknob. In the car, I turned the defrost on high and pulled out of the parking lot—thick forest swinging away from me—and onto the road. My head throbbed with sleep. Cold and wet have always been my least favorite physical states. The doleful landscape rushed past as I maneuvered my Sube around the slick contours of Mountain Road. Within ten minutes the woods gave way to Mariana's sweeping lawns, now covered in snow and blank silence.

I turned onto school property and realized I'd inadvertently pulled into the student carpool line instead of the faculty entrance. Twelve years of the same daily routine were hard to shake.

Inside the building I ran into Headmaster Pasternak conducting a tour for parental hopefuls. Most of the fathers were slicked and shined, their suits impeccably tailored, their bodies smelling of expensive aftershave. Despite the weather, the mothers wore high heels.

The group walked down the hall with the detached confidence of CEOs. They paid no attention to the students who, in their haste to make the bell, did look a little like underlings sent to make Xeroxes and fetch coffee. Only one couple, clearly the outsiders of the group, seemed genuinely intrigued by the commotion of students changing classes. The wife wore a hemp tunic shirt and a gray braid down her back. Her husband had a dearth of hair on his head and a great deal of it over his lip. They whispered back and forth like kids on a field trip—the ones who lag behind and make trouble. They reminded me of my own parents.

As I approached, I heard Headmaster Pasternak intone: "The Community Code is the foundation of this school, Mrs. Simpson, and our students—"

Then Pasternak saw me and threw his hands up with joy. "Mr. Kaplan! Good morning!" He beamed as if I'd just sold him a winning lottery ticket. "Mr. Kaplan teaches freshman biology and sophomore chemistry," Pasternak told the parents. "He's an alum of the school and quite distinguished — BA from Stanford, PhD from UCLA, and quite a few publications at the young age of twenty-eight. We call him *Mr. Kaplan* at his own insistence, by the way . . ."

Pasternak shook his head like he couldn't believe a PhD would voluntarily choose not to flaunt his title. Whether he really believed this or whether it was for the parents' benefit, I couldn't tell.

"Mr. Kaplan is here as part of the College-Based Education Initiative I was describing."

"Excuse me, Mr. Kaplan?" A man in a pinstripe suit raised his hand like he was signaling for the check. "I'd like to know what you think about the school's science facilities. I mean, are they up to date, technologically speaking?"

"Mr. Hughes," Pasternak butted in, "our laboratories are brand new. We've taken great pains to provide the most up-to-date equipment."

"But Mr. Kaplan, what's your take? I can't imagine that students at an elite school in the twenty-first century are still playing around with Bunsen burners. What about new computer technology or scientific digital systems or — well, you know the lingo better than I do."

All eyes turned, including Pasternak's. I knew what he wanted me to say.

"To be honest," I replied, "I believe critical thinking is ultimately more important than fancy technology." And then I was waxing eloquent about the simple beauty of the high school labs. The black-topped lab tables, the map of elements that always hung over the chalkboard and would snap up with a satisfying *thwap* no matter how aged and battered it was. These were rooms full of wonder and the excitement of mixing chemicals together without ever knowing exactly what would happen. These were rooms that sparkled in my mind's eye like untarnished petri dishes. "Don't you remember how much *fun* science class was?" I asked.

Pasternak's eyes narrowed. I'd given the wrong answer. But I was the expert, so there was nothing he could do about it. He pressed forward with his sycophantism. "Mariana is at the forefront of technological advancement. This fall we'll introduce Aciview, a grade catalogue system through which parents can observe students' academic progress via an online password-protected site."

I imagined this dad perusing Aciview over his morning coffee: *Looks like Bobby was down from a 3.6 to a 3.45 this week.* And Mom, flipping the French toast: *Oh, honey, education is a long-term investment. You can't expect immediate dividends.*

Pasternak ushered the parents down the hall, pausing to take hold of my arm. "Can you stop by my office sometime this week, Jonah? At your convenience, of course."

Before I could respond, he was hurrying after the man in the pinstripes, attempting further damage control. The hippie parents followed the group toward the stairwell, but before they entered, the mother turned. Her eyes met mine with a sorrowful expression, though I couldn't tell whether the look was for me or for her soon-to-be-matriculating children.

I headed off in the opposite direction. There were a million things Pasternak might want to discuss: new textbooks, my role as Academic League advisor, the rising price of wheat. But at the moment when he'd gripped my arm with his bony fingers, I felt the unmistakable muscle memory of my past: I was still a naughty student in trouble.

Iris

A FTER THE PHONE-THROWING incident, my parents called Dr. Patrick faster than you can say paranoid schizophrenic. I saw the landline light up, so I pressed the speaker button to listen in. Since they were discussing *my* mental health — without me! — I decided snooping was justified. Dr. Patrick wanted to know whether I was still talking to my "imaginary friend." (The nerve of him, belittling Murrow like he was an invisible playmate!) He also said my involvement with the school paper was a positive indicator of my "growing social integration and emotional rehabilitation," but he advised my parents to monitor me for "further signs of erratic behavior or delusion." He reminded them to be patient. "Remember, she's grieving." On the few occasions that Dr. Patrick nixed the psychobabble, he actually made sense.

The next morning, classes were shortened for the "Community Forum," Mariana's fancy name for a school assembly. So far, we'd had speakers from MADD and SADD as well as GLADD (yup, Gays and Lesbians Against Drunk Driving). This time, HM Pasternak had brought in a "nationally respected psychologist and teen counselor" named Dr. Marcie Putz ("pronounced," she assured us, "with a long *u*") to talk about bullying. After forty-five minutes, I'd learned the following lesson: Don't bully. A better message, I thought, would be to warn against saying any single word too many times in a row. The more

Dr. Putz (long *u*!) said "bullying," the more the letters morphed into a collection of meaningless sounds. *B-u-l-l-y-i-n-g,* I thought, trying to bring the meaning back. Bully pulpit. Bully Brooks. I tried to say "other people being bullied" three times fast, but I couldn't do it.

"Dr. Putz?" The short *u* echoed through the theater like a bull(y) horn. We all turned to see the Community Council president, Henry Landon, leaning against the theater door, his hands in his pockets. He was trying to look nonchalant, but his eyes told a different story. "Could a large group of people be bullied at the same time—like a collective bullying?"

"I suppose," Dr. Putz said into the mike. "Do you have something specific in mind?"

"Well, I think we're all being bullied right now. Outside."

"Excuse me?" Dr. Putz said, but she'd lost her audience. Everybody was jumping up and pushing toward the hall like Black Friday barbarians. Meanwhile, Pasternak shouted into the microphone demanding order, but to no avail. The crowd was drunk with disorder. Then all at once I was swept up and out of the theater. People crowded the windows. I squeezed myself in between two bulky football players and caught a good look outside.

"Holy shit," one of the football players breathed.

"Jesus Christ," the other one said.

The athletic field was burning. The fire shot up as though from the snow itself, and flames licked the air. Smoke blew every which way. On the snow, maybe six feet in front of the flames, were three large words drawn in red paint: BROTHERHOOD. TRUTH. EQUALITY. Behind me, the teachers were attempting to round us up, but we weren't moving. We were pressed to the windows, searching for the source of the flames.

Then the wind must have shifted; the smoke blew away to reveal three wooden posts more than ten feet high, thrust into the ground. Hanging from each was a body strung up by its neck. The bodies were on fire. People were shouting. Someone was crying. Were those actual people? Who were they? Who had done this? Fire trucks and an ambulance sped through the school gates. Just then the fire burned through one of the ropes, and its body fell.

"Get to your homerooms!" a frantic teacher yelled.

The firemen and medics took off across the field, dashing through the red paint, turning TRUTH and half of EQUALITY into a pile of bloody-looking snow. One medic picked up the fallen body from the ground, raising it with ease. It was a dummy. They all were.

At the end of the day, I hoisted my book bag and set out for the Historical Society. I didn't tell my parents I was going; I just walked off school property.

It was a cottony gray afternoon, and the air smelled like wood smoke. The plow had done a good job on the roads, but there are few sidewalks in Nye, so I had to walk a narrow line between the pavement and the thick banks of snow on the shoulder. It was slow going, but the crunching of my boots helped me relax. It felt good to be away from the school, out in the world where nobody was watching me or sending me cryptic, frightening messages. Every time I shut my eyes, I saw the incinerating bodies and their snapped necks.

"Always confront your fears head-on," Murrow advised me now. I imagined him walking beside me in a fedora and long wool overcoat. He had no cigarette; his hands were thrust into his pockets for warmth. "I aired *London after Dark* during the Blitz," he continued, "because I wanted to show people's fortitude along with their fear. I wanted to scatter the shadows."

"Tell that to Katie Milford," I said. "I asked her about reporting the hangings, and she shooed me off like I was a squawking crow."

"Editors can be a real pain in the ass," Murrow said, shaking his head. "But what can you do?"

The trees stretched tall and straight on the roadside, like soldiers at attention. I thought about the difference between driving to a destination and walking there. Murrow grew up in a log cabin without electricity or running water, and if he needed to get somewhere, he walked.

From now on, I decided I was going to be like Murrow — through sheer force of will, I would take myself wherever I needed to go.

I did wonder, however, if Murrow had been this cold. My lungs hurt and my fingertips burned. To distract myself from the discomfort, I thought about the wizened old person who probably ran the Historical Society, someone who greeted visitors with cocoa and cookies and would love me automatically because I reminded them of their grandkid. I picked up the pace.

Finally, after forty-five minutes, I saw a wooden post that read, *Nye Historical Society. Founded 1982.* The date was disappointing; I'd been hoping for a much earlier century. Still, I looked past the sign and saw a two-story white clapboard house sitting at the top of a steep hill. I puffed my way toward it and arrived with burning legs.

The Historical Society windows were crusted with dirt. The slanted, splintered porch looked like something out of a horror movie, and I couldn't help but think of myself as the lost little girl who stumbles upon the witch's cabin in the wood. But I'd come all this way, so I rang the doorbell. Soon the door swung open, and there before me was not the elderly person I expected but a young woman with startling green eyes, cat's-eye glasses, and so many freckles that I felt dizzy just looking at her. She had thick wavy auburn hair, and her fingers were covered with rings.

"Well, hello!" The rings flashed as she gesticulated. "Come in or you'll freeze."

I hesitated but stepped into the foyer. The woman closed and locked the door. She flipped on the lights, illuminating cabinets and display cases. "Welcome to the Nye Historical Society." She sounded like an overjoyful telemarketer. "I'm Hazel."

I introduced myself and held out my hand. Hazel looked surprised and amused; she probably didn't get many hand shakers. I told her I was researching a story for my school newspaper.

"A reporter?" She raised an eyebrow. It arched to an astounding point.

"I heard you had a series of letters written by Charles Prisom, the founder of Mariana Academy," I said. Hazel frowned and the freckles around her mouth slid toward her lips, as though they might fall in and be swallowed. "I'm very careful with historical documents," I added.

"Oh, I'm not worried about you!" Her laugh was like ice tinkling in a glass. "It's just that nobody has asked for those letters in years. I'm not even sure I know where they are."

She turned and walked back into the house. I followed her past a photo series labeled *Decades of Nye* and a glass-topped table bearing a velvet box, laid with six pewter spoons. *Cutlery, 1765,* the card read. Then I was following Hazel down a narrow hallway. She had some serious hips and her gray sweater and blue scarf bulked her up quite a bit, but she glided in front of me as though upon a litter. Then she opened a door, and I stopped short. An enormous room was spread out beneath exposed rafters, as colorful and cluttered as the backstage of a Victorian period play.

"This is my studio," Hazel said. "The Historical Society provides me with room and board. Feel free to nose around. I'll make us some tea."

I stepped inside and was immediately enveloped by the scent of musty clothes and rose perfume. Threadbare Persian rugs lay upon the scuffed wooden floorboards, and scarf-shrouded lamps cast a golden, shadowy light on chipped gilded mirrors. The walls were cluttered with prints—peacocks, exotic flowers, and Renaissance-style paintings where men in tights wooed women in billowing dresses. A bowl of juicy-looking pomegranates sat on a cluttered side table. I touched one, but it was fake. Beside them was a bound folder with a cover page that said, *The Interfering Goddess: Power, Manipulation, and Sexual Politics in Classical Literature. A Master's Thesis by Hazel Greenburg.* I read the first few lines, but it was thick on the theory, so I turned my attention to the phenomenal clutter of books. They were stacked on tables, inside the fireplace, and in tall piles by the bed.

The bed itself was covered with a quilt that resembled a wall tapestry. It depicted a naked, muscular man standing beside a tree. Tied to the tree was a white cow with large sorrowful eyes. But the really strange thing (if a naked man hanging out with a cow wasn't strange enough) was that the man's body was covered in eyes. There were eyes on his forehead, his nipples, and his stomach. I bent over to see if he had eyes on his penis.

"Iris."

Startled, I expected to see Hazel right behind me. In fact, she was across the room on a chintzy couch of faded blue silk. I lingered by the bed until Hazel smiled and held out my tea. "I don't bite," she said.

I went to her and took the mug. I sat down, and the cushion sagged like I was trapped in quicksand.

"So why are you interested in Charles Prisom?" Hazel asked, blowing on her tea.

I told her about my Charles Prisom article, but I was feeling unusually shy, and my voice sounded small. "One of my sources suggested I come here," I squeaked.

"Your sources, eh?" For a moment I thought Hazel was patronizing me, but then she nodded. "You sound like a serious journalist." Hazel looked deep into my eyes, her green irises glowing like light refracted through sea glass. It was preternatural, that color. "So tell me," she said, curling and uncurling her fingers around her mug, "what would you like to know about Mr. Prisom?"

"Well, my source said Charles Prisom wrote a bunch of letters about his motivations for founding Mariana Academy. She — I mean, my source — said there might be information here about the origins of the Community Code." I hoped Hazel hadn't caught my slip-up. When a source is secret, you're not even supposed to reveal the gender.

Hazel placed her hand over her heart as though she were about to sing the national anthem. "I pledge to follow the wisdom and forbearance of my father, Charles Prisom, in building a community of Brotherhood, Truth, and Equality for All."

I blinked. "How do you know that?" Hazel had just spoken Mariana's hallowed school pledge. Before every test, students sign their name to it as a promise not to cheat. Before every assembly, we stand

and recite these words. I thought about the burning figures in the snow. The bodies of Brotherhood, Truth, and Equality disintegrating into ash.

"I'm a Mariana lifer," Hazel said. "K through twelve."

Thirteen years in Nye! I nearly groaned out loud. I did not envy Hazel at all. But then, she was still here, so she must have found something to like about the place.

"Can I make a guess about your source?" she asked.

"All right, but I'm really not at liberty to say if you guess right or wrong."

"I'd put my money on Mrs. Kringle."

I managed to keep my face blank for about two seconds before gasping with surprise. Immediately thereafter, I shielded my face, horrified. There was nothing particularly secret about Mrs. Kringle, but I was practicing for the day when I'd have to pull a Judith Miller. How could I have failed so miserably?

Everybody makes a mistake sometime, Murrow whispered. *Do I even have to remind you about the* Person to Person *fiasco when I stupidly let the sources preapprove the interview questions?*

Your sources were celebrities! I thought back. *Nobody expects honest answers from famous people.*

"So you're not from here, are you?" Hazel said, not realizing she'd interrupted a conversation with Murrow.

"We just moved from Boston," I said, and told her about my old school.

"I tutored students at University School between 2002 and 2004, when I was getting my master's!" She seemed genuinely thrilled to have this in common with me, and I felt a rush of warmth toward her.

"So I would have been in kindergarten and first grade then. Do you think — I mean, maybe I even saw you there."

"It's certainly possible. University School is pretty small, right? But you don't sound thrilled about the move."

I shrugged.

Hazel looked like she was going to ask me another question in that vein but then seemed to change her mind. I was very curious to know what she was thinking about me.

"Tell me," she said, "have you ever been to Greece?"

I shook my head, wondering at the digression.

"It's an extraordinary country," Hazel said. "I was there for a couple of years, working on archaeology digs, waitressing, traveling around the islands. And of course, I met plenty of Greek men . . ." She stopped, curling the corner of her lip.

Non sequitur though it was, this was getting good.

"Well, maybe that's a story for another time."

I sat back, disappointed.

"But how about you? Anyone at school strike your fancy?"

"I'm focusing on my reporting right now," I said.

"Well, I guess it's good to have priorities."

"So — the people you met in Greece?" I prompted, trying to lead her back to the Greek men.

"The people were lovely, more or less . . ." Hazel bit her lip, looked past me into the room. Her eyes glazed over in the dim, wavering light. Half the lamps in Hazel's studio flickered as though they were on the verge of burning out.

"Your life is so interesting," I said, still hoping for more on the men. "I mean to travel like that, meet so many people."

She shrugged. "When I was your age, I had everything planned out, but sometimes, you just have to let the Fates guide you."

"You mean things didn't turn out the way you wanted?"

The way Hazel looked at me, I worried that I'd offended her. But then she said, "I returned from Greece five years ago, and I tutored classics at Mariana and worked part-time as an assistant for Mr. Renquist, the previous curator here at the Historical Society. And then one morning about three years ago, I came in to work to find Mr. Renquist sitting at the kitchen table." Hazel nodded at the table by the sink. "His face was lying in a bowl of scrambled eggs."

I looked at her, confused.

"Heart attack," she said, shrugging as if it was perfectly usual to find your employer dead in his breakfast. "Anyway, the town hired me as full-time curator."

"So you stopped tutoring?"

"Eventually, but not because of my job here. At the time that I took this position, I was tutoring a girl named Mary—one of the brightest students I have ever taught. She was a loner and shy, but we'd been reading Cicero's orations and I could see how much they excited her. She became interested in Roman politics and government, and soon enough she announced that she wanted to run for junior class representative. We spent months writing speeches, working on Mary's oratorical skills, and designing a strategic campaign. She gained confidence. She blossomed. People at school started to take her seriously. Before she decided to run, most of her classmates barely knew she existed."

"Did she win?"

"No." A low growl vibrated in Hazel's throat. "Mary was accused of rigging the election. It's a long story, but essentially the Community Council brought evidence to Headmaster Pasternak proving that she'd tampered with the ballots."

"Wait—" I said, and sat up as straight as the sagging cushion would allow. "Mary? You're not talking about Mary Breckinridge?"

Hazel nodded, and my body swelled with adrenaline: the feeling of making an unexpected investigative link.

"The Community Council Disciplinary Board recommended that Mary be thrown off the campaign and receive a two-week suspension," Hazel continued. "I talked to Pasternak on her behalf, but he said the evidence proved her guilt. And it ruined her reputation. Afterwards, not a single teacher agreed to write her a college recommendation. She repeated her senior year at another school."

I was starting to understand why Prisom's Party was so active at Mariana. I thought about the mob of students, chanting at Marvin, berating him. And if his sister was innocent, I couldn't even imagine how indignant she must have felt, knowing she'd been wronged and having no recourse to prove her innocence.

"How do you explain the evidence against Mary?" I asked.

"Evidence is fabricated all the time. Think about governments that also control their country's media. Think about Russia and China. They're masters of manipulation. It's not for nothing that the students who accused Mary of rigging the election also tried her."

I thought about Katie Milford shooting down all my stories and understood Hazel's indignation.

"When I came back here after all that time away," Hazel said, "I'd hoped the system had changed. It hadn't. In framing Mary Breckinridge, the students on the Community Council were sending a message: 'Don't mess with the system or you'll get burned.' But enough of this depressing talk!"

Hazel rose from the couch and took our mugs to the kettle for more hot water. I tracked her graceful movements—how she poured the milk, the way her fingers untangled strands of her wavy hair. She was womanly but also girlish. The woman part made me feel young and nervous, while the girl part made me feel as if she and I could be close friends.

She returned with the tea, and my eyes fell on her fingers, curved around the mug. "That's an interesting ring," I said, pointing to the thick silver band she wore on the middle finger of her right hand. Perched atop the band was a silver fly with globular eyes and sharp, flexed wings.

"It's a horsefly," she said. "The Greeks called it the gadfly. A good friend gave it to me." She leaned toward me. "In ancient Greece, Socrates was called the Gadfly of Athens. No matter how hard his opponents tried to swat him away, he kept biting them with difficult questions."

"He sounds like a journalist."

Hazel nodded, a sly smile creeping across her lips. "So he was. Not unlike yourself, I'd think."

I glowed with the compliment. But then Hazel grew serious. "Do you know what it took for Socrates' enemies to make him stop pursuing the truth?"

"Hemlock," I said, eager to show off my knowledge of the classics. But Hazel regarded me with concern, like I was about to drink a cup of the poison myself.

"Yes," she said slowly. "That's right."

For a moment neither of us spoke. Then I blurted, "I think certain students at the school are trying to intimidate me. They think I'm a gadfly." I told Hazel about the note in the Trench and the computer virus. "Not that I think I'm as smart as Socrates, of course. And truthfully, he was pretty annoying the way he kept pestering everyone and — "

"Fear allows a ruling regime to thrive." Hazel's stare made me snap my mouth shut. "But you don't strike me as easily intimidated."

She was right. Woodward and Bernstein didn't back down in the face of Nixon. And Murrow certainly didn't cower before McCarthy.

"And there's another thing," I said. "I've got this teacher, Mr. Kaplan, and — "

"A teacher? Mr. Kaplan?" she repeated, surprised. I nodded. She raised another arched eyebrow. "So what of him?"

Hazel leaned forward, expectant, her expression strangely voracious. I started to answer, but I couldn't do it. If I shared my suspicion that Mr. Kaplan was involved with Prisom's Party, I'd end up trying to explain the cryptic staring contest he and I had been having since the ice cream social. And then Hazel would think I was crazy. She'd tell me I was hallucinating or paranoid. She'd probably confirm everything Dr. Patrick thought about my unsound mental state. And I didn't want that to happen; I didn't want Hazel to send me away.

"Well," I said, changing tack, "Mr. Kaplan's probably the best teacher I've ever had."

"Oh." Hazel gave one slow nod. She looked unhappy.

I folded my arms over my chest. "What's wrong?"

"It's just that Jonah — Mr. Kaplan — used to be on the Academic League team with me. He never struck me as the educator type."

So they were in school together, an interesting development. Perhaps Hazel would offer up vital details about Mr. Kaplan's childhood in Nye and I could begin to understand his strange behavior through her. "What type was he?"

"Difficult to define." She paused. I thought she was going to explain what she meant, but she said, "To be honest, Iris, I haven't seen the man in over a decade. He could be a totally different person now. So tell me why he's such a good teacher."

I tried to describe how different Mr. Kaplan was. How he cared in a way the others didn't. How I suspected that if he had been running the school, Mary Breckinridge would have been exonerated.

"He wants to run the school?" Hazel sat up.

"Oh, no, he didn't say anything like that. But he and the status quo aren't exactly best friends."

As we talked, the sky grew progressively darker until I could see our reflections in the window, talking like old friends. Just a few hours earlier, I'd been on the road, cold and lonely. But in no time I'd made a sort of ally.

After a while Hazel asked how I was getting home. My parents had no idea where I was, and my phone was broken. They were probably worried, but I didn't care.

"You look like you need a ride," Hazel said, and before I could respond, she added, "Loneliness is worse when you're living with other people."

I'd told her nothing about my mother, and yet she knew exactly what my parents were like. We bundled up and headed for her car, an old rusted Saab that was full of junk: papers, empty Coke cans, shoes, magazines, more books, and gum wrappers spewing dried-up balls of chewed gum. The car also smelled thickly of stale cigarettes, but who was I to judge? Hazel was an artist and she'd lived in Europe. She said the heat was broken and apologized. I wondered why she didn't get it fixed, but I didn't ask.

We were halfway to my house when I realized we'd forgotten all about Charles Prisom's letters. "Oh!" Hazel exclaimed, her breath thick in the air. "It completely slipped my mind. The next time you come we'll dig them up."

I shivered in the cold, cramped car, but I was smiling too. Hazel wanted me to come back.

As soon as my parents heard me come in, they rushed to the front door. "Where in God's name have you been?" my mother demanded.

"Out with a friend," I said, and stormed up to my room.

Lily

L ILY BELIEVED THAT Justin asking her out was only a symptom of a larger existential problem: in order to attract a different type of boy, she'd have to be a different type of person. Her experience with the popular cliques had been instructive, however, so in the weeks after Justin's invitation, she turned her eye toward another social group — one that prized uniqueness.

The Studio Girls were four eccentrics who walked around like movie stars, proud to have every inch of themselves sculpted for display. They discussed movies you couldn't see at the sixteen-screen Cineplex, bands named after bizarre animals, and books written without certain letters of the alphabet. Each day they met in the art studios and threw themselves into their work. Lily wasn't sure how talented they were, but she yearned to know their secret — how to turn her own abnormality into an asset — and so she too began frequenting the art studios at lunchtime. The Studio Girls rarely talked to her, but they weren't usually mean to her, either.

In order to justify her presence Lily needed an art project of her own. In fact, she had two going simultaneously, a real one and a decoy. The former was a notebook, her "sketchpad," in which she wrote detailed observations about the Studio Girls. The latter was a painting that depicted the view from the art room windows: a small courtyard in which a family of ducks had made its home. Lily wondered why the ducks had not yet flown south for the winter and why there was no mallard. Had he run off on the family? Taken up with some hot young swan? In any case, Lily couldn't decide how many ducks to paint. When she first started the painting in late September, there'd been five speckled ducklings waddling in line. Now there were only four. She knew there was a hawk's nest on campus, but she had never once seen the hawk.

Lily visited the art room at least twice a week, and the scene never lost its magic: eight long legs crossed at razor-sharp angles, eyebrows arched, paintbrushes poised like cigarettes between slender fingers.

On this particular day, Veronica Mercy was performing a dramatic reading of the school newspaper. *"Vandal Victimizes School!"* Veronica read the headline in a loud, theatrical voice. She continued:

> "When Mariana Academy students walked into school after Thanksgiving break, they were shocked to find their lockers covered with images illustrating bondage, sex with animals, pill-popping, anorexia, cheating, and violent behavior toward other students.
>
> "Now some of these students are reeling from the consequences of having their personal lives broadcast to the entire community. Since the vandalism, two students have been admitted to a rehabilitation center for eating disorders, and disciplinary proceedings have begun for others found guilty of cheating and illegal drug use."

Veronica rolled her eyes, as though she considered these transgressions unimpressive.

The other girls weren't paying much attention, involved as they were with their own art projects, but Lily was fixated. Veronica was a beautiful mess. She was working with clay, her "primary medium," and wore an oversize work shirt over her school uniform. Her thick dark hair was pulled into a disheveled bun. From her tone as she continued reading, she could have been on stage reciting Shakespeare.

> "The 'Rule of Lockers' tradition, which has flown for years under faculty radar, has long allowed students to group their lockers according to social clique. The system is run by seniors, who collect

everyone's computer-generated locker numbers at the start of each academic year and redistribute these assignments among students, based on their friend groups. The vandalism highlighted this fact with themed images: sports equipment for the athletes, easels and paints for the artists, Bunsen burners and test tubes for the Academic League, and thespian masks for the theater crew.

"But no one was targeted with more vitriol than the students whose first-floor locker real estate is known to symbolize their prime social status. The most frightening pictures were drawn on large rectangular sheets of paper and taped to these students' lockers, their intricacy suggesting months of work."

Lily had taken a good look at these images before the school ripped them down. On Katie Flannigan's locker, a girl with Katie's red hair spewed a thick stream of projectile vomit onto the adjoining locker of sophomore Tad Durban and into a picture of Tad's Hummer. A line of red-eyed crabs scuttled out the Hummer's exhaust pipe, across four lockers, and up into the crotch of a girl with junior Amanda Richardson's black curls. On another locker, students hung from a gallows constructed of books: three torqued necks, six pigeon-toed feet, thirty clenched fingers. The figures' lips were shaded blue. They had black X's for eyes. Tristan Adams's locker was decorated with a pornographic image questioning his sexual orientation. A week after the vandalism, Tristan downed a bottle of prescription sleeping pills. His housekeeper found him and took him to the hospital just in time.

Veronica continued the recitation. *"The faculty was untouched by the vandals' brushes with the notable exception of Headmaster Morgan, who received a quotation from Percy Shelley on his office door: 'My name is Ozymandias, king of kings: / Look on my works, ye Mighty, and despair!'"* Veronica recited this quote with a gargantuan smile and said, "And now for the best part of the story—they interviewed me! Amy, you have to read it."

Amy Chang sat beside a large papier-mâché egg, reapplying her signature red lipstick and smoothing down the sides of her black bob cut.

"Amy!" Veronica snapped, and waited until Amy reluctantly took the article.

"'*The vandals don't understand the nuance of Shelley's Ozymandias,*' said junior Veronica Mercy, '*and they clearly haven't read their Foucault.*'" Amy turned her big dark eyes on Veronica and cooed at her. "Oh, Ronnie, you're *so* intellectual."

"Shut up, bitch," Veronica said, laughing. "Keep reading."

Amy made a big show of clearing her throat. "*Miss Mercy's locker received an innocuous picture of a paintbrush. She said the vandals had shown a 'lack of vision.'*"

"The hullabaloo over all this is a dreadful bore," complained Jocelyn Simon, who, Lily noticed, always spoke like a Victorian-era British person. Jocelyn didn't bother to look up from her own project: a miniature clothesline hung with condoms. "On more titillating topics, did any of you perchance read about that woman at university? The one who slept with all those blokes?"

"I heard it was artificial insemination," Amy Chang said.

"She became impregnated on multiple occasions and then aborted the fetuses," Jocelyn said. "Afterwards, she injected the fetuses with plasticine."

At that moment Krista Stark arrived carrying a pack of construction paper and crayons. Amy looked up from her compact. "They're ironic," Krista said by way of explanation.

Lily scribbled down *artificial insemination project* in her sketchbook and *crayons = ironic*. Then she pulled out her own copy of the vandalism story. The story had just come out and everyone at school was reading it. Rumors about the rebirth of Prisom's Party swirled through the halls. After decades of dormancy, some people said, Prisom's Party had awakened to fulfill its duty of protecting the Community Code. The Rule of Lockers promoted social segregation, and so clearly violated the school's motto of Brotherhood, Truth, and Equality for All. But darker rumors circulated as well. Others believed that the members of Prisom's Party pledged allegiance for life and faced unthinkable punishments should they ever try to leave. According to this theory, popular students like Tristan were members of Prisom's Party who'd made the grave mistake of trying to quit.

And then there was Lily's own father, who believed the vandalism was related to what he called "the Columbine Effect." Elliott Morgan worried that Mariana's students were starting to copycat the two murderers who'd shot up their Colorado school the previous April. "Those boys kept journals," he told his family. "Filled with disturbing pictures that were very much like our vandalism."

Whether Columbine or Prisom's Party was to blame, everyone accused the Trench kids, in particular Jonah Kaplan and Hazel Greenburg. Jonah had always been an outcast and provocateur. But what had happened to Hazel? How had the plump, happy girl who'd befriended Lily back in middle school turned into such a bizarre, intimidating Trench dweller?

Since junior high, Hazel had grown fast, her chunky body stretching into a long, knock-kneed shape before finally settling into its current voluptuous form: all curves and freckles and flashing green eyes. She was like Alice, the way she stretched and expanded and shrunk. And she lived in the Trench, which was its own mysterious rabbit hole. Rumors encircled Hazel like dark clouds: she cut herself; her eccentric artist mother was a drug-addicted prostitute; she'd tried to rub away the multitude of freckles on her body with Clorox. In short, the girl was fucked up. Together, she and Jonah were angry and bitter enough to perpetrate a malicious act like the vandalism. They also provided Lily all the reason she needed not to attach herself to any Trench dwellers. Even kindhearted ones like Justin. Lily didn't want to punish him, so she didn't reject him. But she didn't accept his invitation for a date either. She told herself this was the best approach, that she was minimizing the harm.

Lily looked up to see Veronica Mercy sashaying between the tables. She paused briefly to run her long nails down Amy Chang's arm and kiss Krista Stark atop the head. Then she headed for Lily. Lily shut the sketchbook with her observation notes.

"I wish I had eyes like yours," Veronica said, landing at Lily's table. She gave a perfunctory glance at Lily's duck painting. "I mean, not eyes that moved around all fucked up like that, but the color. That color is so amazingly creepy."

The room had gone quiet and Lily realized that the other girls were watching her.

"Is all your hair that color?" Veronica whispered, leaning toward Lily's pale ear. "I mean, *all* of it?"

Lily blushed.

"Wow. You're like a totally white canvas. The living embodiment of innocence." Veronica's eyes flashed, and then she was sashaying away again, leaving behind the scent of musk perfume and a fluttering sensation in Lily's stomach.

Jonah

IT TOOK OVER a week for the school's so-called collective bully-ing to make the local news, and when it finally did, just after Hal-loween, it was a pitiful excuse of a story. Perusing the local newspaper one morning, I found a short article buried deep inside the B section: *School Flames Quickly Quelled.* According to the piece, there'd been a small fire at a Mariana pep rally back in October and no one was hurt. This cover-up was Pasternak's doing, no doubt, and I was impressed by the reach of his influence.

The day after the event took place, he'd emailed the faculty and parents:

> The fire posed absolutely no physical threat to any teacher or stu-dent. The school-sanctioned pyrotechnic display was meant to il-luminate the virtues of the Community Code. We'd planned to take students into the hallway after the assembly so they could watch from a safe distance and make a public pledge against bullying. A faculty member who was unaware of the project grew concerned and called the fire department. It fills me with pride to know that our fac-ulty are so conscientious about the students' safety that they do not hesitate to act in the presence of a perceived threat.

This email, in conjunction with the newspaper story, made me wonder what Pasternak was doing in Nye. He seemed better suited for a Hol-lywood PR firm or Fox News.

The week after the fire took place, conflicting views of the event circulated through the school. From the number of stakes, to the real identity of the hanging figures, to whether there'd even *been* any hanging figures at all, to what the words in the snow had said—everything was in dispute. There'd been a lot of smoke outside, even more commotion inside, and most people hadn't gotten a good look. Moreover, the people who hadn't seen the fire wanted to be in on the conversation, so they pretended to be in the know.

"Whoever's behind all these incidents," my department head Rick Rayburn commented one day during lunch, "are treating us like chimps. They've given us certain stimuli, and they're waiting to see how we'll react."

"I definitely feel pumped full of chemicals," my colleague Stephanie Chu said.

"Do you think we're giving them the expected response?" I asked.

"Even the administration is lying left and right." Rayburn nodded at the open newspaper on my desk. "The collective conscience is poor, Jonah. Didn't you get the memo?"

Meanwhile, I'd willfully forgotten Pasternak's request for a chat (in high school, "See me" is a universally accepted mark of impending academic doom), so when he unexpectedly opened the door of the teachers' lounge one afternoon, I didn't realize at first why he was scowling at me.

After I stood up and followed him out, he began to speak about a number of scandals that had wracked the school in recent years. First, the three football players who'd been expelled for hazing. "Ghastly things they made the freshmen do," Pasternak said, leading me down the corridor. "Jockstraps and some disgusting Codeine-and-cough-syrup concoction and baseball bats and a bucket of piss." Then the students who'd been expelled after they were caught hacking into Ms. Montgomery's school email account. "They sent offensive emails," Pasternak said. "Detailed sexual content to a handful of students *and* teachers." And finally, Mr. Franks.

"He was caught while—" Pasternak stopped and threw up his hands. "Suffice it to say he's gone too."

Pasternak led me briskly past classrooms inside which students were guzzling information as if their brains were gas tanks. It looked far from healthy.

"We learned about these activities," Pasternak said, stopping at the door to the back stairwell, "because of the *Devil's Advocate.*"

Waves of sour breath blew from his mouth into my face. "That underground paper people have been talking about?" I asked, dodging the putrid airstream.

"Prisom's Party calls it their 'information arm.' Ring any bells from your student days?"

I shook my head. "Legends are malleable," I said. "That's why they're legends."

"Well, the paper exposed the football players and the students who hacked into Ms. Montgomery's email. Last summer, Prisom's Party mailed me a package containing irrefutable proof about Mr. Franks. Photographs of him in the *act!*" Pasternak's body shook like an addict in withdrawal.

So the rumors were true. "It seems like Prisom's Party was helping you," I offered.

"Dammit, Jonah!" Pasty's eyes popped, and his pupils bobbed like black egg yolks. "These kids are trying to run this school behind my back and they've become threatening. Before they were targeting specific infractions, but this year they're reveling in their disobedience. Quoting Orwell is not a good sign."

"I agree," I said. "And I'm wondering why nobody is addressing the problem."

Pasternak shook his head, then turned and entered the stairwell. I followed, our feet echoing against the cinderblock walls. "Do you understand what would happen if any of this wound up in the real newspapers? I can handle the local press, but only for so long. It may be a new millennium, Jonah, but there are plenty of people on the board who would be delighted to replace me with someone named Worthington or Beaumont. Capeesh?"

He had a point. Like me, Garrison Pasternak was Jewish, and his success at Mariana, and in the conservative town that housed it, was an aberration. I had to give him some credit for managing to stick it out in an unfriendly environment for several decades. I'd spent a mere twelve years at this school and nearly went mad.

"Now," he said, stopping at the bottom of the stairs in front of a black door, "follow me." He pulled out a ring of keys and inserted one of them into the lock. We entered the Trench.

At face value, the Trench is nothing more than a long, narrow corridor that once housed lockers, computer labs, and miscellaneous supply closets. But in the biosphere of Mariana Academy, the Trench had been the emblem of Mariana's embedded caste system, the home of untouchables like Justin and me. In some ways it resembled the real Mariana Trench—the one in the Western Pacific. Like the ocean depths, our Trench was freezing. Like the deep sea, where thermal vents pump boiling chemicals from the earth's core, our Trench also had a unique source of heat: vents expelling a noxious cafeteria effluvium. The earth's atmosphere may be 78 percent nitrogen, 21 percent oxygen, and a small percent noble gases, but the air quality in the Trench was about 93 percent foul.

The Mariana Trench (the real one) is nearly 6.8 miles below sea level—that's deeper than Mount Everest is tall. You might wonder what can possibly survive down there, but tons of living things survive at the bottom of the sea. Our Trench was no different. Twelve years ago it was filled with all kinds of bizarre adolescent life (not to mention the hated centipedes that made the subterranean environment their home). As I'd told my class, many organisms need extreme environments to survive. The Trench was the only part of the school where I had felt at home.

Pasternak turned to face me. "I know Prisom's Party is operating out of here, but I can't find them. And let me tell you, I have looked. They are invisible. They're ghosts."

He continued plodding down the hallway, muttering. Finally he stopped. "I know this school wasn't fair to you, Jonah. I know you don't owe me anything. But I need your help. I could have brought a dozen advanced degrees back, but I brought you. Specifically."

Of course. The large salary and suspiciously light teaching load now made perfect sense. He wanted to make sure I signed on. "I still don't understand what you want me to do," I said.

Pasternak sighed like a beaten old man. He was well past the age of retirement, yet he hung on. I looked at his ringless left hand. I didn't know much about him, but I imagined he lived alone in an apartment with newspapers dating back three decades and brownish plants gasping for air. I guessed his medicine cabinet was full of pills for his various old-man ailments and that he ate microwavable meals for dinner. I felt a torque in my chest. How did a person end up like this, so old and alone?

"You used to *live* down here, Jonah. You had plenty of experience sneaking around under the radar. Don't think I've forgotten all those things you did." Pasternak chuckled as though he found the memory of my transgressions pleasant. "Like I said, I can't force you, but I'm *asking* you: perform a little detective work on my behalf."

"I'm supposed to be a role model. I didn't come here to play your Eliot Ness."

"If you'd just consider my request. Jonah, please . . ."

I couldn't bear another moment of his rheumy-eyed desperation. "I'll think about it."

Pasternak looked relieved, but he didn't miss a beat. "Would you take a look around now and tell me if you see anything suspicious?"

Physically, the Trench looked exactly as I remembered it, coat hangers and dusty chairs stacked to my left and the darkened classrooms and lockers to my right. But something was missing. As uncomfortable and dirty as this place was, it always made me feel safe. I would jump down that final flight of stairs, and as soon as my loafers hit the floor, I'd know I was home. So many years later, I felt like a tourist amid ruins.

I walked to the Academic League headquarters, where Justin and I had spent most of our time. It was locked. I peered through the pane. "These rooms?"

"We've searched. But I'll get you keys."

I turned toward the end of the hall where rows of chairs were stacked over five feet high against the wall. I could just make out flashes of orange and green behind them. I turned back to poor old Pasty. "Looks the same to me," I said.

We stared at each other for a few moments. I wondered what he was thinking.

"You go up," I said, itching to get rid of him. "I'll look around a bit more."

"Good. The door will lock behind you when you come out. And for God's sake, Jonah, turn off the stairwell lights. I don't want to encourage anyone else to wander down here."

Iris

AFTER LISTENING TO Hazel, I knew I couldn't let the Trench intimidate me. When an editor rejects a story idea, you must immediately send your pitch to the next publication or risk fearing rejection forever. But as soon as I garnered the courage to investigate, I was suddenly deluged with work. Perhaps to distract me from investigating the mock hangings, Katie Milford assigned me a story on the homecoming game (of course she deleted my references to chronic traumatic encephalopathy!) and saddled me with a special Halloween insert. At least I managed to get my first op-ed published: a Maureen Dowd–style tirade against the sexy animal costume phenomenon.

Finally, after Halloween weekend, I put on my sternest *See It Now* face, let myself into the Trench, and marched down the dark hallway with complete confidence. Perhaps my fear was all from perception. Like Mr. Kaplan said: what humans consider extreme is normal to plenty of creatures on the earth, and vice versa. If I'd grown up down here and this dark, dank hallway were all I knew, then *this* would be the place I felt at home, and the upper world — sunshine, hallways packed with people, fresh air — would be terrifying. On the other hand, what if comfort was actually genetic, and no matter how you were raised, you were wired to fit in only in certain places? And what if I spent my entire life searching for the place I belonged — the place that matched *who I was* — and I never found it? Even worse, what if the place I truly belonged didn't exist?

I was sprawled out on the floor of the *Oracle* archives, paging through old newspapers and worrying about all this, when I heard footsteps—and voices. The fear I'd been suppressing resurged. I jumped up, flipped off the light, and stood in the dark. The footsteps and voices grew louder. I pressed myself against the wall. I wasn't sure how many people were out there, but I could feel the closeness of their bodies in the way some animals sense predators and prey by radar.

But then I saw Mr. Kaplan and Headmaster Pasternak come into focus through a crack in the door. And at that moment a soundtrack started playing in my head. It was on a loop, and it went like this: *shit-shitshitshitshitshitshitshitshitshitshit. SHIT.* I was an idiot to have hidden. I wasn't doing anything wrong, but if I suddenly popped out, how was I going to explain the fact that I'd been hiding?

After a while Pasternak left, and I saw Mr. Kaplan moving a bunch of chairs around. Then he stood in the hallway just looking at the wall. I was dying to see what he was staring at, because he had a strange expression, like he was about to scream. He opened his mouth, but the sound that came out wasn't angry or loud. It was a whimper. The cry of a lost child.

I pressed my palms to my ears and shut my eyes, but the awful sound zinged around my head like a pinball.

And then the hallway went quiet. I don't know how long I stood in the archive room, covering my ears, but when I stepped out, Mr. Kaplan was gone. He'd restacked the chairs, so I began taking them down again. As I did, I began to notice something on the wall behind them. At first I only saw green and orange lines, but soon these lines assembled themselves into a kind of face. And all at once I was looking at an enormous drawing of the four-eyed demon, its mouth set in a gleeful snarl. I crept closer, remembering how pale Mr. Kaplan had looked when he saw the same image in the girls' bathroom. Now, in the long tunnel of the Trench, I could still hear his whimper, vulnerable and raw.

He'd seen the darkness inside of me, I realized, because he harbored a similar pain. But what had happened to him? Why did the demon plague him so?

Jonah

After I ascended from the Trench, I walked around in a daze. I'd been deluded, thinking I could return to Mariana and not encounter my past at every turn, but I had always imagined my adult self and my boyhood as a double helix: twisted threads that traveled in a spiral but never actually made contact. Returning to the Trench had tangled the strands together.

Part of me wanted to bolt the Trench door tight; Pasternak was right, I didn't owe him anything. But my conscience jabbed at me. I owed the students. I'd set myself up as a kind of educational 007, whose mission it was to short-circuit the kids' assembly-line approach to education. That commitment shouldn't be half-assed. Mariana's problems were systemic, and ferreting out Prisom's Party was the first step in targeting the school's culture of hypocrisy. If the young renegades believed that fear was an appropriate weapon to combat immorality, then the collective conscience was indeed poor.

I was heading toward the school office, ruminating, when a woman called my name. I turned around, and there was Hazel Greenburg, gorgeous as a modern Botticelli arisen from the faculty mailboxes. Surely I was hallucinating. But no, this was Hazel in the flesh: her hips a little wider, her face fuller, and her green eyes fiercer than the last time I'd seen her, who knows how many years ago. She looked at me with her usual mixture of interest, mocking, and omniscience. Hazel was the kind of girl who knew things about you that you didn't even know about yourself. My heart beat at hyperspeed. I was still in love with her.

"Hazel." I half swallowed her name. She reached in for a hug and squeezed me tight. It was an indescribable relief. She pulled away. A few strands of her auburn hair stuck to my scruff, and she brushed them away with her long, freckled fingers. Those fingers, I remembered, moved with uncanny precision, like intelligent entities.

"I heard you were teaching here," she said, and shook her head. "But I seriously didn't believe you'd step foot in this place again. How *are* you handling the ghosts, my long-lost friend?"

Hazel was smiling, but my face burned like a man accused. I struggled to sort through the seemingly infinite implications of her question. "What are *you* doing here?" was all I could manage.

"You don't sound thrilled."

I shook my head. "Are you crazy?"

"Well, after a brief hiatus, I'm returning to the tutoring profession." She smirked, already over the surprise of our sudden meeting. "Classics. Pasternak and I agreed on a pretty sick rate."

I nodded, mute.

"You look like you've been bludgeoned by a gladiator," she said. And then in response to my frown, "Cantankerous as ever, I see. But you look good, Jonahlah. All grown up."

"Gee, thanks, Bubbie."

"Oh, Jonahlah, didn't your mother teach you how to accept a compliment?"

"I'm just surprised to run into you like this," I said, hiding the fact that I'd actually been looking for her around town.

She nodded, and her face displayed an openness that seemed new to me. Hazel's expressions sometimes appeared to be constructed entirely from the play of light and shadow. In a moment, all of her features could reconstitute themselves, shape-shift, so you never really knew what you were looking at. But I hadn't seen her in a decade. A lot could have changed. Bumping into Hazel now, I realized, was a great stroke of luck. She and I had once been inseparable. We'd been co-conspirators. Maybe she would help me with the task of finding Prisom's Party.

"I have an appointment in town," she said. "But here's my number." She fished in her bag, pulled out a pen and scrap of paper, and wrote her number on the back. "Call me this weekend. Now that I'm making the big bucks, I can buy you a PBR or something . . ." She seemed to lose her train of thought, and I realized that she was just as nervous at seeing me as I was at seeing her. She was just better at hiding her emotions.

"We'll talk," I said.

"Yes," she agreed, and her lips curled upward in an uncertain smile. Then she turned and walked out ahead of me, her long hair sighing against her back.

For the rest of the day, Hazel elbowed every other thought from my head. I imagined her tutoring students, her freckled fingers correcting some poor kid's bungling of Vergil. I pondered whether I could get her hired as a part-time Academic League consultant. It was a wonder Pasternak wasn't already outsourcing for extracurriculars and hiring tutors to telecommute from Mumbai.

I began to fantasize about what our partnership might be like. I imagined that we'd create mnemonic devices to help the kids remember the ancient Roman rulers and have a running bet over how long it would take somebody to say cunnilingus instead of Caligula. I saw us knocking over a shelf of Bunsen burners while making out in the school's lab closet and cracking each other up with bad science jokes about our explosive sexual activities. But these were juvenile fantasies. Part of me wished I were sixteen again, but an alternate version of my teenage self: silly and intoxicated instead of overly intellectual and conversationally inept. I tried to conjure up a modern-day fantasy involving Hazel and myself, but I couldn't. I didn't know her anymore.

Hazel and Justin and I had attended Mariana from kindergarten on, and though she was a year above Justin and me, we ended up in the same science clubs and computer electives. As kids we romped for hours in the woods behind our homes, enacting elaborate fantasy worlds, building makeshift weapons, battling imaginary Orcs. Hazel was never the damsel in distress; she was the leader of our small warrior band. She issued orders and we obeyed. She even named us. Justin was the cowardly lion, a moniker he didn't mind, because, as he once told me, "That's the kind of thing you expect from an older sister." I was much less reconciled to my nickname—Mr. Tumnus, a reference to my small stature and pointy ears.

When you're young, you don't realize there's a direct relationship between your perceived invincibility and your vulnerability. I may not have had Masters of the Universe biceps, but I had a masterful mind and so, I assumed, I had the emotional armor to match. I didn't know that with a single glance a girl could melt the strongest metal. I certainly did not believe Hazel was capable of such a thing. We were buddies, pals. Allies.

Then one night when I was fourteen, my view of Hazel underwent a dramatic reconstruction. A few headgear-encaged geeks from the science club were sleeping over at our house, watching *Mystery Science Theater* in the basement. Just before this, a science experiment in our kitchen had devolved into a massive shaving cream fight, and my mother had sent us one by one to the upstairs shower. At some point I realized I'd had too much soda and skipped on up to the second-floor bathroom. I must have been in a real hurry, because it didn't even occur to me to knock.

Hazel was standing in the shower steam, not two feet from me, her wet hair dripping onto the bathmat, her breasts level with my face. To my fourteen-year-old eyes, her large pink areolas were like ice cream cones licked flat. She was only fifteen, but she seemed perfectly matured to me. I was struck dumb by the brown, tan, and chestnut spots that speckled her torso, stomach, and breasts. The tops of her feet were freckled as well as her toes. The freckles seemed to be moving, audibly crackling, and suddenly my eyes were drawn to the coarse conflagration between Hazel's legs. The freckles were like sparks shot from that fire.

Hazel's nipples hardened as the cold air rushed in from the hallway, but she neither screamed nor covered herself. In fact, she looked me over like I was the naked one, her eyes zeroing in on my crotch. I wanted to run, but I could only stand there, cupping myself, listening to her hearty peals of laughter.

After this, she acted like nothing had happened. Her laughter hadn't been cruel, I realized years later, but joyous, as though to suggest that my embarrassment was foolish, unnecessary. *After all,* she seemed to say with that killer curl of her lip, *what man (or boy) can look at me and not feel aroused?* It would be another two years before I learned that there was one boy unsusceptible to her charms, and that, sadly for Hazel, he was the only boy who mattered.

Still, from that moment forward, I was obsessed. By high school, we spent all our time together, meeting regularly for the Academic League. Our proximity tormented me, but I kept my frustration bottled up. I did not want to turn out like Justin, decomposing into a lovesick pile of compost. So I turned the Hazel switch to Off and engaged the security lock. I should have known that some doors don't stay shut, no matter how much cement and steel you put over them.

Lily

L ILY'S FAVORITE DAY of the week was Sunday, because this meant brunch with her grandmother. The tradition was sacrosanct. Amelia Morgan cooked a large, unhealthy meal, standing over skillets of greasy eggs and bacon in her silk charmeuse blouse and pearls. After everyone had stuffed themselves full, they lounged around the polished dining room table.

"So how are things at school, honey?" Amelia said on this particular morning.

"The guidance counselor asked to see Lily last week," Elliott said, surfacing from his *Times*. "The teachers believe she has confidence issues."

Maureen shook her head as she turned the page of her *Berkshire Interiors* magazine. "Amelia, we've told Lily again and again that she's no different from anyone else."

"You're the one who won't let me drive, Mom! Who won't—"

In tandem, Maureen and Elliott put down their reading material.

"That is in the best interest of your health," her mother snapped.

"Which we've discussed ad nauseam," her father muttered.

"Lily, what did you tell the guidance counselor?" Amelia asked gently.

"I said as long as nobody had put an Albinos Only sign over the water fountains, I'd consider myself equal."

"That was an inappropriate thing to say!" Her father shook his head but couldn't contain an amused smile.

"The guidance counselor told me not to joke about the 'trials of other minority groups.'"

"My goodness." Amelia licked her lips and her lipstick glistened. "Before long, the school will be calling you Melanin Challenged."

Her grandmother was right. And yet despite Mariana's attention toward political correctness, Elliott had grown quite upset the year Mrs. Kaplan sent him a letter asking him to add a menorah to the Christmas display or remove the tree. "What's next," he'd said, "a Buddhist shrine and some Wiccan doodad?"

Lily had always known the few Jewish families at Mariana to be different. As children, the Kaplan twins were the ones eating chalky Oreo-cookie knockoffs at lunch and refusing ham-and-cheese sandwiches on playdates. Of course, now that she was older, she understood the real implications of being Jewish at Mariana. Neither the Kaplans' parents (both scientists) nor Hazel Greenburg's mother (an artist) belonged to the local country club. Neither Mrs. Kaplan nor Mrs. Greenburg attended the exercise group or book club that Lily's mother organized. When Mrs. Kaplan did make an appearance at a school event, Lily saw how coldly deferential the other mothers were toward her. She could tell the exact moment when they noticed Mrs. Kaplan's ring finger, bedecked by a slim gold band and a noticeable lack of Mariana housewife bling. Over and over, she saw their eyes lift ever so slightly, their distaste mingled with pity.

"Lily's doing just fine," Elliott told his mother and his wife. "And Lily, two years from now you'll be off to a terrific college in a city where you won't need a car."

Lily's mother nodded her approval. "Lily, you know we'll drive you anywhere you want to go."

After breakfast, Lily and her grandmother went for a walk. Amelia walked a mile every day regardless of the weather. The afternoon was frigid, but Lily would happily submit to extreme levels of discomfort for one-on-one time with Amelia. So grandmother and granddaughter bundled up in thick shearling coats and set off. There was no one else outside, and the world was gelid. Even the chimney smoke seemed frozen in place above the rooftops.

They walked for a while without speaking. Then Amelia said, "You've been sighing every thirty seconds since we left the house."

Lily kicked a pebble on the ground.

"So come on, honey. Spill."

Lily shrugged. "It's complicated." And it was. Her project in the art studio was progressing. Since she first started observing Veronica Mercy and the others, she'd filled half a sketchbook with notes. The pages resembled detailed mathematical proofs. If Lily could only crack the code, she'd figure out the girls' secret. And she was getting close. Veronica was paying more attention to her these days, drifting over frequently to examine the truly ugly ducklings in her painting, or comment on her skin and eyes.

On the other hand, the Justin situation had declined. Her non-answer policy had only encouraged him. He watched her unabashedly, his pale blue eyes shining with an intolerable mixture of anxiety and elation.

Amelia raised her head to the frosted sky and examined the quiet street as though seeing it for the first time. "I'm seventy-three, kiddo. I've been around more blocks than you can imagine, and most of them weren't half as attractive as this one."

Lily wished there were no Justin in the world. "Well, there's this b—"

"A boy!" Amelia clasped her mittened hands together, delighted.

Lily pursed her lips against the cold and shook her head.

"It's one of *those* situations . . . Lily, if he can't see you for who you are, he's not worth it."

Amelia's eyes were bright with cold, but stern. As elegant as her grandmother was, Lily knew her philosophy was encapsulated in the simple belief, *Don't take shit from anyone.*

"It's not like that," she said, and began to explain about Justin, about his longtime crush, about how he'd slammed his foot into the gym wall after losing the last Academic League tournament and fractured his foot.

"Well, is this Justin unattractive?"

"No."

"Does he treat you poorly?"

"He treats me too well. He's always giving me things and offering to help me with my homework. Once when I tried to thank him, he shook his head and thanked *me.* Like I'd done him this big favor. He's so awkward." They walked in silence for a moment; then Lily said, "I just want a normal boyfriend."

"What's your young man interested in?"

Lily remembered the dragonfly. "I think he collects bugs. And he reads everything."

"An intellectual."

"A loser." And then she thought, but didn't say, *Like me.*

Amelia frowned.

"His brother was responsible for the locker vandalism, Grandma."

"Your father said the vandals weren't caught."

"I know, but —"

"How would you feel if people judged you because of things your father did?"

"Oh, they do, Grandma. You have no idea."

"Then you don't need much convincing. This young man sounds like a good person. A genuine person. And popular boys are vain."

"Not all of them."

"Okay, for argument's sake then, let's assume the popular crowd isn't any more superficial than the unpopular crowd."

"Okay. That seems fair." Lily stopped and looked up at Amelia's house. They'd already made it four times around the block, but neither of them wanted to finish the conversation in front of Lily's parents.

Amelia looked squarely into Lily's eyes and smiled. "Well, given that assumption, everybody is exactly who they are."

"Real deep, Grandma."

"It's actually quite simple. You meet somebody, you get to know them, and you judge them based on your own standards. Your opinion of this boy may turn out to be completely valid. But as of yet, you don't have enough evidence."

"He broke his own foot, Grandma!"

"Lillian, you don't really *know* him. You haven't had a single substantive conversation with him. And I know high school runs by different rules than the rest of the country — I was once your age, I get it. But honey, out in the real world, your attitude makes you a snob."

Lily's face burned. As usual, Amelia was right.

"You know why the world is filled with war and misery? It's because people let their emotions lead them this way and that when they should be using their minds. Like I said, your suitor may be totally wrong for you, but you'll never know if—"

"If I don't try him on? He's not a sweater!"

"Point taken. But you're acting as though you must make a definitive decision about this boy and stick to that decision for eternity. One date, Lillian, isn't the be all and end all."

That evening, Lily sat on her bed, staring at the phone. She picked it up and put it down half a dozen times. When she was talking to her grandmother, life seemed straightforward, like a well-organized closet. Rationality, she thought. Common sense. If only these things defined the parameters of her life.

Lily looked around the bedroom that her mother had furnished for her: at the curtains and the carpet she did not choose, at the bedspread that had appeared one day, many years ago, as though randomly deposited from the sky. She hated this room, yet she'd never complained or tried to change it. The guidance counselor was right; she wasn't assertive. She did what was expected of her, and the expectation at Mariana was that you didn't date from the Trench. But that wasn't rational. And in all honesty, Justin wasn't bad-looking. Lily dialed his number. This wasn't the be all and end all, she thought to herself. But then why were her hands shaking?

Lily and Justin set their date for the night of the school's fundraiser auction, which meant Lily's parents would be out late. That Saturday afternoon, Lily prepared for the evening. She wanted to wear a new dress, but to get underneath a dress Justin would have to go up from the bottom, and that didn't seem right for a first date. He could reach under a T-shirt, but that seemed anticlimactic without some fancy bra waiting for him — something Lily most definitely did not own. If she wore a button-down, would he reach under it or undo the buttons? Lily considered each option. She was excited and wished she wasn't. This date wasn't supposed to mean anything. So why was she fussing over the details — buttons and bras?

In spite of herself, she made a mix CD and repositioned the candles on the shelf. She deliberated over whether candles were too cliché. On television, when two people came into a bedroom, the candles were already lit. She tried out lighting combinations, draping a variety of sheer scarves over her bedside and desk lamps. She made her bed. Then she showered, shaved, and rubbed on the fancy lotion Dipthi had bought her for a birthday present. When she was dressed, she looked at the clock. It was three in the afternoon.

Justin arrived early in a dark blue Peugeot station wagon. Lily, who had been standing by the window since seven thirty, saw him stop a couple of houses away and loiter there. His apparent anxiety irked her, even more so because she felt the same way. Maybe she should pretend to be sick. Maybe she could fabricate an emergency.

At five to eight, Justin pulled up in front of her house and parked in front of their large oak tree. His crutches were gone, but he was still wearing the plastic boot. He walked slowly toward the door, favoring his good foot, carrying a monstrous bouquet. She couldn't feign sickness now.

Lily checked her hair and adjusted her necklace. She wore a dark blue V-neck with three-quarter arms and jeans that Dipthi said gave her a "tight ass." Her boots were black suede, like Doc Martens but less austere. She smiled at herself. It was possible that at this moment she was actually pretty.

"You look really nice," Justin said, handing her the flowers. She didn't know what to do with them, so she carried them back out to the car.

At the pub in town, Lily checked for anyone she knew, but all of the young families who usually filled the restaurant had already finished their meals and headed home to put their kids to bed. They looked over the menus in silence. Lily kept thinking about the locker vandalism, and Jonah's culpability, and what people would say if they saw her on a date with the vandal's brother. She looked around again to make sure she didn't recognize anyone.

"Are you okay?" Justin said.

"What? Yeah."

Justin began chatting about their Latin class, and they managed to fill the time until the waitress arrived for their orders. When she left, they circled around the Latin discussion again. It seemed to Lily they could simply keep spiraling—Caesar, Ovid, Cicero, Caesar, Ovid, Cicero—for the rest of the meal. And yet soon enough, she knew, they'd have to swim away from their small island of safety. They'd have to *talk*.

The food arrived. The waitress set a grilled chicken sandwich and fries in front of Lily and a cheeseburger in front of Justin. If Justin was going to kiss her later, wouldn't he be more concerned about his breath? But he was working on the burger the way only a boy could, and for the first time the date started to feel somewhat like regular life.

"What's your favorite Latin word?" she asked, and winced at her own ineptitude.

Justin looked up from something he was examining under the table and smiled. *"Amo."*

Lily blushed. *Amo, amas, amat,* she thought. *Amamus, amatis, amant.* Their Latin teacher had made them march through the halls chanting conjugations. I love, you love, he, she, or it loves. *It* loves?

That made no sense. We love. You (plural) love. They love. And then, of course, the perfect passive subjunctive — would that I had been loved — the saddest conjugation of them all.

"Did you drop something?" She noticed Justin staring at his lap again. *Please God,* she thought, *let him not have a hard-on.* After an awkward pause, Lily excused herself and headed toward the bathroom. When she returned, she saw that Justin was bent over, reading something in his hand. She crept up behind him and snatched the paper away. Then, before she knew what she was doing, she'd slid into the booth next to him. She had never made such a forward physical move toward a boy. And now their arms and knees were pressed together, their first touch all night. She smelled his aftershave and freshly laundered flannel. She felt the heat rise from his body. They looked at each other, surprised. Lily inspected the scrap of paper she'd stolen. It was covered with bullet points: *family, school, religion, parents' jobs, favorite books, religious beliefs.* He'd written a conversation crib sheet! Only instead of feeling annoyance or pity, she was overcome with relief.

"I was nervous too," she said. "I got dressed an hour early."

His look of humiliation deepened.

"And I changed my clothes three times."

Justin refused to look at her.

"And I made a make-out mix CD."

The corners of his mouth turned up just enough. He thought she was joking; now *she* was the pathetic one. "I changed my socks five times," he said.

"I can't even see your socks."

"My feet get really sweaty," he said.

After dinner they returned to Lily's house. She'd rented a movie days ago, because on a Saturday night they were likely to encounter other kids from school at the video store. Standing among the racks, she'd debated movie selections. A comedy seemed the obvious choice, but Justin seemed too erudite for the slapstick flicks she liked. An action movie wasn't right — you couldn't make out to people shooting each other. And most dramas were too serious. Finally she chose *Dead Poets Society*. At least they could laugh at how much worse the school in the movie was than their own.

In the den, she motioned Justin toward the special loveseat near the TV. "I'm sorry we have to sit so close to the screen," she apologized as she went to put in the movie. "My eyesight is terrible." When she turned around, Justin was still standing. "You can sit down, Justin." He sat, pressing his body into the couch arm as though trying to dissolve into it. She joined him, hugging the opposite arm. She reached for the remote, using it as a pretext to shift a few inches toward him. She didn't get very far. Justin was sitting stark upright, staring straight ahead.

She started the movie and edged closer to him until there was less than half a foot between them. Now they were both staring at the television, avoiding each other. Lily felt electricity vibrating between them, invisible energy shooting between their shoulders, elbows, and legs. They still weren't touching and yet she felt fused to him, as though by magnetic force. She sensed Justin trying to look at her without turning his head.

A flock of birds exploded across the screen and Lily thought about the ducklings outside the art studios. The last time she'd seen them another baby had disappeared. She felt inexplicably sad for those ducks, but there was nothing she could do for them.

"What's wrong?" Justin said.

Lily shook her head. "Nothing."

"This is going to be a sad movie, isn't it."

"You haven't seen it already?"

He shook his head.

"Then how do you know it's sad?"

"Unforgiving adults and bright-eyed boys. It doesn't bode well."

She paused the video. Suddenly the house felt very quiet and still. "What are you talking about?"

"I get these ideas in my head." He shrugged. "They don't always make sense to other people."

"Try me."

"There are these signs. The bells on their campus are really ominous. And those boys are so eager and naïve. I just have a bad feeling about it. But Jonah says I overinterpret everything."

The locker vandal, Lily thought. "Your brother —" But she stopped herself. She had nothing nice to say about Jonah. Meanwhile, Justin was looking at her.

"So which one of these guys is going to kill himself?"

"You're creeping me out, Justin. Just admit you've seen the movie before."

He shook his head.

"Then how can you possibly —"

"Well, for one thing, it's got death in the title." He smiled.

Lily did not smile back. "You said suicide. How could you know that?"

"It's the tone, I guess. If the movie were asking us to get angry or to grieve for these kids, then I'd put my money on an accident. A *Separate Peace* kind of scenario. But so far, the tone is setting us up for something else."

Lily waited for him to continue.

"The movie wants us to mourn."

"Are you always this serious?" She didn't understand the difference between grieving and mourning. She didn't understand why Justin had become all philosophical with her. Had he forgotten that this was a date?

But over the course of their discussion, they'd inadvertently shifted toward each other, and now his thigh was a mere six inches from her own. She rested her hand on the cushion halfway in between them, and electricity flowed up her arm and exploded in a starburst through her body. She did and did not want him to reach out and touch her. She focused her eyes on the hand in his lap, willing it to move, willing it to stay.

"Are you bored?" she mumbled.

He looked at her like he was staring off the edge of a cliff. Vertigo, she thought, wasn't the fear of heights but the fear of jumping.

Her heart pounded. She heard bells echoing, though the movie was stopped. The flapping of wings. Justin swallowed. Then his lips were against hers. His warm tongue pressed against her own. He shifted forward, murmured a low sound, cupped the back of her head with his hand. She saw herself sitting on the picnic table watching the soccer team. She was wet again. Justin made another low sound. She shivered. His tongue was strange, so much larger than her own. Her arm, attached to the palm still pressing the couch between them, was growing numb. He pulled away and looked into her eyes. Then he began to cry. What had she done wrong?

"I've wanted to do that for so long," he said. "You have no idea how I—"

At that moment, the sound of voices, keys. The front door opened.

Lily's parents found Justin at one end of the couch holding a *New York Review of Books,* his eyes oddly red, and Lily at the opposite end perusing a coffee-table book titled *Idyllic Greens of Ireland.*

"Justin. I didn't know you were coming over." The curve of Maureen's mouth gave away her surprise and, Lily thought, not a little disdain.

"Justin," Elliott said with a nod.

"What time is it?" Lily demanded. How were they back already? She'd planned on getting Justin out of the house long before her parents returned.

"Nine thirty," her father said. He took off his coat and draped it over a chair. Even across the room Lily could smell his cologne. "Your mother had a headache."

Lily's parents turned to leave. Lily heard her mother in the hall—*Elliott! Do you think they were*—and then the creaking of the stairs.

"Fuck."

Justin looked hurt. "I'll go."

She nodded. They walked to the front door and stood in awkward proximity.

"I had a really good time," he said.

"Me too."

"So I guess I'll see you on Monday."

She nodded.

"Can I call you before that?"

She nodded.

"Okay." He leaned down. His lips again. His tongue. The air rushed from her chest, sucked out by the force of his mouth. Then he was closing the front door behind him. She turned off the front hall lights and watched in the dark as he drove away. She realized she'd left the bouquet of flowers in his car.

Iris

L ONG AFTER MR. KAPLAN left the Trench, I stood before the demon on the wall, transfixed. I forgot how afraid I'd been of this place. I forgot that a long and lonely hallway stretched out behind me, exposing my back to the dark. I forgot I'd been warned.

And then hands grabbed my arms, a sock was pushed into my mouth, and a black cloth was thrown over my head.

"Stop squirming," a voice hissed. "You don't have to make this so difficult."

Like fuck I don't, I thought, and kept kicking. Hot tears slid out of my eyes. My tongue pressed uncomfortably against the sock in my mouth.

Then I felt somebody's breath beside my ear. "Don't worry, Iris." This was a new voice — low and calm. "Nobody's going to hurt you." But all I could think about were the stories of journalists gunned down in Russia or murdered in Pakistan. Anna Politkovskaya and Daniel Pearl. *Murrow,* I thought, panicking, *this can't be happening!*

After what seemed like eons, the hands put me down. The sock was pulled out of my mouth. Someone led me over to a chair and pulled the black cloth off my head. I rubbed my wrists and wiped my eyes. There was snot on my face.

I was in a chair in the middle of a windowless, concrete room with a single door and a lamp in the corner. My captors sat in a line about five feet from me. There were four of them, and I could tell by their school uniforms that they were three boys and one girl. I couldn't see anybody's face, however, because they all wore pig masks. Normally, I like pigs. I once begged my parents for a micro pig. But these were not cute E. B. White pigs. These were *Lord of the Flies,* rotting-head-on-a-stick pigs: the epitome of evil.

I jumped up to dash for the door. "Sit down!" a beefy male student yelled, and I sank back into the chair. Again I ordered myself to calm down. Murrow wouldn't have cried in this situation, and if my captors were students, how dangerous could they be? "Oink," I said, and hiccupped.

The large beefy kid stood up. I could hear him breathing like Darth Vader behind the mask. "O'Brien, sit down," a cool female voice said. "This isn't Gitmo."

"Oh, really?" I was starting to feel more angry than scared. "You grab somebody and gag her and throw a sack over her head and you're not trying to scare the shit out of her? Now you've got me holed up in some undisclosed location. What is this place? Do you guys have Dick Cheney hiding in the next room?"

"Iris," the female pig said, "we're sorry for the way we brought you in here. Just give us a chance to explain, and I assure you that everything will be illuminated."

The others nodded. I scanned their bodies in search of identifying features—any clue about who they were. But I saw no jewelry or nail polish. Not even a strand of exposed hair. Five hundred students attended Mariana's high school. These four could be any of them.

"Now on the end there is O'Brien," the female pig said. "Beside him is Syme. And Winston's to my left. I'm Julia."

"These aren't your real names, right?"

The four of them laughed. "I thought you said she was intelligent," said the pig called Syme, snickering.

Julia ignored this comment and crossed her long legs with tea-party poise. "We know you're researching a story for the *Oracle* about Charles Prisom or, to put it bluntly, us."

"Prisom's Party," I breathed. "You're responsible for the flash mob and the flaming effigies! What's wrong with you?"

"Slow down, Iris." Julia's voice was unnaturally calm.

"You're telling me you weren't responsible?"

"I'm not denying anything. But just because something *looks* sinister doesn't mean it is."

"Katie Milford said you're some kind of secret society."

There was more laughter from behind the masks. "We find that particular appellation rather juvenile," Julia said.

Her diction was crisp, pretentious. I slumped down in the chair. "You couldn't have anything to do with Charles Prisom."

"Quite the contrary." Julia stood up and walked toward me with a large, leather-bound album. "This contains the story of Prisom's Party in letters, clippings, and photographs. It has been passed down to us through the generations." The book smelled of old libraries and brought to mind fountain pens. Its cover was wrinkled and worn but as soft as you'd imagine a newborn colt's skin to be. It wasn't so different in appearance from Lily's *Marvelous Species*.

Pressed to the paper on the first page was a handwritten letter. The paper was thick, unlined, and yellowed with age. The black script was slanted like rushing waves. It was difficult to read, but I made out the following:

January 13, 1906

To my courageous and trustworthy disciples,

As you know, I founded Mariana Academy according to the ideals of Brotherhood, Truth, and Equality in the hopes that no student should ever feel ostracized for his physical and mental idiosyncrasies or for his particular background. Since 1885, when we admitted our first group of students, we have remained true to this promise.

On the eve of my death, I have every faith that my son Henry will prove a strong and competent leader. But the lifeblood of this school is not the adults — it is you, the students. Time distorts the past. History can too easily slip through our fingers, and there may well come a day when my legacy is corrupted and, ultimately, forgotten. This may seem unbelievable to you now, but it is all too possible.

To guard against such an occurrence, I am appointing you, Prisom's Party, to be the bearers of my legacy. You will be the eyes and ears of this school — its very conscience — when I am departed.

In the name of the Community Code, I bestow upon you the following responsibilities:

* You will swear a lifelong unwavering oath to Prisom's Party.
* You will cloak yourselves in secrecy, and through clandestine measures you will induct new members to ensure the survival of Prisom's Party throughout the generations.
* You will fight for those students who find themselves disenfranchised.
* You will be vigilant, and when my legacy is threatened, you will rise as a beacon of light to restore the Community Code. Upholding my Code requires heroism in action and thought. You will be the first generation of these heroes.

With sincerity and hope,
Charles Prisom

I looked at Julia. My brain was buzzing, *Holyholyholyholy SHIT!*

"We brought you in here the way we did," Julia said, "because we must take the utmost precautions to ensure our secrecy. Like you, we are working undercover. I assure you that we are not duplicitous. We are simply following the dictates of Charles Prisom."

She sounded sincere enough. "All right," I said. "So what am I doing here?"

"All in due time, little flower," Syme said with a sneer.

"If you'd permit us," Julia said, "some history first."

"All right," I said again, trying to broadcast healthy skepticism, but even I could tell I sounded more like a petulant little kid than a seasoned reporter.

Julia folded her hands in her lap and began to speak. "Prisom's son Henry had been head of school for fifteen years when he hired a young Marine to teach English. Later, it was discovered that this Marine had been dishonorably discharged from the military, but nobody knew that at the time. In any case, the young Marine was charismatic and brilliant, and in a couple of years he had worked his way up in the administration. When Henry Prisom grew ill and announced his retirement, the Marine was unanimously voted to become head of school."

"And a new king arose over Egypt who did not know Joseph," Syme said, and then in his serpentine lilt he spoke two words: "Thelonius Rex."

"Come on," I said. "That's not a real name."

O'Brien stood up. "We're not pulling shit out of our asses here."

"Perhaps he changed his name," Julia said. "But he was definitely going by Rex when he arrived here." She took the book from my lap and turned to a grainy black-and-white photograph of a handsome young man with a thick head of black hair and what a cliché-riddled writer might call a "sinister glint" in his eye. On the very next page was a piece of Mariana stationery bearing an August 1921 date and addressed to the school board. The letter began, *I humbly accept the position of Mariana Head of School.* It was signed, *Thelonius Rex.*

Julia closed the book. "Strange doesn't mean impossible," she said. I supposed she was right. *Just look at these kids in their pig masks,* I thought. *And look at me sitting here with them, lapping up their words.*

"The first year of Rex's leadership went well," Julia continued, "but when Henry Prisom died, Rex grew unhappy with how the school was run. The rules were lax, the faculty permissive, the students undisciplined. So he set about making certain changes, small ones at first. You have to understand that under the Prisoms' supervision Mariana felt very much like a liberal arts college, and it was still a boarding school. Students had tremendous freedom. There were many innovative student clubs, including the *Oracle.* You'd barely recognize the paper from even a decade ago. In the past the stories were both well-written and timely . . ."

"Very funny," I said, but I felt a twinge of the indignation that now accompanied all my dealings with the *Oracle*. Stories abounded at this school. Students were kidnapped and dragged to secret lairs! And yet every time I pitched Katie, she gagged me. It might as well have been 1932, when a singing bird was trumpeted as the year's most entertaining overseas broadcast! I really felt for Murrow, who begged CBS to cover the Anschluss in 1938 but was ordered to report on choirboys instead.

"Iris, are you listening?"

I nodded. I was starting to feel glum.

"Rex began running the school like a basic training camp. He shut down the clubs, implemented strict curfews, and imposed harsh punishments for minuscule infractions. He shuttered the *Oracle* and censored student mail. He fired the teachers he didn't like and brought in educators who sympathized with his disciplinarian style."

"My parents would have sicced a pack of lawyers on this place."

Julia shook her head. "Back then, parents deferred much more to the schools. And Rex was a master manipulator. He scared students into keeping mum by preying on their worst fears and insecurities. And all of this would have continued—if it hadn't been for Prisom's Party."

As impossible as Julia's story sounded, it seemed that some part of me had known this tale from the moment I first saw Mariana's dark, weathered walls. I could see the events playing like a movie against the concrete backdrop of the Party's secret room: Rex with his hard-set mouth and obsidian eyes, marching students military style to breakfast, commanding silence as he sat stiff and proud at the headmaster's table.

Julia continued. "Prisom's Party had watched Rex rise to power, but they hadn't done anything about it."

"Why not?"

"They were just a small group of students, subjected to the same rules as everyone else. They had to meet in secret. If they were caught, there'd be no one left to defend Prisom's legacy, and they knew full well that the victors write history."

The other pigs nodded. I imagined they wore grave expressions beneath their masks.

"During Rex's rise to power, Prisom's Party was headed by a student called Edmond Dantes. This wasn't his real name, of course, but the secret one he used for Prisom's Party. And Dantes realized that if he didn't act against Rex before he graduated, no one would."

I was sitting on the edge of my chair but slid back, feigning lack of interest. "So?"

"In 1923, two years after Rex's ascension, Edmond Dantes started the *Devil's Advocate,* an underground newspaper. We don't know how Prisom's Party managed to print and distribute these pamphlets, but for months the newspapers served as the only voice of dissent."

I imagined cloaked figures running through the campus under the cover of night, their hearts thumping as they slipped between shadows while rushing to their secret meetings. I saw the cautious looks in the refectory, boys with dark circles beneath their eyes transmitting coded information through the placement of plates and spoons.

"The problem, Iris," Julia said, "was that a lot of students resented the *Devil's Advocate,* because after the paper began appearing, Rex's punishments became seriously twisted. He made students stand up at meals and renounce allegiance to their roommates and best friends."

I imagined being told to stand up in front of the entire school and proclaim my hatred for Dalia. I'd never do such a thing, no matter the punishment. "But why?"

"He believed lessons in suffering, hardship, and fortitude would help students become strong individuals. He was also clearly a psychopath."

"And Dantes?"

"Rex didn't know who Dantes really was or where he was hiding. But he devised a plan to make Dantes come forward. One night he walked into the refectory, carrying a bowl of bright red strawberries, and he called for Timothy Keaton, a freshman, to join him at the front of the room. Now, everyone knew that Keaton was seriously allergic to strawberries. If he ever ate one, his face would swell up and his throat would close. Awful stuff. So Rex said he was going to make Timothy eat the entire bowl of strawberries unless the leader of Prisom's Party revealed himself."

"Come on, a teacher wouldn't do that. Somebody would have reported it to their parents. Or to the police."

"I agree," Julia said. "It's quite possible that Rex was bluffing. But we think he'd decided that if he couldn't identify the members of Prisom's Party, he'd discredit them instead. He knew Prisom's Party would lose all credibility if they saw a student in harm's way and did nothing. Edmond Dantes knew this too, so he had no choice. He jumped up and knocked the bowl of strawberries from Rex's hands. Rex lunged back. And then chaos erupted."

"No such thing as a peaceful revolution, dear Iris," Syme said, wagging his finger in a manner that was both pedantic and lascivious.

"Dantes was tall, but Rex was built like a wrestler. Students rushed to Dantes's aid, but the faculty — remember, these were Rex's teachers — fought against them. Rex and Dantes ended up fighting by that large window near the kitchen door, and it looked like Rex was simply going to beat Dantes to death. But then Rex suddenly pitched out the open window. Nobody knows whether Dantes pushed him or whether Rex tripped, but Rex fell directly onto the gate."

A wrought-iron fence separated the campus from the road, and certain embellishments on school grounds were patterned after it. The most notable feature of this fence was its spadelike spikes.

Julia held up two fingers. "Two of them. In the chest."

For a moment, nobody moved.

"The thing is," Winston said in low voice, "Rex's death changed everything."

This was the first time Winston had spoken. I'd been wondering about him, sitting there silent throughout these proceedings.

Winston continued, "Mariana parents pulled their children out, and the school closed. Dantes finished his senior year elsewhere and slipped off the radar."

Julia flipped to another page in the photo album and showed me the newspaper clippings from 1923 announcing Rex's death and the closing of the school. On the following page an article reported the school's reopening as a co-ed day academy in 1940. So that was why the *Oracles* between 1921 and 1940 were missing, I realized. First Rex shut down the student paper and then the school closed.

"Prisom's Party lived on through the siblings of former students," Julia said. "But again, it lay dormant until the turn of the century."

It was strange to hear this phrase used outside of a history book. But it was accurate. We'd passed from one century to another in my lifetime. This would be the stuff of history one day.

"For too long, this school has been obsessed with social climbing, success, and power. We may not have a Rex on our hands, but the strong are still taking advantage of the weak." As Julia said this, I could feel waves of frustration radiating from the four of them. "Ask anyone about the scandals going on around here, Iris, and you'll see that the administration doesn't give a damn about the Community Code. The Community Council is like the Mafia. Nobody questions them, because they know they'll wind up discredited, their reputations ruined. It's happened more times than you can imagine. And most of the kids here only care about getting ahead anyway. Brotherhood, Truth, and Equality for All is a sham. We're the only voice of dissent."

"Except" — Winston stood up — "for you."

His voice made me shiver. "Me?"

Now Syme jumped from his chair and began hurling verbal missiles at me. "We know you've been pitching serious stories to the *Oracle* with no success. We know you've been writing essays for European history on CBS's coverage of the Second World War. And we know you worship Edward Murrow like he's Jesus."

My mind buzzed with questions: how did they know these things, and why did they even matter? Meanwhile Syme stood over me, like a cocky prosecutor cross-examining a hostile witness. I realized I was hoping that Winston would defend me, but he said nothing.

"Iris," Julia said. "We know you don't care what other people think of you. You value the truth, period. Even if it means you're . . ." She dangled the unfinished sentence before me, as though for sport.

"Even if I'm what?"

"A freak of nature."

I tried to protest, but Julia continued, "That's a compliment, Iris. And we've brought you here because we need your help. Prisom's Party is facing a serious problem."

I waited.

"His name"—she leaned forward until I could see two dark eyes through the slits in her mask—"is Jonah Kaplan."

My mouth fell open.

"Pasternak hired him in order to hunt us down," Syme said, "and if he outs us, then you can say goodbye to the legacy of Charles Prisom."

"And your remedy for this is—?"

"Blackmail!" O'Brien burst out.

"We have reason to believe Mr. Kaplan is hiding damaging information," Julia said icily. "If we can find out what, we can give him an incentive to back off."

"But Mr. Kaplan's not like Thelonius Rex. What could he possibly have done?" I remembered my mother telling me that Mr. Kaplan was almost kicked out of Mariana as a student, but that was a long time ago.

"Jeez, Iris, I don't know," Syme said, snorting. "How about put his students through a perverse psychological experiment in which he manipulated a bunch of fourteen-year-olds into giving one another fatal electric shocks?"

"It wasn't real. It was a simulation to show us—"

"It was sadistic," Syme snapped.

"And you guys are so full of love? Look what you did to Marvin Breckinridge!"

"We did that for the school's benefit!" O'Brien growled.

Julia stepped forward. "You're a smart person, Iris. I think you know that Mr. Kaplan isn't all he seems." Her face was very close to mine, the pig's rubber snout almost touching my cheek. "Look at his reaction to that book of yours," she whispered.

Had one of them been hiding in the stacks or behind a carrel when I showed Lily's book to Mr. Kaplan? And if so, how did they know about our meeting in the first place?

"None of this makes him guilty of anything," I said, but Julia ignored me.

"You have now seen him react to the Prisom's Party symbol twice — on the first day of school in the girls' bathroom and again today in the Trench. He's afraid of us, Iris. And the only reason to be afraid of Prisom's Party is if you have a black stain on your past."

Winston nodded at Julia to take a seat and knelt by my chair. "Look, we could be wrong about all of this. But we owe it to ourselves and to this school to investigate."

I didn't know what to say. My brain was reeling.

"We don't want to hurt Mr. Kaplan, Iris. We just want to be left alone."

I looked from face to face, but of course the masks revealed nothing. "But why me?"

"We need someone on the outside, someone Kaplan would never suspect. One of us snooping around the *Oracle* archives would look suspicious. But you're a reporter. Everyone *expects* you to be asking questions."

"You want to use me."

Winston shook his head. "We could have gone to anyone else on the paper. But you share our values. We can trust you."

"But you don't. I don't even know where I am right now! I don't know who you are!"

"If you prove yourself," Winston said in a whisper, as though we were having a private conversation, "you'll become part of us, part of this extraordinary history."

"A member of Prisom's Party?"

Winston nodded. "Fully sworn. Become a steward of the truth, Iris. Help us."

I so badly wanted to believe that somebody my age could say "steward of the truth" without rolling his eyes or making a sarcastic crack. I wanted to believe all this was real.

"It's quite simple," Julia said. "You can go back to your old life and you'll never hear from us again."

"Or," Syme said, "you'll just be alone out there. Four years without friends, without parents who understand you. Four years pining after ghosts."

"We're fighters," Winston said. "We won't give up on life."

"What are you talking about?" My heart drummed inside my throat.

"She left you." Winston's voice was quiet but firm. "She gave up. We won't do that to you. Ever."

"How do you know about Dalia?"

"We have resources, access to student files, psychological reports," Julia said. "That's why we always break the important stories."

"Iris." Winston touched my shoulder. "Think about what being a member of Prisom's Party would mean for your journalism career. You'd be able to write whatever you want for the *Devil's Advocate* instead of being Katie Milford's pawn."

"Who do you want controlling the flow of information around here?" Julia added. "The people who only care about being powerful or the people who want to use their power for good? It would be irresponsible — wrong, in fact — to do nothing. Don't you think?"

Winston squeezed my shoulder, and I knew that behind the mask he was smiling. There was something about the strong, comforting pressure of his hand that filled me with a sudden and overpowering desire to see his face. O'Brien's rage, Julia's highbrow diction, and Syme's creepy sibilance gave me the odd sense that the three of them were acting. But Winston, despite his mask, somehow seemed to be himself.

"We don't want to pressure you," he said. "So we'll let you go and you can decide for yourself. But if you turn this offer down, you won't have another chance."

What would Edward Murrow do? But of course I knew. In the Blitz, he refused to hide in bomb shelters. He rushed to Vienna during the Anschluss to await the arrival of the Nazis. He wasn't afraid to stick his neck out even if there was a guillotine hovering overhead.

Winston dug into his pocket and produced a small white pill. "This is a sleeping pill," he said. "Once you're conked out, we'll take you back."

The pressure in my chest was about to burst. "Can't you just blindfold me again?"

"Sorry, kid. Company policy. You can't come in and out the same way." Winston gave me the pill. "Everything is going to be all right, Iris. *I'll* make sure of it."

I turned the pill over in my fingers and thought about Julia's earlier comment: *Just because something* looks *sinister doesn't mean it is.* At first this had seemed a convenient excuse — but then I remembered a passage from *Marvelous Species.* The microorganisms metabolizing toxic chemicals in the earth's core had created and shaped human life. So what seemed harmful to us was just the opposite; it was the source of our existence.

The Party members looked at me, their masks expressionless and cruel. I closed my eyes and popped the pill into my mouth.

III

INVESTIGATING THE UNKNOWN

Over three hundred species of extremophile life, including tube worms, blind shrimp, and giant white crabs, live among the poisonous hydrothermal vents of the Mariana Trench. Since laboratory conditions often prove fatal to such creatures, scientists wishing to study them must travel into the ocean depths and observe these organisms in their natural habitats.

— *Marvelous Species: Investigating Earth's Mysterious Biology*

Lily

DECEMBER 1999

TWO WEEKS AFTER Lily and Justin's first date, the Queen of the Geeks requested an audience with them. "In the Trench?" Lily asked Justin. She'd heard the rumors. Most troubling was the story about a student from the 1950s who hanged himself from a Trench light fixture. His girlfriend found his body turning slowly from a jump rope. Lily's father assured her no such thing had ever happened. But the fact that she could never enter the Trench without wondering exactly which light the boy had chosen meant that *something* awful had happened there. You could remove the physical evidence of an event like that, but you couldn't erase the eerie feeling that remained.

On the appointed day, Justin met her outside the Trench door. "Ready for your descent into Dis?"

Lily frowned.

"It's the underworld. Aeneas walks through 'Dis's empty halls.'" He squeezed her hand and led her in.

Indeed, the Trench was dark, cold, and quiet. Lily kept glancing behind her, certain she could hear a creaking rope. Justin put his arm around her shoulder. "There's only one really frightening thing down here," he said. "And that's a four-foot-ten-inch troll with a big puff of orange hair and a bad attitude."

But Jonah didn't worry her. She was far more concerned about Hazel.

They arrived at the Academic League room, where Jonah Kaplan

141

sat with his back to the door, a sea of note cards between him and his friend Toby, an equally diminutive boy with little-kid dimples. Eric Randall zipped his fingers across a laptop keyboard and absent-mindedly picked at an infected pimple on his cheek. Ellen Day lay on her stomach, reading a beat-up copy of *Dune*.

"Hey, guys," Justin said. "You all know Lily?"

As soon as Toby saw them, he began scooping up the note cards. Jonah swung his head around with such force it looked about to spin off his neck. "What's she doing here?" He helped Toby gather the cards. The others watched anxiously.

"Hazel told me to bring her."

"Well, she didn't tell us. Jesus. A little notice would have been nice." Toby unlocked the bottom drawer of a file cabinet and deposited the cards.

"Shove over," Justin said, but nobody budged. "Move!" The color rose in his face.

Toby whispered into Jonah's ear like a lawyer conferring with his client. It was obvious who in the room was the prosecution and who was the defense. Jonah ran a small hand through his huge hair. He shook his head. "Look," he finally said aloud, "this isn't going to work."

"Why not?" Justin demanded. "This is just a team meeting."

"Jonah's right," Eric said.

"Nothing personal," Ellen murmured, turning the page.

Jonah ran his fingers through his hair again and muttered, "Not to you."

Lily looked at Justin. "I can go. It's no big deal."

"You're my girlfriend." Justin's mouth cinched up like he'd bitten into a lemon. "She's not going to tell—"

"Shut your fucking mouth before you get us in a shitload of trouble," Jonah snapped. "She's Morgan's daughter!"

"Hypocrites!" Justin shook his head in disbelief. At that moment the door opened. "Oh look," he snorted. "Your queen arrives."

Hazel smiled broadly as she entered the room. Then she saw Lily, and something in her smile shifted. "Lily!"

Lily couldn't tell if it was excitement or disapproval she heard in Hazel's voice. Hazel scanned the unhappy congregation. "What's the matter?"

Justin led Lily into the hall, but Hazel overtook them and pulled him into a private conference. Seconds later, Jonah followed. The trio huddled together: Jonah's flaming head, Justin's sandy-red crown, and Hazel's auburn locks bent into a multicolored sun. Lily stood alone, a distant white star, and watched them. From what she'd observed over the years, Hazel treated Justin like a best friend and Jonah like a beloved younger brother. The twins—one big, one small—were like repellent magnets. But somehow Hazel held them together.

Jonah slunk back into the Academic League room, passing Lily as though she were invisible. Then Hazel took Justin's hand in her own and squeezed it. Lily's stomach torqued at the sight, but here was Hazel walking toward her with a smile. As Hazel passed, she muttered, "Hades receives many, but few return."

Justin arrived at Lily's side. "I'm so sorry," he said.

"What did Jonah mean, it wasn't just a practice? And why do you lock up your materials? And what's that thing painted on the wall over there?" Lily had noticed the large, frightening face when she came out of the Academic League office. The image was partially covered with stacks of chairs, but she could see a couple of crazed eyes and a gap-toothed mouth.

Justin tucked a strand of hair behind her ear. "You know how little kids play house? Well, my friends are playing popular. Finally they have somebody to exclude." He put his arm around her shoulder. "Come on. The underworld's getting on my nerves."

• • •

Lily wasn't certain about Jonah and the others, but she suspected Hazel was no child innocently donning adult clothing. The girl was complicated and capricious. And her intentions were far from clear. She was like an ominous storm head hovering in the distance, but whether the threat was real was impossible to know.

Lily had never been close to Hazel, but for a short time they'd been friends — of a kind. The particular moment of their entanglement lasted less than a day, and it should have been one of those painful childhood memories that eventually come to feel so dreamlike you question whether it happened at all. But for Lily — and quite possibly for Hazel — the memory was a living, feeding thing. A memory made flesh.

Until she turned thirteen, Lily spent her summers at the expensive day camp popular with Mariana parents. It was called Camp Sunshine, and Lily hated it. She wasn't allowed to play outside. (Lily's doctor said she could spend time in the sun with the proper precautions, but her mother distrusted doctors as much as she did sunlight.) And perhaps as a result of her indoor confinement, she had no camp friends.

Hazel Greenburg, a roly-poly girl one year ahead of Lily at Mariana, had no friends either. She designated herself Lily's partner in all camp activities, and stuck to her like a barnacle. As far as Lily was concerned, the only thing the girls had in common was their status as biosafety hazards. Coarse hair sprouted like a fungus between Hazel's eyebrows, and freckles swarmed over her arms and legs like a bad case of chicken pox. Lily reeked of sunblock, and her coloring resembled that of the undead. People kept their distance.

The year Lily turned eleven, the camp announced a special field trip to Water World, and the Morgans granted their daughter permission to attend, as long as she promised to remain in the park's indoor complex. On the morning of the trip, Lily stood before her mother in a metallic purple bathing suit and rainbow flip-flops.

"Turn around," Maureen ordered, and Lily turned. "Hair," she said, and Lily held up her ponytail. The lotion made sucking sounds between her mother's palms and was cold and slimy on her skin. "Pull your suit down so I can get your back," Maureen said, closing the cap on one bottle and opening another.

"Can't you just rub it around the edges?"

"The sun goes right for the tan line. Pull it down."

"Can't I do it myself?"

"If you want to go on the trip, you're going to do it my way."

Slowly, Lily pulled the spandex straps off her shoulders as though she were peeling them from a bad burn. Maureen yanked the back of the bathing suit down. "Hold still." She braced her daughter's shoulder with one hand and rubbed with the other. "Turn."

"Mom!"

"I'm just doing your neck and sides. I'm not *looking* at anything. And anyway, it's not like there's anything to see."

Finally Maureen snapped the bottle shut. "Now get your things." She sent Lily out with a slap on the butt.

Not long after that, Lily sat on the Camp Sunshine bus, slick and smelly from her mother's morning rubdown, reading *The Scarlet Letter.* Her father had given her a set of The Classics for Christmas. The phrase conjured a hoary man droning in a large auditorium, and it wasn't long before Lily grew bored with *The Mill on the Floss* and *Bleak House.* But *The Scarlet Letter* was different. Lily envied Hester Prynne's dark, glossy hair and eyes, but more than this, she was in awe of Hester, who wore her stigma with so much pride. She loved escaping into Hester's embattled, heroic life, and she did so now as the bus rumbled down the highway. Hazel sat beside her bubbling with excitement. "It's going to be the best day ever!" Hazel exclaimed, and Lily shifted toward the window.

An hour later Lily was jolted from her book by Hazel's finger jabbing her shoulder. Beyond the haze of the interstate, monolithic towers rose against the blue sky, their metal structures gleaming in the sun. Tubes of intricate slides encircled these structures, winding hypnotically toward the earth. It was a fantastical new world, a realm of unforeseen possibility, a place where anything could happen. The bus turned in to the massive parking lot, and with a hacking cough, stopped outside the ticket booth. The kids streamed out. Lily followed Hazel into the women's changing room, carrying her towel, knapsack, and special prescription sunglasses. Her flip-flops slapped against the tiled floors.

The changing room was a maze of blue lockers, its air sharp with chlorine and filled with the noise of clanging metal and screeching children. Lily crept around the tepid puddles and wormy strings of hair. She'd never seen so many naked bodies in one place. Lily's body was bony with nipples the size of small buttons, and she gaped at grown women with dark beards between their legs and eggplant breasts. Some of the women had fatty thighs. Hazel's thighs touched, and her bathing suit was so tight that it cut into her plump buttocks. She wondered if Hazel would one day resemble the locker room women or, worse, if she herself might. Lily hoped not.

Lily stood in the shade underneath an overhanging roof as her counselor, Jenny, told the group to choose buddies. Hazel grabbed Lily's hand and thrust it in the air.

"That's nice of you," Jenny cooed. "Staying indoors with your friend." Lily pulled her hand free. Jenny bent over and rested her hands on her knees. Lily removed her thick black glasses and stared at Jenny's white-toothed smile and ribbon-tied pigtails.

"Now Lily, it's very important that you stay inside," Jenny said. "Do you understand?"

Lily nodded. Over Jenny's shoulder, she saw the popular girls run off into Water World's white glare. When Jenny was gone, Lily walked to the edge of the roof's shadow. A line ran down the pavement. On one side was cool shade; on the other side, bright sun. A concrete ocean stretched before her. She lifted a foot into the light and gingerly tested the pavement. Heat sank into the padding of her big toe and sent a flash of warmth into her foot. Wonderful.

"Let's go into the park!"

Lily recoiled from Hazel's mouth so close to her ear. She turned to find the girl smiling brightly and wondered how Hazel could be so oblivious to what other people thought of her.

"I'll look out for you, Lily," Hazel said. "I'll tell you if you're getting burned."

Lily stared out at Water World. *All right,* she thought, and plunged into the light. The heat burned like a scalding bath. Then the sharpness broke and sunlight washed over her. A light breeze raised the hair on her arms. This wasn't so bad. And besides, her mother had slathered her with so much sunblock, she might as well have been wearing armor.

Hazel coaxed Lily into trying some of the slides. They started with the tubular intestines and gradually sought out the straight tongues that shot you into the water like spitballs. They tried slides that made Lily's stomach fly into her throat and her heart sink to her feet. Slides that left her feeling simultaneously terrified and invincible. Afterward, the girls stumbled on gelatinous legs toward a bench. They sat there catching their breath.

"You're a little pink," Hazel said.

Lily took off her dark glasses and examined her arms and legs. It wasn't so bad. Her skin didn't hurt.

"Let's go swimming," Hazel said. "Your skin'll be more protected under water."

Lily slipped her glasses back on and followed Hazel to a pool in a corner of the park. She felt dizzy from the slides and heat, but the water was an instant relief.

The girls pushed across the pool on their backs: Hazel's pudgy, speckled body beside Lily's skinny white one, drifting like flotsam. They didn't speak. They moved only to keep afloat. Sometimes they collided, but they let it happen and didn't laugh. They allowed the water to lap over them. Lying on her back under the blue sky, darkened just enough by her glasses, Lily felt an unfamiliar sense of calm. She wondered if this was how Hazel moved through the world, her green eyes protected from other people's judgment as though by special glasses. Did it matter how other people saw you if you weren't aware of them looking?

Lily opened her eyes to find herself alone. Most of the families had cleared out for lunch. Her throat felt parched, too dry to cough. She started to speak Hazel's name, but Hazel was no longer beside her. Lily spun around. At the deep end of the pool, an old man swam laps; at the shallow end, a mother bounced her water-winged baby. Then, in a corner, Lily spotted Hazel's magenta bathing suit. She called out, but Hazel didn't answer, so she swam over. As she neared, she could see Hazel struggling at the pool wall. Her wet hair hung in a heavy knot down her back and swayed with the motion of her undulating body.

"Hazel?" Lily was only a couple of feet away now, treading water. Hazel's hands gripped the edge of the pool. Her body arched, bent inward, arched again. She looked like she was having trouble holding on. "Hazel!"

Lily kicked over to the wall and grabbed the edge with one hand. Hazel's cheeks were flushed, her eyes clenched. She gasped, the sound so quiet Lily wouldn't have heard it had she not been inches away. It was a sound unlike any she'd ever heard, at once feathery and full. Suddenly Hazel pushed herself away from the pool wall, dunking her head beneath the surface.

"What were you doing?" Lily demanded the moment she reappeared. "Are you okay?"

Hazel squinted the water from her eyes. She looked at Lily, and her face went pale. "Am *I* okay?"

"Yeah."

"I'm fine." Hazel shut her eyes, opened them again, as though she was expecting to see something different from before. "Lily?" she said, but Lily interrupted.

"What were you just doing?"

Hazel was quiet for a moment. The color rose in her cheeks. "I'll tell you something," she said tentatively, "but you have to promise not to tell anyone. You have to swear."

Lily nodded uncertainly. The water-winged baby and the old man were gone. Hazel leaned forward and whispered in Lily's ear.

Lily glanced over Hazel's shoulder and saw the water jet. Small bubbles rose to the surface and popped. She shook her head.

"You've never tried it in the bath?"

Of course Lily was curious. At night in her room, when darkness hid her from herself, her fingers wandered to the edge of her underwear. Once or twice she'd slid her fingers down the white slope between her thighs, *over* the underwear. Because this — the M-word — was the most embarrassing thing a person could do.

Mariana's guidance counselor had told a room full of uncomfortable sixth graders that it was "natural." But the lesson had upset some parents, who believed that sexual education shouldn't deviate from strict lessons of anatomy and reproductive function. Shortly thereafter, Lily overheard her father on the phone.

"Well, I insist the, ah, the term should be taught, though perhaps we could include its derivation. The likely etymology is *manstuprare,* which comes from *tubare,* to stir up. *Manus* is Latin for 'hand,' and *stuprum* means defilement or dishonor. That would send an implicit message, and no harm in getting a little Latin into the lesson."

This was so typical of her father, whose lifelong mission was to "get a little Latin in" — to any conversation, whether it belonged there or not. Still, Lily wanted to know what it was like. Once, riding a bicycle, she'd felt a tingle inside her body. In the darkness of her room this feeling glowed like light around her. If only she could reach out and catch it, harness its energy. And Hazel was offering her this. Without taking off her clothes or using her hands. Was it the M-word if her hands were above the water, innocent bystanders? Not according to the Latin.

"I'll be the lookout," Hazel assured her. "And you can always push away from the wall into a backstroke. They'll never know."

"How will I know it's working?"

Hazel only grinned and swam into the center of the pool.

Lily positioned herself in front of the jet. The water beat against her stomach. She opened her knees wider, then narrowed them. She tried raising her hips, lowering them, easing them forward, tilting them back.

The whole process felt oddly scientific, as though she were conducting an experiment on herself. Then bursting water hit her between the legs. She looked over her shoulder to check on Hazel. Hazel smiled and nodded, then turned away. Lily closed her eyes and felt the sun beat down on her face. Suddenly she felt an unexpected hiccup. She moved again, and the feeling disappeared. With shaking arms — the truth of Hazel's confession making itself suddenly apparent — she moved until she found the hiccup again. She leaned back slightly and the sensation grew. Like small bubbles ballooning and bursting against some invisible apex of her body. And beneath these bubbles, a growing pressure, a warmth, like light, beginning to spread out from that invisible point. The sun warmed her face. Her head reeled in the darkness behind her eyes. She pushed herself into the pressure; the heat on her face fused with the heat between her legs as the largest bubble of all began to bloom. Larger and larger it grew, threatening to burst, to split her body apart. She gripped the concrete. A wave rushed upon her, thrusting her body into the bubble . . .

"Lily!"

"What is she *doing?*"

"Wait, no! Wait!"

Lily snapped her eyes open. Panic doused the heat in her body, and she pushed back from the edge, but it was too late. Jenny stood by the side of the pool, her face stricken. Campers gathered at her side, giggling.

Hazel kicked over. "I didn't see them coming."

Lily swam madly to the shallow end, and climbed out. Her limbs felt like wet rags. Her head spun. The campers were now silent, gaping at her like she was a hideous creature slithering from a swamp. *They saw,* she thought. *They know.* She stood on the hot pavement, her bathing suit, dripping hair, and tears forming a puddle on the concrete.

Jenny led Lily from the pool, cursing, saying she'd be fired. Lily's head throbbed. Her mouth felt full of water. Why would Jenny be fired? Was it illegal to do that thing with the water jet or just perverted? Would all of Camp Sunshine get kicked out of Water World?

"I should have been watching you," Jenny moaned. "Does it hurt? Here's First Aid."

"Jesus!" the lifeguard said when he saw Lily, and led her to a chair.

"Put your head between your knees, honey," Jenny coaxed. "Let's take off those glasses."

Light filled Lily's eyes, and then she saw something that looked like her legs but couldn't possibly be. Swirling waves of sickness rose in her gut. She began to shiver. Her head lolled on her neck like it was only partially attached. Then it seemed that the entire room—from the chair, to the first-aid cabinet, to Jenny herself—was tipping over.

Lily opened her eyes to a white cubicle, a white bed, and white curtains. She was stretched out on the bed with damp white cloths covering her arms and legs. Nausea lapped at her, and she was grateful for the blandness of her surroundings. In the space between the bottom of the curtains and the floor, she saw three pairs of shoes in a triangle: her mother's sandals with the toe that poked through the front like a little tongue, the doctor's black clogs, heavy and hooflike, and her father's loafers with their mustache of leather fringe.

"There's a good chance that whatever chemicals that place uses to sterilize its water ate right through your daughter's sunscreen," a male voice said. "And I'd guess she probably spent some time in direct sunlight. You'll have to keep an eye out for signs of heat exhaustion."

"Heat stroke?" her mother burst out.

"Heat exhaustion," the doctor corrected. "Which is significantly less severe."

"Heat stroke," Maureen whimpered.

Then the feet broke formation and the curtains parted. Lily's father approached the bed. He reached out his hand as if he was going to touch her forehead, and then quickly retracted it.

"I want to know what she was doing in that pool!" Maureen demanded from where she cowered behind her husband. Suddenly Lily remembered Jenny and the group of kids pointing at her. She remembered the water jet. Hot, embarrassed tears filled her eyes. And then she remembered Hazel. Hazel was supposed to warn her. But Hazel had betrayed her and said nothing.

"I want a mirror," Lily croaked, and the doctor handed the object to Elliott.

"I don't want you to be frightened," he said, and turned the mirror toward her. Maureen shut her eyes. In the instant that Lily saw herself, a billion needles seemed to puncture her arms, legs, and face. She wanted to claw her skin off, but the smallest movement sent searing pains over her body. She recognized the color immediately: Scarlet Letter red.

After two agonizing weeks spent soaking in oatmeal baths, Lily finally returned to camp. Hazel followed her at a distance all day, floating behind her like a balloon. At the end of the afternoon, after most of the kids had gone home, she approached Lily in the parking lot.

"I'm sorry," she said, coming up beside Lily, who was scanning the road for her mother's car. "I didn't mean for you to get hurt."

Lily said nothing.

"I got scared when I saw your skin burning." An urgency had crept into Hazel's husky voice. "I didn't know what to do. I'm so sorry, Lily."

Lily bit her lip. There was something prickly beneath Hazel's words, a tightness she hadn't noticed before.

"Please, Lily, you have to forgive me!" And all of a sudden Hazel was crying, a messy eruption of tears and phlegm.

Hazel, who had promised to protect Lily, had lured her out into the sun and then betrayed her. Was she really to believe that Hazel — the same girl who'd shown her the water jet — had been scared?

Lily's mother pulled up, and Lily climbed into the car. Hazel continued to weep. Lily watched the girl's body disappear in the mirror, dissolving into the waves of asphalt heat.

She'd never told anyone what had really happened at Water World. But the fact that Hazel knew made her feel sick inside.

Jonah

I WAS LEADING AN Academic League practice after school one afternoon when the door opened and in walked Iris. We all stopped what we were doing and stared. Iris was wearing a gray suit and black heels. Her hair was done up in a bun. She looked like an adult, only smaller.

"Can I speak to someone from PR?" she said.

"Excuse me?" I looked at the team. They were thoroughly enjoying this.

"You know, public relations for the Academic League."

"Hey!" I shook my head at the team. "Do you guys want to get back to work?" They resumed their scrimmage prep, but they were keeping one eye on the action. "We don't have a PR rep, Ms. Dupont. This is just a school club."

Iris glanced uncertainly around the room. "Well, I'm considering an immersion story on you guys. I want to spend time with the team and interview them—and you, of course—to get the inside scoop. Hunter S. Thompson style."

"You want to write a piece of Gonzo journalism about the Academic League?"

Iris nodded.

"If the kids don't have a problem with you doing some interviews, it's fine with me."

"Thank you so much, Mr. Kaplan. You won't regret—" But Iris

snapped her lips together and stared at me with wide, startled eyes. She then clasped her hands primly and walked out of the room. Something odd was going on with her, but trying to pin down a fourteen-year-old girl's problems was like trying to identify the exact location of an electron. According to the Observer Effect, the minute you actually looked at the electron, it wasn't there anymore.

"Wrap it up, guys. And please," I implored, "be respectful to Iris when she comes back."

The team nodded, reluctantly. You'd have thought the Academic League would be more understanding of Iris's quirkiness. They weren't exactly the social crème de la crème. But contrary to popular belief, high school did not run according to a horizontal social hierarchy with the nerds as serfs to the popular despots. The alliances and antagonisms were more complicated than the political dealings of a Third World country. In high school, you never knew who was your enemy and who was your friend.

Later that evening, Hazel called to make dinner plans. When she suggested the Sidecar Café, however, I panicked. The Sidecar is first-date central. This probably wasn't a date—I hadn't seen Hazel in years—but the mere prospect that it might be set my serotonin levels into free fall. *I don't understand your bad luck with women, Jonah,* my mother once said. *Your father snagged the hottest entomologist in the lab.* But my father is an astrophysicist, a field that has ranked at the top of *SciGuy Magazine*'s Sexiest Scientific Field Index for fifteen years. (Stephen Hawking barely has the use of his hands, but to see the female PhD candidates chasing his electric wheelchair, you'd think he had more sex appeal than James Franco.) Microbiologists rank second to the bottom, only one tier above the comp sci guys who can't get laid because they only know how to communicate in zeros and ones.

Still, on the appointed day, I showered and shaved and drove into town to meet Hazel. I rapped my fingers against the wheel, feeling both anxious and sour. It was a dismal night, with an icy rain falling.

It seemed that even the atmosphere was pissed off. But succumbing to the pathetic fallacy was my brother's realm, not mine. I turned up the radio to snap myself out of the funk.

I turned onto State Street, drove past the library, the Nye Grocery-Drug, Main Street Hardware, and the Decatur Pub, where the science department went to play trivia each week. Nye wasn't exactly bustling, though we did get a student crowd from the nearby college where my parents had once taught. Tonight, the rain had kept most people indoors.

The buildings along State Street were reminiscent of Mariana's gray stone, though they'd been constructed more with medieval implacability than with Gothic flair. The squat, chunky blocks gave the place a thirteenth-century feel, like we were all tribal Scotsmen protecting ourselves from foreign invaders (in this case, antique-hunting Bostonians). Nye required only a fifteen-foot stone wall with flaming torches and a trebuchet plunked down outside the post office.

There's plenty of wealth in our general vicinity — we're not far from the glimmer of the Berkshires — and that wealth does seep through the cracks. But most affluent families who send their children to Mariana Academy reside in the less isolated towns to the southeast. People in Nye proper have either been here for a very long time or are transplants (like my family) who couldn't afford to live in Stockbridge and Lenox. The small college where my parents taught is even more remote than Nye, so many of the faculty settle here, moving into one of the ramshackle Victorians on Church Street as the current inhabitants die off one by one.

When I returned last summer, I spotted several efforts to lure in visitors by increasing the town's quaintness quotient. For example, a new sign had appeared outside the bookstore: a black iron arm, exploding with curlicues, from which hung the silhouette cutout of a large book. Matching curlicues spelled the name, NyeTime Bookshop. The Sidecar Café displayed a similar emblem from its doorway, this one a jaunty sidecar and a man sporting a newsboy cap. The Sidecar had claustrophobic low-slung ceilings and lighting so dim you felt like a blind geezer trying to read the menu. The café served wine but no other alcohol. Not even sidecars.

I immediately spotted Hazel at the bar, leaning flirtatiously toward the bartender. The sight of her coiled updo and beautiful freckled neck ratcheted up my nerves. Maybe this was a date after all. Her laughter rose, resonant and deep. She hadn't seen me yet and I hung back a moment, taking in the scene. The bartender was tall with scraggly facial hair and a fitted shirt that advertised his pectoral muscles. Approaching the bar, I spotted a dark tattoo on each of his forearms. They might have been of skulls, or the logo of some indie band, or a fashionably obscure Nietzsche quote like "Idealism is mendaciousness in the face of necessity." A rhinestone belt glinted around the Nietzsche wannabe's skinny hipster waist. For all these reasons, and because I was wearing only corduroys and a button-down from the Gap, I hated this man. If Hazel was into this guy, I didn't have half a chance.

He noticed me with a cool nod. "What can I get you?"

Hazel turned her head but did not get up. She looked like she was stuck there, like she had no intention of moving away, ever. "Hi, Jonah," she said, and gave a tug at a loose strand of hair. Like magic it all came tumbling down over her shoulders, unfurling like coiled lengths of silk. (I was pretty certain that women played with their hair when they were seeking male attention — but which man was this display for?)

Nietzsche Man refilled Hazel's glass. "On the house," he said, smiling a row of crooked bottom teeth.

"Thanks, Marcus." She returned the smile.

"Hey," I said, responding to a greeting that already seemed long gone.

"So can I get ya something?"

I looked at Hazel. Maybe this wasn't a date at all. Maybe she, Friedrich N, and I were going to stand around all night shooting the shit.

"Mar, we're going to sit down. Thanks for the wine."

He nodded and proffered a pair of menus. "Lentil's really good tonight," he said. "Just the way you like it." He refilled the two sips she'd taken.

I would have preferred something much stronger, but *Mar* produced a wineglass from under the counter. I reached for my wallet.

"That's on me." Hazel grabbed my wrist. I tried to protest, but I was too preoccupied with the sensation of her hand squeezing my pulse point. "Shall we?" she said after she'd paid. I could still feel the pressure of her fingers as she led me to the back of the café. The ceiling was so low that I could reach up and touch it with my hand. I looked out the window but saw only streaks of rain. I took a big gulp of wine.

We chatted about the Academic League until our soup came. "So tell me, Jonah," Hazel began, as though this was a business meeting, "why on earth are you teaching at Mariana? I had high hopes for you, sonny."

I ran through the litany: the UMass entomology team, Pasternak's generous offer, my plan to be a better teacher than the ones we'd had. "I'm saving student lives," I joked, and then remembered the speech I'd given my class about being ill equipped to do just that.

Hazel nodded, but she knew as well as I did that a microbiologist didn't just wake up one morning and decide to switch fields. I didn't feel like elaborating, however, so I changed the conversation to my parents. Hazel's home life was more than a little erratic, and my parents had treated her like a surrogate daughter. I told her about my mom's NSF grant to study a rare beetle in the Cook Islands and how my dad had gone along to kick off his retirement. Hazel asked if I was living at home, and I told her about my apartment in Forest Acres. The whole time, I was fixated on her tongue, soft and pink, testing the lentils.

"Let me guess. Your apartment features track lighting and beige carpets?"

I nodded and took a bite of soup. It scalded my tongue. I pushed the lentils around to cool them, but it was no use. When I swallowed, they burned my throat. I took a gulp of water. Hazel watched, amused, clearly unconcerned with my scalded papillae.

"It's total wilderness outside the bedroom window," I mumbled through the pain.

"Is that a good thing or a bad thing?"

"Depends on the season," I said, and Hazel chuckled. "The woods felt more homey when we were kids."

"We can still play, Jonahlah." She met my eye for a quick second before plunging her spoon back in the bowl.

"Is that so?"

But she didn't return the flirtatious volley. "Why aren't you living at your folks' place?"

"And wake up every day in my Transformers bedsheets?"

Hazel put her freckled palms on the table, her face thoughtful. "I'm an adult now, too," she said without a hint of irony or innuendo. I started to hope that she'd wiped away her old animosity and forgiven me for our falling-out. I knew I should appreciate this moment—that I shouldn't worry too much about the past—but I still had so many questions about what had transpired between us. "It's really good to see you, Hazel," I said.

Hazel blinked, her eyes tired. "Jonahlah, you have no idea."

The more we drank, the more information Hazel offered up about the last decade. In high school she'd been the most confident, self-assured person I knew. Even her teachers were a little intimidated. (Me, they just wanted to kick in the ass.) She'd been the epitome of success, walking out of Mariana with a perfect GPA, a feat practically unheard of. But I had no idea how difficult a time she'd had after high school. She'd attended Bates, and she now explained that she had few friends there, none of them close. She focused doggedly on her work, and lost herself in a bramble of Latin and Greek literature. Immediately after college, she left for the Mediterranean.

"I couldn't stand to be anywhere near this town," she said. "Not even California was far enough." Hazel eyed me. I started to respond, but she cut me off. "When your brother died, it wasn't just the following months and years that changed, Jonah. Everything that came before was suddenly different. But maybe that wasn't the case for you."

I regarded her, not sure what to say. This was the first time since I'd been back in Nye that anyone had mentioned Justin's death outright. Of course, hardly anyone at school, aside from Pasternak and a few other teachers, knew about it.

"Hazel, I—" But at that moment, Marcus arrived with our dinners. Hazel didn't even look at him as he placed her mussels and French fries on the table. *Ten points for the underdog,* I thought cynically. Because Hazel's eyes, though fixed on my face, were not happy.

"Anyway, I became a different person in Greece," she said, as Marcus left.

I nudged my salmon. I wasn't hungry. Hazel raised her eyes at me. Freckles dotted the creases of her eyelids.

"I was so starved for contact," she continued. "And every night I'd go out to some bar and drink cheap Greek wine and wait."

I imagined Hazel sitting on a rickety barstool, her long hair gleaming in the candlelight, her cotton dress rustling in the breeze. And all around her a sea of men, captivated and entranced. I imagined myself—pasty and pale—among those burly, dark-haired Greek suitors. At least in Nye the pickings were slim.

"Sometimes I'd get into a fling for a week or two," she continued. "But I didn't really care about any of them. I'm not sure they cared much about me."

I knew how Hazel felt. Justin had died in a car crash the spring of my sophomore year, and the accident site was uncomfortably close to both my parents' home and the school. After graduation, I'd wanted to purge myself from Nye in order to purge it from me. Everything in the East felt brittle, like I was walking on a tremulous crust.

I told Hazel now how I'd wanted to be in a place where the sidewalk was hard beneath my feet, a place where nothing ever froze: California. "Not that I spent much time in the sun," I added. "The lab microscope was practically fused to my eyeball."

"You always had a talent for blocking out what you didn't want to see, Jonahlah."

"So why did you come back?" I asked, trying to ignore the jab.

Hazel picked a French fry from the paper cone. "I was running out of money, and I started to feel aimless." She put the fry, uneaten, on her plate. She told me about the Historical Society, her tutoring, and the Community Council scandal with her former tutee. She claimed not to regret relinquishing her dream of becoming a classics superstar. I didn't buy this for a second; Hazel took what she wanted, by force if necessary.

"Now tell me," she said, her eyes flashing mischievously as she leaned over her still-untouched mussels, "why are you really here?"

"You mean in the metaphysical sense?"

"You hated Mariana, Jonah, and they hated you."

All true. I refused to conform and therefore was considered dangerous. In entomology terms, I was an endoparasite: an exploitative entity sapping the life force from its host. But to Helen and Jeffrey Kaplan, the only adjective that belonged in front of the word "education" was "good," so forget public school. Their Jewish social conscience did not extend that far.

"And by the way," Hazel added, "you can't change that place."

"Have a little optimism, why don't you?"

Hazel shook her head. "Think about it, Mr. Science. The school may be giving you free rein over a couple dozen students, but the organic building blocks of its composition are exactly the same."

"I agree. And finding Prisom's Party is the first step in changing that composition."

"Prisom's Party?" She looked like I'd mentioned some ex-fiancée. Indeed, it was crazy how the myth had persisted into the new millennium.

I explained my discussion with Pasternak in the Trench. "Those kids need help, Hazel. They're caught in the system, just like I was, and look where the system got me."

Hazel sat back, indignant. "It *got* you Stanford and UCLA! Only now you're getting all worked up over *saving student lives.*" The way her mouth tightened gave me a glimpse of my friend as a future mother. She'd clearly be the family enforcer.

"Who says I'm worked up?"

She shrugged. "This Prisom's Party thing—it's made you all emotional."

This felt like an accusation, so I threw one back at her. "You hated Mariana as much as I did. I'm surprised you agreed to work there in the first place, let alone come back now after what happened to your tutee."

Hazel twisted a spiral of hair around her finger with a coyness I found excruciating. I finished off my wine and refilled the glass. Hazel raised her hand and Marcus came running. "We need another bottle. Any chance you have something stronger?"

Marcus flashed a wicked grin. "My dear, you know we only serve wine at the Sidecar." He disappeared and returned a moment later with bourbon-filled shot glasses. "What are we toasting?"

"Old friends," Hazel said. I blinked. Had she just winked at me? We clinked glasses and tilted our heads. The bourbon shot hot and fierce down my throat. Marcus put another bottle of wine on the table, collected the shot glasses, and left.

"How do you know him?" I asked, pouring myself a glass and drinking it too fast.

"He's an artist," she said as though this answered the question. I poured us both more wine. "Don't worry about Marcus."

Hazel held my gaze longer than was comfortable. Millions of unspoken possibilities flashed between us. I wanted to touch her and solidify the connection. But it was too soon. It had taken supereons for the biological potential encapsulated within single-cell organisms to blossom into complex life. There was hope for Hazel and me, in our Precambrian phase, if only I was patient.

By this point Hazel's freckles were buzzing all around, and when I excused myself to the bathroom I had to focus on my balance. Was I too emotional? I stood over the leaky sink, inspecting my grim expression.

My ex-girlfriend at UCLA had dumped me three weeks before graduation precisely because I wasn't emotional enough. "Unavailable" was the term she'd used. I scoffed at this rebuke. I was career-oriented, I argued. No different from her or any of our colleagues. We'd been accepted into this highly prestigious doctoral program because we were dedicated and directed. If the prospect of the next publication, the upcoming grant, did not pull her from bed in the morning, then what did?

"Relationships, Jonah!" she exclaimed. "Life!" And then, knowing I required clarification, she added, "*Human* life!"

She slammed the door and was gone. I turned over and went back to sleep. I'd been at the lab until 3 a.m. the previous night, and my headache, the perennial throb of recent months, felt like a bulldozer overturning the gray matter in my brain.

Not long after this, graduation weekend arrived, and with it, my parents. Somehow I'd forgotten to set my alarm, and they woke me up with a persistent banging.

"Jonah, are you sick?" My mother gasped at the sight of me and pushed into the darkened studio. My father peered into the kitchen nook. Without a word he began bundling up garbage, throwing bags of chips and empty soda cans and candy wrappers into a plastic bag. As I watched him stomp around, it occurred to me that I'd been subsisting on a diet of MSG and high-fructose corn syrup. My mother yanked the window cord and the blinds shot up with a brisk *thwap*. Searing light cut into my face. It was, apparently, a beautiful morning.

"We have news," my mother said. "We're moving to the Cook Islands!" Her eyes shone. "I've won an NSF grant."

"You've quit your jobs?" My parents had taught at the college for as long as I could remember. They were natural inhabitants to Nye. They couldn't just up and change environments.

"Your father's going to retire in style. Drink cocktails on the beach. It's the opportunity of a lifetime, Jonah."

I felt off balance, as though the whole apartment — the whole state of California — was tipping over. My father sat down beside me. "It's our turn to start over, Jonah," he said. "And I know you can't appreciate this . . ." He stared at his Birkenstocks. "But we went from having two sons to one. And then, when you came out here, from one to none."

He meant that I'd run away, and he was right. But I needed distance from my brother's death and the constant panic it produced in my gut, even if it took three thousand miles and ten years of intense, focused study to do so.

"Jonah, what are you doing?" My father surveyed the studio, and for the first time I saw what he must be seeing: how the place was full of clutter and yet utterly empty. When he met my eyes again, I knew he saw the exact same contrast in me.

"I know you've got a postdoc, but is that really the best thing for you?" My mother edged closer to me. I was now sandwiched between my parents, their warm bodies radiating concern. "And by the way," my mother said, "I bumped into Hazel at the supermarket. Apparently she's home again — or has been home for a while? She wasn't very talkative. Have you spoken to her recently? She didn't look terrific."

"She's back in Nye?" I could feel the blood rushing to my face, my fingers tingling. My parents knew that Hazel and I had grown apart after Justin's death, but they didn't know the extent of our estrangement.

"You look strangely energized," my father said. "Remarkably healthy, all of a sudden. Why might that be?"

"I'm getting over a breakup, Dad. Remember?"

"Exactly," my father said.

My father was correct: The pure excitement I felt upon hearing Hazel's name was anathema to the deadness I'd been feeling for months. And once I realized how numb I'd been — once I saw my middle-aged parents upending *their* lives — I couldn't go on as before, hunched vulture-like over the microscope. As my ex-girlfriend had said, I needed to live. But how? I considered applying for teaching jobs abroad or offering my knowledge of radiation-resistant microorganisms to some clandestine DOD lab. Meanwhile, Hazel lingered in the back of my mind, pulling me homeward like a tractor beam. Why not find work close to Nye, conduct science of the natural world *in* nature, and re-boot my outdated operating system? Why not make things right with my former best friend? I had a moment of doubt—how would I feel being home after all this time? But I'd secured enough distance from the past. My advisors thought I was ruining my career, but I didn't have a choice—either leave the lab or be buried in it. Not long after signing on with the UMass entomology project, Pasternak came calling.

I'd navigated around explaining all this to Hazel; things were going well between us, and I didn't want to make myself seem vulnerable. I wasn't, really, but I knew that the story of my return suggested otherwise. I *was* drunk now, however, and everything was rotating. I splashed water on my face and returned to the table.

As I approached, something odd happened. Hazel was on her cell, and she didn't see me until I was practically standing over her. When she did notice my presence, she abruptly ended the call. Just snapped the phone shut on whoever she was speaking to.

"Is everything all right?"

"Absolutely, Jonahlah. But what about you?"

Her tone reminded me how drunk I was, and I instantly second-guessed what I'd just seen. After all, the room was hardly in proportion.

"How about I drive you home and bring you back in the a.m. for your car," she said. "We can get brunch in town."

Despite the state I was in, I recognized how unusual this offer was. Hazel wasn't selfish (she'd been a good friend, especially to my brother), but she was fickle. She didn't make plans in advance or offer promises, even little ones, because she didn't like to be tied down. The old Hazel would have let me call a cab in the morning. Was this merely the new, adult Hazel I was seeing, or something else? *Don't worry about Marcus,* she'd said. I tried to read her face, but I could see only the flickering candle and her freckles dancing.

Lily

JUSTIN AND LILY stood on the concrete front steps of Hazel's house. The structure was half log cabin, half postmodern museum with diamond-shaped glass windows set into dark splintery planks. Hazel opened the door wearing a long brown sweater, a thick green scarf, and at least a dozen jangling bracelets. She ushered them in to a large room with three tapestry-covered couches and skylights filtering snowy light. The room contained many large paintings, most displaying women in various states of undress. The canvas over the fireplace showed a woman who resembled Hazel, minus the freckles. Her hair curled like vines across her naked breasts.

"That's my mom," Hazel said when she saw Lily staring. "It's a self-portrait."

Justin had explained that Lorna Greenburg ran a big-deal artists' colony and that she was "eccentric." Clearly, Lily thought.

Hazel took Justin's hand—just picked it up like Lily wasn't there—and led him out and down the hall. Lily followed.

The kitchen smelled like paint. Jonah sat at an island, clutter encroaching upon the magazine before him. Clotted paintbrushes leaned out of Mason jars like wilted wildflowers, and the curled-up paint tubes resembled half-used toothpastes.

"Hi, Jonah," Lily said. She was making an effort to be congenial.

Jonah grunted, hopped off the stool, and opened the fridge. Inside sat a few Diet Cokes and a rotting banana.

"I haven't been to the store in a couple days," Hazel said. "Order us a pizza, Jonah."

"You do the shopping?" Lily said, amazed.

Hazel shrugged. "So what did you lovebirds do last night?" She perched herself on one of the island stools and leaned forward on her elbows. Lily and Justin looked at each other. "Aw, Jonahlah, look how shy they are!" Hazel was staring at Lily's and Justin's intersecting fingers. Meanwhile, Jonah was staring at Hazel. What, Lily wondered, was going on with the three of them?

The front door slammed. "Hazel!" An operatic voice echoed through the house. Everyone's gaze broke and shifted toward the kitchen door, as of that moment empty, but quickly filling with the sound of clicking heels, stomping boots, and low laughter. A thin cloud of smoke appeared, followed by a man — bearded and flanneled, wearing silver earrings — and, finally, a woman with wavy hennaed hair who was dressed in gauzy, diaphanous black.

The man looked startled to see the four teenagers in the kitchen. "I thought you only had one child, Lorna?"

"Three of these must have wandered in." Hazel's mother flicked her cigarette into an ashtray on the island. "Justin, Jonah," she said smiling at them. "Pleasure as always." Then she turned to Lily, the burning tip of her cigarette held high beside her face, its bright point like a third eye. "I haven't seen you here before."

Hazel's mother hardly resembled the fireplace portrait. Lines creased her mouth and eyes. Her foundation was like poorly mixed acrylic paint. She was her daughter's height but only half her daughter's size, her shoulders slim as bird bones.

"This is my girlfriend, Lily."

"Well, it's about time!" Lorna exclaimed, her cigarette sweeping through the air.

"Who are you?" Hazel demanded of Lorna's companion. "The painter or the sculptor?"

"For God's sake, Hazel! I didn't raise you to be rude to my guests." Lorna pointed her cigarette at her daughter. The smoke curled around

Hazel's face, but Hazel didn't blink. Lorna shook her head. "A kid's sole purpose in life is to make *your* life difficult. Isn't that right, baby?" Suddenly playful, Lorna kissed her daughter on the head. "You all have fun!" she sang, and hungrily grabbed her man's hand, much in the way, Lily noticed, that Hazel had grabbed Justin's hand when they first arrived.

The man looked over his shoulder. "I blow glass," he said in a tone suggesting that this didn't mean much to him.

"I know what else you blow," Hazel muttered. "Lorna's all crazy now," she continued. "But she'll crash in the next week or two and then things'll be quiet." She turned to Lily. "She's manic-depressive."

"That must be tough."

"Could be worse."

Lily wasn't sure what could be worse about it. "And that man?"

"Hazel, baby," Hazel said, imitating her mother's singsong voice and itinerant cigarette, "you can't rely on men for shit, but you can enjoy them." Hazel flicked the imaginary cigarette at Lily. "Just make sure you throw them out before they get the same idea about you."

"And your dad?" Lily asked meekly.

"Must be somebody walking around with the other half of my DNA. I used to get birthday cards, but I don't anymore. Jonah!" Hazel snapped. "I thought I said to call for pizza."

The next day Lily and Justin lay in the Kaplans' family room, buried under itchy blankets. This was a rarity. In four months, Lily had been to Justin's house only half a dozen times. Lily's house was safer; she had no siblings to disturb them. On this afternoon, however, Jonah was at Hazel's, and the Kaplans were working in their college labs.

Lily was asking Justin about Hazel's empty refrigerator. There were so many art supplies in that house, but so little food. "She's been taking care of Lorna for a long time," Justin said, stroking Lily's hair. He seemed much more interested in her head than in the conversation.

"But doesn't Lorna have meds that keep her, I don't know, sane?"

"Yeah, but she doesn't like taking them. She says they ruin her ability to create. The weird thing is that Lorna knows she has to make money and put food on the table."

"Not very much food."

"You know what I mean. She provides. So when she has to start running the artists' colony—accept applications, deal with the foundation that funds the place, all of that—she gets all serious and starts taking her meds. It's like a cycle. From April to October, she's pretty much together. From November to March, she's a mess."

As Lily mulled this over, Justin resumed his stroking. He was fascinated with her hair, always touching it, turning the white strands over in his fingers like magical thread. He kissed her, but she pulled away.

"Are you and Jonah equally close with Hazel? I mean, is there ever any—I don't know—any competition?" She'd seen how easily the three of them teased one another. They were prone to spontaneous laughter as if their minds were linked by some mental open-source network. Just as often, though, Lily noticed that one of them would try to send a non-verbal message to just one of the others—Hazel to Justin but not Jonah, or Jonah to Hazel but not Justin. These were messages communicated by looks, the subtle raising and lowering of eyelids, brief gestures. Lily wondered about the dynamic when she wasn't around. Was the subterfuge necessary then?

Justin locked his fingers with Lily's. "My mom wanted you to know that Hazel's always been really physical with us, you know, because she doesn't get affection at home."

"Why does your mom care?"

Justin didn't answer but pressed his face into Lily's hair. "You smell so good," he said.

"Do you spend a lot of time with Hazel when I'm not around?"

"I'd always rather spend time with you." Justin reached under Lily's shirt.

"Hey!" An unexpected voice caused them to jerk apart. "Did you guys make any babies today?" Neither of them had heard the front door open, but here was Jonah standing before the couch, shaking his head.

"You know, he has a bedroom. It's very nice. The best thing about it is the bed."

"Get out, insect!"

Jonah ignored his brother. "You know why he won't take you upstairs, right, Lily? He's a fake. He's worse than a girl faking an orgasm."

It was true. In their few visits to his house, Justin refused to bring her to his room.

"Shut up, asshole." Justin threw a pillow at his brother and missed. "Wait, where are you going?" he said when Lily stood up and started toward the door.

"Upstairs. To avoid another interruption." She was angry at both brothers. What sixteen-year-olds behaved this way? Outside the family room door, however, she paused. "You may think so," she heard Jonah say. "But you'll regret not listening to us. In the end."

Lily felt, more than understood, what Jonah meant by this comment, and she hurried toward the stairs. Why *did* Justin insist that they stay downstairs? It wasn't like entering his bedroom meant an immediate loss of their respective virginities. They hadn't even seen each other naked! His penis frightened her. She understood that it was connected to him, that there was a direct correlation between her touch and his response. Yet even after she finally came to stroke it, the smooth spots and ridges coalesced into little more than an abstract shape, something that brought to mind, of all things, modern art. In any case, it was time to move things forward.

But with each step she took toward the second floor, Lily felt an increasing discomfort. The upstairs walls were covered with something, but the lights were off and her poor eyesight made it difficult to see. Were those picture frames? But then why was her skin prickling? At the top step, she froze.

Insects swarmed the walls, crawled from the ceiling to the floor, and swarmed over her body, skittering up her arms and legs. She swatted madly at herself, but there was nothing on her. The insects were frozen, pinned behind the glass frames that covered every inch of the walls. In a rectangular frame to her right was the largest scorpion she'd ever seen. Nearly half a foot long, its pincers were spread open, and its stinger-tail curled over its body like a whip. Lily tripped away from the wall, backing into an even larger frame behind her. Inside was a tarantula covered in thick black bristles. She whimpered, and stumbled again.

Justin brushed past her and walked down the hallway. He stopped in the middle, faced her, and stretched his arms out so that his fingers brushed the glass frames on opposing walls. He looked like a god commanding the insect swarms.

He pointed to the scorpion. "That's *Hadrurus arizonensis,* the largest scorpion in North America." He took the frame off the wall and thrust it toward her. "Do you see that bulb at the end of its tail? That's the poison gland. It sinks into its victim." He moved closer. "And releases the poison into the blood."

Lily wanted to turn away, but she couldn't move.

"*This* used to be our pet. You know how most kids have dogs or cats? Our parents gave us a scorpion. It stung me right here." He pointed to the center of his palm. "It's not lethal."

Her throat felt swollen. "It must have hurt."

"Yeah. Kind of like somebody plunging a two-inch rusted needle into your palm." His blue eyes glowed with anger. "It hurt like a fucking scorpion!"

Jonah had rankled Justin more than Lily realized. Now he was mad, possibly at her. But what had she done?

"How about slamming your foot against the wall because you lost a stupid competition?" she snapped. "Did it hurt like that?"

They stared at each other. Somewhere in the house, a burst of laughter echoed and died.

"No," Justin said evenly. "It didn't hurt like that." He turned away from her and replaced the frame. "I told you not to come up here." His voice wavered. "I didn't want you to see this."

"Why did Jonah call you a fake?"

Justin inhaled. He appeared to be holding his breath.

"Why?" she demanded again.

Justin finally exhaled. "He thinks I'm pretending to be a different person to keep you interested."

"Are you?"

"I don't know."

"Well, either you are or you aren't."

"Lily, my mother is an entomologist. She studies bugs for a living. Imagine telling *that* to the kids in school when we were little. Imagine telling it to their parents! That was bad, but the fact that my mother chose to decorate her house with a bunch of insects is so much worse. It meant Jonah and I couldn't have anyone over whom we didn't totally and absolutely trust. You were terrified when you came up here, and you know what? That's a normal reaction. But this," Justin said flinging his arms wildly around, "this isn't normal!"

Lily wanted to say something, but Justin seemed so upset that she couldn't fathom an appropriate response.

"And it gets better, Lily. You know why? Because I *killed* half these insects. This was how I spent my weekends growing up. *This* was an average Saturday. Instead of playing sports or collecting baseball cards, or doing whatever it was that we *should* have been doing, we were asphyxiating bugs." Justin's mouth twisted into a Jonah-esque snarl.

"So your mom forced you to do this? You said, 'Mom, I want to go play soccer,' and she said, 'Not until you murder a bunch of bugs'? Because you're talking about all of this like you hate it and always have."

Justin's chin stiffened. He looked past her, and she could see his eyes skimming the insect frames.

"Sure, if you're looking at all this from the outside, it's pretty screwed up," Lily said. "But have you looked at *me* lately? Did you ever stop to think that people treat me like an insect, like some kind of alien life form? Maybe the reason you like me so much is because I'm as creepy-looking as all these bugs." And then she laughed. She'd meant this as a joke, but it wasn't. She remembered Justin stroking the dead dragonfly at school. It was obvious now—he'd chosen her because he was obsessed with the bizarre.

Justin said nothing. His face pulsed pink, then strawberry.

"You're making all of these assumptions about me—what I'll like, what I'll hate—but you won't give me the chance to decide for myself."

"I'm sorry." His chin sank to his chest, his neck boneless. But then his head snapped upright. "Don't move!" He squeezed her shoulder and hurried off down the hall.

Lily waited, her arms pressed to her sides, imagining the insects skittering behind their glass panels. Maybe Justin was right to want to keep her from all of this. Maybe *that* instinct was the right thing. The normal thing.

Only then he returned. He held a large book with a thick leather cover. *Marvelous Species: Investigating Earth's Mysterious Biology.* "My mom gave this to me," he said. "According to the bookseller there were only a few printed, so it's rare." He handed it to her. "It contains everything you could possibly want to know about entomology, extreme life forms, you name it. Look inside."

She balanced the heavy object between her hands and opened the cover. On the title page she read, *To Lily, marvel of my life. Justin.*

"I don't understand."

"I wrote that a long time ago. Years ago."

For a brief moment, Lily remembered her grandmother's assurance—*It's only one date, it's not the be all and end all*—and then forced the words from her mind. "How did you know you'd be able to give it to me?" she said.

"I didn't. I guess you could say it was aspirational."

"What are all these blank pages at the back?"

"That's for entomological and botanical drawings—if you want to add them. Now, are you ready for your first lesson?" He turned to chapter one and began pointing out insects, their scientific names and habitats, what they ate, and why their coloring was useful. He told her about the expeditions he and Jonah had taken with their parents, trekking through forests in search of specimens, capturing them and preserving them. Without a hint of discomfort, he described the killing process, detail after sick little detail.

Jonah

T HE MORNING AFTER our dinner at the Sidecar, Hazel came to get me as promised. It was a cold day but clear, and we drove past the snowdrifts, shielding our eyes from the glare. We ate breakfast at a diner in town, and afterward, just when we'd said goodbye on the sidewalk, Hazel called me back. She looked shy, almost sheepish, and a small place inside of me melted. "Do you want to go for a drive?" she asked.

I would have preferred to take my car. I did not trust Hazel's geriatric scrap of metal any more than her driving. She sped, as always, swinging us madly around the curves. But even as I clutched the seat, I felt exalted. The world around us glimmered, coated with new ice from the previous night's rain. The shadows of tree branches slid over Hazel's serene face, and I was struck by the extraordinary fact that we were only feet from each other, breathing the same air.

I told her about my early grad school days in California, drinking microbrews and playing darts with my friends on the weekends, laughing about science jokes so rarefied only a handful of people on the planet could understand them. She was surprisingly interested in these friends. What held us together? she wanted to know. Was it just the science?

As I mulled this over, we entered the heart of the Berkshires. The houses here were much grander than those in Nye, like pictures in a glossy catalogue. I was about to answer Hazel when she spoke again. "Did you tell your friends out West about Justin?'"

So this was at the root of her questioning. "He came up a few times."

The way Hazel glanced at me, I knew I'd given the wrong answer. "I didn't want to share him with a bunch of strangers," she said. "Not like you apparently did."

Remembering that Hazel's moods could swing wildly, I tried not to worry about this dig. "I thought about presenting myself as an only child," I said. "I mean, that's what the West is for, right? Reinventing yourself. But any time I was put on the spot, I just couldn't do it."

Hazel sped past a gabled house whose lawn looked pristine even at the onslaught of winter. I couldn't tell if she was still listening or not.

"Isn't it ridiculously rich out here?" I said, trying to deflect her criticism elsewhere. Hazel didn't answer.

We visited a gallery showing Lorna Greenburg's latest artwork. The show featured silver tool-like sculptures resembling the torture implements of a sadistic dentist.

"You could do some damage with those," I said, looking at the sharp, flashing objects.

"Like mother, like daughter," Hazel murmured. I asked what she meant and she looked at me like she'd just surfaced from a trance. "I don't know." She shook her head. "I don't know why I said that."

We walked out of the gallery. "Let's do something for old times' sake, Jonah. Something childish." Her cheeks were pink with cold and her hair fell in curls from beneath a bright blue snow hat. Her teeth matched the snow.

"You're gorgeous," I said, but Hazel feigned annoyance and shook her head.

We bought Chanukah memorabilia at a drugstore and then went to a boutique that sold expensive Christmas tchotchkes. Hazel chatted up the cat-hair-covered saleswoman as I infiltrated the Santa Claus figurines and gilded ornaments with dreidels, gelt, and Stars of David confetti. Under the cover of a six-foot synthetic Christmas tree, I strung up a HAPPY CHANUKAH banner. I snapped some photographs and then took Hazel by the hand. "Shabbat Shalom!" she called to the quizzical clerk as I pulled her out the door, the two of us giggling like kids.

On the way back to Nye, I told Hazel about my students: the snobby ones, the wickedly smart ones, and, of course, Iris. I was surprised to learn that Iris had found her way to the Historical Society on assignment for the *Oracle*.

"Sounds like she has a crush on you," Hazel said after I explained Iris's interest in the Academic League and the way she was always spying on me in class.

I protested, but Hazel was adamant. "Girls get carried away, Jonah. Especially girls as lonely as Iris. You need to watch yourself."

I wouldn't have described Iris as lonely—a loner, maybe. "Girls are perplexing," I said. "They're like an alien species."

"How so?"

"Oh, I don't know. The insanely complicated sociopolitical organizations they build. The weird substances they excrete, the bizarre protuberances."

"You're going to talk about substances and protuberances in the context of *women*?"

We pulled into the center of town, and I was trying to garner the courage to ask Hazel home with me. The bright blue color was draining from the sky, a stretch of gray encroaching like a storm front. I wanted to wrap both of us up in a large blanket, but Hazel leaned over and kissed my cheek. It was time to say goodbye.

"I'll call you," I said. "You promised me a PBR."

"Dammit," Hazel moaned, with mock disappointment. "I guess I did."

Iris

Thanksgiving morning I packed myself a bagged lunch, put on my snow boots, and told my mom I was going to Hazel's house. "Why not invite your friend Hazel over here?" she asked. And I thought, *Not a chance.*

People were taking advantage of the unusually warm weather. I passed husbands stringing up Christmas lights and kids building snowmen. At a park called Potter's Hill, I stopped to watch the little kids in puffy coats riding their silver saucers and plastic sleds. They'd come shooting down the hill, scarves flying, and crash-land in the snowbanks. For a few minutes they wouldn't move, just lie on their backs, playing dead. Then all of a sudden they were up again, magically resurrected, and climbing the hill with these dutiful, earnest expressions, their sleds trailing behind them like security blankets.

I walked toward the hill, found a patch of snow just off the sledding tracks, and lay down. Above me the sky was milky blue; the snow under me felt like a firm mattress. Dalia would have liked this place. Back in Boston, she and I used to lie on our backs—on the grass or the snow—and watch the clouds overhead. Sometimes we'd lie there for an hour or more thinking our own thoughts. Could she see me now? Did any part of her remain in the universe? It would have been nice to think of her and Murrow together somewhere, but I knew that wasn't possible.

I closed my eyes and listened to the kids shrieking and playing. I wondered if Potter's Hill was actually a potter's field, where people used to bury their unidentified dead. If so, were all these kids sledding over a bunch of bones? At this very moment, somebody could be decomposing just a couple of feet beneath me. Mr. Kaplan told us that with all the dead skin cells and falling leaves, the world is dying as much as it's living, even though we only like to consider the living parts. He said to train our minds to see past façades — to let our eyes penetrate. Sometimes he's so clueless. A teacher shouldn't use the word "penetrate" with freshmen. *Ever.*

Still, I considered his advice a lot after Prisom's Party kidnapped me. I had awakened in the *Oracle* archives curled on the floor. My head felt stuffed with cotton balls, and my wrists were still sore. I'd missed three periods. I had never skipped a class before, and my small act of defiance thrilled me. Had I dreamed about the kidnapping, the pigs, Thelonius Rex? But then I felt something around my neck: a silver flash drive hanging from a piece of string. I pulled my laptop out of my briefcase and inserted the drive. It was named "Chestnut_Tree," and inside were documents titled A and B. Document A contained a short note.

> Our email: W3AR3WATCH1NG@gmail.com
> Your email: littleflower1998@gmail.com. Password: Murrow.
> Use these addresses to submit your intel or contact us on gchat. You are NOT to share this information with anyone, and you MUST be discreet. Contact us only when you are alone and NEVER during class.

Did they think I was stupid? I was sure I'd seen as many spy movies as they had. I opened document B.

> Your assignment, should you choose to join us, is to figure out Mr. Kaplan's secret. To start, do a thorough search of the *Oracle* archives and see what you can find. You'll want 1998 through 2002. We hope you'll choose the path of Charles Prisom. Sincerely, Prisom's Party.

Just hours before, I'd known nothing about Prisom's Party. But suddenly I was on the *inside*. Suddenly I had the chance to be part of something spectacular. But then I thought about my aching wrists, and the sound of Syme's centipede voice, and the flash mob and the assignment I'd been given to uncover Mr. Kaplan's secret. WWEMD? But Murrow didn't answer. He seemed less accessible to me in the Trench, as if the place had shoddy ghost reception.

I stood up from the archive floor. My head ached, but soon an idea began to rise up, as though from a deep pool. It floated toward the light, breaking the surface and sparkling before me. I would investigate Mr. Kaplan for Prisom's Party, and if my doubts about them were unfounded, I would serve them loyally. But if I discovered they were using me for some evil end, I would expose them. And this time, I wouldn't bother with Katie Milford. This was a story for the *Nye County News*—at the very least.

I sat for a minute in the archive room, waiting for this decision to settle, to see how it felt. It wasn't long before a lot of murky seaweed began clotting up my brilliant plan. Murrow once said that a journalist can't make good news out of bad practice. Well, lying to the Party seemed like pretty bad practice, and blackmailing Mr. Kaplan definitely seemed wrong. On the other hand, didn't investigative journalists lie all the time? And didn't Charles Prisom instruct the Party to take all necessary means to protect itself? Weren't the ideals of Prisom's Party more important than the career of one individual? I wasn't sure I knew the answer to any of these questions. But I also knew there was only one way for this fearless reporter to go, and that was forward.

With trembling fingers, I logged into the gmail account and sent a message to W3AR3WATCH1NG. The near-immediate reply—*Hello, Iris*—made my fingers quiver above the keyboard. *When can I visit you again?* I wrote. If I was going to investigate *them*, I needed to know where they were hiding. *We will give you access in exchange for information*, the response said. I was trying to decide what to write when another message came in: *Good luck, Iris*. And I knew—at least I hoped—Winston was on the other end.

I pulled out the newspapers from Mr. Kaplan's high school years. There were a number of articles by a Justin Kaplan. Was this Mr. Kaplan's brother? And then a familiar adrenaline rush swept through me. A Justin had written the inscription in Lily's book.

I started into the papers from Mr. Kaplan's sophomore year. Among the general school news, I found a bulletin reporting a horrific vandalism of the school lockers — students depicted in disgusting acts of violence and sex — and the fallout of expulsions and hospitalizations that resulted from it.

SUSPECT EVADES EXPULSION, BUT SUSPICION REMAINS
by Laurence LeSueur

NYE — The students responsible for Thanksgiving's locker vandalism remain a mystery, but the school's primary suspect, sophomore Jonah Kaplan, has been removed from the Community Council's most-wanted list.

The Community Council had used Kaplan's reputation as a cruel provocateur and his frequent disciplinary run-ins with Headmaster Morgan to build the case that he was the locker vandal.

Kaplan denied any involvement in the vandalism and was exonerated after his parents testified that he'd spent the entirety of Thanksgiving break under their supervision.

A poll conducted by students found that 93.3% of the student body does not believe this alibi. Over 60% of students believe he is responsible for the attempted suicide of an upperclassman.

"Even if he isn't directly responsible," one member of the Community Council said, "it is people like him who bastardize Prisom's legacy and the sacred ideals of this school."

When asked to comment on the situation, Headmaster Morgan said, "We are doing the best we can to bring the vandals to justice."

But for many, the headmaster's best may not be good enough.

As I read this article and the others in the series — all of them so forthright and critical — my anger at the *Oracle*'s current editorial staff exploded. I'd done my best to write with a lucid, vibrant prose style, but Katie Milford always edited my stories to oblivion. In my last assigned piece (a review of the new TV drama *Xcess High*), she'd actually *added* clichés to my copy! Even worse, she was guilty of censorship, what Murrow called "a denial of every human institution we now defend." I pitied the reporter who came searching for clues in my stories ten years from now.

In any case, the article from 1999 only added credence to the Party's belief that Mr. Kaplan was hiding something. "We can deny our heritage and our history," Murrow said, "but we cannot escape responsibility for the result." If Mr. Kaplan was trying to deny a secret from his past, he'd be held accountable eventually. Murrow continued, "There is no way for a citizen of a republic to abdicate his responsibilities." Like it or not, I was now a citizen of this republic—this school—and as such, I was responsible for how the events of the past affected our present and future. I was desperate to believe that Mr. Kaplan hadn't bullied a kid into attempting suicide. But as Mr. Kaplan himself told us on the first day of school, belief wasn't good enough. Only Truth mattered. *Please, Murrow,* I thought, *let Mr. Kaplan's secret be unimportant. Let his transgressions be inconsequential.*

From Potter's Hill, it was another twenty minutes to the Historical Society. When I arrived, I stood at the door for a long time waiting for Hazel to answer. Since the kidnapping, I had called the Historical Society's phone number and left multiple messages but hadn't heard back. I was starting to worry. Hazel lived all alone, and if she'd gotten into trouble, who would help her? I pressed the doorbell over and over and was just deciding that I would break one of the windows if necessary when she opened the door.

She looked awful. She was dressed in an oversize flannel shirt and jeans, and her hair resembled a knotted ball of chestnut yarn.

"I'm sorry . . ." I stammered.

Hazel didn't say anything. She just looked at me with these lusterless eyes the color of a mildewed pool. Her freckles looked like splattered mud.

"I was worried. You didn't call me back and . . . Are you okay?"

Hazel nodded, though the motion seemed to require tremendous effort.

"Are you sick? Do you need a doctor?"

"I was sleeping, but come on in and I'll put the kettle on."

"Are you sure?" I lingered on the porch. "I can come back another day."

"You trekked all the way here, didn't you?" There was a bite in her voice. I suddenly remembered that I didn't know Hazel at all. She opened the door wider and waited for me to enter before shuffling to her studio without turning on any of the lights. Her room was mustier-smelling than the last time. She pulled aside the curtains over the sink and turned on a couple of lamps. I leaned against the kitchen counter as Hazel filled the kettle.

"I took your advice," I said, thrusting some enthusiasm into my voice. "I went back into the Trench."

Hazel turned to face me, her thousands of freckles like eyes inspecting my face. It was only a trick of the light but disconcerting nonetheless.

I recounted the secret conversation in the Trench between Mr. Kaplan and Headmaster Pasternak. As I spoke, Hazel grew less cranky, and I was about to launch into the demon and the kidnapping when the kettle burst like a warning siren. I stopped talking.

"Are you all right, Iris?" Hazel asked, pouring me a cup of tea. I nodded and took a sip. The tea tasted like minty roses. "It's an herbal infusion from Nepal," she said. "It calms the body and loosens truths from the heart." I gave her a blank look. "Toxins build up in the body, which is why so many cultures believe in purifying sweats. But we're all filled with emotionally toxic thoughts and memories—the things we don't like to speak about. This tea helps shake those thoughts loose."

"Like a truth serum?"

Hazel frowned. "Of course not. Now drink up."

My head was telling me to keep mum about Prisom's Party. It was too soon to reveal that part of my investigation to Hazel or anyone else. But my heart was ordering me to confess everything. I decided to compromise. The *Oracle* articles about Mr. Kaplan were in the public domain, so why not share them with Hazel? I handed her the Xeroxes I'd made and watched her carefully as she read.

"I remember all of that," she said when she was finished reading. "And in fact, I have a few other documents that might interest you." Hazel told me to wait and disappeared from the studio. She must have been upstairs, because I could hear the ceiling creak overhead. I thought I heard her muttering to herself, though it might have been the wind rattling the windows.

Within five minutes she had returned and begun spreading five-by-seven-inch photographs on the coffee table. The locker vandalism blazed to life in all its horrible detail.

"I took these shots before the school ripped down the images," she said. "Just look at the detailing . . ."

She seemed awed by the pictures, like she was an art critic appraising a brilliant body of work. It seemed strange that Hazel had these pictures in her possession after so many years, not to mention after all the traveling she'd done. But my overwhelming response to the display was disgust.

"Iris?" Hazel looked at me suddenly. "How did you come across the locker vandalism in the first place?"

"I was researching my Charles Prisom story." My face flushed with the lie, but I pressed on. "You mentioned that you knew Mr. Kaplan. Do you think he could have been the locker vandal?"

"Well, as I told you last time, Mr. Kaplan was a difficult person to understand. He was always troubled, and you never quite knew what he was capable of, so I guess —"

"I don't want him to be guilty," I burst out, and then, embarrassed by my lack of professionalism, I added, "I mean, I'd like to exonerate him."

"A virtuous instinct," Hazel said, and rose to reheat the kettle.

A virtuous instinct but a faulty one, Murrow whispered in my ear.

What do you mean? I thought back, watching Hazel across the room. *And P.S., this isn't a good time for a chat.* It occurred to me that I hadn't asked Murrow a question. Was he so deeply embedded in my subconscious that he was now giving unsolicited advice?

You're following Mr. Kaplan as a reporter, he continued, *not as a friend. Friends can afford to have their biases, but reporters — well, I don't need to talk to you about the importance of objectivity.*

But you said I was lucky to have Mr. Kaplan as a mentor.

That was before you started investigating him.

I considered this, feeling that I'd made some fundamental miscalculation, but before I could send any more thoughts Murrow's way, Hazel returned. She eyed me strangely, like she sensed something was off, and asked again if I was all right. I nodded and described my faux immersion story about the Academic League. She advised me to address the vandalism more directly. "Get out that reporter's notebook of yours and let's create a strategic plan to determine his innocence. What do we need to know about the vandalism?"

I chewed my pen cap. "Whether there were any witnesses or evidence."

"Yes, but it's been a decade since the event. The trail is probably cold."

"What about figuring out how he entered the school?" I thought about Prisom's Party and the Trench. Who knew how many keys were floating around, changing hands between students. Maybe there was even a skeleton key that could open any door in the building. That might explain how Prisom's Party was able to sneak around so easily.

"Also important," she said, "but still difficult to figure out."

We looked at each other and suddenly I knew the answer. "We need to know whether he can draw," I said. Hazel looked energized for the first time since my arrival, and I knew I'd found the right approach. I opened a fresh notebook page and we assembled a plan.

"You're smiling," Hazel said a while later, as she finished her tea. "What's going on in that brain of yours?"

"I have all these lab partners and study partners, but it never feels productive, you know? Everybody either wants to control the group or do as little work as possible. But this feels like a team." I lowered my head. "I know how silly that sounds."

"It does not! Two minds working on the same wavelength are a marvelous thing. Human beings may all share the same emotions, but we don't all *think* alike. Never take a kindred spirit for granted."

Dalia, I thought, and swallowed hard.

"And Iris . . ." Hazel cast her eyes downward. "When you do find that kind of connection with someone, you must protect it fiercely. You never know who might seek to destroy it."

What Prisom's Party was asking me to do would surely destroy my connection to Mr. Kaplan. I felt sad knowing that I might break this link before I even had the chance to fully understand it.

"Alone we are nothing, Iris. We're invisible. But when you find someone who sees the world as you do, you become visible."

I turned my head to the window. It wasn't yet dark, but I could just make out our shapes — Hazel's and mine — like ghosts in the glass. With her, I felt visible. And with Mr. Kaplan. They were the only living people who made me feel this way.

"You must have had friends back in Boston who really saw you, right?" I nodded, and all at once I began to cry. A small inside crying that just happened to show up on the outside, too.

Hazel scooted over and put her arm around me. "You had someone," she whispered. "But you lost her."

"How did you know?" I gulped and looked up into Hazel's speckled face. For just a moment there was an oddly sanguine look in her eyes, but I blinked and it was gone.

"Oh, I just know what that kind of loss looks like." She sighed. "What happened?"

Aside from Murrow, I hadn't talked to anyone about Dalia's death. Dr. Patrick had attempted to pry my mouth open, but my lips were sealed like a shuttered crustacean. Of course, everybody at my old school knew. The *Boston Globe* ran a front-page piece about teenage mental illness with a photograph of me and Dalia together when we were thirteen. My parents were furious that the paper didn't ask my permission, but apparently that job had been left to an unpaid intern. After the story broke, people began to recognize me. This didn't last more than a few weeks, but it was one of the reasons my parents were happy to leave Boston.

Dalia was the perfect lede for the *Globe* story, I told Hazel now. "There was a whole debate about whether her medications were responsible for what happened or whether it was the illness. And a tragedy's great for the news."

"How did she do it?"

No one had yet had the guts to ask me this. Now that Hazel did, I wanted to crawl into her arms and never come out again. It was the same urge I'd felt looking up into the Morgans' oak tree for the first time. "Her wrists," I said. "In her bathroom at home. Her mom found her."

We sat for a moment without talking. I wasn't crying anymore, but I felt terribly tired. Hazel looked exhausted, too. Her ringing phone startled us both.

"Well, hello," she said in a way that suggested she knew the caller well. "No, I'm busy right now." She paused. "Really?" She stood up and moved away from the couch. "This is an excellent opportunity." Silence again, then she moved farther away from the couch. I realized I had no idea what Hazel's social life was like. I didn't even know if she had a boyfriend, though she was so striking, I figured she must. Hazel finished her conversation and sat down.

"I'm so sorry, Iris," she said as though the interruption hadn't occurred.

"It's okay."

Hazel's mouth tensed, and for a moment I thought she might be angry, even angry with me. But then all at once the exhaustion returned to her face. "It's getting late. And I'm sure you have a family dinner. You'd better get going."

I didn't want to leave. I didn't want to go back into the cold by myself.

"I'd offer to drive you back," she added. "But I can't. Not tonight."

"Wait," I said, feeling suddenly helpless. "What about Prisom's letters?"

"Still looking." Hazel seemed distracted. "Do you mind letting yourself out?"

I shook my head. "Well, thanks." I sidled to the door. Hazel went into the bathroom. I stood for a moment listening, afraid that she was in there slitting her own wrists. But that was crazy. "Bye, Hazel," I called out.

There was no response, so I walked back through the darkened house and let myself out into the graying afternoon.

Jonah

NOVEMBER 2012

I N T H E T W O weeks after our Sidecar dinner, Hazel and I were together often. I even brought her to trivia, where she quickly became
the locus of my colleagues' attention. It turned out, however, that she
didn't mesh well with everybody. After our second game night, Stephanie Chu approached me in the department.

"So you've known Hazel a long time?" she asked. I told her yes,
though we'd been out of touch. Stephanie nodded, but her skepticism
was transparent. I wondered if some underlying female competition
was at play; Stephanie was the kind of woman I usually went for — nerd-
ily attractive, A-cup, Asian.

"Look, Jonah," Stephanie said, "it's clearly none of my business,
but there's something odd about the way she looks at you. I mean, it's
intense. Really intense."

My heart swelled. If Stephanie had noticed this, it could only
mean that Hazel's feelings toward me were developing. And Stephanie, through no fault of her own, simply wasn't accustomed to Hazel's
forthright manner. "Hazel's an intense person," I said. "She's always
been."

"Okay, Jonah. Like I said, none of my business."

And it wasn't. I was ecstatic over my new, adult relationship with
Hazel. I felt liberated, free of my previous teenage angst. Though I
once believed my superior intelligence would protect me from this
Salinger-induced adolescent cliché, it had not. Angst is like the chicken

pox—anyone under the age of twenty-five is susceptible. But as with chicken pox, once you've had your angst, you become more or less immune. How else could high school teachers do their jobs?

Only then Hazel disappeared, and the angst returned. I'd last seen her at game night, when she'd bested the entire science department in Settlers of Catan, quickly grabbing up every inch of vulnerable territory. After four days and no response to my texts and phone messages, I grew concerned and more than a little anxious. On Thanksgiving Day, I called again to hear the now-familiar recording: *This is Hazel. You've missed me.* The deep, embracing timbre of her voice convinced me that I had, in fact, missed her in some fundamental way. Still, I left her a message inviting her to join me for dinner.

I spent the day perusing *Discover* and *Scientific American,* hoping the pretty pictures would distract me. They didn't. I commenced pacing, but that didn't help, so I perused microscopes on eBay. I commenced pacing for a second time. I felt like one of those scientists who thought they'd discovered signs of life on a Martian meteorite that landed in Africa a few decades back. The meteorite turned out to be an inert pile of intergalactic dust. And my relationship with Hazel? No signs of life there either.

At 6 p.m. I grabbed two bottles of red wine and set out for Thanksgiving dinner. Rick Rayburn, my department head, and his wife, Mary Ann, the school librarian, lived in a neighborhood of midsize houses with backyards just large enough for a small patio, a swing set, and a grill. Crayon drawings decorated the small, bright rooms, and the kitchen was stocked with the organic equivalents of Kraft and Chef Boyardee.

The Rayburns liked to host faculty potlucks. My colleagues in the science department would drink beer and eat homemade guacamole while children ran around. I always left those evenings in awe of the Rayburns: how they negotiated the chaos of raising three kids and built a home infused with so much simple joy that even the inevitable disappointments served only to enrich the fabric of their family life.

"Vladimir Ilyich!" I said when Rick Rayburn opened the door. He was a decade my senior, and tall with receding dark curly hair. The combination of his beard and wire-rimmed glasses made him look like a card-carrying member of the Communist Party.

"Rasputin!" Rayburn shook my hand. "But where's your plus one?" He peered outside.

"She couldn't make it." I handed him the wine and Rayburn took it with a sympathetic smile. He'd invited me over because he knew I had nowhere else to go, and though I'd declined the invitation about four times, he'd finally worn me down. "Just come and eat," he'd said. "And stop making things awkward for yourself."

I'd just walked inside the house when I felt a tug at my pant leg. Staring up at me with wide brown eyes was Oliver, age six, his hair exactly like his father's must have been before it started falling out.

"The kid remembers you from the last potluck," Rayburn said. "I think you're his favorite adult."

I put my hand out and Oliver slapped me five. Strangely enough, I'm a little-kid magnet. It takes very little — a pinch of melodrama and a funny face — to make children laugh. Even better, you can do the same joke over and over again and they'll never get bored. This technique often causes any adults in the room to wander elsewhere. Perfect for me, because I am then freed from endless annoying conversations about subjects I have no interest in discussing.

"So what's shakin', bacon?" I blubbered my lips and Oliver burst into convulsions. Rayburn shook his head. "Don't drive Jonah crazy," he said. At which point I made the blubbering sound again and Oliver went ecstatic.

I followed Rayburn through the warm, fragrant house. In the kitchen, Mary Ann Rayburn appeared to have spoons swirling in half a dozen pots, like that circus act where the man spins china plates on chopsticks.

"Jonah!" She kissed me on the cheek. She was a diminutive woman with a dark brown ponytail and what my mother calls yoga arms. "My favorite mad scientist! Oops." Mary Ann grabbed a napkin and pushed it against my face. "Lipstick. Thirty-five and I'm already turning into my mother."

"My grandmother always licks her finger." I licked mine and moved it menacingly toward Oliver, who broke into convulsions a third time.

"Okay, everybody out," Mary Ann ordered. "Ricky, get Jonah something to drink."

"Don't you need help?" I asked.

"I'm afraid you'll make something explode." She smiled. "Now out!"

Every time I came here, I had the same argument with myself. It was unwise of me to romanticize this life. Who knew whether Rayburn was really content or had ambitions much higher than high school teacher and father of three.

Oliver pulled me into the family room, where his siblings, Corey, eight, and Eliza, ten, played Connect Four on the carpet. I was introduced to the McCaffrey family, including Peter McCaffrey, a junior in my advising group. I flashed Rayburn a look. "I didn't tell you?" he said jovially. "Pete here is Mary Ann's nephew." Rayburn liked playing little tricks. He was relishing this. Peter looked sheepish. He was studious and polite, but painfully shy. I'd been trying to get him to join the Academic League for weeks now, convinced I could help him overcome his timidity. So far, I'd had little success. The other thing I knew about McCaffrey was that he had a hopeless crush on Iris Dupont. It must have been some kind of "opposites attract" thing. She was so tiny, and he was tall as a knobby pine — all knees and elbows. It was an unlikely pairing, but I thought they'd be good for each other. Iris needed someone her age who appreciated her, and Peter needed someone to draw him out of his shell. Earlier in the year, I'd encouraged Peter to talk to Iris. Start by saying hello, I'd instructed, and he'd looked at me like I'd asked him to perform open-heart surgery.

Halfway through dinner and after the kids had abandoned their plates, the conversation turned to school, and from there it was only a short jaunt into a discussion of what Rayburn had dubbed "the troubles." I told him we weren't dealing with the IRA. He said I was underestimating the situation.

"Rick, maybe we shouldn't . . ." Mary Ann nodded at Peter.

We all looked at Peter, his fork poised in midair.

"It's okay, Aunt Mary Ann." It was the first thing he'd said since we all sat down.

Rayburn turned to me. "We're all family and friends here tonight. I say scrap the teacher-student designations for a little while and let's just be ourselves." He took a sip of wine. "Jonah, for the evening why don't you think of Peter like . . ." He paused, turning his glass on the table. "Like your little brother."

It was strange to think of myself as an older sibling. Justin was five minutes and twenty seconds older than me. He quickly grew to be more physically mature and, at the end of his life, was significantly farther along with his love life, not a small point of contention between us.

"Do you have any siblings who would be offended by making Pete here family?" Rayburn added.

"I'm an only child," I said without thinking. It seemed Hazel was exerting some invisible force over me. And yet for some reason the lie felt right, almost like a relief. "You mind being my little brother for the night?" I asked. Peter returned an uncomfortable smile.

"So, Prisom's Party," Rayburn said, and took a bite of sweet potatoes. "Mary, this is so good."

Mary Ann turned to me. "He knows I don't like talking about this stuff, but he fancies himself an amateur detective. He would just love to be the one to find these kids and turn them in. Reap all the glory."

"I'm a physics teacher," Rick protested. "I've got to take my glory where I can get it." He took a rather large sip of his wine, and I wondered if buried in this remark was an actual note of dissatisfaction.

"Here's the question," Bill McCaffrey said, scratching at his mustache. It was the most amazing accessory I'd ever seen adorning a man's upper lip: thick, black, and bristly. "Is it so important to assert our authority that we can't let these students operate under the radar and do some good for the school?"

Peter's older sister, Jamie, home from college, leaned over to me and whispered, "My dad was about five years too young for the Dow protests at Wisconsin, and he's been trying to make up for it ever since. He calls Pete and me 'Generation A.'"

"Generation Apathy," Bill McCaffrey clarified. Apparently he'd heard Jamie. "My kids don't care about changing the world." He glanced at his son pushing mashed potatoes around his plate. "Let me ask again: What harm has this Prisom's Party really done?"

"Mary, tell him the rumors—" But Rayburn was interrupted by a loud crash from upstairs, followed by silence, followed by a child screaming. Mary Ann slid her chair back.

"Talk about entrenched gender roles," Bill McCaffrey said, spooning string beans onto his plate. "Jesus, Rick, don't you do *any* of the cooking or childrearing?"

Rayburn shook his head, but he pushed his chair back and followed his wife upstairs. This left me alone with the McCaffreys, and Bill didn't miss a beat. "You know anything about the rumors?" He leaned toward me on his elbows. His mustache twitched.

"No, sorry."

"Ignore him, Jonah," Linda McCaffrey said.

"I heard you were quite the hell-raiser back in the day."

"Bill!" Linda McCaffrey looked up from the asparagus spears she'd been slicing into ever-smaller sections. For the first time Peter was showing interest in the conversation.

"I was pretty tame," I said, and happened to catch Peter's eye. He blinked like he hadn't heard me.

Rick and Mary Ann returned. "Nuclear war averted," Rayburn said, reclaiming his seat.

"We were just discussing Mr. Kaplan's illustrious history at the school," Bill McCaffrey said. "Or should we say notorious history!" He leaned over and nudged my arm.

Rayburn sipped his wine and shook his head. "Kaplan's straight as an arrow," he said, winking at me. I noticed that Peter had perked up again. He looked like he might ask me something, but before he could, Rayburn plunged ahead. "Back to your story, my darling wife."

"Well, I've heard a few things about blackmail."

There was a loud clatter. Peter had dropped a spoonful of cranberry sauce on the table, and the spoon fell into his lap. He looked mortified and started wiping at the mess.

"Oh, honey." Mary Ann took the napkin from him. "There's some club soda in the fridge. Bring it back and I'll help you with the stain." Peter slunk into the kitchen.

"Who's blackmailing whom about what?" Bill McCaffrey said. This guy was insufferable.

"Well, you all remember Matt Sheridan, of course." Mary Ann turned to me. "Matt was a senior, full load of APs, a soccer star, president of half a dozen clubs, and last year he was elected president of the Community Council."

"Impressive," I said.

"But you know kids like Sheridan," Rayburn said. "Fool's gold."

Mary Ann shook her head. "Did you know my husband has categories for all the students? 'Fool's gold' means Sheridan looked fantastic on the outside—"

"But he was empty on the inside," Rayburn cut in. "He was a jerk, Jonah. Arrogant, entitled, Abercrombie good looks. I'm sure you've figured out that to get elected to the Community Council, you especially have to *look* like leadership material."

"Anyway," Mary Ann continued, "one day last year toward the end of first semester, somebody destroyed the Prisom Artifacts."

The Prisom Artifacts was a collection of memorabilia preserved from the early days of the school: time-glazed portraits of Mariana, Charles, and Henry Prisom; sepia photographs of the school's first class, twenty-five stern-eyed boys, their hair slicked, their mouths unsmiling; the Prisom cup, a crystal goblet engraved with the school's motto—*Brotherhood, Truth, and Equality for All*—that was symbolically bestowed upon the head of the Community Council each year;

and an original copy of the Community Code booklet, bearing Charles Prisom's signature. These were kept in a glass display case in the lobby. Or had been. Only now did I realize that the display was gone.

"The case was toppled, the goblet smashed, the pictures shredded to pieces, and the Community Code booklet burned." Mary Ann shook her head. "Then a few days later a *Devil's Advocate* appeared with photographs of Matt Sheridan trashing the stuff."

"Jesus," I said. "What happened?"

"We think Sheridan just snapped. Too much pressure, I guess. He left school and took the rest of the year off. We heard he had a breakdown. I think he's now at the Melville School."

"Talk about a downgrade," Bill McCaffrey said. I looked at Bill and his mustache, and my chest welled with antipathy. With a father like that, no wonder Peter walked around like he was constantly ducking for cover.

"Mary, tell them about the girls in the library," Rayburn said.

Mary Ann sighed. "Well, I overheard some girls gossiping a few weeks ago." She lowered her voice so Peter wouldn't hear her in the kitchen. "They seemed to think that Matt Sheridan was *forced* to destroy the Prisom Artifacts. It doesn't make a lot of sense." She paused. "Did you find the club soda?" she called to her nephew.

"Yes." Peter's voice sounded like it was coming from just behind the door.

"So, Jonah," Rayburn said, folding his hands on the table, "what's your take?"

The adult in me wanted to believe that these rumors were outrageous, but the child in me knew otherwise. "Actually, I'd like to know why some of our students are stressed to the point of meltdown and why others feel so marginalized that they've taken up vigilante justice as an extracurricular activity."

An uncomfortable silence fell over the table. I hadn't meant to sound so defensive. I glanced at the pillaged side dishes and the bones sticking out from the turkey carcass, and began to feel ill. Peter returned with the club soda.

"Don't worry," Jamie said, and tousled her brother's hair. "Dad's disappointed that there's no grand conspiracy happening at school. Other than that, you didn't miss much."

Peter smiled at his sister like she was his only friend in the world. Had I ever smiled at Justin like that? I combed my brain for a memory, just one carefree, uncomplicated moment. I couldn't remember much before junior high, when Justin started outgrowing me. Even playing in the woods was competitive practice for us. My chest grew tight, and I felt a dense ball of pressure in my throat. I watched Jamie noogie Peter and Peter swat her away, the grateful smile still plastered across his mouth. The ball in my throat pushed its way up; I could feel it behind my nose, spreading outward, heading for my eyes. I excused myself.

In the bathroom, I stood over the sink, closed my eyes, and took a couple of deep breaths. Gradually I forced the ball of pressure back down.

When I returned to the dining room, plates were being cleared. "You all right?" Rayburn said, putting a hand on my shoulder.

"Too much turkey," I said.

"Well, go in the other room and take a load off. We'll have dessert out in a few."

I walked into the family room to find Peter sitting on the couch with a book. "So, how are things going?" I said, trying to engage him. "You haven't come by office hours in a while." Mariana teachers had mandatory office hours. Along with academic majors, office hours were supposed to help acclimate the students to the "college mentality." Of course, this raised the question of when the kids were supposed to get into the high school mentality. Had specific measures been taken in elementary school? Kindergarten?

"I'm on top of everything, Mr. Kaplan."

I nodded. This kid was not easy to talk to. "Hey, I know we've discussed the Academic League," I said, watching for his reaction. This subject required a gentle tread. "And I know you're concerned about public speaking. But you could start out as researcher. You don't have to compete right away." Peter was listening. He wasn't protesting yet.

"And I thought you might be interested to know that we've recently made sort of a new addition to the team."

"What do you mean?"

"Iris Dupont is doing a story on us for the *Oracle*. She's going to be sitting in on our practices and interviewing team members."

"So?" he asked, the color rising in his face.

"Well, if you joined the team, she might want to interview you. And maybe an interview would be a good way to break the ice."

Peter nodded slowly. "And I wouldn't have to get up in front of an audience?"

"Start off behind the scenes and see how you like it. But I'm telling you, Pete, competing might win you some points with the ladies."

Rayburn stuck his head into the room. "Petey, how are you getting on with your big brother? He's giving you good advice, I hope."

Peter blushed.

"Okay, lads, dessert time."

Peter followed Rayburn into the dining room. I pulled out my phone. I had missed a text from Hazel. *Having a bad night. Can you come over?* Finally. I wrote her back and asked for the address. I hoped dessert wasn't going to take very long.

Lily

I T WAS FEBRUARY, the bleakest month of all. As Dipthi told Lily one day during lunch, February had the highest rate of relationship failure and heart failure. More homeless people froze to death in February, Dipthi said, than in any other month.

Lily and Justin had been dating for four months, but Justin's friends continued to shut her out. They plastered duct tape over the little window of their Trench lair and made her knock before entering. Lily couldn't figure out what they were hiding, and Justin parried whenever she confronted him. "They're just territorial," was his constant excuse.

Lily returned to the art rooms at lunchtime, now recording her observations of the Studio Girls in the back pages of *Marvelous Species*. She didn't tell Justin about it. She wasn't sure if this was wrong, but it certainly felt illicit—like something Veronica Mercy would do.

Still, Hazel remained a problem. Whenever Justin left the girls alone, the silence was toxic. One night they sat on opposite sides of the Greenburgs' couch while Justin gathered snacks for a Monty Python marathon. Unwilling to meet Hazel's challenging gaze, Lily instead studied the ring on Hazel's hand: a thick silver band with a horsefly mounted on top. Justin had presented this ring to Hazel on her birthday the previous year. He'd recently given Lily her own ring, a silver monarch, in honor of the first insect he'd ever preserved. The monarch was regal enough, but it lacked the horsefly's ferocity. She wished that Justin's gift to her had been similarly aggressive and strong.

"Veronica Mercy told me she's applying to artist apprenticeships this summer," Lily said now, unable to stand the silence any longer.

Hazel pressed a pillow to her chest. "So?"

"I thought you might have an opinion because your mom's an artist."

"My opinion?" Hazel laughed as though she found this a ridiculous question. "Veronica doesn't have a chance in hell of making it in the art world. Her work is crap."

Lily sat up. "What's wrong with it?" Veronica had recently presented her friends, including Lily, with a photographic compilation of her work, and Lily had pasted the pictures into *Marvelous Species*. "Because I'm trying to get my art out there," she'd explained as she handed Lily the album. Lily, of course, was thrilled that Veronica had included her. "I think her stuff is pretty good," she said now.

At that moment Justin arrived, struggling to balance three full glasses of soda and a plate of cookies. Hazel looked at him, her face inexplicably sad.

"What's wrong?" Justin said, carefully laying the goods on the coffee table.

"*Odi et amo,*" Hazel mumbled and then proceeded with a string of Latin words Lily didn't recognize. That first part, *I hate and I love,* was all Lily was able to catch. She was certain that Justin had understood, but he did not react.

The next evening Lily curled up beside Justin with *This Side of Paradise.* A single lamp lit the room, and shadows collected on the walls. The Kaplan parents were out to dinner and Jonah was at Toby's house. In the cocoon of Justin's bedroom, she finally felt safe and calm. Justin, on the other hand, was frazzled. He was studying for the Academic League division championship. The tournament was two months away, and already the stress pulsed in his face like a vein.

"Lily?" he asked.

"Hmm?" She was absorbed in the book and barely noticed when

Justin didn't respond. A few moments later he repeated her name. She looked up this time and their eyes met. "Are you okay?" she asked.

"Fine." But then a few minutes later he said her name again.

He probably just wanted to kiss her and was feeling shy. Only the next instant he was on top of her, pressing her back, holding her arms against the bed. The book fell out of her hands. She tried to speak, but her voice was muffled beneath him. He was kissing the sides of her neck, her throat. "Justin," she gasped.

He pulled off of her. "What's wrong?" He looked terrified. "Did I hurt you?"

Lily shook her head. They sat for a moment without looking at each other. "You never did anything like that before," she said, finally.

"You didn't like it."

"No — I just — I didn't know what was happening."

"I'm so fucking stupid. So stupid. *Stupid.*" He clenched his fists. "It's just that she — "

"*She* who?"

"She said you'd want me to be more aggressive, that you'd be afraid to ask for it."

"You were talking to Hazel about us?"

"Only because she asked me how things were going and I said good, but . . . well, maybe I wasn't doing things right. Because we still don't take off a lot of clothes."

"I can't believe you told Hazel about our — "

"Don't you talk to Dipthi about us?"

"It's different."

"How?"

"I don't know."

Justin hung his head. "I'm sorry. I'm stupid. So stupid."

"Stop saying that!" Could Hazel have put Justin up to this, knowing it might scare her? But Hazel wasn't malicious, she was just messed up. Being Queen of the Geeks didn't make her a master manipulator.

"I promise not to talk to Hazel about this stuff anymore. I swear."

Lily squeezed her legs against her chest. Justin inched forward on his knees, like he was about to bow down before her. "Tell me what you want and I'll do it."

She shook her head. He placed his hands on her knees. Then he laid his head in her lap. "Am I hot or cold?"

A long time seemed to pass. Lily's heart galloped in her chest. What if she spoke and he recoiled in disgust? But then she pictured Veronica Mercy lying on this very bed, her thick dark hair flared around her shoulders. She imagined she was Veronica Mercy, a girl who did not hesitate.

"Hot," Lily said.

Later that night, Lily walked into her house to find her parents at the dining room table, a mess of papers between them. Her father whispered into the phone, rattling an agitated pencil against the tabletop. His eyes were red. Her mother stood up, and for a brief moment, mother and daughter only stared at each other through the heavy silence.

"What happened?" Lily could barely get the words out. It was as if she already knew. Her mother rushed to her, but Lily backed away.

"She'd just come back from her afternoon walk . . . The doctors said aneurysm . . ."

Lily fled to her room and climbed into bed fully clothed. She lay there in the dark but soon was reaching for the phone and dialing Justin's number. It was as if her grandmother had prepared her for this moment, had prodded her not so gently toward Justin Kaplan's arms for this very purpose.

Jonah

NOVEMBER 2012

I ARRIVED AT THE Historical Society and found Hazel crying at the front door. I took one look at her — the wild mane of hair and raw nostrils — and remembered what my mother had said about Hazel seeming depressed.

"Jonah." Fresh tears spilled from her eyes, and her head tipped forward into my chest.

Leaning into my armpit, she led me to her living quarters at the back of the building. A single lamp lit the room. Crumpled tissues dusted her sheets. I noticed three prescription bottles on the nightstand. I sat Hazel down on the bed and propped some pillows behind her.

"Jonah—" Her voice was hoarse. Her tears were hot and wet through my shirt. "I disappeared on you." She was crying harder now.

She wasn't talking about the last two weeks, I knew, but her previous disappearance, after Justin's death. Back then, she'd begged to know what killed him — accident or, as many people believed, suicide? But I refused to talk about it. Not even if she'd sworn her undying love for me. So she cut me off, stopped speaking to me entirely.

The following year, her last one at Mariana, she quit the Academic League and stopped hanging out in the Trench. I'd see her in the halls sometimes, but she ignored me. If I couldn't answer her questions, she wanted nothing to do with me. All of this left me feeling not only heartbroken — I would never have a chance with Hazel now — but utterly

201

alone. In an instant my brother had disappeared. Within weeks of his death I'd lost my best friend too.

Now, a decade later, she was suddenly owning up, which for Hazel was equivalent to an apology. "Did something happen today?" I asked. "What set this off?"

She pulled away and sat up. "I won't do it again, Jonah." She shook her head. "I promise. I'm going to stay right here. I'm not going to let you down. We're the only ones who know what it's like."

I nodded. She didn't need to finish. We were bonded over my brother's death, tied together as no one else would ever be tied to either of us. It was scary, acknowledging this need for another person, a person for whom there was no replacement. I was sure this was why Hazel had vanished for the last two weeks. She was independent to her core; she didn't want to believe that she needed me.

"I won't leave you again," she said, as though she hadn't already made this promise twice over. "But you can't leave me either. You have to swear that you'll stay. Promise me, Jonah. Please!"

I ran my hand down the length of her thick hair, and turned my head away. I was grinning. I wasn't happy to see her like this, but she had suddenly vindicated my most deeply held conviction: that our compatibility was not merely a hypothesis but a result. Quantifiable and repeatable. "You and me," I whispered in her ear. "From now on."

I woke some time later to the touch of Hazel's lips, so soft and buoyant they made my whole body feel afloat. Soon we'd shucked off the covers. A ball of emotion—the same one that I'd fought against in the Rayburns' bathroom—pumped in my chest. I pressed myself against it, and Hazel kissed me harder. She dug her fingers into my back as though trying to tear through me. I kneaded my fingers into her spine. We were fighting each other, physically confronting a decade of loneliness and disconnect. But we were also struggling together, desperately trying to grasp what we'd lost. Did we think we could retrieve it now that we were together? Because we were fighting Zeno's Paradox: No matter how many times you halved the distance, you'd never reach the destination.

The following day, Hazel was still out of sorts. She didn't fall asleep until dawn, hours after we'd exhausted ourselves on her bed. After she woke up in the late afternoon, we sat on the rumpled bed, talking and drinking tea. She showed me photographs from Greece. For the first time since I'd arrived at her house, she seemed to relax.

"I loved it there," she said, pulling the blankets around her legs. "That hot, white sun bleached out my whole previous life."

When she said this, I remembered something. "That thing that happened when you were twelve — with the bleach . . ." We'd never discussed this, but I recalled the afternoon my mother told me Hazel was in the hospital. She'd had an accident with a bottle of Clorox, but was going to be all right. Later on Justin informed me that Hazel had purposely tried to wipe out her freckles.

"I never told you what happened with me and Lily at Water World, huh?"

"You and Lily went to a water park together? You mean, like in a parallel universe?"

Hazel wasn't amused. "Remember that fancy camp your parents refused to send you to? Lily and I were kind of friendly back then."

"Come on."

"It's true. I was going through a seriously awkward phase. I looked like a babushka doll in neon spandex."

"Yes. That may have been the one time in our lives when I was better-looking than you."

"A moment that lasted approximately five minutes." She patted my leg. "Anyway, Lily was the only person there more clueless than me."

Here Hazel paused and looked down at the white sheets covering her legs. She ran her fingers up and down the slopes of her thighs, as though brushing them clean of some invisible residue.

"Anyway, I promised to look out for her and make sure she didn't burn, because she wasn't supposed to be outside at all. And when she did burn, I got scared. So I just pretended nothing was wrong. She thought I'd intentionally betrayed her—that I was jealous of her, because she had this perfect white skin and I looked like a walking disease."

"You used to think that about your freckles?" I said. Hazel shrugged. "But they're beautiful."

Hazel shook her head. "I tried to apologize. But Lily wouldn't even *look* at me. So I did that thing with the bleach."

"But why?"

Hazel pulled the sheet away and stretched her legs out on the bed. I ran my eyes down the length of her strong thighs and muscular calves. "It was really stupid, I know. I guess I was trying to punish Lily for not accepting my apology. I remember thinking, *See how you feel when you hear what you've made me do.*"

"My mom told me it was an accident."

"Lorna spread that around. I mean, Jesus, think about the alternative. *Crazy Lorna Greenburg let her daughter rub out her freckles with a bottle of bleach.* Somebody would have called in child services."

"But you told Justin the truth." I still felt a twinge of jealousy knowing that Hazel had taken her secrets to Justin before me.

"The conclusion of this pitiful tale is that because everyone thought it was an accident, the whole reason I'd done it in the first place was completely moot. Which made me really, really mad—" She cut herself off. "I don't want to talk about this. Don't ask me any more questions about Lily."

I felt reprimanded, so I looked around the studio and directed my frustration there. Everything appeared to be crumbling, like we were surrounded by mounds of decomposing matter. Why was Hazel living in this glorified junkyard?

"It doesn't help to dredge up everything, Jonah. It doesn't make dealing with my mother's genetic baggage any easier. You grew up with me. You know what to expect."

Be patient, I ordered myself. *Think geological eras and thank evolution for those beautiful legs in front of you.*

"I don't expect anything, Hazel," I said. "I'm just happy to be here."

The next morning, while Hazel slept, I went grocery shopping and stopped by my apartment for clean clothes. Then I took a detour. My childhood home was a white colonial built in 1862. From afar it was a work of country perfection: white clapboards, glossy green shutters, fancy molding over the front door. All illusion. Up close, the clapboards were scratched and the paint had been flaking off the molding for years. The front lawn was usually a soggy mess of carpetweed and crabgrass. The bathroom fixtures were rusty, the door frames warped, and the floors slanted at preposterous degrees.

When I pulled up that afternoon, I felt a stab of guilt. My parents knew I'd chosen to rent an apartment instead of living at home. They understood I needed to "separate" (my mother's word) and "build my own life" (my father's). But I'd done little in the way of home management—none of the raking, mowing, dusting, or periodic anti-burglar checkups my parents had requested. The truth was, I'd been avoiding the place.

I pulled my hat down over my ears, noosed my scarf around my neck, and hurried up the front walk, careful to avoid loose bricks. Entering was like stepping inside a mausoleum. A cold, unused feeling pervaded. I walked through the living room into the kitchen. Out of habit, I opened the fridge. Just as you can date a tree by its rings, you could tell the age and events of our home by our condiments: rows of crusted ketchups, jams, and mustards that no one had bothered to throw away, each jar a putrid microbial breeding ground.

I climbed the stairs and walked past the insect display, the dark, still bodies frozen in their frames like prehistoric mosquitoes preserved within amber. My room was similarly preserved. Sci-fi novels filled the shelves along with the requisite model vehicles and Academic League trophies. My father wished we'd added a few athletic trophies to this collection. He convinced us to play a season of baseball under the pretext that it would improve our understanding of physics. (Somewhere in my room was an article titled "How to Hit Home Runs: Optimum Baseball Bat Swing Parameters for Maximum Range Trajectories.") Of course, we were awful. Justin was distracted by grasshoppers in the outfield, and I usually got thrown out for attitude. Our combined batting average was an imaginary number.

I'd come here to find a certain Airwalk shoebox filled with materials my friends and I had collected on secret societies. The collusions, pledges, and religious rites fascinated us, and we filled notebooks on the Skull and Bones, Freemasons, the Sufis and Druze. We were drawn to these groups for the same reason we were drawn to science fiction: the legends and myths made us feel powerful. But this time around, I wasn't looking for power. I wanted clues to ferret out Prisom's Party.

My room yielded nothing, and I moved on. The door to my brother's room was framed by two long-horned beetles, *Macrodontia cervicornis,* each of them half a foot in length. The mandibles resembled miniature lobster claws, and wings sheathed their abdomens like wooden skirts. They were brilliant, these wings, decorated like cave drawings and varnished in shades of brown, chestnut, and gold. My parents used to call the beetles "mezuzahs" and joked about our having to kiss them before we entered Justin's room.

My brother's room no longer felt like his, and hadn't for a long time. It had once been the very definition of entropy: mounds of paper, clothes, school supplies, and Academic League materials dumped on every available surface. Now a couch had replaced the bed, and there wasn't a stray paper to be seen. I had to give my mother credit. For months after the accident, the littlest thing ignited her tear ducts: pouring a cup of coffee, tying her shoes, shoveling the front walk. Her every action was filtered through Justin's absence. "It's a different world altogether," she'd told me. "Everything is stunted, elongated, or just blurry. It's like looking at the world through an unfocused microscope." In her place, I would have barricaded Justin's room, or set fire to it, or thrown his possessions away.

Now, only the books identified the room as Justin's. They rose to the ceiling in impeccable rows, organized by an algorithm Justin had written that accounted for the text's subject, author, and physical height. Each book was pushed to the exact edge of the shelf, the spines flush. Justin was incredibly OCD on this point. I used to torment him by sneaking in and pushing random books back, some of them by just a few centimeters.

There were undoubtedly still parts of my brother here: skin cells and nail clippings that the vacuum cleaner didn't catch. Plenty of DNA. But his odor faded a week or two after his death, and now I could no longer remember what my twin brother had smelled like.

I sat down in the desk chair and looked up at the inscrutable expression of Albert Einstein. Given Justin's literary sensibilities, I'd have expected him to choose Walt Whitman or F. Scott Fitzgerald, but the image of the physicist was the single poster on Justin's wall. Taped up beside Einstein's furrowed brow, thick mustache, and cotton-tuft hair was a piece of college-ruled paper.

> "The individual feels the nothingness of human desires and aims and the sublimity and marvelous order which reveal themselves both in nature and in the world of thought. He looks upon individual existence as a sort of prison and wants to experience the universe as a single significant whole."

This was Einstein's Cosmic Religious Feeling, his belief that the pursuit of science and art was enough to make us feel connected to each other and, ultimately, would save us from isolation and despair. I thought about my brother sitting at his desk, copying out these words and taping them to his wall. I thought about *his* isolation and despair. He believed a connection with Lily could lift him from the abyss, shoot him like a rocket toward the sublime. But according to Einstein, a person could achieve this connection only if he gave up his individual desires. And who lived without desire? The desire for scientific distinction had left me disconnected and exhausted. My brother's desire for Lily had killed him. We all desired what we could not have. Justin, Lily, and myself. Even Hazel.

I searched through Justin's dresser and cabinets but found nothing. Meanwhile, I started to feel panicked. The house ached and groaned, as though complaining about my presence. Wind gusts rattled the windows, calling to mind the clicking and snapping of insect exoskeletons. Finally, in Justin's closet, I located the Airwalk box. I'd bought the shoes early in high school, one of my few (and fruitless) attempts to feel cool (I didn't ride a skateboard, had never even tried), and the shoes themselves had long since disappeared. Now that I'd found what I wanted, I grabbed the box, tucked it under my arm, and fled. I ran down the stairs and out the front door like something was chasing me.

I sat panting in the car, waiting for the heater to warm up. I lifted the shoebox lid and quickly realized my mistake. My mother, utilitarian to the core, had chucked the material on secret societies and filled the box with papers related to Justin's accident instead. There were news clippings, condolence notes, and mathematical equations that my father had collected at the crash site—his desperate attempt to determine exactly what had killed my brother.

So now what?

I did not want these reminders nearby, but I wanted to go back inside the house even less. I pushed the box beneath the passenger seat and drove away without looking back.

Iris

T HE MONDAY AFTER Thanksgiving break, I reported first thing to the *Oracle* office for a new assignment: covering the Jimmy Get Well campaign. Jimmy Cardozi was a freshman who'd been diagnosed with cancer over the summer, and I was supposed to interview the juniors and seniors in the premed major who'd been handing out pamphlets on childhood leukemia and selling chocolate chip cookies. Contributions went into the lockbox that sat in the school lobby beside a life-size cardboard cutout of Jimmy. This was Jimmy pre-cancer: six feet tall, rotund and grinning. He hadn't looked like this for a long time.

I wondered how Jimmy felt walking past the Jimmy Get Well table every day. I know if I'd lost fifty pounds and all my hair, I wouldn't want to be reminded of my former healthy state. I doubted anyone had bothered to ask Jimmy for permission to use his likeness, just as I doubted the teachers knew that as soon as the picture went up, kids started saying things like "Hey, Jimmy Get Thin," or "Jimmy Get a Clue," or "Jimmy Get a Life!"

I wanted to present the truth of Jimmy's experience. I planned to accompany my written story with a podcast modeled on Murrow's program *This I Believe.* But Katie Milford said the story should cover how successful the JGW campaign had been and how it exemplified the tenets of the Community Code. "Don't give me your self-righteous free-press crap, Iris," she told me. "There's a lot of money in that donation box."

Maybe so. But money didn't tell the whole story.

I was about to raise these concerns when our features editor ran in, flushed and panting. *"Devil's Advocate!"* he exclaimed. Katie snatched the paper from his fingers, and she was suddenly magnetized—the entire office practically stuck to her. Clearly enjoying her newfound popularity, Katie cleared her throat and read the headline, *"Technology Lends Immorality a Hand,"* and then continued:

"MARIANA ACADEMY—First there was Wikipedia; now there's Wikicheatia, an online encyclopedia for students seeking the 'non-study' option. This password-protected site (access comes with a $500 price tag) offers pages for a variety of classes at Mariana Academy, each with the questions and answers for major tests. Like the actual Wikipedia, users can edit information or create new pages. As the tests change, students who have taken those tests can update information for future users.

"But what's the point, you might wonder, if the exam questions change each year? How could Wikicheatia help? The answer is simple. The exams don't change that much. Wikicheatia relies on faculty laziness. And so far it's been pretty successful. Because our exams are not proctored, students can easily whip out their smartphones and search sites like Wikicheatia.

"But Wikicheatia, like its mainstream counterpart, runs into trouble with accuracy. Wikicheatia's head editors are supposed to supervise page content, but they can't keep tabs on everything. And so, sophomores Reagan Rodriguez and Madison Morrison are about to find themselves in cyber-trouble. The girls paid the five hundred bucks each and copied the answers from Wikicheatia onto Mr. Harley's most recent trigonometry exam. They did not know that all of the Wikicheatia answers for Mr. Harley's trig test were off by two numbers. Oops."

"Cocky bastards," Katie said, crumpling up the *Devil's Advocate* and tossing it in the trash. "Now get back to work!"

I headed out to find a crowd of students gathering around the math department. I pushed my way through until I had a glimpse of the door window. Inside, Reagan Rodriguez huddled in a chair, her head bowed while Mr. Harley screamed at her. He flailed his arms like a boat motor, his face red and shining. The atmosphere at school was turning downright hostile, but I couldn't worry about that now. I had work to do.

The plan Hazel and I had come up with would prove Mr. Kaplan's innocence via the scientific method. Just as he'd taught us in class, I started by defining the question: Was Mr. Kaplan the locker vandal? Next I gathered information and resources, such as *Oracle* articles and discussions with Mr. Kaplan's classmates (i.e., Hazel) and the observations of his students (i.e., myself). Third, I formed a hypothesis: Mr. Kaplan is not the locker vandal. And finally, I planned to test the hypothesis with an experiment—a drawing test. It was an innovative approach, and I thought Murrow would have been proud.

The science department was blissfully unaware of the chaos just one floor below them. The journalist in me wanted to break the news, but I couldn't risk them all losing focus. I called for attention and explained that I was reporting a science story on the relationship between left-brain individuals and artistic ability. Then I gave everyone a list of objects to draw. The goal was to see whether Mr. Kaplan's pictures resembled those from the locker vandalism and to observe his response to the images. I had everyone participate so he wouldn't get suspicious.

I couldn't instruct a bunch of teachers to draw students sodomizing each other, so I adapted the images to a PG-13 rating. Mr. Kaplan's rabid dog resembled a cloud-eating sausage with feet; his tarantula looked like an amoeba, and his frightened schoolgirl bore a striking resemblance to a banjo. He seemed perplexed by the assignment—not the reaction of a guy with something to hide. The teachers joked about their pictures. A few looked annoyed. Finally Mr. Kaplan asked me what was going on.

"You're not the locker vandal!" I exclaimed, and then clamped my hand over my mouth, stunned at my imprudent reaction.

The teachers looked at each other, then at Mr. Kaplan. "What's she talking about?" Mr. Rayburn said.

Mr. Kaplan's initial bafflement quickly morphed into consternation. I approached him and motioned that we needed to speak confidentially. "Just say what you need to say." His voice was clipped.

I explained about the *Oracle* articles I'd found in the Trench, and how I was hoping to exonerate him. "I thought you'd be proud," I said, my voice starting to quaver. "Because I used the scientific method."

Mr. Kaplan's face was hard with disappointment. "Iris, nobody would be asking questions about me if you weren't."

He never used my first name, and it made me feel like a child. "I'm sorry," I said, working hard to keep my voice steady.

Do you see the problem of trying to report as a friend? Murrow whispered. *Your lack of professionalism has been disappointing.*

I bit my lip.

"Iris, are you listening?" Mr. Kaplan was eyeing me. "I need your cooperation on this. I need you to promise you won't bring the vandalism up with anyone else. Can you do that for me?"

I swallowed. "What vandalism?"

Mr. Kaplan sighed. "Now, are you still planning to come by the Academic League practice tomorrow afternoon?"

"I'll be there," I said. *I'm a hard-nosed reporter,* I thought to Murrow. *I'm not a friend.* "Oh, and by the way"—I turned back to the room—"you guys just missed the latest *Devil's Advocate*." I let the door shut on their startled expressions.

I went to the third-floor bathroom and wrote to Prisom's Party.

A good start, they wrote back. *But we're going to need more evidence. Even if Jonah Kaplan didn't paint the lockers he still may have masterminded the project. Have you searched his desk? His faculty box? His car? Start using that investigative brain of yours!*

It's not like I've done this before, I wrote. *And anyway, you were the ones who tapped me. Maybe you should have hired a professional!*

Fair enough, they responded. *But you want to come back and see us, don't you?*

You guys said access in exchange for information. So how did you get to be involved in the Party? I prayed my correspondent was Winston. I was sure he would answer honestly.

A few seconds later the response came: *I was tapped.*

I wrote back immediately: *By whom?*

I can't tell you that.

Do you test out all your potential inductees? Are there others like me?

There was a lengthy pause. My heart flipped inside out as I waited for a response. I was starting to realize that I had a serious crush on Winston, which was really weird, considering that I'd never seen his face.

There's no one like you, my flower.

It wasn't Winston but creepy Syme. I logged out as fast as I could.

IV

MICROBIAL INVASIONS

Just as melanin protects human skin from the sun, melanin polymers defend microorganisms against radiation, extreme temperatures, and heavy metals. A microbe with low melanin levels can easily fall prey to pathological bacteria.

— *Marvelous Species: Investigating Earth's Mysterious Biology*

Lily

M ARCH ARRIVED, SOGGY and slick. At the end of February, the weather shot upward—from the twenties into the high forties—and the natural world, reeling from this abrupt shift, sank into muddy depression. Weeks before, thick, blinding blankets of snow had covered Mariana's fields. Now this snow melted into fetid bogs. In those early days of March, you couldn't walk two feet without accruing diarrhetic splatters on the backs of your legs or hearing the sucking, slurping sound of your shoes in the muck.

These dark stains were far more pronounced on Lily's snowy skin than on anyone else's, but she didn't care. She swung madly between the loss of her grandmother and relief at Justin's presence. Everywhere she went, he was there to help her skip over a puddle or sidestep a watery rut. Ever since her grandmother's death, they sat side by side in class, surreptitiously slipping notes between their desks. For the first time in her life, Lily felt exactly as she'd always wanted to feel: included. It wasn't about being part of any specific clique; it was the simple knowledge that she was living as a normal teenager was supposed to.

But her parents were concerned. Elliott had instituted a father-daughter bonding regimen, wherein one night a week they did an activity together. It was an obvious ploy to glean information about her life. Her new, normal life. On this night, she and her father played gin on the living room carpet while her mother drank coffee and read the paper on the couch.

"When it comes to dating," Elliott was saying, "there's a lot of pressure."

"You sound like a sex-ed pamphlet." Lily selected a card from the center stack.

"People like Justin can't always keep the ups and downs in perspective."

"What do you mean, people like him? He's not retarded."

"You haven't seen Justin's file. We just want to make sure that if things don't work out between you, then — "

"Who said things aren't going to work out?" Lily looked from parent to parent.

"Your mother and I just don't want anyone to get hurt."

"Oh, my Lord!" Maureen gasped, as though responding to the mere mention of pain.

"Maura, what's wrong?"

Maureen placed her coffee cup on top of the newspaper. She closed her eyes for a moment, then opened them and forced a smile. "Just a lot of nastiness in the world."

A litany of tragedies flashed through Lily's head: war, terrorism, earthquake, disease. But papers were always filled with these things. "What happened?"

"People killing each other over in Africa. Same old thing."

"Mom, people kill each other over here, too."

Elliott glared at his daughter: *She's not trying to be insensitive.*

Lily glared back: *Well, she sounds insensitive to me.*

Elliott sighed in a way that indicated a truce.

"Just forget it." But then Maureen began to cry. Elliott rose from the carpet and went to his wife. He reached for the newspaper, and in an attempt to stop him Maureen's hand knocked over the coffee. Dark liquid ran across the coffee table and onto her lap. Cursing, she jumped up as Elliott fished for tissues. Amid the commotion, Lily grabbed the newspaper and scurried into the hall. Her mother had been reading a story about Kenyan albinos, a tiny population ostracized for its freakishness.

"Lily, put that down!" her mother yelled from the living room. "Lily!"

But Lily heard her mother's voice as if through a pane of glass. *Africa's Albinos Decry Ancient Superstition,* she mouthed to herself. *Mercenaries are kidnapping and killing albinos and selling their skins on the black market. Some people in Africa believe albino skin to be good luck.*

Akeyo Mundi, 15, had been forced to drop out of school because of her albinism. She suffered from nystagmus, an eye condition which prevents the eyes from focusing on faraway objects and causes extreme nearsightedness. Mundi couldn't see the chalkboard or read books without extra-large print.

"People say my daughter is lucky, because of her skin," Makena Mundi, Akeyo's mother, said. "But the men do not want to marry her. No one will hire her for work."

Two weeks ago, the Mundi family was eating dinner when men armed with machetes broke into their house. They grabbed Akeyo from the table.

"Her father tried to stop them, but they sliced him in the shoulder," Mrs. Mundi said.

One of the men held Akeyo by the arms as the other sawed off her legs. The men collected the stumps and ran away. Akeyo died.

Lily's parents were still calling to her, but what were they saying? She looked at her pale palm with its violet veins, and imagined a knife slipping beneath the tip of her middle finger and slicing a thin line toward her wrist. She imagined the skin peeling away, like chicken fat. She saw her parents' bodies beside her, watched them gesticulate, but their actual words made no sense. Suddenly she vomited onto the floor.

"Here, honey." For a moment, Lily thought it was her grandmother rubbing her back, but it was her mother holding her. "I'm so sorry, Lily. I didn't want you to see that."

Lily broke from her mother and rushed to the bathroom. She

swooshed water around her mouth, washed her hands, and dried them on her mother's plush hand towels. She looked at herself in the mirror. Why was she crying? She didn't live in Africa. That article had nothing to do with her life.

"Lily, are you all right?"

Lily stared at the mirror. But wasn't it possible that she felt sick in a different way from how most people would?

"Lily, I'm so sorry. I didn't want you to see that. But I'm here for you."

"I'm here too, Lily!" her father echoed. Then both her parents were talking at once, assuring and reassuring her. *We won't ever leave you. We're right here. We're not going anywhere.* But as they pleaded and comforted, an idea swept through Lily with great force: her parents feared that *she* was going to leave *them*. How naïve they were, Lily thought. How much like frightened children. She opened the bathroom door and let her mother and father embrace her.

Whereas the Morgans were concerned about Lily's relationship with Justin, Mrs. Kaplan was elated. The next evening, she intercepted them as they were coming down from Justin's room. She stood at the bottom of the stairs, and Lily had the uncomfortable feeling she'd been waiting there for hours.

Mrs. Kaplan clasped her hands to her chest. "I've just ordered a pizza, Lily. Would your parents mind?"

Lily and Justin glanced at each other, silently assessing the potential damage this offer could do. Before either one could answer, however, Mrs. Kaplan put her arm around Lily's shoulder. It felt strange to have someone else's mother touching her, but she let Justin's mom lead her into the kitchen.

"Justin thinks we're embarrassing," Mrs. Kaplan said, opening the refrigerator door. "But we're not that bad. Honey, do you have any idea how old these Cokes are?" Justin rolled his eyes. "Well, if this soda is flat or tastes funky, let me know." She handed Lily a Coke can. The aluminum was sticky.

"Thank you, Mrs. Kaplan."

"Oh, no. It's Helen."

Lily opened the Coke. A sharp *pop* echoed in the silence.

"Justin, will you get your father?" Justin didn't move. "Justin!" Justin slunk out of the room. Mrs. Kaplan began setting the table with paper plates and napkins. When Lily's parents ordered pizza, a rare occurrence, her mother still used china. "Jeffrey loves pepperoni," Mrs. Kaplan said, "but we don't officially allow pork in the house, hence the paper. We're horrible Jews."

Lily leaned against the wall, trying to understand this confusing statement.

"So." Mrs. Kaplan smiled at Lily as though waiting for her to say something. But Lily was only sixteen and Mrs. Kaplan was an adult; wasn't it her responsibility to keep the conversation going?

Mrs. Kaplan stood by the table, her hands knotted together. "I'm just so happy that you and Justin have been spending time together. These last few weeks, he's been a different person." Mrs. Kaplan sat down at the kitchen table and began folding a paper napkin in front of her. Her hands were chapped, her nails short and unglossed. "He's always been so hard on himself . . . I don't know why."

Lily did not move from her spot against the wall. She watched Mrs. Kaplan's fingers smooth out the napkin.

"After he broke his foot in the fall, we worried that—" She paused, looking intently at the napkin. "Well, I was beginning to think this would never happen for him." Mrs. Kaplan nodded to herself. "But everything's all right now." She kept nodding. "Finally, he's happy and—"

Lily spotted a box of tissues and brought them to the table.

"Thank you, honey." Mrs. Kaplan wiped her eyes and went to the sink. The doorbell rang, and Justin entered with the pizza box.

"I'm sorry that took so long. My dad stumbled into some insane tirade about string theory." He leaned toward her ear and said, "Is my mother crazy?"

Lily glanced at Mrs. Kaplan's back. "She's fine."

Just as Lily and Justin sat down, Mr. Kaplan walked into the kitchen. He stood a solid five foot ten and bore a strong resemblance to Jonah — or how Jonah might look as a man: narrow, angled face, small, quick eyes. He wore a T-shirt and khaki pants with a braided leather belt. Red hair grew in abundance on his face and arms and, like Jonah, from his head. His eyebrows resembled furry crimson caterpillars. His feet were bare and his toes sprouted long red hairs. Jeffrey Kaplan was not a boy like Justin, or a dad like her father, but a *man*. Justin touched her arm and she flinched.

"Good to see you, Lily," Mr. Kaplan said, and scratched his beard. His fingers sounded like sandpaper against the scruff. Lily began to stand. "No, don't get up." He waved her back. "You ordered pepperoni?" Mrs. Kaplan winked at Lily, no sign of tears. "Where is my prodigal son?" he said, licking pizza grease off his fingers. On cue, Jonah walked in, grabbed a slice of pizza, and without a word walked back out.

Lily, Justin, and the Kaplans ate in silence, their mouths masticating bread and cheese.

"So, Lily." Mr. Kaplan folded his hands on the table. "How do you like Mariana? Do you see your father often at school?"

"This isn't an interview, Dad."

Mr. Kaplan coughed. "Take Your Daughter to Work Day must be pretty boring," he said, smiling. "Or does your dad let you play disciplinarian?"

"Jeff!"

Justin looked desperate. "Lily, don't you need me to take you home?"

"I need to grab my bag upstairs." She smiled apologetically at Justin's father. He turned up the corners of his mouth and nodded.

"Oh, Lily," Mrs. Kaplan said, eyeing her husband and son. "I'm so sorry to hear about your grandmother. Justin told me how close you were."

"Thank you," she murmured, and hurried from the kitchen.

The upstairs hallway was cast in early-evening gloom. She walked a straight line toward Justin's room, trying to ignore the insects. She felt like Aladdin, warned by the genie that to touch the treasure chamber walls meant sudden death. Justin's room was just a few steps away.

Only then Jonah appeared before her, animus radiating from his diminutive body.

"You scared me," Lily said.

"What the hell are you doing?"

"Getting my bag."

"No—with my brother." Jonah shifted his weight and ran a hand through his hair. "Why did you decide, after all this time, that you were interested in him?" As he spoke, a tight feeling built in Lily's chest. "Because I think you're only using him to climb your way out of your pathetic existence. You only care about Veronica. And Alexi."

"I'm allowed to have different friends." She wanted to back away, but she felt an irrational fear of accidentally touching the insect frames. As though they'd curse her forever.

"You feel guilty, though." Jonah smiled. "About something."

"You're jealous. Your brother has a girlfriend and you don't. He's doing things you've never done." Jonah opened his mouth, but Lily kept going, fueled by a peculiar energy she'd never felt before. "Have you kissed a girl, Jonah? Have you touched a girl's breasts? Have you stroked a girl's hair? Has any girl ever pressed her mouth to your ear?" She couldn't believe she was saying these things. "You wish you were your brother. And you're a hypocrite, pretending to care how other people treat Justin when you treat him like shit."

Lily marched past Jonah and stood heaving in Justin's room. When she heard Jonah's door slam, she grabbed her bag and hurried downstairs. In the foyer, she heard voices.

"God, Mom!" Justin was saying, "You're even worse than Dad. She's already self-conscious about her appearance and all you did was stare at her like she was some freak."

"Oh, honey, I'd never—I was trying to be friendly. And I know how important she is to you. I've seen how you've changed."

"Oh, God!"

"Honey, don't be embarrassed."

"I'm the same person."

"But honey, you're not."

The voices stopped. Chairs scraped. Justin stormed into the hallway but stopped short when he saw Lily standing there.

"Let's go," he said, and walked past her out the door.

Iris

I STOOD ALONE IN the Trench. The four eyes bugged out at me, their red veins like trickles of blood. "What are you?" I shouted, but the craggy mouth only smiled, sinister and calm. A rush of air gathered in the darkness behind me. Those eyes had seen things and that mouth held vital information. Something was approaching, and those eyes could see it. They were watching, waiting for it to happen. And just as I felt the black sack thrown over my head and the cold fingers on my neck, I woke up.

My sheets were tangled and soaked with sweat. I switched on the light and flipped through my collection of Murrow's broadcasts until I came to "A Report on Senator Joseph R. McCarthy," from March 9, 1954.

> We will not walk in fear, one of another. We will not be driven by fear into an age of unreason, if we dig deep in our history and our doctrine, and remember that we are not descended from fearful men — not from men who feared to write, to speak, to associate and to defend causes that were, for the moment, unpopular.

I read the words again and again, like my own Lord's Prayer. My history was the legacy of Charles Prisom. And Prisom stood for courage and truth. But nobody was being truthful. I was hiding the truth from Mr. Kaplan, and I feared that Prisom's Party was hiding it from me.

And what about Mr. Kaplan? What was he hiding?

Only in the classroom was he confident and self-assured. In fact, it amazed me how the class dynamic had begun to change. We were learning a lot, but it didn't feel forced. One day we'd be out in the snow, searching the fields of goldenrod behind the school for the gallflies that withstood extreme cold. The next day we'd be reading the memoirs of men who'd climbed Mount Everest and plunged their high-tech subs to the ocean floor, after which we'd discuss survival techniques from both human and microbial perspectives. In teams, we searched through scientific journals and magazines to learn about the latest practical applications for extremophile research. We started writing our own homework assignments and test questions, and we led part of the class discussion almost every day. Of course, now that we'd been exposed to all this cool, creative stuff, nobody wanted to hunker down and memorize the basic biology come exam time. But it felt like we were a team and Mr. Kaplan was our coach.

But out of class, Mr. Kaplan flip-flopped more wildly than a presidential candidate. How could he be one person in the room and another person outside of it? Which Mr. Kaplan was real? Could these two identities coexist, or was one just masking the other? I worried about this. I worried a lot.

As a case in point, I'd recently collided with him at the entrance to the Trench. I was coming back from the *Oracle* archives and he was heading down.

"I have a terrific interview subject for you at Academic League practice," he said, but when I asked who, he seemed not to hear. "You do understand what I explained to you the other day?" He was patronizing me, which wasn't like him. "Because it's not appropriate to get involved in a teacher's personal life. I know you have good intentions, but—" Mr. Kaplan ran his hand through his hair. "Do you understand what I'm trying to say?"

I nodded.

"Good." Then he unlocked the Trench door and disappeared.

I continued up the stairs.

"Hey!" Murrow shouted in my ear. "Don't you want to know what he's doing down there? If he's really looking for Prisom's Party, maybe he'll inadvertently lead you to their lair."

"I'm going to be late for class. Some of us don't have the luxury of being paid to do what we love."

"Suit yourself," Murrow said, and snapped his suspenders.

I walked up a few more stairs, paused, groaned, and retraced my steps. I let myself into the black door with Katie Milford's key and slunk quietly along the wall. I couldn't see Mr. Kaplan, but I could see light emanating from the *Oracle* archives at the end of the hall. After a short time Mr. Kaplan stepped into view. He put his satchel on the floor and stood for a moment looking at the back wall. Then he unstacked the chairs until the demon became visible. How long, I wondered, had Mr. Kaplan been sneaking down here to look at that thing? Weeks? Months? And then I thought: *Why not just ask him? Why not pop out right now and say you've forgotten something and then ask him what that creature is?* But just as I started to announce myself, Mr. Kaplan picked up his satchel and hurled it at the wall. "Bastard!" he shouted, his voice echoing through the hallway. "Bastard!"

I gasped, but Mr. Kaplan hadn't heard me. He stood with his back to me, heaving like a boxer readying for the next round. I thought about the night I'd thrown my phone against the wall and how furious I'd been. How all I'd wanted to do was smash something to bits.

I walked into the AL practice that afternoon terrified that Mr. Kaplan would take one look at me and know that I'd spied on him in the Trench. Instead, his face lit up like a Times Square display. "Meet your interview subject, Ms. Dupont. Our newest team member, Peter McCaffrey."

When I saw Peter's rag-doll body, untucked shirt, and sheepish expression, I suppressed a groan. Peter was a couple of years older than me, and his locker was near mine. He always seemed to be hanging around whenever I retrieved books, loitering like a vagrant. Since school started, I hadn't heard him utter so much as a compound sentence.

I sat down at the back of the classroom and motioned for Peter to join me. I thought the kid might have potential in the looks department—if he stood up straight and looked you in the eye. So far, I hadn't been able to test this theory.

"Have fun!" Mr. Kaplan said, like he was sending us off on a date.

I held out my digital recorder. "Could you please state your name, age, and year at school?" Peter mumbled his answer. He was sweating. "So, tell me why you joined the Academic League," I said.

Peter drew circles on the desk with his finger. "Thought I'd try something new."

"Look," I said. "I'm at least going to need you to speak in complete sentences."

A droplet of sweat rolled down the side of his face. He swept his dark hair from his eyes and waited for the next question. He had a bomb defuser's look of intense concentration.

"What kind of coach is Mr. Kaplan?" I asked.

"Manic."

"Excuse me?"

"He's on hyperdrive. Everything is super important with him, super serious, like our lives are at stake in here." Peter glanced behind him, where Mr. Kaplan was indeed gesticulating at the team members like he was preparing them for battle. Then I saw him catch Peter's eye and give a conspiratorial nod. Peter was so obviously a plant, chosen by Mr. Kaplan to observe *my* behavior. Perhaps this was the reason he'd been loitering around my locker. But I was on to him.

I asked Peter mundane questions about the AL to throw him off track. Then I thanked him for his time and left. I went immediately to the science department.

I walked over to Mr. Kaplan's desk and opened the drawer. I'd become disconcertingly comfortable with snooping since arriving in Nye.

"I'd say you've become disconcertingly comfortable with a number of things."

I turned to see Murrow smoking in a swivel chair, perusing a biology textbook. I gasped. Had I subconsciously summoned him?

"You're really about to search through a man's desk?" he said. "You're a journalist, Iris, not a detective."

"This is hard enough for me without your input," I said, trying to shake my unease.

"You can't make good reporting out of bad practice."

"I have to do this. I need access. Didn't you recently advise me not to think of Mr. Kaplan as a friend?"

"Yes, but that doesn't mean you should invade his privacy."

"What else am I supposed to do?"

Murrow looked around for an ashtray and, finding none, tapped his cigarette into the textbook. "The world blackens even the most innocent hearts," he murmured.

"Who are you talking to?"

I whipped around. *Shitshitshitshitshitshitshit. SHIT!* Peter walked into the office and sat down in Mr. Kaplan's chair.

"Mr. Kaplan asked me to look for something," I said, glancing at the chair where Murrow had been. It was empty.

I pulled a stack of *Oracle*s and old yearbooks from Mr. Kaplan's desk, affecting an air of purpose. Peter said nothing. He just swiveled.

"You want to cut that out?"

Peter swiveled to a stop. "I'm not going to tell on you, Iris."

"There's nothing to tell."

"Did I offend you?"

"I don't like people spying on me."

"I came to get note cards." Peter looked genuinely hurt. I thought Mr. Kaplan had sent him to follow me, but maybe that wasn't true. "And anyway," he added, "you're a hypocrite, going through Mr. Kaplan's desk."

I stared at him, fuming. I had no rebuttal. "Sorry I snapped at you," I said.

Peter looked surprised. "It's okay. I'm working on a project for my engineering major on digital modeling and video surveillance."

"Spying," I said, and smiled.

Peter leaned over me. "Hey, can you hand me one of those newspapers?" But he'd already grabbed one. "These bylines say Justin Kaplan," he said, rustling the pages. "Who's that?"

"Mr. Kaplan's brother?"

"Mr. Kaplan doesn't have a brother. He told me at Thanksgiving he's an only child."

I looked up. Peter had spent Thanksgiving with Mr. Kaplan? He'd had an opportunity to sit at the same table with Mr. Kaplan for hours, talking like two regular people? Only Peter had probably wasted the opportunity. He could have delved the depths of Mr. Kaplan's brain, but he probably just sat there, pushing his turkey around. I was phenomenally jealous. "Maybe there were two Kaplan families at Mariana?" But I knew how unlikely this was.

Peter knelt beside me and my pulse jumped. He reached across me—static from his sweater giving me a shock—and picked up one of the yearbooks. He flipped through the opening pages. "Look at this, Iris. Right here!" He tapped the book. The heading read, *In Memoriam. Justin Kaplan: 1983–2000.* Below a portrait showed a plaintive face with strawberry blond hair and blue eyes.

Mr. Kaplan's brother was dead? Something fluttered in my chest, something that pushed against the muscle.

"They were twins." Peter pointed to a photo of two boys beneath a banner that read, *Happy Fourteenth, Justin and Jonah.* "Fraternal."

"You don't say."

"You know, Iris, I'm not even upset that you're being rude. And the reason I don't care"—Peter paused and took a deep breath—"is that I like you, Iris."

I looked at him, stunned. *Dalia,* I thought, *a boy likes me.* And I almost burst into tears. Because I wanted to run and tell her. Because she should have been here and she wasn't. *Keep it together, Dupont!* I ordered myself. I grabbed the yearbook from Peter's hands and returned it to Mr. Kaplan's desk drawer. Then I jumped up and headed for the door. The song on loop in my head was: *I like you, Iris. I like you, Iris. I like you.*

I should have been happy that a boy liked me, especially a cute one. But I just wanted Peter to back off. He was a distraction. He made me uneasy. He was confusing. But he followed me, trailing through the halls and into the Trench stairwell. "You're going down there?" he asked.

At this point I should have opened the black door and locked Peter out. But my body was jittery with a feeling somewhere between anger and elation. It was as if some other girl—a much more experienced girl—had usurped my identity. And that girl liked the thrill of taking this boy somewhere she shouldn't. That girl liked the idea of giving Peter a hard time.

"Buck up and be a man," I said, and felt quite satisfied with myself until I realized that "buck up" is a cliché and, worse, refers to the rutting season for deer, when stags fight each other for the attention of fertile females. The last thing I wanted was for Peter to put me and fertility anywhere in the same Zip Code.

"But how are you going to get in?" he asked.

The girl, the one who was me but not me, held up Katie Milford's key and dangled it in front of Peter's face.

"But the rumors . . ."

"Poor Peter's scared," the new girl said, and laughed, because Peter had no idea what was really in the Trench. But I *did* know, so I was happy to have him with me. As much as I wanted Prisom's Party to take me back into its lair, I wasn't in the mood for a kidnapping.

Sure enough, the *Oracle*s in Mr. Kaplan's desk were missing from the archives. Was grief the reason he'd removed the newspapers with his brother's byline? Why he'd lied to Peter about being an only child? But Justin had been dead for twelve years.

Twelve years from now I'd be twenty-six, which seemed inconceivable. I already felt that the older I grew, the farther I traveled from Dalia.

I saw her growing distant in my memory, like an object in the rearview mirror. I couldn't imagine looking back and no longer being able to see her.

"Are you okay, Iris?"

I'd almost forgotten Peter was there. We were standing outside the archives, so close together that I could smell the detergent on his clothes. A freckle in his left eye sparkled like a speck of gold, and the confident girl of a few minutes before had vanished. "Look at this!" I said. I hadn't planned on showing him the demon, but I needed to squash the awkwardness between us.

"Holy shit," Peter said when I'd finished unstacking the chairs. "That's the same picture as in the bathrooms."

"I know. But it looks like it's been here for a long time. See how the paint's faded?"

"I can't believe you've been hanging around down here by yourself."

Peter spoke with such sincerity that my stomach dropped like a water-filled balloon and went *splat. I like you, I like you, I*—I shook my head a little, hoping to empty Peter's words from my brain. Meanwhile, the demon went on grinning, its mouth wide and dark. I felt an amorphous fear as though some ill-intentioned force was leading me along. And where did that path lead? *Well,* I thought, *you're staring at it! These four eyes, this gaping mouth.* It seemed only a matter of time before the monstrous mouth sucked me in and swallowed me whole.

Peter stepped closer. He was tall, I realized. Very tall. "Iris?" He touched my shoulder, and thousands of shocks zipped through my body.

"I have to go," I stammered, and fled.

Coming out of the Trench was like surfacing from a mineshaft, and as I climbed the stairs, I realized I'd made an important discovery. I now knew the origin of my ineffable connection with Mr. Kaplan—what he'd seen in me that first day at the ice cream social and what continued to bind us together over the weeks and months. He'd lost his brother, his twin. I'd lost my best and only friend. Our pain was the same. I stopped in the middle of the hallway. Students walked by on their way to sports practices and play rehearsal. The ordinary after-school world in motion.

Reporter, not friend. Don't forget what you are.

Whose thought was this? Murrow's or mine? There was an acrid smell in the hallway. Camel cigarettes? I looked around, but there was no one there.

I'd come to think of the third-floor handicapped stall as my private hideaway. The stall was spacious with a wide ledge above the heater on which I could curl up like a cat. I settled in and called Hazel. I was nervous about talking to her after our awkward parting on Thanksgiving. But we were friends, I reasoned, and friends checked in with each other.

"Are you all right?" she asked when she picked up the phone. Hearing her concern, I felt silly for worrying.

"Actually, I wanted to ask you something." I explained about locating Justin Kaplan in an old yearbook. "And I have this feeling that Mr. Kaplan's trying to hide his brother, or is pretending he never had one."

There was a long silence on Hazel's end. "What makes you think he's pretending that?" she said finally.

"Well, a friend of mine overheard him say he's an only child. Plus he removed all references to Justin from the *Oracle* archives. What happened to Mr. Kaplan's brother, Hazel?"

"Car accident." She paused again, and I could hear her breathing on the other end of the line. "Grief has a way of worming inside of some people, Iris, burrowing into their heart's core. Sometimes when a person's in pain, he'll behave in uncharacteristic ways. Dangerous ways, even." She paused. "But you know all of this already, don't you?"

"Yes." I swallowed. "I guess I do."

"If you need me," she said, "you should call. Any time."

I thanked her and we hung up. Outside, I saw two girls walking arm in arm across the playing field toward the Outpost, the old dorm at the edge of campus where upperclassmen went to smoke. I followed the girls as they made their jaunty trip across the field, and I remembered my parents coming into my bedroom in Beacon Hill last December saying, "We have something to tell you." I knew right away what had happened. And before they said another word, I started asking, *How?* But they wouldn't tell me. They were always trying to protect me. So I screamed, *HOW?* And finally my dad turned his left palm over and tapped his wrist, like he was giving me some stupid baseball sign. *Where is she?* I screamed. *I need to see her!* I jumped up and ran out the front door, even though I wasn't wearing shoes. And I started running down the street toward Dalia's house, though she lived many blocks away. My feet burned with cold, but I kept going until my dad caught me in the middle of our street. He swung me into his arms like I was a baby, and carried me back to our house. I kicked and screamed the way Dalia had the night she'd run into the cold, wearing almost nothing. And I kept screaming for her and crying, and my parents sat in my room all night long because they didn't trust me to be in there alone. Not long after that, they sent me to Dr. Patrick.

Hazel talked about grief like it was a carnivorous parasite, destroying the person you'd been before it infected you. And it was true. Who was I, sneaking around and lying to people? Was I even a good person anymore? And did I even care? The girls down below disappeared into the trees. At that moment, I wanted nothing more in life than to be out there with Dalia, arm in arm, escaping into the woods.

Jonah

W HEN IT COMES to problem solving, I've always preferred
written materials. Unless I'm out in nature or working in a lab,
inanimate sources are more efficient and they eliminate the inherent
awkwardness of face-to-face interaction. But sometimes you just need
a live source, a conclusion I came to after rooting around in my parents' house and coming up with nothing relevant to my Prisom's Party
mission.

The week after Thanksgiving, I headed out to Melville, Vermont,
a small, lifeless town over the state line. I was going to talk with Matt
Sheridan, the student who had supposedly destroyed the Prisom Artifacts. "Melville's worse than the state pen," Matt told me over the
phone. "This boarding school is like the sixth circle of hell. Get me out
of here for a night, and I'll tell you whatever you want."

I drove along winding roads, past forests of brittle trees and shadows sprawled across snow. I should have been preparing for my interview, but I couldn't stop worrying about Iris's drawing test. Her reli-
ance on the scientific method reminded me of a book I'd read, *Seven
Clues to the Origin of Life: A Scientific Detective Story*. The author, a
Scottish chemist, had conflated scientific exploration with detective
work. He'd even opened his book with a reference to Arthur Conan
Doyle. Now, I couldn't help but wonder if my curriculum—investigating the distant past—had somehow encouraged Iris to look into *my*

past. I'd told my students to think for themselves, to strike out for the unknown. And Iris, unfortunately, was doing just that.

The locker vandalism that she'd discovered almost caused a student's death. If I was again associated with the incident, my PhD could not protect me from the ensuing parental wrath. At the same time, I was heartened to see Iris getting along with Peter. Individually they were unstable elements — say, sodium metal and chlorine gas. Bonded together, they'd be predictable as salt.

Matt Sheridan was skinnier than I expected him to be. He had an archetypal prep school face — chiseled cheekbones — but with ears just a little too large for his head. The Melville School had not been good to him. He walked from the dormitory to the parking lot with the defeated hunch of a person who'd once stood up straight.

"Sometimes I wish I'd stayed at Mariana," he said, absently drumming his fingers on the window as we drove through town.

"That bad out here?" But it was clear. The buildings were dark. A factory must have shut down sometime in the last decade and the town shuttered with it. The Melville School no longer had a good reputation.

"Melville's super strict," Matt said. "But I deserve it, right, Mr. Kaplan?"

Was he being sarcastic? This was not the jerk Rick Rayburn had led me to expect. I didn't know how to respond. "Call me Jonah," I said.

"I prefer Mr. Kaplan," Matt said. "If you don't mind." He turned away and stared out the window.

The diner — the only one in town — glowed like a fluorescent fish tank. The booths were sheathed in sea-green vinyl that made a crackling sound whenever we shifted our weight. In the awful light, I could see the hollow depressions of Matt's cheeks. His eyes were red, as though soaked in chlorinated water.

"You look tired," I said. Matt shrugged. The hamburger he ordered arrived on a waxy bun. It resembled a child's mud pie. I dumped a couple thimblefuls of half-and-half into my coffee.

"So you went to Mariana?" he said, chewing. "Did you like it?"

"It was a good education."

Matt flashed a snide smile. "Exactly. A good education, and a shitty everything else."

"Matt, what happened with the *Devil's Advocate*?"

"Not one for smooth transitions, huh? But okay. Which version of the story you want?"

"All of them," I said.

The official account was exactly what Mary Ann had described. A week after the destruction of the Prisom Artifacts, a *Devil's Advocate* published photos of Matt smashing glass and burning the Community Code booklet. The headline ran: MARIANA COMMUNITY COUNCIL PRESIDENT STRIKES SYMBOLIC BLOW AT COMMUNITY CODE. "*Matt Sheridan knows better than anyone that the Community Code means nothing these days,*" he quoted to me now. "*His violent act smashed glass and the veneer of Brotherhood, Truth, and Equality for All.*" Matt snickered. "Their use of zeugma was a little forced, don't you think, Mr. Kaplan?"

Every time he said my name, it sounded like he was mocking me. "Was the *Devil's Advocate* right?" I said. "Was it a symbolic act?"

"Oh, who the fuck knows why I did it?" Matt rubbed his eyes.

"I don't understand."

Without looking up, Matt told me that last fall a girl named Sonya Stevens friended him on a social networking site. According to her page, she was a sophomore at Hanley Prep, one of Mariana's main rivals. She was a cheerleader and the treasurer of Hanley's Honor Society, the equivalent of our Community Council. Matt and Sonya struck up an email exchange. She was funny and smart and extremely attractive. They had an ongoing game in which they'd send each other close-up photographs of various body parts—an earlobe, elbow, half a nipple—and then guess what anatomical feature they'd shot.

"She really understood me," Matt said. "We talked a lot about our schools, our families, the kids we didn't like. I guess that doesn't make me look too good, but it's the truth. Sonya and I felt the same way about a lot of the people we went to school with: how high-strung they were, how jealous. If you're popular, there's a reason. If you're unpopular, there's a reason. So don't get on my case about it, you know? Don't tell me I'm not 'nice' enough to be CC president. I accomplished things and I won us a bunch of soccer titles. I was good at my job."

I listened, trying to maintain control of my facial muscles.

"And I was under a lot of pressure, Mr. Kaplan. To keep up with everything. And Sonya understood, because she was under the same pressure. She understood that I wasn't an immoral person or a mean person or whatever — that I was doing what I needed to do to get by."

I exhaled. "All right," I said. "So then what happened?"

"So we kept sending each other these pictures, and hers became more and more — well, you know . . ." Matt glanced up, then back at his plate. "She'd be touching herself and doing things to herself . . . and she started asking me to do the same. It was stupid of me, I know, but I was totally obsessed with her. She was so beautiful. I mean fucking gorgeous."

He pushed his plate away as though suddenly disgusted and started tearing up. It felt uncomfortable to see this young man, barely eighteen years old, crying in a sea-green diner booth. And I didn't know what to feel toward him — sympathy, pity, contempt.

"Did you and Sonya ever meet?"

"No. We emailed, gchatted, talked on the phone a few times. And sent those pictures. It was gross, I guess, but I couldn't believe a high school girl was into that kind of stuff — that she wanted to see *me* doing it. And there was something awesome about the mystery of the whole thing — because we'd never met, and because no one at school had any idea what was going on." Matt paused. "And then one day she said she wanted me to destroy the Prisom Artifacts. I thought she was joking. But when I tried to laugh it off, she got all serious and said I'd better do it."

"She had all those pictures."

Matt nodded.

"But you had pictures of her too."

"That's right, Mr. Kaplan. I told her if she brought me down, I'd bring her down with me. And then she wrote me saying that she didn't actually go to Hanley. And I checked on it. There was no Sonya Stevens at Hanley, or the local public school, or even in the whole state."

"So you did what she said." I could just imagine what was happening in Matt's brain at this moment, the receptors of memory and shame overloading in his amygdala.

Matt looked at me, pleading. "I never thought I was being set up. I never thought I was that stupid. What kind of person lets a girl do that to him? I mean, what does that say about me, Mr. Kaplan? And when the *Devil's Advocate* came out, I thought to myself: Well, they're right. I do know better than anyone that the Community Code is a lie. I'm the fucking Community Council president and I'm putting up this front, when really I'm just this stupid, disgusting person. So fuck it. Fuck all of it."

Matt banged his fist on the table. The silverware and plates clattered. A couple of loners at the counter turned their wide fish eyes on us, then slunk back to their dinners. "Disgusting," he muttered, and his fingers fell inert into his lap.

I drove Matt back to the Melville School. Before he left the car I asked why he'd decided to tell me his story. He looked at me, and for a split second I saw the kid he'd probably been a long time ago, before he screwed up, before the awful possibility of this — who he was now — was even a glimmer in his mind. "I told you because it doesn't fucking matter anymore," he said. Then he got out.

Matt's story was troubling on so many levels. Prisom's Party had used blackmail to send him a message: *You are gullible and disgusting; you brought all of this on yourself.* And after he did their bidding, they exposed him anyway, using him to send the school a message: *Your moral foundation is a sham.* Bill McCaffrey had asked me what harm Prisom's Party had done, and now I had the answer. These kids weren't concerned with truth so much as punishment. And that was dangerous, especially when the primary actors were children.

Iris

H AZEL HAD GIVEN me a warning. I should be wary of my grief,
or it would possess me like it had possessed Mr. Kaplan. I had to
protect myself. So no more tears wasted on Dalia. No more analyzing
Mr. Kaplan's every look and movement. No more ruminations about
Murrow's Platonic ideal of morality. I would put my overzealous mind
on lockdown and become a woman of action.

Once I made this decision, I felt energized and ready to move forward with my investigation for Prisom's Party. I assessed the random
information I'd gathered. Rooting around Lily's room, I found the
same yearbook I'd discovered in Mr. Kaplan's desk. I learned that she
and the Kaplan twins were in the same class, so the Justin who'd signed
Marvelous Species must have been Mr. Kaplan's brother. His death was
the tragedy my parents mentioned. Of course, the elder Duponts had
kept this event from me — this morbid connection between Lily and
myself.

Mr. Kaplan's strange behavior was likely related to his brother's
death. And his brother was linked to Lily. Which meant that by the
transitive property, Mr. Kaplan was somehow linked to Lily. Perhaps
she knew something about him that could help me. But contacting Lily
directly was impossible. According to my parents, she was living in a
remote Kenyan village with sporadic Internet access, and in any case,
I couldn't simply email her requesting secret information about Mr.

Kaplan's past. I needed to come at Lily slantwise, investigate the periphery of her world, and see what new threads I discovered.

In the yearbooks, I recognized a girl with thick dark hair and heavily lined eyes. Veronica Mercy, according to her portrait: the same girl who was the centerpiece of Lily's *Marvelous Species* appendix. *Well, Veronica,* I thought, *let's see what's become of you.* I found her website—she made documentary films in New York—and saw that she looked much the same except for her hair, which she'd chopped into short pixie spikes. It was nearly 11 p.m., but I was a woman of action.

Veronica picked up after a couple of rings. "Yeah?" Her voice was chalky.

I introduced myself as a freelance journalist working on a magazine story about the children of prep school principals. "I understand that you attended Mariana Academy," I said, "and that you knew the headmaster's daughter, Lily Morgan."

"Lily Morgan?" she said. "How in God's name did you connect me with her?"

I swallowed the prickling in my throat. "She suggested I contact you."

"No shit."

"She did. She said you could provide an alternative perspective on her life at Mariana." I was deep in the bullshit, but feeling confident.

"Who the fuck are you?"

"I told you, I'm—"

"You sound like you're ten, so stop fucking with me or I'm hanging up."

Goddammit! I beat the comforter with my fist. I told her I was a student investigating for the *Oracle*. "Look," I said, "I'm not screwing around, so please don't screw with me."

"You've got balls, kid."

"I'm a reporter. It's my job."

Veronica laughed, which I did not appreciate. But then she said, "Lily was a loner and she followed me around like a goddamn puppy until I finally threw her a bone. A total disaster for both of us, but whatever. She deserved what she got."

"What do you mean?"

Veronica snorted. "A bunch of those Trench freaks said Lily was behind her boyfriend's suicide. Normally I wouldn't trust a word from their mouths, but Lily wasn't exactly a loyal girlfriend. Also she skipped town pretty soon after the guy died. Her parents must have sent her away to fend off suspicion—you know, about her role in her beloved's demise. But if I were you, I'd give up on this little project and get the hell out of Nye before it sucks your soul out through your eyes."

"What do you mean, disloyal? Did she cheat?"

"In a manner of speaking." Veronica cackled. "Hey, if you really do know Lily or ever meet her, ask if she still has a copy of *Sacrificial Lamb* lying around. If you want to know about her sordid past, that's all the insight you'll need." Veronica hung up.

Justin Kaplan killed himself? Outside, the bare branches pointed their skeletal fingers at me. I watched them whip in the night. I had the awful feeling of my insides being drained out, the way a body gets emptied of fluid in preparation for burial. I pulled down the shades so I wouldn't have to look at the branches anymore. Then I curled up in the fetal position on top of Lily's bed.

Hazel called Justin's death an accident, but Veronica claimed much worse. And to think that Lily might have been responsible . . . I looked around at the flowered wallpaper, the incongruous CDs. *Who was she, Murrow?* I sat up and my eyes fell on *Sacrificial Lamb,* the heavy-metal mix, the one Veronica Mercy had mentioned. I slid the disk into my laptop. But *Sacrificial Lamb* wasn't music. It was a movie.

Lily

F OR THE FIRST time in her life, Lily understood why the popular cliques had been so cruel to her: meanness was sustenance. She'd finally lambasted Jonah, and the experience was delicious. She now saw how once you had the taste of meanness in your mouth, you might crave it all of the time. Except Jonah had not even allowed her to enjoy this small bite. *You feel guilty,* he'd said. And he was right. Lily wanted to be with Justin, but she felt like an impostor in his life.

And so, for the next week, Lily spent most lunches and afternoons sitting at the paint-splattered table at the back of the art room, staring out the window. The mother duck was nestled on the ground beside some spindly shrubs. The ducklings were down to three. Was there nothing the mother could do to protect them?

One day, Veronica motioned Lily over to the large canvas she was painting. Its swirling pattern of white strokes made Lily feel seasick. "This piece was inspired by *Moby-Dick,*" Veronica said. "You know, 'The Whiteness of the Whale'?"

Moby-Dick was the one classic novel Lily's father hadn't given her. In fact, when she started high school, he'd eliminated it from the English curriculum.

Amy Chang said, "Ronnie's become obsessed with albinos. She's having a very productive 'white' phase."

"So, Lil," Veronica said, and the room fell quiet. "I'm putting together a submission for summer art apprenticeships. Next weekend I'm hosting a mock eighth-grade sleepover party. The idea is to illuminate the hypocrisy of clichéd teenage social interaction by actively confronting those clichés and thereby subverting them. We're working on four different characters with Krista as our cinematographer. Would you be the fourth body? The part is perfect for you." Veronica turned on her all-consuming smile, and Lily basked in its brilliant light.

Veronica Mercy lived in Bethlehem, in one of the new residential communities popping up throughout the western part of the state. The red brick houses commanded sweeping lawns, and Victorian-style streetlamps punctuated lengths of white sidewalk. At the heart of the community was the Village Square, a tree-lined park that reminded Lily of a college campus but was bordered by various chain stores.

It was well after dark when Maureen dropped her off at Veronica's. The lamp lights flickered behind their glass enclosures, illuminating the line of cars parked outside. Lily looked at the clock — 8:55. Veronica had told her 9:00, but everyone else was already there.

Veronica had already provided details about the evening. Upon arrival Lily would receive an identity, which she would assume for the night. Lily had asked for some hints about her character, but Veronica said advance preparation would ruin the project's authenticity.

"Just remember that we're creating a dialectic," she'd written back. "A semiotic discourse between the subject and the gaze. You'll be fine."

Lily had no idea what this meant, but she didn't care. Veronica had said her "artistic future" depended on this project, and she'd asked Lily to play a central role. Lily stood outside Veronica's front door as though on the threshold of a new life.

A woman in tapered khakis and a green sweater set answered the door. Her smile was the width of the door frame. "You must be Ronnie's new friend, Lily! Come in!"

Lily followed Mrs. Mercy through the house in a state of bewilderment. The place was like a Laura Ashley catalogue on LSD. Every view offered a profusion of objects flowery, fluffy, and pastel. Lily wondered how a woman like Mrs. Mercy could have produced a daughter like Veronica.

Along the back wall of the mint-colored basement was a massive entertainment system with the largest television Lily had ever seen. The screen was mounted on the wall, its black face lording over three adjacent couches like an aloof god. The TV wall and the couches formed a square, in the center of which sat a huge pile of sleeping bags and backpacks. Lily remembered the line of cars parked outside. Perhaps the other girls came early to help Veronica set up. This kind of art project probably required a lot of preparation.

Lily dropped her things and headed back up the stairs. When she reached the top, Mrs. Mercy handed her an envelope. "Ronnie wants you to read this before you go upstairs. If you ask me, she's doing one of her crazy projects . . . but don't reveal I'm on to her. She's very secretive about this kind of thing."

Lily turned the envelope over in her hands. Inside was a note.

Dear Lily,

We're so excited you're working with us! Below, you'll find your identity. You should begin acting as your character as soon as you walk into my room. Krista is our cinematographer, so just ignore her. We're all keeping our own names. Go upstairs to the guestroom, second door on the right. You'll find your costume and props. My room is next door.

Cheers, VM
P.S. Hope the clothes fit.

Name: Lily Morgan
Age: 14
Identity: Lily Morgan is the typical "good girl." She has never had a drink or done drugs. Her parents forbid her to date. She's not allowed to watch R-rated movies. Because Lily is albino, she feels different from the other girls at school, but she's doing her best to fit in. This sleepover is a chance for her to break from her parents' mold. Lily can't wait to express her true identity.

Her outfit lay on the guest bed's periwinkle comforter. She dressed in the black stirrup stretch pants, the black-and-white-polka-dotted skort, the Jewel concert T-shirt, and the polka-dotted headband. She slipped on the white scrunch socks, black flats, and celestial-themed clip-on earrings. Finally she picked up a boxy leather purse with a long strap. Inside Lily found a small pink book labeled *Diary*. The diary had a small brass lock but no key.

The stretch pants were tight and the shoes a size too large. She would never wear any of these things, but this was art. If she wanted to impress Veronica and the others, she'd have to play her character as faithfully as possible.

Veronica jumped up from a beanbag chair when she saw Lily in the doorway. Her lithe body was decked out in tight jeans and a white baby tee. The others didn't look up. Jocelyn was sprawled on the bed in Umbro shorts, a Hypercolor T-shirt, and Vans sneakers, and Amy sat cross-legged in ripped jeans, an oversize flannel shirt, and Doc Martens. "Smells Like Teen Spirit" played on the stereo. Krista crouched in the corner, filming.

"Lil, sit down," Veronica said. "Jocelyn, shove over."

"Look, guys, she's matching!" Jocelyn pointed at Lily's polka dots. She'd dropped her British vernacular for the night.

Lily blushed. But they were snickering at her character, not her. She had to remember to keep herself and her character separate. They were all playing roles. Veronica was stuck up and popular. Jocelyn was a smart-aleck jock. Amy was grunge. And she was the designated wannabe. Not the choicest role, but it made sense. Like Veronica's note said, this was Lily's chance—her character's chance—to become something new.

"So, Lily," Amy said. "Before you got here, we were talking about Juggernaut. Do you like Juggernaut, Lily?"

Lily had no idea what Juggernaut was. It sounded like a band but could easily be a new movie. In junior high, she would have agreed with the majority opinion; she liked the way her voice blended in with the others, as though it counted.

Jocelyn lit a cigarette and inhaled. "Well?"

Lily was certain her character would lie, but something stopped her. "I don't know what Juggernaut is," she said.

The girls exchanged glances. Veronica sucked in her cheeks, inhaling and exhaling a painfully slow breath. For a second no one spoke.

"I'm sorry," Lily stammered. "I know my character wouldn't have—"

"I don't know what you're talking about, Lil." Veronica eyed Lily. "You're crazy. No wonder you only have, like, two friends."

Lily felt the sting of this insult, but then Veronica winked at her—at the real her.

A new song came on the stereo. "R&B? Really, guys?" Amy said. "Now, Nirvana! I'd do Kurt Cobain in a second."

"You'd do a dead guy?" Veronica said.

"I know he killed himself," Amy said, scowling. "But Cobain's still *alive.*"

"Um, no, he's not."

"Yes, he is. He died in 1996, and right now it's *1995.*"

"Krista, cut the tape." Veronica stood up from the beanbag and stared down the group. "This isn't going to work if we can't keep our characters and the *year* straight. Amy, Kurt Cobain died in 1994. I thought you'd researched grunge."

"They knew their characters in advance?" Lily tried to sound casual.

"What?" Veronica looked flustered. "Yes. I mean, no. Just Amy. Since she's supposed to be representing a specific type of person from a specific time. Lily, your role here is more . . ." Veronica snapped her fingers. "What's the word I want?"

"More 'stock'?" Amy said.

"No," Veronica said, annoyed. "More *universal.* I mean, yes, you are unique: you live in western Mass., you go to Mariana Academy, you're albino. But there's always someone like you at these kinds of parties. You're the Other. Basic Lacan. Understand?"

Lily nodded.

"Look, too much explanation cuts into the authenticity of the experience we're fabricating. Forget what year it's supposed to be. Just focus on the sleepover paradigm." Veronica nodded at Krista, who raised the camera to her face.

"This is so fucking meta," Amy mumbled.

The doorbell rang.

"Chinese." Veronica groaned. "Thank God."

Krista hurried out ahead of them so she could get shots of the girls stampeding down the stairs. Once they'd all collected in the kitchen with the food, Veronica produced a shampoo bottle from beneath her sweatshirt and began squirting alcohol into each girl's drink. Lily had no idea what had happened to Veronica's mother.

"I'm not sure I — I mean, no thanks," Lily said when Veronica came around to her. The refusal seemed in line with her character, but she wasn't sure she wanted a drink anyway.

"Look at her," Jocelyn said, climbing onto one of the kitchen stools and crossing her legs. Even in Umbros she looked sophisticated. "She's obviously a prude."

"Well, she can't be a prude with us," Veronica said, and put her arm around Lily's shoulder. "I'll be honest. We invited you over tonight because we know you want to be different. You don't have to do everything your parents say."

The real Lily didn't bow to her parents' every command. She was dating a guy they didn't like. And even if she was playing a character, her presence at this party was somehow part of her new self. Tonight, it seemed she could go back in time — return to the past and catch up on all she'd missed. "I'd love a drink," she said.

"Cheers, ladies!" Veronica raised her cup and downed its contents. Then she poured herself another. With an asthmatic wheeze, the shampoo bottle coughed up its final drops.

After slurping up lo mein and gnawing greasy spareribs, everyone headed down to the basement. Within seconds, Veronica, Amy, and Jocelyn had claimed the three couches and were dumping out their overnight bags. Soon the floor was covered with everything they'd brought to re-create and mock the authentic sleepover experience: oversize nightshirts, padded bras, aerosol deodorants, eye shadows, hair sprays, teen novels, boy-band calendars, glitter stickers, flavored lip-glosses, scrunchies, gummy bracelets, teen magazines, M&M's, Doritos, Oreos, Pixy Stix, and a Ouija board.

Lily watched the scene and realized she had no place to sleep. She wasn't the only one having this thought, because there was Krista training the camera on her ambivalent face. *Ignore the camera,* she thought, and looked away.

"Do you guys think you could . . ." She pointed at the pile.

Veronica hopped off the center couch and pushed crap aside until it formed a ring. Then she laid Lily's sleeping bag in the center of the ring and returned to the couch. Suddenly Lily saw the scene as through the camera lens: there she was, standing on her sleeping bag, in the center of a bull's eye. The girls were silent, almost like they'd rehearsed the shot. But that was completely at odds with Veronica's plan. This evening was supposed to be organic. Lily pushed down the queasiness in her stomach. For the first time in her life, she was at the center of the circle.

The girls made a list of "hot" kids, and ranked them by physical attributes, intellect, and character traits. They did the same with their "not" classmates. Under Dipthi they wrote: *Beware the unibrowed Indian. Will bite.* Under Justin, they wrote: *Future occupation: serial killer, child molester, and/or commits suicide by age 30.* Lily didn't protest; trash-talking was Sleepover Etiquette 101.

Veronica pulled a couple of shampoo bottles and a carton of OJ from her bag. "Ready for the vodka course?" She constructed a wall of pillows and carried the containers behind it. "In case my mom comes down," she explained, and brought out cups for Amy and Jocelyn. Then she came back with one for Lily and another for herself.

"Cheers!" They tapped the red plastic cups together. Lily took a sip. Her eyes bugged. This was her first screwdriver. Her first experience with vodka, period. They gossiped and gobbled junk food and finished another round of drinks. Just after 1 a.m., Veronica looked around the room. "Ready to go?" Immediately the girls started searching for their jackets. Lily stood there dumbly, watching. "Well, come on, Lily!" Veronica said brightly. "It's field-trip time."

Outside Lily shivered in Veronica's miniskirt. The girls walked single file around the side of the house and across the street to Jocelyn's Jeep. Amy slid into the back. "You next, Lily," Veronica said. Krista stood beside her, the camera pointed at her face. Lily looked inside the car, hesitating. How much had Jocelyn had to drink? "Come on!" Veronica nudged her. "We don't have all night." Lily got in.

Bethlehem was separated from Nye by a small, steep range of forested hills. The long route between them (parentally dubbed the "safe" route) was a county highway that curled around the base of the hills, passed through an ugly smattering of strip malls, and, after a steep climb, deposited drivers in Nye's center. The short route (parentally dubbed the "dangerous" route) was the preference of most young drivers because it plunged directly into the hills, taking drivers on a joy ride of slopes. This was the route Jocelyn chose.

Cold air rushed through the car as Jocelyn careened around bends in the road, and Lily braced her feet on the floor. At one point Veronica reached for Lily's hand. Her eyes flashed in the dark. Her long hair whipped Lily's face.

They climbed into the hills, dipped suddenly, and climbed again. There were no other cars on the road, no streetlights here, only forest rushing by and Jocelyn's brights sweeping wildly across the trees. The girls laughed and sang to a rock album, wailing with abandon. They didn't seem to mind the cold. Amy puffed on a cigarette, and Lily's head reeled with the alcohol and the speed and smoke. Finally they sped downward, the road dumping them out on the other side of the range. Jocelyn cut a sharp corner and then they were in town, rushing past Nye's dark, ponderous buildings. Windows morphed into more trees as they headed toward Lily's house and the main road to school.

Then, suddenly, Jocelyn veered onto a side road, the trees so close and thick that Lily could not see the sky. Branches gave way to branches, and behind them more branches. Abruptly, Jocelyn cut the wheel and the Jeep bounced onto unpaved ground. After ten minutes or so, Jocelyn braked and killed the engine. The music was swallowed up. The girls hopped out of the car. Lily followed and stood beside the Jeep, listening to its insides settle. The woods were silent. There was no wind. Amy struck a match and the sound hissed in Lily's ears.

"Where are we?" Lily wiggled her toes in the too-big shoes.

Jocelyn linked her arm with Lily's. Amy came over and linked up on the other side. The two girls pressed against her, and she was thankful for their body heat. She noticed that Krista was no longer filming, and she felt relieved; she would have looked like an escorted prisoner.

"I hate this walk," Jocelyn said.

"You wouldn't last five minutes in the real wilderness," Amy said.

"Wilderness is a fabrication," Veronica retorted as though they weren't, at that very moment, walking through black, brambled woods. The ground was flat but uneven and Lily kept stumbling in the oversize shoes. Veronica led with a flashlight, though now and then she'd stop, the path having suddenly disappeared. Lily imagined the forest floor as a long tongue, licking up their trail. She thought of bread crumbs and candy houses. Witches and ovens.

Then, all of a sudden, the woods turned to stone. Veronica scanned her light along the face of a wall and up toward the sky, illuminating darkened windows. She led the group a few feet along the wall, until her light reflected in a series of windows. Then her light swept down, as though into the earth, and Lily saw stairs descending toward a door.

Jocelyn and Amy withdrew their arms from Lily's, the warmth evaporating as their bodies moved away. They walked down the stairs and waited for Veronica to get out the key. The air smelled of dead, wet leaves.

"*Entrez!*" Veronica said, holding the door open, and one by one they walked into darkness. Veronica swung her light around—she seemed to be treating it like a light saber — and its bright circle revealed an empty concrete room. It was much colder than outside, and the place smelled like a garage. *Where the hell are we?* Lily thought over and over, but she dared not ask.

She followed the girls across the room to another door; they stepped through it into more darkness. They were now standing in a tunnel. The floors and walls were concrete, but rusty pipes snaked along the low ceiling. Veronica was first in line, followed by Amy and then Jocelyn. Lily came next, and Krista walked behind her.

"How are you doing?" Krista whispered, with such kindness that Lily felt an outpouring of warmth for her.

"Scared," Lily said.

"Great, can you say that a little louder for the video mic?"

Lily swallowed and didn't answer. Suddenly everyone stopped.

"Okay, Lily," Veronica said. "We're almost there, but because you're not fully initiated yet, we're going to have to blindfold you."

For a second, Lily panicked. What if they left her here, alone in the dark? But Amy was already tying a bandana over her eyes and yanking the knot extra hard. They guided her another few feet, walked through another door, and then stopped again. They seemed to be in a confined space now. The girls were pressed close. Lily breathed in their sweet perfume and shampoo. This reminder of the outside world — the regular world in which these types of strange adventures did not happen — reassured her.

Lily heard the sound of scraping wood, and the group shuffled forward a few feet. Immediately she felt the change. They were in another open space, cold though not freezing, with a familiar burnt smell. Amy walked Lily in one direction, then back the way they'd come, then turned her around a few times. When she was sufficiently disoriented, Amy walked her forward and removed the blindfold. They were standing in a Trench classroom.

Jocelyn flicked on the lights, bathing them all in a harsh hospital glare. Krista resumed filming. Veronica pulled a dozen airplane bottles of hard alcohol from her purse. She handed one to each girl and put the rest on a desk. Everybody removed the caps and drank. Lily took a small sip.

"How'd you find that tunnel?" she asked.

"Wandering drunk one night over summer break when Alexi and I were—" Veronica frowned. "You need to drink more than that!" she ordered. Lily tilted her head back and the liquid burned in her throat. "Good girl," Veronica cooed, patting Lily on the back.

The girls sat down on stiff army blankets that Amy had brought in from somewhere, and they huddled together for warmth. In the fluorescent light the girls' skin was sickly pale, their makeup clownish. They looked like children in a pageant, at once too young and too old. Lily reeled from the alcohol and piercing light, but she shut her eyes and the nausea passed.

"Ready to play?" Veronica said. Amy pulled the Ouija board from her backpack. "So who are we calling first?"

"The boy who hanged himself," Jocelyn said.

"Shouldn't we turn the lights off?" Lily asked, trying to be a good sport. The girls looked at her, and she realized they couldn't because of the camera. They all put their hands over the arrow.

"We wish to commune with the boy who hanged himself," Veronica whispered. "We wish to know your name."

At first the arrow didn't move. Then it began to slide. At first Lily was certain they were moving it. Then she wasn't sure. The arrow skimmed across the board and lingered on a letter: *J.* The arrow moved again, landing on *U.* Lily watched the girls' wrists and forearms for tautness, but their hands were relaxed—the arrow pointed to *S*—like they were simply letting this happen. The arrow landed on *T.* Lily's heart beat faster. Electricity buzzed around the circle, fusing their bodies into one breathing collective. *I . . . N.*

"Holy shit," Veronica whispered.

Justin? Lily thought. *This must be a joke.*

"Last name," Veronica said.

K was followed by *A,* then *P.* Only then the arrow stopped. The girls waited. "Is that it?" Amy whispered. Nobody replied. The arrow did not move. And then it did. The last three letters. When the arrow got to the *N,* Lily stared at it, not realizing the girls were staring at her.

"Did you do this?" Veronica demanded.

"What?"

"Mess up the game?"

"No."

"You're lying."

"No, I'm—"

"She's lying," Amy said.

"She's lying," Jocelyn said.

"You manipulated the arrow," Veronica said. "It's obvious."

"The rumors are true." Jocelyn's baby-doll eyes grew wide.

Lily had the feeling of string unspooling. There was nothing she could do to stop it.

"I knew Justin was boning you," Veronica said.

"What? I'd never do that," Lily said. "I don't like to break the rules. Remember?"

Jocelyn tucked her legs up to her chest. "Maybe the good girl isn't so good after all."

"Tell us the truth, Lily," Veronica said, and handed around more airplane bottles.

"I swear."

Veronica ignored her. "I think she keeps a diary. Check in her purse."

"Already got it!" Jocelyn held up Lily's purse like a trophy. Veronica grabbed it and pulled a small hammer from her own bag. She put the diary on the desk and smashed the hammer against the lock. Her face was set with total focus and the others looked on, riveted. *It's not my diary,* Lily told herself. And yet she felt the impact of metal against metal, like she was the thing Veronica was trying to crack open.

The lock burst. Veronica tossed the diary to Jocelyn.

"'Dear Diary,'" Jocelyn read in a singsong voice.

"It actually says 'Dear Diary'?" Amy snickered.

Veronica brought Lily another drink. *Here,* she seemed to say, *have some refreshment at your own execution.*

"'The people at Mariana suck,'" Jocelyn read. "'The artsy girls are fake and obnoxious, especially Veronica Mercy. And the boys are disgusting. There's this one boy, Justin, who's the biggest loser in the whole school. But the weirdest part is that I think about him at night. I touch myself and imagine him eating my pussy.'"

Jocelyn lowered the diary. The three girls stared at Lily. *Stay in character,* she thought, frantic. Krista crouched down nearby, the camera angled on Lily's face.

"You perverted bitch," Veronica snarled.

Tears welled in Lily's eyes. *It's not me. It's my character. It's not me.* She forced the tears back, took a deep breath.

"She's using Justin Kaplan for sex!" Jocelyn burst out with a wild look.

"Lily," Veronica said with icy calm, "are you using Kaplan for sex?"

Lily shook her head.

"Don't lie to us. Are you using Justin Kaplan for sex?"

Lily looked from face to face. Three pairs of eyes and the camera's blank lens.

"Are you?" Amy demanded.

Lily shut her eyes. She knew what she was supposed to say. But she couldn't speak. She just couldn't say it. The three girls pressed toward her. Lily opened her eyes to find their faces just inches away. In the garish classroom light, the Studio Girls looked etiolated, white as Lily herself.

"Are you?"

"Are you?"

"Are you?" they shouted at once.

Lily swallowed hard. "Yes."

"We were nice to you," Veronica said, "and you not only shit all over us, but you took advantage of this poor lonely kid."

"It's sick," Jocelyn said.

"Please," Lily heard herself pleading, though the person talking sounded far away. Her cheeks were damp with tears. But were the tears hers or her character's?

Veronica shook her head. "We should send you home."

Was Veronica going to make her walk home in the dark, in the middle of the night? Was Veronica that cruel? Or that committed to her project?

"But that would be idiotic," Veronica continued. "I think you need to leave us alone for a while. Then you can come back later and apologize. Make it up to us."

"But how?"

Veronica sighed. "I don't know, Lily. You really hurt our feelings."

"Where do you want me to go?"

The girls looked at each other. "Outside," Veronica said. "Fresh air might give you some clarity on this . . . situation."

Lily didn't move.

"Come on!" Veronica stood up and walked to the door.

"Can I take the flashlight?"

Veronica sighed like a parent who's been asked one too many questions. Lily picked up the flashlight. Veronica and Krista walked with her down the long Trench corridor, up the stairs, and into the stairwell. They didn't speak until they'd gone out the back door of the school, propping it open with a textbook.

"You can wait by the picnic tables next to the soccer field," Veronica said. Lily hesitated. If only Veronica would wink again and remind her this was just a game. "We'll get you when we're ready." Veronica and Krista disappeared into the school.

Lily sat on the picnic table where Justin had first asked her out. Beyond the fields and woods loomed the hulking Hoosac Mountains. Somewhere out there was the end of the world—a place where sky and earth fused, where you could stand on solid ground and dive into space. Lily imagined floating through the expanse, watching the stars, soaking up the infinite black. She'd always wanted to be with others, in the center of a group. But without other people there'd be nothing to want.

It was her character, not the real Lily, who craved this acceptance, she told herself. Then again, even though the diary didn't belong to her and she hadn't written those lines, she felt an uncomfortable ownership over them. She was wearing a costume, but she felt exactly like herself.

Lily looked toward the sky, at the scattered stars and fulsome moon. She pulled off Veronica's earrings and threw them into the grass. Her character wasn't the stars or the moon. Her character was a little satellite orbiting a large planet. A girl who went around and around, trapped in somebody else's gravitational pull. The real Lily wasn't alone, because the real Lily had an ally. Justin. But she didn't feel connected to him now.

"I'm a freak!" she yelled into the night. "A fucking freak!"

"Who are you talking to?"

Lily jumped off the picnic table and whirled around to see Alexi Oppenheimer standing a few yards behind her. His face emerged from the darkness, his sharp cheekbones coming into relief. He wore his soccer jacket, with the neck unzipped and the sleeves pushed up. The strength of Alexi's body was contained within those firm, sculpted forearms, and he knew it.

"Are you okay?" Alexi reached out as though she needed steadying.

"What are you doing here? Are you part of this too?" She looked wildly around for Krista hiding with the camera.

"What are you talking about?"

Lily shook her head. A rush of tears came.

"Did the girls do something to you?"

She didn't answer.

"Let's see. Did they put your hand in hot water while you were sleeping? Or cover you in whipped cream? This is a sleepover party. What did you expect?"

She stared him down. "You're part of this!"

"What? Listen, can we just talk a little?" He crept toward her like she was a wild animal. He reached out his hand.

"Get away from me." But she didn't move. With surprising steadiness, Alexi brushed away the tears on her face. Her body broke out in goose bumps. Then, suddenly, she wanted to hurt him. She wanted to punch his self-assured, smiling face. "Fuck you, Alexi."

He shook his head. "Hold on a sec, okay?" He fumbled with a small object and then tossed it to her. It was a digital tape recorder. "Krista couldn't come out here and still have this be 'organic.' You know Ronnie."

Lily nodded. Her knees buckled. Was she drunk? When had that happened?

"Jeez, Morgan. Sit down before you fall over."

Lily loved the way he called her by her last name. She walked toward him and lowered herself to the ground.

"How's the weather over there?"

She scooted a few feet closer. And suddenly the immensity of the moment hit her. She was alone in a dark field with Alexi Oppenheimer.

"Alexi, what's happening?" Her head throbbed. She put her head in her hands.

"It's part of the project," he said. "Ronnie wanted to diversify the content, or something like that. Audio without video. A twist in the plot, i.e., me. I'm supposed to seduce you, get you more drunk. And then I'm supposed to offer you this." He held up a flask. "There's a sleeping pill dissolved in it. After you pass out, I'm supposed to carry you back in. Ronnie has this whole plan for editing the video—with you getting more and more intoxicated over the course of the night, and a final shot of you passed out on the floor of the school. She's calling the whole thing *Sacrificial Lamb*. Or something."

Lily looked up, feeling the sky rush away from her. "So what now?"

Alexi looked at her intently, and she flushed again under the weight of his gaze. He pulled out an airplane bottle, drank half, and handed the bottle to her. She hesitated. "Just alcohol," he said, and she finished it off. "You can lie in my lap if you want." She didn't move.

"Come on, Morgan. I've confessed everything. There aren't any more tricks."

"But what about Veronica's project?"

"I'll tell her I erased it by accident." He reached out and stroked Lily's hair. At his touch, she felt her entire body swallow. He mistook her reaction for a shiver and moved closer to her. "I'll warm you up."

"I have a boyfriend."

"I know. That Kaplan kid." He stroked her hair again. She closed her eyes. Hot tears fell down her cheeks. Everything was confused. She bit her lip, but the tears wouldn't stop.

Maybe she was like her character. If she really loved Justin, she wouldn't want to be here with Alexi. But she did love Justin, or felt something real for him. If she was more like Veronica, she wouldn't worry about these conflicting emotions. She'd embrace her feelings, no matter how messy they were. She'd revel in her confusion.

"I want a drink," Lily said, and Alexi handed her another airplane bottle. "No," she said. "I want the one with the pill in it."

"Okay. If you really want to," Alexi said. He didn't sound convinced.

Lily switched the recorder back on. He looked at her and she nodded. He hesitated but she nodded again.

"Here, Lily," he said. "Have a drink."

She took the flask and drank deep.

"Why don't you lay your head on my stomach," he said.

"I don't know if I should."

"You've got to relax, Lily. Have another drink."

Lily drank again. Then again.

"Now put your head here," Alexi instructed. She could feel his stomach muscles beneath the soccer jacket. He rested his hand on her abdomen. She imagined his fingers running across her belly button, slipping into her skirt. She shivered, then flushed hot.

"How about one more drink?"

"All right."

The next thing she knew, the flask was floating out of her hands, drifting away as though weightless. There was a soft pressure against her head. A comforting motion, moving down, down her scalp.

"Doesn't it feel good to break the rules, Lily? Doesn't it feel good to be yourself?"

"Mmmm." She was vaguely conscious of Alexi holding the tape recorder closer to her mouth. "Mmmm," she mumbled again.

"Look at those shooting stars. Aren't they beautiful?"

Lily opened her eyes to the sky. Her eyesight was too poor to see anything as particular as a shooting star, and yet she felt them moving above her: bursts of light that shot across the sky and burned up in the black.

"How about another little sip?" Alexi whispered.

Lily's head rose and fell on the waves of Alexi's breathing. Something flashed by her. A star or the glint of a flask?

Her skull felt like lead. Up . . . and . . . down. Her head approached the sky, lingered at the edge of space, and began its slow descent to earth. Then she was moving, soaring through the night, the wind rushing over her face.

Jonah

DECEMBER 2012

P ASTERNAK TOLD ME that under no condition was I to further
investigate Matt Sheridan's case. "I'd be deposed in a second," he
said, "if people discovered I'd misconstrued the facts. Let's just find
Prisom's Party and stop this unpleasantness from happening in the
future."

Pasternak was a coward. It was wrong to let Matt wallow at Melville.
In addition to which, I knew that finding Prisom's Party wasn't an end.
If treated like one, this "unpleasantness," as Pasternak called it, would
only repeat itself, like the seasons and the carbon cycle and most other
natural processes of decay and rebirth.

It was December 7, my twenty-ninth birthday. I was never much for
birthdays, and I hadn't told anyone, including Hazel. I almost wished
I'd forgotten the date myself. Twenty-nine seemed momentous, the
last year before I entered full-fledged adulthood. I'd gone a good distance in the journey toward financial independence and professional
success, employing the various tools and weapons I'd collected along
the way. But then I made a faulty step, ran smack into some evil-eyed
mushroom, and was forced to start over. The irony, of course, was that
even though the game had reset (literally sent me back to home base), I
already had the princess within my sights.

I drove to the Historical Society after school. Part of me wanted
nothing more than to spend my life with Hazel, creating a replica of

Rick and Mary Ann Rayburn's home, a perfectly calibrated fusion of bright lights and finger paints. This image grabbed me so hard that I had to take a moment in the car before going inside. I'd taken the hint from her once already: too much emotion would push her away.

As it turned out, Hazel had baked me a cake. She was not the Martha Stewart type, which was clear from the product, a Betty Crocker confection that emerged from the oven desiccated, despite its being engineered to turn out moist no matter what you did to it. The cake had chocolate frosting and said, *Happy Birthday, Jonah,* in blue letters.

"I can't believe you remembered," I said.

Hazel looked like I'd said something ridiculous. "You deserve to celebrate your life, Jonah. You're almost a man."

"I thought I was a man at thirteen."

Hazel smirked. "I forgot how we Jews insist on torturing our young."

She didn't sing to me (she was tone-deaf), but she listened attentively as I told her about my meeting with Matt Sheridan and how, more than ever, I felt compelled to drag Prisom's Party into the open. "They've crossed a frightening line with the Sonya Stevens business," I said. "I'm worried about what's coming."

Hazel shook her head. "You're going to believe what some screwed-up kid told you?"

"Yes."

Hazel poked at the brown and yellow lump on her plate. She pulled a pack of cigarettes from her pocket and offered it to me, knowing I didn't smoke.

"We're talking criminal activity, Hazel."

"Your crusade to save the souls of these students," Hazel said, blowing smoke over her shoulder, "is a lot of bullshit." She rose and walked over to the sink.

"Not to me," I said, hurt. "And at least I have a crusade. I'm teaching these kids how to *think,* which is more than whatever it is you're doing, holed up in here. You had ambitions of your own, remember?"

Hazel stared out the window. I couldn't see her face, but I noticed the cigarette shaking between her fingers. Suddenly I realized it wasn't my birthday she'd remembered. It was my brother's. "You could have put his name on the cake, too," I said. "You don't have to pretend like he's not here."

Hazel slammed her fist on the counter and walked out of the room.

Only once had Hazel and I talked about her feelings for Justin. It was a Sunday night in March of my sophomore year, a few months before the accident. Lily had been at our house for dinner that night—the first time she'd ever sat down to eat with my parents—and I'd run into her alone in our upstairs hallway. I remember her eyes glowing and the veins running along her pale forehead, like purple weeds trapped beneath ice. She seemed to be constructed from glass.

Lily had always been shy and accommodating (an obsequiousness I detested), but when I accused her of manipulating my brother, she lashed back with unexpected vitriol. Furious, I called Hazel to commiserate, and within half an hour we were speeding away in her car.

"I'm fucking sick of this," she said.

In the dark, I struggled to suppress a smile, certain that Hazel was furious at Lily on my behalf. But something was wrong. Hazel was driving too fast. She swung us recklessly around the curves in the road, jerking the steering wheel in her hands. I asked where we were going, but she ignored me.

"Could you slow down a little?" I said, gripping the seat as she accelerated. She scowled but eased up on the gas. "Listen," I said, thinking she'd calmed down some, "we just need to take a different approach to this whole Lily situation—whoa!" We'd crested a hill, and the dip felt like momentary free fall. We were in the hills, heading toward Bethlehem. A bunch of kids from school lived in Bethlehem, but we weren't friends with any of them.

"Maybe if we could find another girl," I continued. "You know, someone who could show Justin that Lily's not so great."

Hazel said nothing, which I took as a sign that she was listening.

"Like Marina Malby, on the debate team. She's pretty cute. Or what about that girl who goes to Blessed Sacrament—you know, the one we met at the math bowl. Anna?"

Suddenly the car jerked right and swung wildly onto the shoulder, spraying gravel. I was wearing my seat belt, but the sudden movement threw me against the door. I banged my shoulder on the window.

"What happened?" I said, holding my throbbing arm. "Was it an animal? Are you okay?" Still Hazel said nothing. She gripped the wheel, stared straight ahead. I realized she'd veered off the road on purpose. "Are you trying to kill us?"

She turned to face me. Her eyes flashed like an animal stalking in the dark. "Shut up, Jonah!"

The rebuke startled me so much that I sank back into my seat. "I'm just sitting here talking," I mumbled to myself, knowing full well that she could hear me, "and all of a sudden we're flying off the road. And she's telling me to shut my mouth?"

"It fucking has to stop!" Hazel slapped the steering wheel. Her voice cracked, and she started to cry. Then I really did shut up. Hazel was not a crier. We sat for a moment in silence. An SUV pulling a trailer sped by, and our car, parked dangerously close to the road, shuddered.

"What did I do?"

Hazel slapped the wheel again, then clenched her fist and pressed it against her stomach.

"You're so naïve, Jonah." She chuckled through her tears. "You're like this little kid, just trying to keep up."

A burning sensation rose up my neck and into my face. My whole life she'd called me Mr. Tumnus, but it had never occurred to me that she equated my underdeveloped body with an underdeveloped mind.

"Fuck you, Hazel," I said under my breath, tears burning my eyes.

Hazel sniffed. "Another girl? A distraction? Brilliant ideas, Jonah. Congratulations on being the single most brilliant person I've ever met in my entire fucking life."

She was staring at me now, her face blazing mad.

"Did it ever occur to you that there already *is* another girl? She's right in front of him, and he doesn't see her. All he sees—all he wants—is some ghost. Why is that?" She leaned in close, and her breath was hot on my face. "Can you tell me why, Jonah? Can that brilliant mind of yours figure it out?"

I looked at my lap. I turned my hands over and studied them. I imagined my hands caressing Hazel's wide cheeks and full breasts. I imagined my fingers, so small and unsure of themselves. Hazel was right. Compared to her, I was just a kid. My brother, however, had the hands of a grown man, even if he didn't know what to do with them any more than I did.

We pulled back onto the road and continued our drive in silence. Soon we emerged from the hills and entered Bethlehem. After a few minutes, a development of large obtrusive houses rose before us. Hazel stopped outside a brightly lit monstrosity looming over a wide lawn. She turned the car off but didn't move. Timidly, I asked where we were.

"Veronica Mercy lives here." She closed her eyes for a minute. She seemed far away.

I stared out the window at Veronica Mercy's house. The Mercys probably threw extravagant Christmas parties. I bet they'd bought Veronica a new car for her birthday. Still, I thought, whatever class differences existed between us were immaterial; I could own a hundred cars, but that wouldn't change my biology. My little-kid hands.

"I'm going to deal with this Lily situation right now," Hazel said. "Trust me."

"What are you going to do?"

"I have it on good faith that Veronica is applying to art apprenticeships this summer, and I have decided to become her muse."

"Why?"

"Because my mother's colony has a new apprenticeship program, only it's very competitive."

"Lorna accepts teenagers?"

Hazel shrugged. "Unexpected things happen all the time, Jonah."

"And this has to do with Lily because . . ."

"If the gods don't direct the hands of men, they have no business being gods." Hazel slammed the car door and left me alone in the dark. Whatever scheme she'd concocted, I couldn't even begin to guess.

I found Hazel in the Historical Society's darkened antechamber, staring out at the snowy landscape. Winter's drab and lonely monochrome stretched for miles, unbroken. I walked toward her and rested my hands on her shoulders. "I'm sorry," I whispered. "This isn't an easy day."

"I'm not like you, Jonah," she said, her voice even less forgiving than the scene outside. "I couldn't just start my life over like it didn't happen."

"That's what you think I did?"

Hazel sucked in a breath, but she didn't answer. I couldn't stand this. I needed to make things right. "Let's not judge each other," I said. "Let's just be happy that we're together." I nuzzled her neck. She turned and I cupped my palms on either side of her head. She was capable of fierce beauty and even fiercer life. She burned hot at her core. If only she'd let me help her, I could restore her to her natural state.

"You should go," she said, and led me to the door. I was reluctant to leave at such a tenuous moment, but at least Hazel seemed placated, no longer angry with me. "Happy birthday, Jonah," she said. "I'm happy you're here." Then she kissed me a final time.

I'd never be my brother, but I was the closest Hazel would ever get to him. Without me, I wasn't sure she had anything else.

Iris

DECEMBER 2012

I WAS MAKING MYSELF a salad in the refectory when Peter sidled up to me carrying a tray with seven glasses of juice. He didn't play any sports, but he drank like a jock. He said nothing, just shadowed me as I piled tomatoes and cucumbers and feta cheese onto my plate. Then he followed me to the other side of the bar, where I added dressing. "Do you want something?" I snapped.

"How's your investigation going?"

"You mean in the last fifteen hours? Half of which I spent sleeping?"

I wasn't pissed at Peter, but the video I'd watched the night before had given me awful dreams and kept me tossing for half the night. Lily was no longer a figment. She was an actual person whose skin was pale as a fish belly-up on the beach. But even though I saw her more clearly, I didn't know her any better. Which side was she on? Was she acting or was she the victim of a cruel prank? And regardless, how could she have declared such vicious things about Justin Kaplan, even in jest? *Sacrificial Lamb* was like absurdist theater, and it had the mark of Prisom's Party all over it. I tried to follow up with Veronica Mercy, but she'd turned off her phone.

"A lot can happen in a night, Iris." Peter's voice shook me back to the present.

"Is that some kind of innuendo?"

"No."

Iris Dupont, you are an idiot, I thought as I headed to my table. It was the one day each month that students were allowed to sit wherever they wanted, and I'd been looking forward to forty-five minutes of uninterrupted reading. But Peter followed me and sat down.

"You're actually on page 623 of this thing?" He pointed to the Mike Wallace bookmark tucked inside *Marvelous Species.*

I grabbed the book from him. "I'm supplementing my biology homework."

"Mr. Kaplan's class." He nodded. "I see."

"You see what?"

"You were going through his desk yesterday. You're after something."

I was trying to get inside Mr. Kaplan's mind, but I couldn't tell Peter that. "There are some people here who are suspicious of Mr. Kaplan," I said. "But they just don't understand him."

"And you do?"

I told Peter Hazel's theory about kindred spirits, omitting the details about Dalia and Justin's possible suicide. As he listened, his face changed; his eyes widened like something was welling up inside of him and was about to burst out. "What's going on?" I said. "Are you okay?"

Peter nodded. He looked upset but asked me to continue. Finally I told him about Mr. Kaplan's reaction to the four-eyed demon.

"That kind of behavior is bizarre, Iris. Especially for a teacher."

Which is precisely why you must keep your friends and your sources separate, Murrow added, his voice floating down from the refectory's cathedral-like windows. *Your emotions will cloud your judgment. You cannot allow that to happen.*

I know! I thought back. *I'm a woman of action, remember?* I was frustrated with Murrow. It was worrisome how frequently he'd been popping up, whether I wanted him there or not. Was this the anxiety and depression that Dr. Patrick had warned about?

"I'm sure Mr. Kaplan is a good person," Peter continued. "But you don't know what mental and emotional problems he's suffering from. I mean crying, throwing things . . ."

"You think he's dangerous?"

"Definitely unstable. What do you know about him, really?"

I looked down at my salad. The connection between me and Mr. Kaplan was as ephemeral as Murrow's cigarette smoke.

"Do you think . . ." Peter began, then paused and ducked his head. "I mean—I was thinking, I could help you."

I looked at him, puzzled.

"I don't think you should be on this investigation alone. Not because you can't take care of yourself," he added quickly. "It just seems . . ."

I waited.

"Well, it seems like you could use a friend."

I nodded, and Peter looked as though he'd just run a marathon—relieved and a little bit sick to his stomach.

I wrote to the Party about the contents of Mr. Kaplan's desk. *We are planning to bring you back soon,* they responded. *Keep the intel coming.*

After school I interviewed more Academic League students, slipping in questions about Mr. Kaplan. I learned his favorite food (tuna), his favorite element of the periodic table (lithium), and his favorite extremophile (radiation-resistant, salt-loving halophiles), but no helpful clues about his past. After practice, Peter asked if I wanted to go get some coffee.

"Like a date?" I said.

His face colored. "Maybe."

"Can we go to the public library instead?"

"Jesus, Iris. You're a workaholic."

I love old libraries. Scrolling through microfilm is like hunting through history, and the clickety-click of the spool is the sound of progress. Also, if I was simply searching the Internet at home, my voicemail recording wouldn't have to say, *You've reached Iris Dupont, reporter for the Mariana Academy* Oracle. *I am out searching for the truth.*

Peter and I found a few stories about Mr. Kaplan's dead brother. He was killed in a car crash at approximately 4 a.m. on May 2, 2000, in a "head-on collision due to severe weather conditions." We found nothing about the location of the accident or what the car had hit.

"I suspect foul play," Peter joked.

Or suicide, I thought, remembering my conversation with Veronica Mercy. My gut began doing a salad-spinner maneuver. If Justin had seen *Sacrificial Lamb* or found out about it, might that have caused him to end his life?

While Peter made a phone call, I looked up information for my Charles Prisom story. In my excitement I'd nearly forgotten that this assignment was supposed to be my cover for the Prisom's Party investigation, and my deadline was approaching. Hazel had still not located Charles Prisom's letters, and a microfilm search yielded nothing new. Then I ran a search for Dantes and Rex. Nothing came up. Until I found this:

PRESTIGIOUS SCHOOL REOPENS AS DAY ACADEMY
by Charles Collingwood

July 13, 1940

NYE — Seventeen years ago, Mariana Academy, a boarding school for boys, closed its doors amid financial scandal. When it reopens this September, it will do so as a co-ed day school — but its new school board promises to continue the focus on academic achievement that once made Mariana one of New England's most prestigious preparatory institutions.

"Our student body has changed, but the values at the heart of Mariana remain," said Edward Dumas, chairman of the school board, during yesterday's announcement of the school's reopening. "We expect the best of our students, both in mind and morals. That's what Mariana founder Charles Prisom stood for, and it's what we're committed to."

Mariana closed at the conclusion of the 1922–23 school year, after its board discovered that then-board president Thaddius Reginald had covered up the school's sinking finances — $1.2 million of debt. Reginald had already shut down most student clubs and athletics in a desperate attempt to save money, and students and faculty grew suspicious. The school board voted to depose its president, and Mariana's headmaster resigned. Lacking leadership and finances, the board closed the school indefinitely.

I read the article three times. Each time, the salad-spinner feeling swelled. Edward Dumas and Thaddius Reginald. A budget deficit? The *Oracle* shut down for financial reasons, not to suppress free speech? Was this a joke? The oppressive headmaster, the *Devil's Advocate,* the tussle culminating in Rex's gruesome death—all of it invention. The microfilm article included a picture of Thaddius Reginald, and sure enough, it matched the picture of Thelonius Rex I'd seen in the Party's book. Prisom's Party had promised never to leave me, but these lies felt worse than abandonment.

"Are you having fun on our date?" Peter said, returning. "We could hit the Northern Massachusetts Grammarians' Hall of Fame or the Nye County Historical Society. I hear they have an excellent display of pewter spoons."

In fact, I was eager to visit Hazel. I needed her help.

"You don't really want to go there?" Peter said in response to my silence.

I shook my head, because the truth was, the thought of taking Peter to see Hazel made me uncomfortable. I didn't want to share Hazel with anyone else, and, I was starting to realize, I didn't want to share Peter either. "I'm going to take a walk," I said.

"Oh." He sounded disappointed, like I might be heading to a tryst at the local postage-stamp museum. I was starting to think there were two Peter McCaffreys: one of them awkward, the other confident. But there were multiple versions of me, too. The brazen girl, the shy girl, the good girl, and the grieving girl. Could all of these personalities exist in an integrated whole, or would one ultimately take over? And what if the wrong identity asserted itself?

Peter and I stood on the library steps, our hands thrust into our pockets. "This was the best fake date I've ever been on," he said.

"Yup," I said. "Let's do it again." We looked at each other.

"Will you let me know if you find out anything else about Mr. Kaplan's brother?"

I nodded.

"When I said I wanted to help you . . ." He looked at the muddy library steps, then back into my eyes. "Well, I meant it."

But if Dantes and Rex were lies, what was I trying to find?

"Iris?"

I looked up and was struck by a terrifying notion: Peter was going to kiss me. "Well," I heard myself say, "see you in school." Then I bounded down the steps. *Idiot, idiot, idiot!* I thought as I walked through town. *You fumbled your first kiss. That would have been a story for your grandkids, but you ruined it.*

Dejected, I picked my way along the splotchy patches of snow, trying to keep the snow mush off my shoes. Prisom's Party had seemed so serious about their book of historical documents, but it was all an elaborate ruse.

Twenty minutes later, I puffed my way up Hazel's steep, snowy drive. But when I was level with the house I froze. Hazel and Mr. Kaplan stood on the porch, kissing. I slipped behind a couple of trees. Mr. Kaplan buried his face in Hazel's neck and she ruffled his hair. They kissed again. Then she went back inside and he drove away.

I felt like I'd been punched in the chest and my heart had exploded into small bits of muscle and blood. It was just like Veronica Mercy told me. *Don't trust any of those Trench freaks.* I dug my fists into the snow until my knuckles burned. Hazel was allowed to have a boyfriend, and why not Mr. Kaplan? But she'd lied to me too, telling me they hadn't seen each other in years. All the times I'd worried about her, she'd been just fine with Mr. Kaplan for company.

I scooped up a fistful of snow, packed it into a hard ball, and hurled it at the front door. It missed and hit the window. I packed another ball and threw it. I wasn't wearing my gloves, and my fingers were red and raw. I wished the snow was harder and sharper. I wished it could cut my skin and make me bleed. I wished I had enough blood to turn Hazel's front yard red.

I sank into the snow. What had made Dalia slit her wrists? Was it just a side effect of the medication, or did she really believe that letting herself drain away was the better option? The only option. And how would things be different if, at the moment she decided to step into the bathtub, I'd been there?

I wiped the tears from my face. I had no right to cry. Hazel hadn't lied to me; she just hadn't told me the entire truth. Well, I hadn't told her the whole truth either. She had no idea that I was a Prisom's Party operative.

Jonah

To our Fearless Leader, Garrison Pasternak:
We declare a vote of No Confidence.

Sincerely,
Prisom's Party

"It was on my desk when I came in this morning," Pasternak said, handing me the note. It was currently morning, but Pasternak arrived as early as 7 a.m., and he'd intercepted me when I walked into the building. Now he motioned me to his side of the desk, his expression grave. "I turned on my computer to find this."

He angled the screen toward me. I saw a grotesque caricature of Pasternak, his rheumy eyes ringed red and his teeth yellowed and rotting. A word bubble from his mouth said, *Come and tour my school.*

"It's the Mariana home page," he said.

The last time I'd checked, the school's website displayed photographs of our campus, populated by children resembling a United Colors of Benetton commercial. But now Pasternak clicked on the word bubble and a new page appeared. Up came the football team's hazing photos. Pasternak clicked again. Here were pictures of a man sitting at a computer, his hands clutching his erect penis, his eyes rolled back in his head. Pasternak clicked. Here was the wreckage from the Prisom Artifacts, over which Matt Sheridan stood with a baseball bat. Another click: the three hanged figures burning in effigy — Brotherhood, Truth, and Equality.

"I've left a dozen messages for the IT guy," Pasternak said. "He won't pick up his cell."

"So you need me to take the site down?"

"Don't be flip, Jonah. Not now." Pasternak paused. "You can take it down?"

I told Pasternak what I needed to make the site go away, and he found me the relevant passwords. I sat down at his desk to operate. I typed in the FTP log-in and password, and the inner workings of the school's website loaded onto the screen. "I'm not going to be able to put the old site back," I said. "You'll have to find your tech guy for that."

Pasternak didn't answer. He stood by the window, watching the students get out of their parents' cars and lumber up the steps. Each kid wore a monstrous backpack, a kind of freak-show stomach that grew from the wrong side of the body, and was grossly distended with academic glut: The Annals of America (dubbed The Anals) and the Norton Anthology of Every Last Word in the English Language.

"Okay," I said. "I'm finished."

Pasternak turned, his face dour. "What happened to this place, Jonah?"

What was I supposed to tell the man? He was talking about Mariana as though a golden age once existed. And maybe it had, early on, when Prisom's vision was still pure. But more likely there'd never been such an era. Most good things in life came prepackaged with nostalgia; otherwise nobody would appreciate anything. But maybe I wasn't giving the headmaster enough credit. Maybe he was only trying to survive in this hostile environment as best he could. Just like the rest of us.

That afternoon I sat at my desk in the science department, perusing the old *Devil's Advocate*s that Pasternak had given me. I flipped through pictures of Matt Sheridan, a baseball bat in his hand, his face twisted in anger. In another picture he bent over a small fire smoldering amid piles of smashed glass. I looked through the photos of Jeffrey Franks. These had not come out in a *Devil's Advocate* but were mailed in an anonymous envelope to Pasternak over the summer. Franks had not been set up like Matt Sheridan; months of pornography traffic showed up on his office computer. The photos before me now displayed Franks at his desk, ogling wide-eyed Japanese cartoon women, their breasts and asses like flesh-colored beach balls, their limbs entwined with tentacles. The expression on his face was nauseating. *He sat right here at my desk,* I thought, and shuddered.

But where had the photos of Franks come from? Prisom's Party could have stolen footage of Sheridan from the school's security cameras, but there was no reason for such cameras in the science department. This meant a photographer had been in the office at the time. But that seemed unlikely. I could see someone hiding behind Franks's chair, snapping pictures of his computer screen, but what about the photographs of his face and lap? The only way to get those shots would be to stand in front of Franks, *on* his desk. This was a mystery, but one I could solve.

When my brother died, the police called the car crash a weather-related accident. My parents weren't convinced. They knew Justin. Only seven months earlier, he'd put himself on crutches by slamming his foot against a wall. After that, a shrink had given him a bottle of antidepressants, but Justin refused to take them. He said he didn't need them, that he didn't want chemicals dictating his behavior.

"You masochistic moron," I'd said. "You must really like being unhappy."

"I like being me," he said.

If Justin's history wasn't reason enough to doubt the police report, my parents also knew how distraught he was over losing the final round of the Academic League semifinals — a tournament for which he'd spent months preparing. There were enough insinuating factors to make my parents wonder whether, in the moments before impact, my brother had pressed the accelerator instead of the brake.

The police agreed to leave the car alone for forty-eight hours, the exact period of time Jewish law allots mourners to bury the deceased. My father spent those two days in the bitter cold, measuring and analyzing Justin's car tracks and the black ice at the crash site. He covered sheets of paper with calculations, becoming so consumed that the earth ceased to be made of hard matter but dissolved into angles and degrees. A purely mathematical plane. He was hoping to draw a line from the impact point backward up the street, thereby determining whether the crash was accidental (Justin hit black ice and lost control) or intentional (Justin hit a metaphorical wall, past which his life, the planet, the very universe, dissolved into nothing). Like my father, I would now measure the angles at which Prisom's Party captured Franks with his pants down, and those angles would show me where the photographer had hidden.

I was sketching out my plans when Rick Rayburn and Stephanie Chu entered. Stephanie's desk was next to mine. We shared a passion for Orson Scott Card novels and spent many an hour debating the minutiae of the Shadow series when we should have been grading exams.

"You've been working hard," Stephanie said, collecting notes for her next class. She bent over my desk. "What's all that?" Rayburn joined Stephanie, peering over my shoulder.

"When was the last time anybody used the books from that top shelf?" I asked. We all looked up at the old textbooks, their spines sagging.

"Beats me," Rayburn said. "Isn't that a book by Albertus Magnus?"

Stephanie laughed. "Let's tell the kids we're now offering AP Alchemy and see how many bite!"

Rayburn and I seconded this notion. Then he sat down and Stephanie went to class.

I inspected my calculations. When the three of us glanced at the bookcase, I'd let my eyes wander to the spot from which I believed Franks's photographs were taken. Sure enough, peeking from between a large textbook and a couple of manuals was a small black lens. Casually, I turned around in my chair and asked Rayburn a question about midterm exams. There was another small camera tucked into the book-case behind my desk.

"By the way, Jonah, my sister-in-law tells me that Peter came home all excited yesterday. Seems he finally garnered the nerve to talk to Iris Dupont."

"Is that so?"

"I hear you gave him a little encouragement."

"It's possible."

"Well, if they get married, we'll make you an usher."

"I can't wait," I said, rising from my desk. The temptation to look at the cameras was too strong. I walked down the quiet hallway, wondering where the other cameras were. Was I being watched right now? It was entirely possible. I could be certain of only the two cameras pointed at my desk, however, so I would have to make those cameras my weapons.

Lily

APRIL 2000

L ILY OPENED HER eyes. The ceiling spun like a frantic carousel. Her head throbbed with a mud-colored pain. She pushed herself upright, and her stomach plummeted. She doubled over and sat unmoving until the sick feeling passed.

Slowly, she raised her head and looked around. She recognized Veronica's basement: the large television and mint-green walls. The overnight bags spewed their stuffing like abused teddy bears. Feminine detritus littered the floor. Candy and chips were crushed into the carpet. Cold, gray light filtered in. She was alone.

Lily remembered drinking from Alexi's flask, but nothing afterward. Had anything happened with Alexi? The previous night seemed like a distant memory: half dreamed, half true. The art project. *Sacrificial Lamb.* What she'd said about Justin.

She forced herself to stand. The world spun away from her, but she stumbled to the bathroom. The tiles were cold under her feet. In the mirror, her under-eye circles were like dark thumbprints. She'd just lifted a hand to fix her knotted hair when she saw a flash of black on her wrist. She yelped and shook her arm, but the black spot didn't move. She held her wrist up to her face to find a dark smudge. Then, in the bathroom mirror, she noticed a couple spots of black on the hem of her T-shirt too. She lifted the bottom of the shirt and saw more black on her lower abdomen. *What the . . . ?* she thought, realizing her stomach was speckled with dark splatters like ants. Lily rubbed at the black spots, but they seemed to be imprinted on her skin. What had happened to her? Was this some kind of rash? An allergic reaction? Had the girls spiked the flask with more than just a sleeping pill? She pushed down the rim of her pajama pants. More black. An awful coldness seized her. She pulled down her pants all the way. Her quads were their usual creamy color, and she breathed a sigh of relief. But then, on her inner thigh, she spotted a black dot. With shaking hands, Lily pulled down her underwear. She screamed. Her pubic hair, once white, was now jet black.

At that moment the ceiling began to shake. "Lily?" Feet pounded on the stairs. A chorus of voices called out, "Lily! Are you awake?"

Lily pulled up her pants, wiped her eyes, and came out of the bathroom to find Veronica, Amy, Jocelyn, and Krista clustered around the door.

"Oh my God!" Veronica shrieked, throwing her arms around Lily's neck. "Last night was amazing. You were perfect!"

"She's not perfect anymore," Amy muttered.

"Lily." Veronica cupped her palms over Lily's shoulders and looked deeply into her eyes. "You're okay, right? I'm sorry it got messy, but it's not permanent dye. It'll wash out."

Lily nodded, bewildered.

"I'm sorry I couldn't tell you what was going to happen. But if you'd known in advance, it would have ruined the effect."

Exactly what Alexi had said. But Alexi had also promised no more tricks.

"So listen, I'm going to edit the tape and then give you a copy."

"Wait—what are you going to do with it?"

"Like we discussed. I'm sending it with my application to the artist apprenticeships. But Lil, don't worry, they'll keep the materials private."

"But—"

"What?" Veronica's face hardened. "What's the matter?"

"Headache," Lily stammered.

Veronica brightened. "Go lie down and I'll make you my hangover special. You'll be feeling great in no time." The girls made room for Lily on the center couch, according her unexpected deference. She felt like the virgin about to be handed to the sea monster, except that for her, the sacrifice had already taken place.

Veronica returned with a glass of something green and frothy.

"Don't inquire about the elements of this particular concoction," Jocelyn said. Her accent seemed to have returned.

Lily took the glass and sipped. The liquid was chalky but otherwise tasteless.

Veronica could hardly sit still. "Last night was just amazing. And to do the whole thing at school? Perfection."

Lily put down Veronica's drink. She was feeling worse. "School?"

"Where the film's climax takes place, Lil. In the Trench."

"We're all ready for the raw footage," Krista said.

"Yeah," Amy smirked. "It's raw all right."

"I'm going to go home," Lily said. "I'm going to call for a ride."

"Already?" Veronica pouted, then looked doubtful.

A few minutes later Lily was changing her clothes in the guestroom when Veronica walked in. She leaned her lithe body against the door, and her dark hair fell down over her shoulders. Lily could just make out her naked breasts beneath her white tank top. She tried not to stare.

"Listen," Veronica said. "Alexi told me how he screwed up out there in the field, and I just want to say — thank you for staying in character."

Lily nodded. She couldn't look at Veronica.

"It really means a lot that you've been part of this."

Lily concentrated on her feet. It felt good to have her own shoes back.

"But Lil?" Veronica came to the bed. "It's really important to keep this between the five of us. The material is sensitive, you know? We don't want to hurt anyone or get anyone in trouble."

Lily stared into Veronica's sable eyes and for a moment became stuck there, as though in tar. She nodded numbly and let Veronica lead her downstairs.

"I don't understand why girls your age wanted to have a sleepover party," Maureen said when she picked Lily up. She'd just come from running a wedding brunch, and her car, including the floor of the passenger seat, was packed with vases and flowered centerpieces. Lily shifted uncomfortably among the profusion of petals and turned away from her mother.

"Your father says Veronica and her friends are artists."

Lily pressed her eyes shut. The girls must have stripped her. They must have touched her. And what about Alexi? Had *he* touched her? Lily shivered deep inside and bit her lip to keep from crying. The thought of Alexi touching that part of her while she was passed out sent sick waves rushing through her. But thinking about his fingers touching her, his eyes examining her — that also made her wet. Right there in the car with her mother. Lily wanted to tear the heads off the flowers at her feet. What Veronica had written in the diary was true; she was a sick, disgusting person.

At home, Lily refused her mother's offer to "brighten her room" with leftover wedding roses. She locked herself in the bathroom and turned on the shower as hot as she could stand it. As promised, the dye began washing out, running in black streams down her legs. The water in the tub turned muddy. She soaped up and scrubbed. After a few minutes, the dye on her skin was mostly gone, but her pubic hair remained the color of smoke. *It's not permanent,* she told herself, and scrubbed harder. There was no change. Panicked, she tried a different soap. "It's not permanent!" she whispered again and again. But the color had set.

At school that week, Lily avoided Justin and spent lunch in the spacious handicapped stall on the third floor where she didn't think anyone would look for her. She sat on the ledge over the radiator and stared out over the fields or straight down at the familiar courtyard where a single duckling sometimes poked at stale bread.

In the quiet, Lily dreamed about escape. She imagined walking through days of sunlight, her arms stretched wide beneath the open sky. In this fantasy there was no one to send her inside, but it didn't matter, because she never burned.

Midweek, someone walked into the bathroom. "Hello?" It was a male voice. Justin. Lily held her breath. "Lily?" She heard the first two stall doors creak. Then his face appeared beneath the door of the handicapped stall. "You're hiding from me?" When she didn't move from the window ledge, he slithered under the door. She turned her head to the window.

"If you just tell me what's wrong, I know we can fix it."

Lily pressed her body against the window. She couldn't make herself small enough.

"I brought you something." Justin pulled a brown box from his backpack and handed it to her. She opened it and peeled back the tissue paper. Inside a picture frame, pinned to a white backing, was the dragonfly he'd found under the picnic table.

"You can't make me better." Her eyes were full of tears.

"I can try."

"Your tournament's coming up." She ran her finger absently around the frame. "Don't you have useless information to cram?"

"It's not useless."

Why the hell wouldn't he get mad? She'd insulted him. He was supposed to lash out! Lily looked out the window, her eyes drifting over the woods and hills to where the mountains bled into the horizon. She thought of Justin filling his brain with libraries of facts. The information was endless. He'd never learn it all.

"Don't you ever get frustrated? Don't you ever just want to stop trying? Doesn't that sound like a relief?"

Justin's blue eyes opened into wide circles, as though this question had never occurred to him before. "No," he said, blinking. "It doesn't."

Iris

MURROW WASN'T HAPPY with me. I was continuing to investigate on behalf of Prisom's Party, he argued, because I was angry with Mr. Kaplan for canoodling with Hazel behind my back. He said there was no way that anybody with half a conscience would continue spying for that organization after I'd discovered their lies about Edmond Dantes and Thelonius Rex.

But I didn't care. In the forty-eight hours since I'd discovered Hazel and Mr. Kaplan kissing outside the Historical Society, I'd decided to finally nab his car keys. "If I'm going to solve the mystery," I said to Murrow as I made my way toward the science department, "I'm going in whole hog."

"So now you're using clichés?" he asked. "Iris, I'm surprised."

"I'm not using the phrase as a cliché," I snapped. "'Whole hog' is a literary allusion to *Huckleberry Finn.*"

"Somebody ate a bowl of Pretentious-O's this morning," Murrow murmured. I ignored him and directed my attention to the current task. The science department was usually empty at this hour, it being just long enough after school that the student-teacher meetings were over. Mr. Kaplan, meanwhile, was coaching an Academic League scrimmage in the theater. I knew where he kept his keys, because I'd seen him pull them from his jacket pocket on multiple occasions. I stood before the parka now, reached my hand in, and, sure enough, felt the rough serrations of metal.

"You'd think he'd be more careful," I said. "I mean, just leaving his keys lying around like this? It's idiotic."

"A certain level of passion, even indignation, is useful, Iris. But you're on the warpath." I turned to see Murrow, sitting in Mr. Kaplan's desk chair, watching me.

"Go away! I don't want you here. And 'warpath' is a cliché!" I headed for the door and marched into the hallway. Murrow followed, skulking just behind me.

"Your mother is right about the whole cliché-czar attitude. You shouldn't fault people for every verbal imperfection."

"If I'm not going to be vigilant, then who will?" I stopped and turned to face him. "I mean, if you give an inch, they'll take a— Shit!"

"You expect too much of yourself, Iris."

"No, *you're* the one with the impossible expectations. I've read all the books about you, all the transcripts, seen all the video footage. I've spent hours, Ed—hours absorbing your life, trying so hard to be like you, to live up to your standards, to be the kind of person—the kind of reporter—you'd be proud of, but I can't do it. I can't live the way you lived and still function here. I'm just as dirty as everyone else. So just be happy, okay? Be happy that you're still the morality king, the perfect Edward R. Murrow." I started walking again.

"I'm not real!"

"I get it. You're a figment of my imagination."

"That's not what I'm talking about, Iris. There is no Edward R. Murrow. There's only the myth of him."

I halted. I couldn't speak. And Murrow just stood there, in stark relief before a panel of lockers, observing me, like he was waiting for me to make a decision. I'd never really seen his face before this moment, never looked at it as a collection of individual features. But now I noticed the mole beneath his right nostril and the crow's-feet around his eyes, and his thick black eyebrows. His hair was parted on the far left and slicked back. I imagined touching it, and feeling the hardened gel flake beneath my fingers.

Who are you? I thought. *Do I know you at all?*

And as I wondered, Murrow began to waver darkly. And then, like a television on the fritz, he went blurry and snapped out.

I stared at the lockers. Just like me, Murrow was a liar. He'd falsified his CBS application, lied about his age and prior experience, even invented fake degrees. He'd carried on a long-term affair with Winston Churchill's daughter-in-law, leaving his wife alone for nights at a time, lying to her, behaving as if his celebrity status exempted him from his basic commitments and moral obligations. I knew all these things. I knew how easily people ignored facts when they needed a hero. I knew that I'd edited out the parts of Murrow I didn't want to see, simply redacted the hurtful information. I just didn't like thinking about it.

I heard laughter and saw a group of girls some feet away staring. "Whack job," one of them snickered. "Was she really talking to herself?" another one said. "Somebody needs to have her committed."

I turned and fled in the opposite direction. What was happening to me? That time at home, when my mother caught me talking to the wall, I'd known Murrow wasn't really there. I'd been imagining, pretending. And maybe I was too old for that, but at least I knew the difference between reality and fiction. And now? My world had become an imbroglio of moral quandaries and deceptions. Maybe I really was crazy. I should have known that Hazel, despite her talk, was no different from any other grownup. I should have expected her and Mr. Kaplan to retreat into their private adult world and leave me on the outside, alone. Good thing I didn't mind being left out. Aloneness is a skill—that's something people don't realize—and I was always terrific at rejecting rejection.

I pushed through the back doors and plunged into the cold afternoon. My eyes watered. I stuffed my hands into my jumper pockets—I hadn't bothered to grab my coat—and marched toward Mr. Kaplan's Subaru, fishing the keys from my pocket. Standing before the car, I hesitated. For a moment I wondered, *What if Ed Murrow could see me doing this?*

But he couldn't see me. And even if he could, so what? He was just a human being like any other. Flawed, imperfect, mortal. I'd been so foolish, treating him like a god.

I unlocked the door, climbed into the back seat, and hunched down. The interior of Mr. Kaplan's Subaru was significantly cleaner than Hazel's Saab. (Talk about a compatibility mismatch. Their relationship was clearly doomed.) I searched the various pockets and compartments. Then, under the seat, I found a shoebox of papers. On top was a handwritten letter on Mariana Academy letterhead.

Dear Jeffrey,

I wanted to tell you again how distraught I am over the accident and how sorry I feel about your loss. I want to do whatever I can to make your lives easier during this incredibly difficult time. Regarding your concern about preserving the accident site for inspection, I have called my contacts at both newspapers and am assured that the details we agreed upon will not appear in print. I, too, would rather this information be suppressed in order to protect Lily's privacy. As for your other question, Lily refuses to say why Justin drove over that evening. I'm sure she knows, and I'm equally certain she'll come around.

My deepest condolences,
Elliott Morgan

So that was why the exact location and cause of death remained absent from the newspapers — Lily's father had made a phone call, and the editors had done his bidding. But why keep this information secret?

Next I dug up Justin's death certificate. It resembled the personal-info section of an application: Name, DOB, Permanent Residence. I imagined what would have happened if this death certificate had accidentally ended up with a bunch of admissions officers. *Well, he went to a good high school, but I'm not sure his death is Harvard material.* I grimaced and kept reading.

Severe fracture to the head, the certificate said. *Victim died on impact.*

But impact with what? The car didn't crash into a pocket of air.

I flipped through more documents, and there it was: the police report. My blood pounded in my ears. The statement described Justin Kaplan driving a 1989 Peugeot down Church Street at approximately 4 a.m. when his car slipped on black ice, spun out of control on the severe slope of the street, and crashed into a large oak tree outside 95 Church.

Ninety-five Church was Lily Morgan's address—my address. Justin had died outside my bedroom window.

I remembered seeing the tree when my mother and I first arrived at the Morgans'. I remembered its imposing size, its lofty, gnarled branches. In my mind's eye I saw these branches waving erratically, as though dancing to a strange and sinister tune. A boy had died beneath them, only feet from where I'd been living.

With trembling fingers I pulled the next pages from the box. It was getting dark outside, and I held the papers up to the window to catch the last light. Now I was looking at a series of numbered sheets. Mathematical equations sprawled across the first few, but as I flipped through the packet, I began to see images too: quick sketches of a car on a hill; markers representing the hill's slope; the hood's angle against a tree; and the location of the black ice. I turned to the last page to find the complete image of the accident site: car, ice, tree—and, drawn in the middle of the page—the four-eyed demon of Prisom's Party.

My brain felt like a hard drive at capacity. But the answer was there, in a few short words scribbled below. *Face spooks J, car swerves, hits ice, loses control, impact.*

Impact.

No wonder the four-eyed monster on the bathroom mirror had spooked Mr. Kaplan. No wonder he'd hurled his bag at the demon's face on the Trench wall. Mr. Kaplan wasn't afraid of Prisom's Party at all; he was furious because their symbol had killed his twin.

I thought about all the things that linked Prisom's Party across the generations. Their members were artists—painters, sculptors, filmmakers, and above all storytellers. The yarns they spun were like spider silk, sticky and ensnaring. Justin Kaplan had unwittingly wandered into their web.

I sat back and shut my eyes, watching a picture swirl up out of the dark and come into bright, digital focus. I saw Justin Kaplan speeding toward Lily's house in the dark, the demon seeming to leap out of the road. I imagined his heart bursting with fright as his hands lost control of the wheel, as his tires hit ice and the tree rushed forward as though to greet him. Justin's death itself had been a kind of performance piece, the climax of a nefarious drama. Was there a video of this too, I wondered, playing in some gallery in New York City or Berlin to audiences who didn't realize they were watching something real?

Was Lily responsible for this? She'd refused to explain why Justin came to her house in the middle of the night. She'd disappeared after the accident. And then, there was *Sacrificial Lamb:* hard evidence of her betrayal. She could easily have drawn the demon on the street outside her home and lured Justin over, knowing the monster would be there to send him on a treacherous collision course. And maybe she had a motive, but maybe she just liked being part of a project, playing the role of creator.

The day I first arrived in Nye had seemed inconsequential, when in fact I'd fallen deeply into Lily's world. It frightened me to look back at my former self and see all the awful ways in which I'd wised up. I didn't want to be like Lily, a pawn of the Party. I was through with them.

But my investigation wasn't over. My journalism was supposed to change people's lives. A naïve goal, maybe, but Murrow had done it. Lieutenant Milo Radulovich was discharged from the Air Force because his sister read Serbian—i.e., "communist"—newspapers. Murrow's first broadcast against McCarthy took up Radulovich's case and led to the lieutenant's reinstatement. Like Murrow, I would be an advocate. Mr. Kaplan and I harbored the same dark shadows, and I understood his grief. So I would uncover what really happened to Justin—accident, suicide, or devious plot—and in so doing, restore Mr. Kaplan to his pre-grief state. I would help him heal.

• • •

After I copied all the relevant documents from Mr. Kaplan's car, I returned his keys and went to tell him everything. The Academic League competition was still in progress, however, so I headed across campus to study in the library and wait.

Sometime later, my phone buzzing in my pocket startled me. I looked up, disoriented. I was sitting in one of the library's reading chairs, my book open on my lap. I'd been asleep for over an hour. Peter's voice was urgent and quick. He'd be out front in fifteen minutes, he said. It was important.

I left the building and headed through the falling snow to Prisom Hall. I had just enough time to see Mr. Kaplan before Peter arrived. But the Hall was locked. I walked down the steps and looked out into the black and blurry white. Snow fell in the lamplight, forming impossibly thin drifts on the stair railings. I ran my finger straight down one of these drifts, imagining a kid sliding down a banister.

Just then, Peter pulled up and opened the window. In his wool coat and fingerless gloves, he looked like a scrappy, preppy mutt. I wanted to tell him he looked fetching, but I felt nervous and instead inspected the falling snow. It took me a moment to realize that Peter was staring at me. He took my hand through the car window. The wool glove was rough, his fingertips cold. "Get in, silly," he said.

Peter snuck sidelong glances at me as we sped away from the school. He refused to tell me where we were going, so I launched into my confession. I told him about the kidnapping, the pigs, and the fake story of Edmond Dantes and Thelonius Rex. I told him about Lily and *Sacrificial Lamb*. And, finally, I told him about the police report and the possibility that Lily Morgan had been a member of Prisom's Party and responsible for Justin's death.

At the next stoplight, I showed Peter the Xeroxes and was about to announce my renunciation of Prisom's Party when he reached out and put his gloved hand on my shoulder. I swallowed, my tongue paralyzed in my mouth. I was vaguely aware that the light had changed. "You're extraordinary, Iris," Peter said, shaking his head in amazement. "You truly are an original."

The car behind us honked, breaking the spell. Peter gunned the accelerator.

"So," I said, flustered, "what do you think the four-eyed demon is? Do you think it means something?"

"You never asked Prisom's Party?"

My reporter's instinct chided me. How could I have forgotten to investigate such a basic detail? Searching now on my phone, I learned that three-eyed skulls were associated with the Mexican Day of the Dead. I typed in "many-eyed monster mythology" and was flooded with sites about mythological Greek characters. There was the Cyclops, of course, as well as a litany of many-headed, and thus many-eyed, creatures: Hydra, Cerberus, Medusa. And then I found a site about Argus Panoptes. A quotation from Hesiod on the home page read: "The great and strong Argus, who with four eyes looks every way, was given unwavering strength by the goddess. And sleep never fell upon his eyes; but he kept sure watch always." Apparently Hera had enlisted Argus to keep Zeus away from Io, the maiden cow. A mythological cock block.

I looked up at the rushing trees and falling snow. I didn't recognize the road, and Peter kept swinging around curves, the car leaning left and then right like a boat slicing through water. "Argus Panoptes," I said. "That's the demon."

"That's right," Peter said. "Same root as in 'panopticon,' a prison where the guards can watch the prisoners without the prisoners knowing it."

I was about to ask Peter how he knew this, but abruptly the ground changed. We were on a dirt road that hadn't been plowed, and Peter maneuvered us through a set of tracks in the snow. I couldn't imagine who had been out here before us. We reached a clearing in the woods and pulled up beside two other cars. Before I could unbuckle my seat belt, Peter had jumped out and was opening the passenger door.

"M'lady." He held out his hand.

"If you're thinking about a picnic," I said, taking his gloved palm, "this is the wrong season."

"Come on!" he said with palpable excitement, and started leading me through the woods along a narrow, uneven path. Multiple sets of boot prints stretched ahead of us and disappeared through the trees, but to either side the landscape was pristine: snow, smooth as a sheet, punctuated by dark trees. My eyes stung in the cold, and for a moment the forest wavered like a heat mirage. I wiped my hand across my face, and the landscape stilled.

"Is this a joke?" I said, sniffing back my runny nose. "Are you a serial killer?"

The snow filled the dark with small shimmering flakes, but the cold was too bitter for romance. When I looked over my shoulder, I could barely make out the tracks behind us. I stopped walking. Peter stopped too, because I was still holding his hand. "I'm not going any further until you tell me where we're going." I clenched my teeth. Even my gums were cold.

Peter touched the crown of my head. "You're all snowy," he said.

"*You're* all snowy," I retorted. "Now where are you taking me?"

"I'll tell you if you let me kiss you." And then Peter's face was hovering over mine. His lips touched down. They were so much larger they could have fit over two of my mouths, and their heat spread up through my face and into my scalp.

Peter pulled away, and immediately I blurted, "You didn't use your tongue!"

"Is that a problem?"

"No. I mean, not that I don't want you to or anything, but I —"

Peter put his hands on my shoulders. The snow fell around us and between us. "Do you still want to know where we're going?"

I nodded.

"Iris Dupont . . ." He reached out his index finger and gently swept some snow from my eyelashes. "We are going to your initiation."

V

PSYCHROPHILES

These extremophiles thrive in conditions of extreme cold by producing a special chemical that keeps their cell membranes from freezing. A frozen membrane can neither allow nutrients in nor expel waste; eventually, such a cell will shrivel and die.

— *Marvelous Species: Investigating Earth's Mysterious Biology*

Jonah

A FTER THE ACADEMIC LEAGUE scrimmage was over, I headed back to my desk. My colleagues had gone home, and the science department was pleasingly quiet and warm. I graded a stack of tests and prepared for the next day's class. Outside, snow began to fall. By seven thirty, large, fat flakes descended in dizzying spirals past the window. We were used to heavy snows in Nye and the plows did a decent job, but sometimes a monster storm blew through that rendered everything immobile. Tonight, I could not afford for that to happen.

After finishing up my work, I spent a long time watching the snow fall on the faculty parking lot out back. Ten years ago this space was filled with balsam firs and towering red spruces that pressed in against the building, close enough to scratch the windows. When a budworm parasite defoliated a large hunk of the forest, the school mowed down the trees. According to Rick Rayburn, the faculty was elated; fewer trees meant more parking.

Back in our day, my friends and I would have vented our frustration over such selfishness by plotting a rumor about faculty-perpetrated ecoterrorism. We would have filled one of the many notebooks we kept locked in our team file cabinet with scenarios about how Elliott Morgan or maybe Pasternak had deviously released the budworms, knowing they'd get parking from the deal. It seemed juvenile now, but it was how we spent much of our time in the Trench. We knew the popular legends about Mariana's secret society: how Charles Prisom had organized a group of stewards to protect the Community Code, and how they'd battled Thelonius Rex. At the end of my freshman year we decided to exhume Prisom's Party and obliterate all traces of hypocrisy from the Community Code. Like Frankenstein, we constructed our creature from disparate bodies: fantasy, religion, and myth. We conjured gods to serve as our guardians and brainstormed methods through which we might target Mariana's rigid, stratified culture. Our makeshift secret society appealed to us the way science fiction did, letting us envision a world in which the forces of good combated the forces of evil. But we weren't fighting *for* anything; we were simply railing against a social order that didn't want us.

What separated us from the current iteration of Prisom's Party, of course, was the fact that we never put a single idea into practice. We were cowards, fearful of getting caught and ruining our precious academic records. In this way, we were as susceptible to the school's culture as the students we claimed to despise.

Then the locker vandalism happened. Hazel and I had plotted a million coups, but they—whoever *they* were—had actually pulled one off. They forced us to consider that Mariana's secret society was real. And if it was, then the kids in the Trench—the social outcasts who *should* have been running such a club—had found ourselves excluded yet again.

We vowed to one-up the locker vandals with the perfect act of sabotage. But the situation had become precarious. Those were the days of Columbine, and the administration was keeping special tabs on me, trying to assess the extent of my malcontent with Mariana and whether I was capable of violence. (Everyone, down to the school nurse, suspected that I'd been the locker vandal.) If we were going to compete with the actual vandals, we'd have to be extra careful to keep our activities hidden. Unfortunately, it was at just this time that my brother and Lily started dating. One word to her father could have upended everything. Justin promised to keep our activities secret, but we didn't fully trust him. "How," I asked him once, "can you maintain an allegiance to us and to Lily? That's a paradoxical state of being. An impossibility."

But Justin only shrugged. "Negative capability," he said. "Ever heard of it?"

The locker vandals were never caught. Nobody could figure out how they'd snuck in and out of the school undetected. Meanwhile, the Academic League continued plotting, searching for the perfect putsch.

Had the vandalism been less vicious, it could have been a great symbol to highlight the hypocrisy of a segregated locker system in a school that professed total equality. But the vandals were interested only in retribution—*We'll show you how it feels to be cut down.* At fifteen, I didn't understand that students had no place designating themselves taskmasters over their peers. I believed the world was divided into two camps—the weak and the strong. In such a world, you exercised power over others when you had it, or you didn't survive. Today, Prisom's Party was acting under a similar misconception.

Much of my revolutionary fervor died with Justin. I'd always existed as half of a pair, but when he vanished from the world, I could no longer define myself in relation to somebody else. I wasn't any better or worse than my twin, any smarter, any stronger, any less lovable. I was alive, full stop. Out in California, I'd collapsed in on myself, because I'd lacked substance. It took coming home and, in a certain sense, starting my life over to evolve from a shadow into a man.

So I knew Prisom's Party and I understood their tactics. They built an identity based on comparison: stronger *than* and smarter *than*. And they weren't alone. Every teenager in every corner of the planet, aside from maybe Iris Dupont, used this approach to combat loneliness and isolation. But not every kid took it to such extremes.

At eight thirty, it was time to get moving. The janitor had finished his rounds and I had half an hour until the automatic timers shut off the lights. I stood up from my desk and stretched. Then I walked down to the first floor. I kept thinking some faculty member or dilatory student would materialize and demand to see a hall pass. But Prisom Hall was empty. Not even my brother's silent eyes followed me from the AL picture in the lobby's display case, because weeks before, I'd removed it.

I'd also removed his articles from the *Oracle* archives and the library's copy of the yearbook with his memorial page. Maybe I was feeling guilty because I'd told Rayburn that I didn't have a brother, or maybe I was anxious because I knew Iris was snooping around in my past. Whatever the reason, I suddenly couldn't bear having evidence of Justin scattered around the school. I felt better — safer somehow — knowing that the relics of my brother's life and death were hidden in my desk drawer. There was just one piece of evidence that I could not collect, because it was painted on the wall in the Trench. One of these days I was going to get a can of paint and erase it.

I entered the school lobby, where there was, in fact, someone looking at me: Jimmy Cardozi. "Hi, Jimmy," I said, walking toward the cardboard figure. "I'm really sorry about this."

Jimmy grinned, as though to say, *Hey, Mr. Kaplan, it's all good.*

I nodded back. "Thanks for understanding," I said.

Iris

═══════════

Y OU'RE WINSTON," I said to Peter, though I was so stunned that
the words felt like lumps on my tongue. Tears welled behind my
eyes, and my mouth collapsed into a frown.

"I had to pretend," he said. "I had to make sure you were fully on
board."

"'On board' is a cliché," I murmured.

He smiled. "So are dates at the public library."

I didn't laugh, and twisted away.

"Hear me out, Iris."

I turned from him. My teeth were chattering and my toes felt glued
together.

"You can walk away right now. I won't stop you. Or you can take
just a few steps forward — with me."

"You lied to me!" I whirled around. "You made up that whole story
about Dantes and Rex. I read the truth in the newspapers."

"Now, just a second," he said. "We did no such thing."

"But—"

"Iris, newspapers get things wrong — and they lie. You saw yourself
how Elliott Morgan controlled the information about Justin's death,
how Pasternak kept the burning effigies out of the local press. If I'm
wrong about all this, it's not on purpose, and I will swear to you on
Edward Murrow's grave if you want me to."

I was heaving mad. "Murrow and I are on hiatus," I said.

"Then I swear on Prisom's grave."

"Where are we going?" I said.

"You'll see really soon." He pulled me in. I felt small and very confused.

"Are you—I mean, is this—part of the initiation?"

Peter shook his head. "This was a coincidence. I'd been trying to talk to you for months. And finally Prisom's Party gave me an excuse."

"Come on. You were never really shy. You were pretending."

Peter shook his head. "You know how superheroes are inept in their regular lives, but become extraordinary once they put on the cape? The Party changes you. You'll see."

I looked up into his eyes. I didn't want to change. But Peter gave me an encouraging nod, so I stepped away to call home and tell my mother I was sleeping at Hazel's. She was so excited that she didn't even complain about it being a school night.

In silence, Peter and I continued through the woods. The darkness curved over us like a dome, the snow falling faster and faster, thousands of flakes swirling out of the black. I felt disoriented, trapped in a snow globe, frantic to figure out whether Peter had dropped any clues about his involvement in the Party. Could I have recognized his voice from the kidnapping? His body? My attraction to him had scrambled my perceptive powers. What if he was lying even now? I looked up at him and he smiled, his face dopey with happiness.

Soon the trees parted and a stone building rose before us. Before I could get a good look at it, Peter led me down a flight of stairs and into a basement. He pulled a bandana out of his pocket. "After the initiation, you won't need this for going in or out." I nodded, and Peter tied the blindfold around my head. He walked me forward, up a set of stairs, and down a long hallway. I began to hear voices. A moment later, the voices stopped.

"Voilà!" Peter pulled off the blindfold. I was standing in what appeared to be a college dorm, lit by a single desk lamp and a string of

Christmas lights strung around the cinderblock perimeter. There were two metal bed frames with dirty mattresses.

"Welcome," Julia said. She sat on one of the beds dressed in a heavy sweater, ripped jeans, argyle socks, and, of course, the pig mask.

"*Ma fleur,*" said Syme. He sat beside Julia with a beer in his lap.

"French? That's kind of affected, don't you think?"

"O poisonous flower! How she wounds." Syme clasped his hands to his chest.

"Shut up." Peter took my hand.

"Help yourself to a drink," Julia said, pointing to a six-pack on the desk.

I'd have expected Prisom's Party to favor martinis or scotch, not to mention more elegant accommodations; they had seemed so mysterious and sophisticated. I felt disappointed.

"You guys should get started," Peter said. "O'Brien and I have some work to do, but I'll be close by." Peter kissed me on the cheek and left.

Julia motioned for me to sit down on the bed. I perched on the mattress edge, avoiding a large yellow stain. I wanted some time to think things through. My mind was working furiously, trying to figure out where we were. The Outpost—the old school dormitory—seemed the logical answer, but then why had Peter picked me up from school in his car? Why not just cut across the back fields? Moreover, during the kidnapping, I was pretty sure they hadn't carried me outside.

"We've all taken an oath of loyalty to Prisom's Party," Julia said. She sat cross-legged on her bed, her elbows resting on her knees. We could have been college roommates sharing late-night stories, except, of course, for her mask. "Prisom's Party learned long ago that swearing to tell the whole truth and nothing but the truth is not effective. People have a tendency to break their promises. So with each person we induct, we make a tape."

I did not like where this was going.

"It has long been the tradition that each new member swears against the person he or she cares for most—the one individual we least want to hurt."

When she said this, I immediately thought of *Sacrificial Lamb*. Had the scene of Lily swearing against Justin been her Prisom's Party initiation?

"Should any of us decide we're unhappy with Prisom's Party or our responsibilities therein, we'll have to think very carefully about exposing the group. Think of it as a kind of mutual assured deterrence."

"In the past, members wrote their confessionals in books—but of course," Syme added gleefully, "videos are much better at keeping members loyal, what with our ability to disseminate the material widely via the Internet."

"But before your confessional," Julia said, "we have something to show you."

She opened a laptop on the desk and turned it toward me. I was looking at an image of the school lobby. Then Mr. Kaplan walked into the frame. He glanced around and headed for the Jimmy Get Well table, where he bent over the lockbox.

"You're using the school's security cameras to spy on people?"

"These are our special cameras," Julia said. "We're a security force of sorts. It's basic surveillance."

So the Party had been following me. All those times I'd descended into the Trench, they'd been watching. When I'd first shown *Marvelous Species* to Mr. Kaplan in the library, they'd been watching.

"Keep your eye on the screen, *ma petite fleur*," Syme lisped.

Mr. Kaplan's back was turned toward the camera, so I couldn't see what he was doing. When he finally stood up and moved aside, the lid on Jimmy's lockbox stood upright.

Syme snorted. "Surprise!"

Mr. Kaplan pulled out a bag and dumped the money in. The picture blacked out, and when it returned, I was looking at the science department office. Mr. Kaplan cleared his desk and then poured the money onto it: all the donations collected over months and including many bills.

Mr. Kaplan ran his fingers through the pile, elated as a kid in a sandbox. Then he dumped it all back into the bag. A few moments later the screen went black.

"Nine p.m.," Julia said. "The school lights went out."

I looked at her and Syme. "It's a mistake."

Syme shook his head. "This happened tonight. Do you need further verification from your lover boy? We can get Petey back in here."

"I could turn you all in, you know. Now that I know who 'Winston' is."

Julia shook her head. "If you tell anyone about us, Peter will have a total memory lapse. He has a video, too, and he doesn't want it released."

I wondered who Peter had confessed against. I didn't think I'd known him long enough for it to be me.

"Your irreproachable teacher has shown his true colors."

That's a fucking cliché, I thought. I wanted to punch Syme in the face.

"You still believe he's innocent." Julia sat down next to me. "You believe there must be a reasonable explanation for what he's done."

She was right. Could Mr. Kaplan need a couple hundred dollars so badly that he'd steal from a kid's cancer fund?

"And that's because he's the person you believe in most," Julia continued. "The whole time you've been working for us, you haven't really believed Mr. Kaplan was capable of wrongdoing. And you still don't."

"Confessing against Mr. Kaplan will make me a full member of Prisom's Party?"

"Almost," Julia said. "Tomorrow we're putting out a *Devil's Advocate* about Mr. Kaplan's little transgression, and you get to distribute the papers."

"You said you weren't trying to get him fired. You said — "

"That was before we witnessed his act of corruption. Circumstances have changed."

On a 1951 episode of *This I Believe,* Murrow said, "There is a creeping fear of doubt of what we have been taught, of the validity of so many things we had long since taken for granted to be durable and unchanging. It has become more difficult than ever to distinguish black from white, good from evil, right from wrong." So much of what I'd seen in the last few weeks had been false. No wonder I'd been doubting myself, fearing that the dark force of my grief was directing me. The truth lay buried beneath these indirections, beating like a heart. I needed to find it, to see it with my own eyes. Because Mr. Kaplan was right when he decried belief on the first day of school. Belief meant nothing. If you wanted to really know, you needed hard facts. I'd keep moving forward until I could look truth in the eye.

I swallowed the sick feeling in my stomach. "What do you want me to say about Mr. Kaplan?"

"Very good," Syme said. "We've written you a script."

Lily

APRIL 2000

T HE NIGHT BEFORE final exams began, Lily lay on her bed, thinking about her first three-ring binder. It was purple with a unicorn on the cover and smelled of plastic and chemicals. Inside, a transparent pencil case bulged with gel pens and reinforcement stickers for Trapper Keeper triage. The binder was an initiation of sorts, because it corresponded with her first locker assignment. To Lily at eleven, the idea of a personal space outside of home suggested infinite promise. It didn't matter if you were awkward or abnormal. In that brief moment when everybody had an empty locker, everybody was equal.

The Rule of Lockers crushed this dream. During Lily's high school orientation, a senior asked the incoming students to turn in their randomized locker assignments. Somebody protested, and the senior flashed a patronizing smile. "Don't you want a locker near your friends?" he said.

Lily and Dipthi were shunted into the third-floor "loner" section, the catchall locale for students who didn't fit elsewhere. Loners quickly absorbed the Rule's cardinal lesson, however: any place was preferable to the Trench.

When the locker vandalism exposed the Rule to the administration, Lily's father abolished it. With some satisfaction Lily imagined all the people who had hurt and rejected her over the years shuffling like a chain gang into the Trench. But then she tried to imagine the Kaplans and Hazel hanging out in the bright fluorescent lights of the school's upper floors. She couldn't. The Trench was their home. What would they do — who would they be — without it?

Someone knocked on her door. "Leave me alone," she said, but the door opened and Justin walked in. His face was pale, save for the blue thumbprints beneath his eyes. He had one hand tucked behind his back.

"This came in the mail." He handed her a CD case titled *Sacrificial Lamb*. "I wasn't going to play it, in case it exploded in my computer." He chuckled, but when she didn't respond, his face stiffened. "I watched it eventually."

If only he had burst in raging, but he merely looked confused. A band tightened around Lily's chest. She'd kept her promise to Veronica, so why had Veronica sent Justin the video? Or maybe it was one of the others? Jocelyn? Amy Chang? But it didn't matter. He'd seen what they'd done — what she'd done — and there was nothing to do but tell the truth.

"I'm responsible for all of it," she said after explaining the art project. "Even for what they did to me at the end."

"What do you mean, 'did to you'?"

For a moment they looked at each other, guarded, skeptical.

"The dye."

"I don't know what you're talking about." Justin was getting angry now. "The last thing on here is you telling those girls that you were . . . using me."

Lily sat up on her knees. "It felt awful, saying those things." She began to cry, fat drops falling onto her jeans.

"What did they do to you, Lily?"

She shook her head.

"What did they do?" he shouted. "What dye?"

"My parents!" she hissed.

Justin knelt down and pressed his palms into her thighs. She flinched. She hadn't let him touch her since the sleepover. "You're hurting me."

Justin removed his hands. "What did they do to you?" he said again, his voice stony.

Fine, she thought, and jumped off the bed. She unbuttoned her jeans and pulled down her underwear. Justin's face went from white to red.

"I don't understand."

"Justin! Listen to me." She grabbed his shoulders. "Just forget about it."

He was looking past her. "Why didn't you come to me?"

She wanted to scream at him, but she had to calm him down. She couldn't let him tell anyone. "I wanted to tell you, but I was too embarrassed." She looked him square in the eyes and willed her lie into a picture of sincerity. He hugged her, and she fought the urge to shake him off. He had to believe he was in control.

When Justin finally went home, she put *Sacrificial Lamb* among her music CDs, where it would blend in with all the other bands. But it would be a reminder to her, every time she came into the room, of what she'd done.

After her math exam, Lily walked into the art studios to find the Studio Girls giving each other Marilyn Monroe birthmarks with a black Sharpie. "Hi, Lily!" Veronica said, waving. "Long time no see. You want one? It'll look fabulous with your complexion."

"Can I talk to you for a second?"

The other girls stopped and fell silent.

"Sure," Veronica said. They went into the hallway.

"I was just wondering how the video turned out." Lily tried to sound casual.

"Fine. And we cut out the dye job. We decided it was too sensationalized."

"Somebody," she began slowly, "sent Justin a copy."

Veronica's face stiffened. "That bitch! Is Justin going to tell anyone?"

"He promised he wouldn't."

Veronica's pupils hardened into small black stones. "You'd better make sure he keeps that promise." Her voice closed up around the word "promise" like a Venus flytrap around a fly.

Veronica returned to the art studio, and Lily watched her through the window, conferring with her cohort. If she was angry with one of them, she didn't show it. Her calculated manner was unnerving; she was plotting a contingency plan. For the first time, Lily felt truly and deeply afraid of what Veronica might do.

Iris

DECEMBER 2012

D O YOU SWEAR to the truth of the story you're about to tell?"
Julia sat across from me on the bed. Syme sat beside her, holding
up the video camera.

I nodded.

"Say it out loud, Iris."

"Yes."

"Good. Now tell us what happened."

I'd read through the script a couple of times, but I couldn't seem
to make my voice cooperate. My insides felt drafty, swept through by a
shivering wind. In my head, I begged for Murrow to come, pleaded for
him to appear. But I didn't want the apparition of Murrow. I wanted the
living Murrow, the one Julia and Syme could see. I wanted him to melt
the camera with his relentless stare.

"Tell us," Julia repeated.

He's dead, I told myself. *He won't come to help you. He never has.*

"Iris, will you please begin?" Julia said, but there was no politeness
in her voice.

I took a breath and began to speak. "This past November, Mr. Kaplan asked me to meet him in the Trench. He said he had a special science project for me."

"And you went?"

I nodded slowly, afraid of what was coming. "When I got there . . ."

I swallowed. "I saw that Mr. Kaplan had set up a video screen and on the screen was Jimmy Cardozi."

"And how did Jimmy look?" Julia said.

"Terrified. He was strapped into a chair and there were wires attached to his arms. I didn't understand what was happening."

"So you asked Mr. Kaplan, and he said . . ."

"He said he was conducting an experiment—on me."

"And what was the nature of this experiment?"

"There was a control panel in the room, and every five seconds I was supposed to press a button on it."

"And then what?"

"That was it. Just press the button. So I did, and Jimmy yelped on the screen. I asked Mr. Kaplan if Jimmy was all right, and he said Jimmy was fine. 'No matter what Jimmy does,' Mr. Kaplan said, 'you must push the button.'"

"And what did you think about this?"

"I was scared, but Mr. Kaplan told me to push the button again."

"And did you?"

I shook my head. "I refused, so Mr. Kaplan went over to the door and locked it. 'You must continue the experiment,' he said."

Julia was sitting on the edge of the bed, leaning toward me, expectant. Syme was on his knees, with the video camera pointed up at my face.

"Look at the camera," he ordered. I didn't move. "Look, Iris!" This time I obeyed.

"It's all right, Iris," Julia said, her voice soothing. "We know this is hard for you."

"After he locked the door, Mr. Kaplan walked over to me and pushed me into a chair by the control panel. Then he grabbed my hand."

"And how did you feel?"

"I was terrified. And Mr. Kaplan . . ." I paused; Julia nodded. "He was hurting me. He was squeezing my hand so hard I thought he was going to break my fingers. And meanwhile on the screen I could see Jimmy twisting and struggling to free himself, but he was strapped in too tightly."

"And then?" Julia and Syme said in unison.

"Then Mr. Kaplan pried one of my fingers free and started forcing it toward the button. And I was crying and begging him to stop, but he just kept saying, 'You must continue, Iris. You must finish the experiment.'"

"And then?" Julia said, breathless.

Tears rose behind my eyes, and all I could manage to do was shake my head. To someone watching this video, I realized, my reaction would only confirm the story I was telling. "Mr. Kaplan . . ." My voice wavered. "Mr. Kaplan pushed my finger down on the button and held it there. And on the screen Jimmy's body convulsed and contorted. And I could hear screams coming from down the hall. But Mr. Kaplan just kept pressing my hand down on the button."

"And he was speaking, wasn't he, Iris?"

"He was saying, 'Look what you're doing to the boy, Iris. Look at the pain he's in!' And I struggled against Mr. Kaplan's hand, but his grip was too strong. I turned away, but he took his other hand and grabbed my chin and forced me to watch."

"And?"

"And then Mr. Kaplan let go. And Jimmy slumped over in the chair, and he didn't move again."

"And did Mr. Kaplan say anything?"

"He said I'd confirmed his hypothesis."

Syme turned off the camera. "What are you going to do with that?" I asked.

"Keep it safe, my flower. Unless you turn on us."

They left me alone and I sat on the bed, seeing images flicker in the air like a stop-motion film. I saw strange insects with poisoned stingers and alien eyes crawl across a powder-pink carpet; I looked at Veronica Mercy's black, liquid eyes, which melted into the single pupil of a video camera; I stared at the implacable oak tree outside my window and its maze of dark branches.

I was desperate for Peter. I needed to see that his face wasn't simply another mask. The others were slippery, but Peter had wrapped his arms around me and kissed me. The air had been cold, but Peter was warm. At that moment, as though by magic, the door opened and there he was. I nearly jumped on him.

"Do you want cupcakes or chips?" He produced two packages. Then I did jump on him.

"I love you!" I cried. "I mean, I don't love you. I'm just hungry. And happy to see you."

Peter chuckled. "Yeah, I get it."

I tore open one of the cupcakes and ate it in three big bites. Peter wrapped his arms around me, and in that moment I almost forgot where I was and what I'd just done. He didn't ask me about the video, and implicitly I knew we were to pretend it hadn't happened.

Julia walked in with a couple of sleeping bags. "Why don't you guys get some sleep. Bathroom's down the hall. And don't go sneaking off. We'll give you the grand tour tomorrow." She nodded at Peter. "The papers are almost done." I was hoping she'd say more about the *Devil's Advocate,* but she didn't.

When I slipped into the hallway, I thought about making a break for it, but I knew Peter would come looking for me. I peed in the girls' bathroom, crouching over the cold toilet seat.

"Climb in," Peter said when I returned. I lingered in the center of the room, my arms wrapped around me for warmth. "Seriously, Iris. We're sleeping. That's it."

"I'm not worried about you taking advantage of me," I said. "I'm worried about contracting a disease from that mattress."

"Fair enough." He unzipped one of the sleeping bags and spread it over the bed. "I promise that not a millimeter of your skin will touch a millimeter of the festering mattress."

I jumped on the bed, and the rusted metal frame made a sound like a trash compactor.

"I think you ate too many cupcakes," Peter said, and I slapped him. He pulled me down and we curled up together. I should have been on guard, planning my next move, but I'd never slept next to a boy before and I wasn't about to squander the chance.

Peter turned off the desk lamp. He stretched out on his back—he was almost as long as the bed—and I laid my head on his chest. His arm curled under and around me, so that the tips of his fingers rested on my back. "You are so little," he said.

"You're so long."

He laughed.

"What is the newspaper going to say about Mr. Kaplan?" I said. "We don't know why he took Jimmy's money."

"It's going to report exactly what happened. An accurate portrayal of events. I made it clear to the others that our intention is not to hurt Mr. Kaplan. With him, we're sticking to the whole truth and nothing but the truth."

"You mean you don't always?" I sat up and the bed creaked.

"Sometimes, when we know something but we can't prove it, we have to engineer the right situation. To help people show who they really are."

"You trick them?"

"People only do what's in their nature."

I was too exhausted to ask Peter what he meant by this. We were quiet for a few minutes and then he said, "Remember I told you how the Party made me different?"

I nodded, but I was looking at the cloudy overhead light. A dark shadow spread along the bottom of the glass.

"It's like I belong now. We all feel that way—Julia, O'Brien, and Syme. And the others before us. That's why you're here, Iris. You deserve to be a part of this. To be inside for once."

My eyes welled. What *was* I doing here? If being on the inside meant I was trapped, I didn't want any part of it.

"Think how awesome it will be . . ." Peter's fingers trailed up and down my back. "You and me, together at school. We'll be a real power couple."

I focused on the shadowy light fixture to keep from crying. Tonight was the only night Peter and I would sleep beside each other. I didn't know how this was all going to end, but it would end. After tonight, he would never speak to me again.

"Iris, you don't have to be lonely anymore."

"I wasn't lonely, Peter," I whispered, and turned over to sleep.

Lily

MAY 2000

LILY PERUSED *Marvelous Species,* trying to figure out what Veronica was plotting. Her appendix on the Studio Girls stopped just before the sleepover, but now Lily imagined devoting an entry to *Sacrificial Lamb,* discussing what the girls had done to her in clinical, scientific terms. It never occurred to her during the months she'd spent in the art studio that if she joined this world, she'd inevitably become part of the appendix herself. A marvelous life form, an organism to be studied. And that was what had happened. During the lost hours of her drugged oblivion, *she'd* become the specimen under the microscope.

A knock on the bedroom door startled her, and she prayed it wasn't Justin. She needed to study; her math final that morning had been a disaster. At first she saw only her father, but when her mother materialized, her body grew cold. They walked in and stood in front of the bed, her father in his trim khaki pants, pressed dress shirt, and tortoise-shell glasses. He looked like he'd been born with patches on his elbows. Her mother wore a long flowered skirt as though in defiance of the weather: rancorous and frigid for May, even for Nye. They looked young. Standing there on her pink carpet they could have been new parents, excited and afraid.

Maureen sat on the bed. Elliott remained standing. "Justin came to see me," he said. "He told me about Veronica's party, the sleeping pill and the dye. Are those things true?"

Lily glanced at the disc among all the others on her dresser.

315

Her father knelt before the bed, as Justin had done the previous night. Her mother hovered specter-like behind him. "I want you to listen to me, Lily. We're not angry with you for drinking."

Like her situation amounted to a common teenage infraction! But Justin was smart enough to keep the art project from them. They wouldn't have understood, and he wanted them focused on the important point.

And on cue her father said, "You were violated."

"No, Dad. That's not true."

Elliott blinked. "This is serious, Lillian. Were you or weren't you drugged?"

Maureen took Lily's hand, but she yanked it free.

"I knew exactly what I was drinking. I took the sleeping pill on purpose."

Her father shook his head. "That's ridiculous."

"Sweetheart, this isn't your fault."

"It is!" She shrank away from her mother's weepy face.

"Stop saying that," Maureen begged. "It's like—like you were *raped*."

"No!" Lily screamed. "You're not listening to me!"

"We *are* listening, and we don't understand why you're not taking this more seriously. Who knows what else happened to you while you were passed out!"

Of course they'd believe only what Justin told them. She had to be the victim.

Abruptly Elliott left. Lily felt his absence like a cold wind.

"Listen, sweetheart." Maureen edged closer to Lily on the bed. "We have to get you checked."

Lily shook her head.

"Tomorrow morning you have an appointment with my doctor."

"Nothing happened!"

"We don't know that."

And her mother was right. The Studio Girls or Alexi could have done anything to her.

"I'm not going to any gynecologist!" Lily jumped off the bed and ran into the bathroom. Sixteen years old and she had no control over her own body. She made her own decisions. But everyone insisted she'd been manipulated and tricked. Outside the window, a violent wind whipped the tree branches, scattering spring petals across the pane. She watched them blow in the air like pink snow. Justin kept calling, so she turned off her phone.

"A little farther," the gynecologist said, and Lily scooted down the rough paper. The metal stirrups of the examination table gripped her feet. She felt like an animal in a zoo. "A little more. I'm going to need you to come all the way down . . . That's right."

At least it was a woman. At least she said nothing about the dye.

"Now I need you to spread your knees. All the way . . . That's right."

Air hit Lily between the legs. She felt split open, bisected.

The exam began. The doctor promised pressure, and there was pressure. She promised a short uncomfortable sensation, and there was that too, as though she'd scooped out Lily's insides with a spoon. Then it was over. "You look fine," the gynecologist said. "Is there anything you'd like to discuss? This is confidential."

Lily sat up. She felt sticky.

The doctor waited a beat. When Lily didn't respond, she left the room.

Getting out of the car at school, Lily saw Veronica and her parents dressed in dark, funereal coats, walking into Prisom Hall. As they disappeared, Justin materialized. In his navy blue parka his hair seemed to glow a brighter red and his eyes a deeper blue. Students streamed around them and up the steps, eager to escape the ferocious May wind.

A strong gust hit Lily's back. "How could you?" She gritted her teeth. "I know I hurt you, but you promised."

"You needed my help!"

The students slowed around them like she and Justin were a traffic accident in the middle of the road.

"Lily, we can't just let the Studio Girls do whatever they—"

"*I* did it!" She dropped her voice to a hot whisper. "I'm responsible for myself."

She wasn't vulnerable. She was dark and disturbed. She'd shown him the physical evidence. But like everyone else, Justin could see only her lily-white skin. Now his head bobbed up and down in small, shallow movements. "I know I did the right thing," he muttered, but he looked lost, like he was trying to prove a simple equation and kept getting the wrong answer.

"Justin, please." Maybe if she hugged him. If she could just squeeze him tight enough . . . She moved forward to embrace him, but at that moment, his head slammed forward, nearly butting her.

The first-period bell rang. The wind lashed Lily's hair across her cheeks.

"Are we okay?" Justin gripped her arms. "If we're okay, everything's okay."

A hollow feeling yawned inside of her. She turned from him and went into the school.

All that day, rumors flew on the wild May wind, landing everywhere and blossoming into hideous shapes. Lily had entered a satanic cult and dyed her pubic hair black. She and the Studio Girls had posted a bondage movie of themselves on the Internet. Alexi had confessed to raping her. Veronica Mercy's parents were sending her to live with a strict Muslim family in Saudi Arabia so she could learn obedience and modesty. If Lily had been less depressed, she would have laughed at these ridiculous stories. But she was too exhausted to care one way or the other.

Now, at the end of the day, she and Dipthi stood inside the auditorium, watching the long-awaited Academic League tournament.

"Your grandmother wanted you to give Justin a chance, not pledge eternal love," Dipthi whispered.

Lily nodded, but she wasn't paying attention. She was watching the stage. There were three teams. Hazel stood in the middle of Mariana's table with the twins on either side of her. The atmosphere felt pressurized.

"Next question," the game master said, and the nine students on stage hunched over their tables. "These rotating neutron stars emit beams of electromagnetic radiation."

Hazel punched the buzzer. "Pulsars!"

"Mariana Academy, twenty points."

Hazel slapped hands with Justin and then Jonah as the audience clapped and cheered.

"Next question. 'Power tends to corrupt and absolute power corrupts—'"

Justin punched the buzzer. "Lord Acton!"

"Incorrect. Mariana down twenty points."

Justin winced. The team had worried this would happen—that Justin would prematurely ejaculate, League slang for buzzing in too soon. But had he screwed up because of her or because he couldn't handle the pressure? How could Lily know? The teams huddled. Kent Hill and Episcopal eyed Justin like predators smelling fear.

"The full question," the game master said, his booming monotone echoing throughout the theater, "is the following: 'Power tends to corrupt and absolute power corrupts absolutely.' This is the first part of a statement spoken by the nineteenth-century moralist and historian Lord Acton. What is the rest of the statement?"

Kent Hill's buzzer flashed. "'Great men are almost always bad men.'"

"Correct," the game master announced. "Kent Hill, twenty points."

Justin looked crestfallen. Hazel put a protective arm around his shoulder.

"Let's go," Lily said, and the girls slipped into the empty hallway. Lily dialed Justin's number and waited for his voicemail. Dipthi stood by like a bodyguard, her arms folded across her chest.

That night, Lily lay awake in bed waiting to feel something—sadness, guilt, relief—but she was numb. In the coming weeks she would have to talk to Justin in person and try to make him feel okay about this. But she would not change her mind.

She switched off the light and went to sleep. Some time later, she was yanked into wakefulness by a noise like a bomb detonating. She held her breath and listened, but her bedroom was silent.

Jonah

A FTER THE SCHOOL lights shut off, I returned Jimmy's money to the lockbox. Then I headed to the Trench. I was hoping the Prisom's Party cameras didn't have night vision.

I was prepared to wait as long as necessary for the paper to come out. I'd sleep at school for the rest of the week if I had to, as long as I could be there when the kids showed themselves. In the meantime, I holed myself up in the old Academic League room. The file cabinets had sat untouched for over a decade. We used to spend hours after each tournament analyzing our performances and writing long critiques of the events. Everyone had a folder with his or her own notes. I pulled out 2002, the year I'd graduated, and read in reverse order until I came to May 2000, the last tournament Hazel, Justin, and I competed in together. Justin's notes weren't there, of course. He'd never had the chance to write them.

On the morning of our final tournament, Justin woke me at dawn so we could get in an early practice. He arrived at my door dressed in khakis and a navy blazer with the school crest. He'd shaved, and his hair was slicked down from the shower. I knew he'd been awake for a couple of hours already, hunched over his books in the half dark. I saw no reason to get up. Justin had been a wreck over Lily all week, Hazel was upset because Justin was ignoring her, and I couldn't stand to see Hazel fawn over my brother. It was a trifecta of failure.

"We have a practice to get to," Justin said, lingering in the doorway.

I jumped up and began pulling up the window.

"What are you doing?"

"It's forty degrees in here and I don't want to freeze my ass off going to the bathroom. Also," I added, ever eager to prove my grand intelligence, "why flush all that potassium, phosphorus, and nitrogen down the drain when it could help fertilize the front lawn? Nitrogen-fixing bacteria *love* urine."

"The ground is frozen."

He was right, of course. Spring in Nye's a real hard-ass. Until the buds break ground in June, the only yellow you see is dog piss on snow. Still, that spring was the coldest on record in over fifty years, and the many conservative crackpots in our town were going wild, certain that the "myth" of global warming had finally been debunked.

"We have to win today, Jonah. We don't have a choice."

"We do," I said. "We could choose to lose." But I was talking to myself, the doorway now empty as though my brother had never come in.

I resumed my journey toward a badly needed nirvana. I pushed up the window, and freezing air burst into the room. I gritted my teeth and dropped my flannels. "Here's to you, Justin," I said to the empty room. *"L'chaim!"* But my urine never arrived at its intended destination. Halfway down it froze and shattered on the walk.

After we lost the tournament, Justin drove himself home and disappeared into his room. An hour later, when he didn't come down for dinner, my father and I went to check on him. We knocked, but there was no answer. "Maybe he's sleeping," I suggested. "Or dead."

My father shot me an angry look and opened the door to find Justin on his bed, surrounded by a snowfall of tissues. My dad walked a few paces into the bedroom. "We're having breakfast for dinner!" he announced.

Justin sat up abruptly. His eyes were so swollen and red they looked bee-stung.

"You'll win the next tournament," my father said. "This is only a small setback."

I shook my head. Here was a physics professor capable of reading equations impenetrable as hieroglyphs, but he couldn't read the face of his own son. A hissing sound escaped Justin's lips.

"He's gonna blow," I said.

"Leave me alone," Justin groaned. "Please!"

My father smiled and nodded with encouragement. He'd always treated "father" like a noun *and* a verb, acting like any problem could be talked through, reasoned out, parented away. This made me sad, for our dad and for us.

When he'd left, I turned back to my brother. "That bitch dumped you, huh?"

"Don't talk about her like that."

"I told you this would happen."

"It's a mistake. She's upset. You have no idea what—"

"It's not a mistake, Justin. She doesn't want you. She never did." It was awful of me to say this. But I was convinced my twin needed my tough love, now more than ever.

Justin climbed off the bed and walked toward me. He loomed over me, six solid feet of him. We looked at each other good and hard, and then, without a word, he shut the door in my face.

I returned to the kitchen. My mother asked how Justin was doing. I said nothing about the breakup. I didn't want my parents heaping loads of sympathy on him.

After dinner I jumped on my bike. My mother didn't like us riding around after dark because there weren't any streetlights and the cars treated the roads like a luge course. The temperature had plummeted in the preceding hours, and I couldn't decide whether to pedal my bike quickly to cut down on time or go slowly and keep the wind out of my face. I wished I were a life form that adapted automatically to its environment, any other species than human.

I was pedaling hard, and my throat burned like I was gargling with broken glass. Just as my energy gave out, I skidded to a stop outside the Greenburgs' house. Hazel let me in. I pulled off my gloves, and the tips of my fingers began to burn. As usual, no sign of Lorna. "You look apoplectic," she said.

We'd wanted Justin to break up with Lily, not the other way around. I thought about my brother and his pitiful hope—*It was a mistake. She didn't mean it*—and felt so angry I couldn't speak. "Lily," was all I managed to say, but Hazel understood.

"Is he okay? I need to see him."

"He doesn't want to see anybody. Not even you, Hazel." I could tell she was stunned, but my fury urged me on. "You said you'd fix this!" I cried. "That night in the car, outside Veronica's. And now look what's happened!"

Without warning, Hazel grabbed my arm and pulled me into her bedroom. She didn't bother turning the lights on, but knelt before a silver laptop on the carpet, her freckled face awash in the computer's blue glow. I sat down beside her, accidentally bumped her knee, and quickly retracted my leg. The blue screen faded to black, then opened to a scene of a room with a mint-green carpet, flowery couches, and an enormous television mounted on the wall.

"What's this?"

"Something I got ahold of. Just watch."

Hazel sped through a bunch of scenes and then I saw a close-up of Lily's face. She looked strung out—whorish eye shadow, eyes glowing acid purple in the sharp light. Tears streamed down her cheeks, but they produced no sympathy in me.

"Don't lie to us," said a voice off screen. "Are you using Justin Kaplan for sex?"

"Are you?" another voice repeated.

"Are you?" a third said.

"Are you?" the voices shouted at once.

Lily blinked and more tears spilled out of her eyes. She stared into the camera, her expression determined. "Yes," she said.

Hazel paused the video. We said nothing, just stared at Lily's too-large face. But I didn't see her exactly. I saw her father fuming, accusing me of the locker vandalism, shaking his head as if I was responsible for every problem the school had suffered; I saw my classmates laughing at me in the halls, calling me Prepubes; I saw Hazel naked in the bathroom, laughing at my hard-on; I saw Lily staring me down: *Have you kissed a girl, Jonah? Have you touched a girl's breasts? Have you stroked a girl's hair? You're jealous of him, Jonah. Jealous.*

"Jonah."

I looked up. Hazel's freckles pulsed in the eerie backlit light. My heart pumped with hatred for one girl and love for another. I was small and weak outside but strong inside. I was going to prove it, do what my brother lacked the courage to do. That was what I told myself, but it wasn't the whole truth. Underneath, I harbored this last hope: that with one heroic act, I could make Hazel choose me instead of him.

I was flying then, back on my bike, pedaling into the night. I vaguely heard Hazel yelling at me — she knew something dangerous was brewing in my brain — but I was already far away, cutting through the woods. My pedals jolted over the uneven ground, skirted the dark stumps and branches swooping inches above my head. Twenty minutes later, I burst from the brush into my parents' backyard, threw my bike on the ground, and snuck into the basement through the back door. Synapses fired in my brain, bright questions bursting like sparks — Why was Lily on a video? Who was asking her the questions? How had the DVD come into Hazel's possession? — but every time a question blazed forth, it fizzled. My heroic act was my only point of focus.

Our basement was musty and dank, a repository for fertilizer and tetanus-encrusted gardening tools. I clanked and clamored around in baskets and bins. My fingers were raw, but I refused to lose momentum. And then, in a box on a high shelf, my hand touched something cylindrical and smooth. My palm closed around it, as though my body knew instinctively that this object was the one I'd been seeking. Then I was back on my bike, pedaling through the same slice of woods by which I'd come.

• • •

I put down the notes. Cold air trickled from the vents, but my underarms were marshy with sweat. Why had I come here? Oh yes, I was waiting for Prisom's Party to put out the *Devil's Advocate*. But I couldn't spend the night like this, carelessly slipping into the past.

I returned the Academic League notes to the file cabinets and left. The Trench was dark and silent. I had never spent the night down here, and I felt like a cave-dwelling creature, a crabby troll, festering in his domain, or Gollum plotting murder in the dark. This environment was no longer hospitable; its crushing psychological pressure made me desperate for air.

Iris

"IRIS, WAKE UP." Peter was squeezing my shoulder. My brain felt packed with rocks. "It's six," he said. "We overslept." I stretched. My legs were pleasurably warm beneath the sleeping bag, but needles of cold pricked my face. "I'm going to get the *Devil's Advocates*," he whispered, and disappeared.

I threw back the covers, hurried into my shoes, and grabbed my coat from the other bed. Then I pulled one of the sleeping bags around me and sat on the bed shivering, waiting for Peter.

I had to think. I would keep one of the *Devil's Advocate*s for evidence and destroy the others. But how? There'd be stacks of papers, too many to flush down the toilet or immolate with a Bunsen burner. I yearned suddenly for *Marvelous Species,* to be holding the thick text in my hands at this moment, searching through the index for a solution. I imagined that the book's information was limitless, that it could solve any problem. But this wasn't the case, and even if it had been, I was out of luck. The book was at home, in Lily's bedroom.

Peter arrived with a backpack slung over his shoulder. I was eager to see what the *Devil's Advocate* said about Mr. Kaplan and Jimmy Cardozi's money, but I didn't want to appear too curious. Peter took my hand and led me from the room. We walked down the hallway and into a stairwell. I wasn't blindfolded this time, but the darkness was fuzzy beyond the glow of Peter's flashlight. At the bottom of the stairs, we crossed a foyer and entered another stairwell. The air grew damp and cavern-like as we descended. Then we were back in the basement. Peter's light illuminated a door at the far end of the room. He opened it, and we stepped into a long, concrete esophagus.

"Doing okay?" He squeezed my hand. At the tunnel's end, Peter took a few steps forward, and then the wall before us seemed to slide away. He reached up and a light clicked on. We were standing in a janitor's closet. The closet's back wall was a sliding panel of wood—and behind that, the tunnel.

Peter smiled at me. He looked tired, and brown tufts of hair stuck out from his head at erratic angles. "I'm going to take you upstairs into the school," he said. "Put stacks of the papers in the locker rooms, bathrooms, and outside all the department offices. When you're finished, go back through the tunnel. You still have Katie Milford's key?" I nodded and Peter opened the door of the janitor's closet. We stepped into the Trench.

Of course! I'd heard of northern colleges building tunnels so students could move around during inclement weather. I remembered the girls in Veronica's video walking through a blackness before stepping into the Trench. In the exact spot I was now standing.

"The lights come on in half an hour, and we need this wrapped up before people start arriving." Peter handed me the backpack and the flashlight. "Good luck." He kissed my lips and was gone.

I hurried from the Trench and unzipped the backpack. It was stuffed full, too many papers to destroy in half an hour. Much better, I thought, to hide them in my locker and get rid of them later. But when Prisom's Party realized I'd lied to them, they'd release the confessional video. And I'd have all the *Devil's Advocate*s in my locker—damning contraband. And then what?

Even if I could convince everyone that my confession was false, I wasn't sure Mr. Kaplan's reputation could recover from the scandal. Everyone from biology class who accused him of sadistic behavior earlier in the year would surely come forward now. He'd be fired, and I'd be responsible.

I needed to get moving, but I couldn't contain my curiosity any longer. I pulled a single *Devil's Advocate* from the backpack and shone my flashlight on the text. The headline, printed in bold black letters, had nothing to do with Jimmy Cardozi.

Jonah

DECEMBER 2012

AFTER I LEFT the file cabinets in the old Academic League office, I hunkered down in a classroom near the Trench stairs to wait for Prisom's Party. I sat in the dark, my back propped against the cinderblock wall, and passed the time by planning a class lesson about gallflies, a species of insect extremophile. The more I tried to focus on my students, however, the more I thought about my brother. As the child of scientists, I had unique ways of tormenting Justin. After putting a few drops of some yellow alkaline substance from our "nontoxic" chemistry set into his orange juice, he lost his sense of taste and smell for two days. I once changed all references of "organism" to "orgasm" in a seventh-grade science paper he'd written. I also called him a gallfly, nature's puniest, most pathetic insect. Or so I thought.

One winter afternoon—we must have been eight or nine—after I'd reduced Justin to tears, my mother decided to teach me a lesson. I was wearing nothing but a sweater, but she pulled me into the backyard. "Come on!" she said fiercely, marching me across the grass, the air nicking at my ears and neck. At a stringy patch of goldenrod she halted. Shivering, I watched her snap off one of the thin brown stalks. In the center of this was a gall, a bulbous gray pod, just smaller than a cherry. "See this?" she said.

I nodded, shaking in my tennis shoes, astounded by my mother's cruel and unusual punishment. She pulled a small knife from her pocket and sliced the gall in half. Inside was a white lump. "Touch it," she instructed.

I did and found the lump hard. Only then it began to move and squirm. And just like that, in front of my eyes, the white lump was alive.

"Touch it again," my mother said.

This time, the lump was disconcertingly soft. It wasn't a lump at all but a larva.

"This is the spectacular child of your puny and pathetic gallfly," my mother said, her breath curling into the air. "It can survive for up to nine months by producing an intercellular antifreeze that keeps the larva's cells from exploding. Does that sound puny and pathetic to you?"

I shook my head. I imagined my lips turning blue and frostbite edging up my toes. I imagined blackened skin and amputations.

"What's the matter?" my mom said. "You're not cold, are you?"

This was my introduction to extremophiles. I never called Justin a gallfly again. If I had, it would have been a compliment.

I must have been dozing, because I was startled awake by voices and a door clanking shut. I grabbed my flashlight and bounded into the hall. The Trench was empty, so I hurried up the stairs and into the school. I threw open the Trench door and my flashlight caught Iris's face, her eyes frozen wide like an animal in the headlights of a hurtling car. She was holding a *Devil's Advocate*. "It's not true!" she burst out. "They're lying!"

At first I didn't understand, but then I saw the headline.

THE DEVIL'S ADVOCATE
"Carrying the Torch of Prisom's Party since 1923"
Mariana Teacher Kills Twin

MARIANA ACADEMY—Science teacher Jonah Kaplan, a Mariana alumnus, has been harboring a terrible secret for over a decade: He is responsible for his twin brother's death.

The deadly car accident that killed sophomore Justin Kaplan on May 2, 2000, shook the Mariana community—but until now, the secret behind this tragedy has never been reported. However, new evidence from that night has come to light. And now that Jonah Kaplan is a teacher here, responsible for the moral and physical well-being of his students, this school deserves to know about his reckless and negligent past.

During Mr. Kaplan's student tenure, he and a group of friends created an image — a four-eyed demon meant to represent the mythological Greek Argus. The Argus symbolized Kaplan's anger toward an administration that turned a blind eye on the school's intense social stratification. Mr. Kaplan harbored particular animosity toward the school's then-headmaster, Elliott Morgan. So on the evening of May 2, he spray-painted the Argus on the street outside Morgan's home.

Hours after this act of vandalism, Kaplan's twin brother, Justin, drove to visit Morgan's daughter. Halfway down the street, his car spun out on black ice, causing him to crash into a large oak tree on the Morgans' property. He was killed instantly.

A thorough examination of the area conducted by the Kaplans' father, a physics professor, determined that the ghastly Argus startled Justin Kaplan, sending him toward the black ice that precipitated the fatal collision.

Jonah Kaplan owes his school, his community, and his friends an honest accounting of the role he played in this tragic event. Instead, he has repeatedly lied about his past — claiming to be an only child and hiding his actions on the evening in question. Even worse, his silence allowed people to believe that Justin's death was a suicide. That Jonah has known the truth for all these years and has not come forward is unconscionable.

I read the story. I read it again. I stared at the words until they dissolved into amorphous shapes. I wanted to obliterate the paper, destroy the very molecules of its making. But the story itself was indestructible. Thirteen years ago, I'd fled my parents, my home, everything I knew, desperate to escape what I'd done. I convinced myself that three thousand miles was far enough, but I could have traveled to another galaxy and outflown asteroids, and still I would have failed to evade the memory of that night. That memory was a parasite. For years it fed on my guilt, secretly thriving inside its host. I'd been sick all along; but I hadn't known it. Until now.

After Hazel showed me the video of Lily saying she'd used my brother for sex, I immediately thought of the Argus, the god my friends had ordained as our protector: the watcher, a powerful deity who saw every transgression and hypocritical act perpetrated by our immoral community. We'd painted our version of the Argus on the Trench wall my freshman year and hidden it behind a stack of chairs. As I searched for the perfect heroic act, my mind returned inevitably to the locker vandalism: those gruesome pictures everyone wanted to blame on me. Why not appropriate the tactic and bring our god to life?

I'd rushed from Hazel's house back to my own, snuck into the basement, and grabbed a can of spray paint. Then I set out again. Lily's house was five miles and three large hills away from ours. I pumped my bike until my thighs burned. The streets were just starting to freeze, but there weren't any cars, so I kept to the center of the road and navigated around the slick patches. I paused like a ski jumper at the crest of Church Street. Then I was off, the wind slicing my eyes. Faster and faster, gravity pulled me toward my heroic act.

At the bottom of the hill, I stared at the Morgans' windows. I was so angry I didn't care whether they saw me. I wasn't in control. I just kept hearing Lily's voice — *kissed a girl, touched her breasts, stroked her hair? You're jealous. Jealous* — and her face as she declared, *Yes, I used him,* and Hazel gripping the steering wheel: *You're so naïve, Jonah. You're like this little kid, just trying to keep up.*

I pulled out the spray can I'd taken from my parents' basement — a garish police-tape orange left over from some science fair display board — and shook it vigorously. The Argus was crude enough that even I could draw it, and I made it huge, half the width of the street. I sprayed the four eyes and gaping mouth over and over until the color leapt up like flames. Then I hurried a few yards up the hill, took a deep breath, and turned toward my creation.

My horror was instantaneous: the Argus was upside down. I'd intended to draw it facing the Morgans' house so Lily would see it first thing in the morning and know that we were watching her — that someone knew all about her fickleness, selfishness, and deception. Instead, I'd painted the creature looking away from the house, up the hill. Of all the careless mistakes I'd ever made, all the numbers I'd forgotten to carry and the negative signs that had vanished from my answers, this was the worst. I had ruined my heroic act. I'd failed Hazel, whom I loved, and my brother, whom I was trying to protect.

I barely registered the ride home. Back in my bedroom, I tossed the backpack with the spray can in the closet and climbed into bed with my clothes on. I lay under the covers, shivering and crying. I must have fallen asleep from sheer exhaustion, because the next thing I knew, my father was shaking me awake.

Elliott Morgan called our house just after four in the morning. *There's been an accident.* My father thought it was me, because I'd been the one to storm out of the house hours before, but I was safe if not entirely sound. My parents and I dressed quickly and headed out.

The night felt hungry, the blackness eager to swallow warm-blooded life. The moon was a white hole in the sky. A freezing rain had fallen, and ice plated our front walk. I slid across the cold, stiff leather of my parents' Toyota and buckled in. Only when we reached Church Street did I understand where we were going. We began a careful descent down the hill, because by this time patches of black ice clearly pocked the street. I had the odd feeling that we were submerging ourselves, only the air seemed to be growing thinner like we were climbing. Midway down, flashing lights spilled onto our car, and then the Argus rose before us like some awful sea creature from the deep.

"What in God's name —" my father said, only we were all distracted at that moment by another sight: our car, its hood smashed like a broken nose against the Morgans' colossal oak. Fire trucks and an ambulance and medics attended to something at the car's driver-side door. The police were waiting for us. My mother struggled against the meaty arms of one policeman, gnashing her teeth and screaming until my father pulled her away. I hovered in a daze. Medics pushed a stretcher toward us. It was covered with a white sheet and beneath the sheet was a six-foot-long lump. At that moment, I remembered the frozen gallfly my mother had shown me and how it had struggled to life before my eyes. I half expected the same thing to happen now. But the stretcher rolled by. The lump did not stir.

Soon words floated by, as though borne on the current of flashing lights. *Ice . . . impact . . . instantaneous.* I wasn't listening. I was thinking about how my parents, with their arms wrapped awkwardly around each other and their bodies shaking, looked a lot like sea life.

Then my parents were pulling me toward them, locking me into their embrace. "Jonah." They sobbed. "Justin."

There was a cough and we looked up to see Elliott Morgan standing on the sidewalk in slippers, flannels, and his winter coat.

"What happened?" my mother yelled.

But Morgan just shook his head. He seemed unable to do anything except move his neck from left to right. Then we were back in the car, driving up the hill.

The rest of the night was a succession of fluorescent lights, signatures, and hard plastic chairs. The police had no reason to suspect that the crash was anything other than accidental, and though we were all considering the alternative, we didn't mention it. We nodded our heads when they explained about the frozen roads, the black ice, the lack of air bags. We said we understood.

We pulled back into our driveway just as the sun rose above the treetops. The wasted night had given way to a cold, drizzly dawn.

Thirty-six hours later, the evening before my brother's funeral, my father returned from the crash site carrying his calculations. "It wasn't suicide," he said, spreading his plans and measurements across the kitchen table. "But it wasn't just the ice. That horrible thing spray-painted on the road. You remember . . ." He handed my mother a photograph he'd taken of the Argus. "I drove down Church at the same speed I believe Justin was going. And that *thing* just flew up at me. Right in my face." My father raised his palm toward his face, like he was about to slap himself. "Justin swerved out of shock, maybe fear. That's why he hit the black ice."

My mother's mouth was moving. At first no words came out, but soon she was mumbling, "That bastard." Her voice grew louder: "That bastard!" Suddenly I realized she was talking about the person who'd drawn the Argus. She banged her fist on the table and screamed, *"That bastard!"* The pain stunned her right hand, so she started in with her left. "That fucking bastard!" My father struggled to hold her, but she kept fighting him and screaming.

I just sat there doing nothing, watching my mother writhe and listening to my parents' tears and my mother's chair scraping against the kitchen floor and the silence of our house and the ringing in my ears and Lily's accusation — *you're jealous, jealous* — and it was like a torrential rushing, like gallons of water filling the room. But then the rushing began to fade and the ringing subsided and Lily's voice went silent. All that was left was a single thought: that it would have been so easy to blame my brother's death on natural phenomena — the freezing of water as a catalyst for tragedy. But we were a family of scientists, so we knew that humans were part of nature too. As catalysts, humans made all kinds of awful things happen.

The *Devil's Advocate* had fallen from my hands. Someone was talking to me, but I couldn't understand a thing. I felt sickened, and there was no cure. If I wanted to end the parasite's life, I would have to end my own. Otherwise, I had no choice but to let the spiteful memory feed.

Iris

I KEPT SAYING HIS name, but Mr. Kaplan was paralyzed.

"Where did you come from?" He suddenly grabbed my shoulders. "Where?" He threw open the Trench door and plunged inside, banging his fists against the lockers. "Iris!" Mr. Kaplan looked deranged. "Show me where you've been hiding!"

"It's not me. I'm undercover —"

"Right now."

I'd left the backpack with the newspapers in the hallway. "Can I just go and —"

"Now!"

I rushed to the janitor's closet and pulled the panel aside.

"This is brilliant, fucking brilliant!" Mr. Kaplan pushed past me and disappeared into the tunnel. I followed, stumbling through the dark, afraid of what he'd do when he caught Peter and Julia.

The tunnel spit me out into the concrete room where the pigs had interrogated me. I could hear the echo of Mr. Kaplan's voice, and I followed it into a stairwell and up into the foyer of the Outpost. I found him in a defunct student lounge lit by dawn. I looked from the dirty blue carpet to the furniture covered with white sheets. Motes of dust twinkled in the streaming shafts of sunlight.

Mr. Kaplan ran to the far corner of the lounge, then back to the foyer. "Hazel!" he bellowed. "I know you're here."

Hazel? But then I turned, and she stood in the doorway.

Jonah

S HE LOOKED LIKE a hologram, her hair gleaming, her freckles crackling like sparks, her green eyes shooting lasers of fury at me. "You," she spat, and her mouth crumpled.

I couldn't speak. I was trying to work out how Hazel had obtained the materials I'd taken from my parents' house. On their own, those documents told a fragmented tale. But the article in the *Devil's Advocate* had supplied the connective tissue. Anatomical material that only Hazel understood.

"You killed him!" she snarled.

For weeks after the accident, Hazel begged to know what had happened to Justin. Had Lily driven him to suicide? Why hadn't I done everything in my power to ensure that he survived the first night of his despair? I knew what had happened, she was convinced, so why wasn't I telling her?

But I couldn't talk about it. It was too painful even to think about, and I dared not risk her discovering my culpability. If she'd only gone to Lily's home before the county power-washed the Argus from the street, she'd have known at once, but she couldn't bear to stand in the place where Justin died. Still, her need to piece together the events of that night had split us apart, the way lightning splits a tree. When it became clear that I wasn't going to tell her what I knew — and my refusal was indication enough that I did know something — she stopped talking to me. I hoped that the Trench would lure her back, but shortly thereafter Headmaster Morgan abolished the Rule of Lockers. Come September, we lost our home.

Now the *Devil's Advocate* had stripped me naked before the school and plunged me into the singularity of my past. This hurt like hell, but even worse was the way in which Hazel had placed me in the center of her universe, as though inside a cocoon. I'd believed that I was maturing and growing strong. But now that the chrysalis had finally cracked open, I was only a weak, despicable thing. Not an adult. Not even a hearty child. And that was exactly what Hazel wanted. I'd killed the boy she loved, so I needed to suffer.

Iris broke the silence. "Hazel, what are you doing here?"

Hazel composed herself. "Why don't you sit down and let me have a talk with Jonah. Then you and I can chat."

"Chat?" Iris shook her head. "Don't patronize me! I knew you were a liar. Pretending you hardly knew Mr. Kaplan. But I saw you kissing him." I started to protest, but Iris cut me off. "Who *are* you?"

"I'm your mentor." Hazel took a couple of steps into the lounge and smiled. "I brought you into Prisom's Party to give you a voice. You've lost so much, but that's what makes you special. Trust me, Iris, I know what it's like. We're kindred spirits."

"You used me to get information about Mr. Kaplan!"

"You made that choice, my dear. You acted of your own volition."

Iris shook her head, her eyes tearing.

This was getting stranger by the second. "The newspapers, the cameras hidden around school, Matt Sheridan — Hazel, you were behind all that?"

Hazel looked at me like I was a lost lamb. "I'm not some cult leader, Jonah. I returned to Mariana for the same reasons you did: to overcome my failures, help these kids."

I shook my head, but Hazel continued, her voice passionate. "Prisom's Party has lived in these walls for over a century, long before my return."

I ran my fingers through my hair. I felt like grabbing it in clumps and tearing it out. "It's a myth, Hazel! Prisom's Party exists only in people's minds."

"You and I vowed to bring Prisom's Party into existence, but we were cowards. I'm carrying on the legacy that should have been ours. Yours and mine. Justin's."

I couldn't believe this. "Did you pretend to be Sonya Stevens, Hazel?"

"They were just photos from some pornography site. They weren't of me."

"But you made Matt Sheridan send pictures of himself!"

"I made him do nothing! You're not listening. Everything these kids have done has been of their own volition. Matt Sheridan symbolized—"

"Matt Sheridan isn't a symbol, Hazel! He's a person. A teenager! This isn't a game."

"You're right," she said. "It's quite serious." She was moving forward, closing the distance between us. I did not like how calm she appeared. "Do you remember us as kids, Jonah? Everybody taunting us in the hallways? Jeering. Do you remember Morgan questioning us, practically accusing us of plotting the nation's next school shooting? Do you remember the signs kids hung over the Trench door?"

I hadn't thought about these signs in years. The worst—*Columbine Breeding Colony*—we'd torn down before the faculty found out. We didn't want to draw attention to ourselves, our inert schemes.

"And fucking Veronica Mercy," Hazel went on. "And her second-rate identity thieves, strutting around in their Outcast Chic. Taking what belonged to us! Usurping our pain!"

The realization came like a flash. "You wanted to be friends with them," I said, and almost laughed. But Hazel's eyes narrowed to small, mean points, and I saw that I was right. The girl who walked goddess-like above us wanted the same acceptance that we did. But she was a Trench kid, so she'd been rejected.

"What happened to you, Jonah?" Hazel began pacing, moving ever closer to me and Iris. "What did you think you'd accomplish as Pasternak's lackey? Did you forget how harsh an environment this is?" She thrust her finger at Iris. "If a kid doesn't fight, she ends up like your brother."

"Hazel, Justin died because—"

"I'm not talking about his death. I'm talking about his *life.*"

I shook my head, grabbed at my hair. "Don't you think I know that? He was my *twin.*" My throat constricted, like I'd been bitten by something venomous. "Why do you think I drew the Argus? I was trying to show you and Justin how strong we could be. How much I . . ."

How much I loved you, I thought. But I couldn't say it. "You're not in high school anymore, Hazel," was all I could manage.

Hazel looked at me, stunned, and in that moment I knew fleeing to California had saved me in some unanticipated but vital way. For all her itinerancy, Hazel had never really left Mariana, never learned to adapt to any other environment. She was trapped in the torturous emotional landscape of her adolescence, despising her alienation but thriving on it all the same. I'd convinced myself that Hazel needed me, but what she really couldn't do without was her pain.

"Where are the others?" came a small, timid voice from the corner. I'd forgotten that Iris was there.

"Gone," Hazel said, and smiled. "Peter ran out on you without a moment's hesitation."

"Peter McCaffrey?" I said, but they ignored me.

"Peter and I are through."

"Don't talk about Peter like there was ever anything special between the two of you. I've been close with Peter for three years, my dear. All the information he learned from you, he passed right over to me."

"Fuck you," Iris said.

Hazel's mouth stiffened. She took an aggressive step forward. We stood just feet from each other now, the three points of a triangle.

"You're a lonely, manipulative freak," Iris said, and the next thing I knew, Hazel lunged. She would have slapped Iris across the face, but I shoved myself between them. Hazel stumbled, but then she was on me, her fists pummeling my body, her fingers scratching. Her nails bit into my forearm and suddenly I was bleeding.

"Get off him!" Iris yelled, and Hazel turned on her like a wild animal distracted by fresh prey. She swung out, and her right fist, adorned with its horsefly ring, made contact with Iris's face. The fly's sharp wings punctured Iris's cheek and ripped upward toward the bridge of her nose. Iris screamed with pain as blood welled lava-like from the gash.

"What's wrong with you?" I grabbed Hazel by the shoulders and shook her, crazed, unable to stop myself.

"Mr. Kaplan! Stop it! Please!"

I was vaguely aware of Iris's pleading voice and her bloody face. She needed medical attention, but the urge to hurt Hazel, physically and brutally, was too strong. Hazel broke free and charged Iris.

"Don't forget your confession, Iris," she snarled. "Don't you forget—"

Iris hesitated, her eyes bright and afraid. Then she bolted. I ran after her.

Iris

DECEMBER 2012

I FLED THE OUTPOST, grabbed the backpack with the *Devil's Advocate*s I'd left outside the Trench, and ran for help. Headmaster Pasternak was in the lobby, still wearing his coat and a newsboy cap dusted with snow.

"They're going to kill each other!" I was breathless, half delirious. Black spots clouded my eyes, and I felt like I was going to puke out my entire stomach. My face throbbed. My neck and hands were sticky with blood.

Headmaster Pasternak was unflinching. "Let's get you to the hospital," he said, and pulled a cloth handkerchief from his pocket. He pressed it to my cheek with surprising care. "I'll call your parents and tell them to meet us at the ER."

I shook my head wildly. My neck barely felt attached to my body. "Come on!" I cried. I saw Mr. Kaplan hurrying toward us, and then the hallway and Mr. Kaplan and the rows of lockers melted into a hazy puddle.

I woke up to the smell of leather and car heat. I was leaning against Mr. Kaplan's shoulder; his hand was pressing the handkerchief to my face.

"She's awake," he said, and I saw in the rearview mirror the headmaster's visible sigh of relief.

"You fainted," Pasternak said. "We're going to the hospital."

"The confessional! Where's the confessional?"

Pasternak looked worried. "Just relax, Iris," he said.

"Mr. Kaplan," I mumbled, my lips thick and gummy. "Where is she?"

He shook his head. "We don't know."

I tried to remember what had just happened, but the pain was like a wall. As Mr. Kaplan walked me to the ER, I thrust my backpack into his hands. "You need this," I said, though I couldn't for my life recall why.

VI

MUTATION

Weak microorganisms that have been exposed to foreign chemicals or ultraviolet radiation will often die. But if they survive, they can mutate into a more robust version of their former selves, able to thrive under new conditions.

— Marvelous Species: Investigating Earth's Mysterious Biology

Iris

DECEMBER 2012

I DON'T REMEMBER MUCH of what happened after Mr. Kaplan and Headmaster Pasternak dropped me off at the ER. I have a vague recollection of waking in a hospital bed — apparently I passed out a second time — and then stumbling into the bathroom and screaming at the dark slug splayed across my face. The nurses came running and found me clawing at the stitches the doctors had sewn into my cheek. There were thirty of them, black ugly things. I was given a sedative, and when I fell back to sleep, I dreamed leeches were stuck to my body, sucking toxins from my blood.

The next day, when I was home recovering, Headmaster Pasternak came over to check on me. He explained that after he and Mr. Kaplan dropped me off at the ER, they'd driven directly to the police station. Not long afterward, the police went to the Historical Society with a warrant for Hazel's arrest. She resisted — she'd been in the process of packing her bags — and spent the night in jail.

I was happy to hear this, but I was disappointed that Headmaster Pasternak had come to visit alone, without Mr. Kaplan. During the hour the headmaster spent with us, my mind marched back and forth past the same questions: Where was Mr. Kaplan? What was he doing? Was he thinking about me? Surely he'd come to see me. Surely our experience with Hazel *meant* something to him. Didn't he realize how I'd saved him, giving him the newspapers to destroy? And hadn't he saved me — or made a valiant effort to — from Hazel? Wasn't this supposed to be the moment where we finally shared the unbreakable bond of our grief?

But Mr. Kaplan didn't come.

It was weeks before I saw him again. My parents decided that I was an invalid (I suspect they'd been talking to Dr. Patrick) and informed me that I was *taking a break.* They arranged for me to complete my midterm exams at home. In fact, for the entirety of winter vacation, they barely let me leave the house.

Not long into my internment, the local papers sniffed out the story about Prisom's Party and Hazel. The *Nye County News* ran two articles: FACULTY-STUDENT VIOLENCE WRACKS MARIANA ACADEMY (talk about a sensationalized headline!) and RESTRAINING ORDER ISSUED AGAINST MARIANA ACADEMY ALUMNA. Soon after these appeared, a reporter from the *Boston Globe* called asking for an interview. My parents urged me to turn him down, especially after the *Globe* mix-up with Dalia. I had reservations about helping the *Globe* reporter all right, but mostly because I didn't want him to scoop me on my own story. I gave in, though; a journalist doesn't write hard news about herself.

"I'll tell you everything," I promised the reporter over the phone. "But only if you get me a summer internship at the *Globe.* And I don't mean fetching coffee for some prima donna columnist." The *Globe* wasn't keen on this at first, but after I sent them my clips and followed up with a number of phone calls, they came around. They knew well enough that prep school scandals are like cheap sex for the American public, and if they didn't have me, they didn't have a story.

I wasn't too worried about the reporter manipulating me, either. I was a journalist; I knew how this worked. So when the *Globe* man came to Nye, I told him exactly what I wanted him to know—the same glossy version I'd given my parents and Headmaster Pasternak. I described the kidnapping, the pig masks, and the legend of Edmond Dantes. I said nothing about my confessional or Mr. Kaplan's brother. At times I wondered what Murrow would think about these half-truths I was telling and whether he was judging me from his heavenly press box. But these concerns were only the superficial remnants of a previous self.

I'd reread Murrow's biographies over winter break, and it was amazing how different he seemed now. I'd missed — really ignored — much of the complexity and the darkness he'd harbored. He was charismatic and moody, openhearted and selfish. A truth-teller and a liar. Like me. I'd tried so desperately to be like him, but after all my worry and ruminating, it turned out we weren't so different in the first place.

Iris

A S EXPECTED, THE *Globe* story gave everyone a five-star or-gasm. The AP picked up the article, and *Seventeen* magazine in-terviewed me for a piece about high school journalists. Some crackpot agent-publicist person even tried to sign me as a client, but I didn't want to kick off my career with a memoir. Take that route and every-body would think I'd invented half the details just to boost book sales.

Peter could have confessed much of what I'd kept secret, but when I turned his name over to Pasternak and the police, he said nothing. He refused to explain how Hazel had recruited the members of Prisom's Party, or her level of involvement in the group. He was expelled for his silence—in addition to everything else. Hazel, too, kept mum. Mr. Kap-lan told the police about Matt Sheridan—I only found out about him from the newspapers—but Hazel denied her involvement in the Sonya Stevens activities. The police searched her computer, but they found nothing pornographic.

Both Pasternak and my parents issued restraining orders against Hazel, but the only charge levied against her was trespassing. Of course, Mariana parents became obsessed with neighborhood men-aces and abusive-teacher stories. For weeks the local papers ran articles to the tune of "Let Your Children Use the Internet and They'll Proba-bly Die." The *Nye County News* published a stream of letters to the edi-tor arguing that the "true tragedy" of this scandal was parental neglect. Suddenly half the town seemed to think my parents and Peter's parents were responsible for what had happened to us — Peter's expulsion, my beating at Hazel's hands. When I explained that I became involved with Prisom's Party *in spite of* my parents, everyone shook their heads at my naïveté.

By the time classes resumed after winter break, the school had sealed up the tunnel and razed the Outpost. They installed new lighting fixtures in the Trench and scheduled classes in the empty rooms. They scrubbed the place clean and painted over the Argus on the wall. Within a month, the Trench resembled any other floor of Prisom Hall. The *Oracle* also published my Charles Prisom story, clearing up all questions about the school's legacy. "On the outside, Mariana may appear to be the setting of a gothic romance," I wrote, "but the fluorescent lights within have not simply chased the shadows into their corners, but illuminated the corners themselves. Our legends have nowhere to hide."

After all this, the other kids didn't know what to make of me. Everyone ogled my nasty stitches, and when the *Globe* article came out, I became a minor celebrity. Kids who'd never spoken to me before were suddenly asking me all kinds of questions about the Trench, and Katie Milford was jealous as all get-out over my *Globe* internship. I didn't care, though. I no longer needed to become the *Oracle*'s youngest editor-in-chief. After my summer in Boston I planned to intern for the *Nye County News* and then *Boston* magazine. Maybe I'd even take a year off before college to intern at *Slate* or *HuffPo* to build up my web journalism chops. By the time I actually entered college, I'd be a working freelancer. (Not that I planned to build a career out of *that* soul-draining slog.) But you couldn't get hired at the *Boston Globe,* or the *Washington Post,* or the mecca of meccas, the *New York Times,* without a thick stack of clips.

The excitement over my scar and the media attention faded, and I sank into the monotony of second semester. The snow sat thick and deep on the school grounds and continued to lie there for weeks and then months, as though spring had forgotten about Nye or decided that our dreary mountain perch wasn't worth the effort. Meanwhile, Mr. Kaplan acted like nothing had happened. When he looked at me, he tried hard to ignore my stitches. I couldn't stop thinking about him, and at night, instead of talking to Murrow, I played through "what if" conversations with him. What if I ran into him at the bookstore in town and we happened to be buying the exact same book? What if my parents invited him over for dinner to thank him for taking me to the hospital? What if we were both in the school elevator when it broke down? I had so many questions for him: about Lily, about his relationship with Hazel, about whether the *Devil's Advocate* had told the truth about Justin's death. Most of all, I wanted to tell Mr. Kaplan about Dalia and explain how he and I were connected in our grief. I imagined us walking along the campus paths, discussing what we'd been through. We each knew how it felt to move through the world alone, harboring dark feelings few people could understand.

Just before summer break, I stopped by Mr. Kaplan's classroom. He was sitting at his desk, grading exams, and I launched into an explanation of what had happened from the time I broke into his car until he found me holding the *Devil's Advocate.* I watched his face, but it was inscrutable, so I explained how Hazel had made me feel visible, but she hadn't seen me at all. "There's only one person who really sees me," I said, "and that's because we share a deep and searing bond, and I —"

"Ms. Dupont."

I clamped my mouth shut. The look of understanding on Mr. Kaplan's face was so sincere that it more than compensated for the betrayal and pain I'd experienced at the hands of Prisom's Party. All of that had been in the service of this moment, when Mr. Kaplan and I would acknowledge the bond of our grief. He pulled a packet from the stack of papers on his desk, and I waited eagerly for what he would say.

"I'm very proud of you, Iris," he began. "You could have used the year's events as an excuse to shirk your academic responsibilities, but you received a near-perfect score."

At first, I didn't understand what he was talking about. Even as I took the exam from him, I wondered: Was this the prelude to our real conversation, the moment when Mr. Kaplan said, *I know you, Iris*? But then I understood. This *was* the conversation—the only conversation we were going to have. I stared at the bright red A inked onto the page. It might as well have been a gigantic X, the universal letter of rejection.

"Ms. Dupont, are you all right?"

I shook my head, too upset to speak. Mr. Kaplan looked at me, concerned. "I thought we . . ." I began—only I couldn't say it. I probably looked paralyzed at that moment, but inside I trembled with the terrible fear that Mr. Kaplan and I shared nothing. Logically, it didn't seem possible—not after Hazel had betrayed us, not after we'd both lost our best friends. But if Mr. Kaplan felt all of this—if he truly felt it—why didn't he say something? Why did he sit there like he was nothing more to me than a concerned teacher and I was nothing more to him than an upset student?

"Iris." Mr. Kaplan reached out and put his hand on my shoulder. His palm felt so much larger than it looked. I glanced up at him, fighting to keep my eyes dry. "Thank you, Iris," he said. "I cannot tell you how much I mean that."

"You're welcome," I replied, even though I didn't know what we were talking about. I rushed from the room before he could see me cry.

Lily

O N T H E D A Y of Justin's funeral, the Morgans took a silent car ride to the synagogue and, after the service, another silent ride to the cemetery. Now, still in silence, they joined the stream of mourners toward Justin's grave. Lily followed her parents, staring at the monarch ring Justin had given her. A butterfly was the first insect he'd ever preserved and, according to his mother, a coming-of-age milestone on par with his bar mitzvah. Lily hated the term "coming of age" and its suggestion of menstrual cycles. But in this case, Mrs. Kaplan was right. The moment you killed something — a living creature or a false hope — was the moment you came of age. Loss of innocence wasn't a passive experience that happened *to* you. It was something you gave up.

"Lily?" Elliott's voice was tentative. She looked up at him and followed his gaze to the grave. Was he asking her to climb inside of it? Then she understood. One by one, people were shoveling dirt into the hole. Her body protested, her limbs jelly-like. How could she throw dirt onto Justin? Wasn't he a human being with skin, and eyes, and organs, still warm? Hadn't he pressed his chest to her chest and put his tongue inside her mouth?

Her heart pounded as the distance between her body and the grave narrowed. The person ahead of her moved away, and somehow a shovel appeared in her hands. She looked at the pile of dirt to her left but didn't know what to do with it. Finally, as though of its own volition, the shovel sank into the soil. Now she was at the grave's edge.

Dirt covered the casket. Was that Justin's head or his feet? *Please God, let it be his feet.* And maybe this wasn't even a coffin. Maybe she was at the beach, burying Justin in the sand. Or maybe the earth was really a warm blanket and she was tucking him in to sleep.

After the cemetery, Lily's parents picked their way down the Kaplans' ice-scabbed street and Lily wobbled behind them, imagining reporters from the *Nye County News* crowding the sidewalk. *Ms. Morgan, how are you coping with this tragedy? Ms. Morgan, was Justin Kaplan's death really an accident?* Antique bulbs popped in Lily's face, each flash capturing a portrait of her guilt.

For two days after the crash, she'd stood at her bedroom window watching Justin's father perform complicated measurements on her street. Her parents refused to say what he was doing, but she could guess well enough. Everyone wanted to know how Justin had died. Everyone had a theory. But Lily had the answer. Justin had slammed his car into the tree out of desperation and maybe, though he wouldn't have admitted it to himself, as retribution for all she'd done to him. Because even though she loved him, they both knew her love wasn't equal to his.

The Kaplan house was full of people, but freezing. Lily followed her parents from the foyer to the living room and watched the sea of black-clad bodies swallow her father, then her mother. She headed in the opposite direction and up the stairs. But as she neared Justin's bedroom, she heard arguing.

"You have to tell me where you went after my house."

Lily recognized Hazel's husky voice.

"Home! I said that already."

And Jonah's nasally pitch.

Lily walked into Justin's room to find Hazel on the bed, her freckled palms pressed into the mattress, her body angled forward like a runner at the starting gun. Jonah glared, his furious blue eyes full of tears.

"You're evil," he hissed at Lily. "Evil!" He was about to charge, but Hazel grabbed him and led him from the room. Lily heard bickering, followed by a slamming door. Hazel returned alone and collapsed on the bed. "How long were you in the hall, Lily?"

"Not long."

"Right. Sure."

"No, really, I —"

Hazel shook her head. "It doesn't matter."

For a moment they were silent. Lily stood awkwardly in the middle of the room.

"It's so claustrophobic downstairs." Hazel frowned. "And all those covered mirrors freak me out."

Lily had noticed the large front hall mirror draped with a dark sheet, though she didn't understand the reason for it. "Yeah, it's pretty creepy," she said.

"You Catholics do plenty of weird shit, too."

"I wasn't . . . I just meant . . ." But Lily knew better than to argue; Hazel had a way of twisting things.

"You're not afraid of Justin's bed, are you?" Hazel flipped onto her stomach.

Lily hesitated, but the older girl smiled with such warmth that she lay down beside her. She saw how many hundreds of freckles Hazel had, how her nostrils flared when she breathed. She realized Hazel must have spent countless nights on this bed, reading Justin's books, and breathing in the sweaty-sweet scent of his room. Lily couldn't even claim a year. "I feel like we're not supposed to be in here," she said.

"That's strange. Of all people, I thought you'd feel the most comfortable."

Lily flushed.

"I mean, you're kind of a big deal to Justin's parents, being his first and only girlfriend. And it's obviously not your fault that Justin was on his way to your house. But what I really want to know," Hazel said, propping herself on a freckled elbow, "is how he was feeling that night when he got into the car. I mean, if he was in any kind of severe distress, you would have known about it. Right?"

Lily's heart was pounding so hard she was sure Hazel could see it.

The girls eyed each other for a long, uncomfortable moment. Then Hazel jumped off the bed. "I'm starving. I think we need some rugelach."

Lily nodded. She felt like she'd completed an important test but had no idea whether she had passed.

The Morgans drove home, and as they descended the steep hill toward their house, the awful demon blazed up before them. The Studio Girls must have drawn the image, Lily thought, because her father had expelled them. They'd been responsible for the locker vandalism, too. It made so much sense now. They didn't give a shit about exposing the hypocrisy of the Community Code, or the superficial nature of teenage social interaction, or anything else. They didn't care who they hurt or even what message they were sending. They simply liked the idea of making a statement.

Elliott parked in the driveway, but Lily was halfway to the house before she realized that her parents were still sitting inside the Lexus.

She let herself in, picked up the mail, and shuffled through it. Among the bills and magazines was a letter with her name on it. In her room, she undressed, hanging up the jacket, sweater, and skirt and slipping off her dark stockings. She removed her bra and underwear and looked at her reflection in the closet mirror. Her nipples were pink as the wallpaper, and down below, what was once the fairest hair of all was the color of dirty water.

She pulled on pajamas and then turned her attention to the envelope, mailed from Boston. The return address read, *Morrissey and Associates*.

Dear Ms. Morgan,

I am terribly sorry I have neglected to contact you for so many months. A number of Mrs. Morgan's files were misplaced, and only now have I fully put her affairs in order. Your grandmother has left monies in the amount of $75,000 for you. She asked our offices to help you with any financial management you may need, but has specified that you — and you alone — are the sole executor of this sum. Again, forgive me for the long delay. Please be in touch with any questions.

Sincerely,
Thomas Morrissey Esq.

Lily read the letter twice. Halfway through the second reading, she heard the front door open and shut. She stiffened. But her parents were not in the room with her. They could not see her. Nor could they stop her. She turned on her computer and started searching the websites of boarding schools in California, and Florida, and even Australia — all of them places far away, where the sun burned hot and bright. The application deadlines had already passed, but she was sure that, with enough persistence, she could convince one of them to accept her for the fall.

Jonah

I KNEW VISITING HAZEL was ill considered, but the talk shows always emphasize closure and I believed I needed some. The town had fired her from the Nye Historical Society, so she'd moved into a cramped studio over the Decatur Pub. I went to see her in early June, my penultimate stop before leaving Nye.

In December, I told the police that Hazel was behind the Sonya Stevens hoax, and explained how she had fooled Iris Dupont, Peter McCaffrey, and the other kids. (I omitted how she'd conned me.) Hazel, however, had an arsenal of excuses at the ready. She told the police she'd found the book with the fabricated letters from Edmond Dantes and Thelonius Rex in a drawer at the Historical Society when she first moved in, and claimed it had given her the idea to revive Prisom's Party. But Hazel was very much Lorna Greenburg's daughter. She had the artistic talent to take the myths about Rex and turn them into physical history, creating an authentic-looking artifact. She was certainly disturbed enough to do it. I think we both felt the intermediary years between high school and adulthood were less significant than what had come before. But whereas I was ready to move on when my future beckoned, Hazel was stuck in the world of our childhood, stunted.

I had a preparatory drink and then I walked up the rickety steps to Hazel's apartment. I pressed the buzzer and heard her padding toward the door. I'd expected her to look depressed, possibly unwell, but not as ill as I found her. She'd lost weight. Her once-full cheeks were gaunt, her bare arms too slim. Her freckles looked like the spots of some rare disease.

"Hi," I said. Hazel leaned into the door frame and glowered. I looked beyond her into the apartment gloom. The place smelled like VapoRub and cigarettes. I wasn't sure I'd be able to sit in that fetid air. "I'm leaving town this afternoon. I wanted to see you. Can we take a walk?"

Hazel picked up a blue shawl from the couch and stepped outside, shoeless. We walked down the sloping hill behind the Decatur to a trickling creek. In the glaring summer sun she seemed to exist in only two dimensions, like a paper doll. She laid her shawl on the spindly grass and sat down on it. I sat beside her. We looked at the cold, murky water. Hazel curled and uncurled her freckled toes. I tried not to let those toes distract me.

"How've you been?" I asked. I knew her situation could have been much worse—she'd avoided jail time—but I suspected that the restraining order was punishment enough. She couldn't hide inside Mariana's walls anymore, which meant that the only other place she had to go was her mind. And her mind wasn't well. "Will you stay here for a while?"

"Probably not." She shut her eyes and turned her face to the sun. "I'm thinking about Italy or Greece."

Her interest in the ancient world was fitting, I realized. Hazel lived for the past and glorified the dead: defunct languages, civilizations, people. To her, the dead possessed greater worth than the living. It made total sense that kids like the one Hazel had been, ostracized and shunned, so often gravitated toward Latin. It was as though by resurrecting the language of Julius Caesar, they could claim some of Rome's glory for themselves. Or maybe Caesar was turning in his grave and thinking: *My legacy is being carried forth by* these *losers?*

"The night we went to Veronica Mercy's . . ." I'd been thinking about this a lot since I realized how manipulative Hazel was. "You persuaded her to make that movie of Lily."

Hazel shrugged. "I invented an apprenticeship position, told her what her application video should include, gave her our home address."

"And then you sent a copy of the video to Justin."

"He needed to see Lily for the cipher she was." Hazel smiled faintly into the light.

I remembered the day Iris brought *Marvelous Species* to school. She said Lily had set the book up like a shrine. In her own small way, she'd honored my brother. "I don't think we were fair to Lily," I said.

"I've been telling you this for months now, Jonah, but you won't listen. People act within their nature. Lily didn't have to participate in Veronica's video or say those things about your brother. But she did."

I swallowed hard. "Your plan didn't work, Hazel."

Hazel shrugged again.

"Why did you show it to me that night?"

"I don't know."

"Jesus, Hazel. You knew how I felt about you. You knew I was already out of control."

"You want to blame the accident on me? Oh, Jonahlah . . ." She shook her head like she felt very sorry for me indeed. I was starting to feel disgusted with her. Only then I imagined her standing at the top of Church Street, looking down at Justin's dead body. Many of us stood at various points in between—me and Lily and Veronica and who knows how many others. So maybe Hazel was right about people acting within their natures. The avalanche had started with her, but we'd helped more than a little to push it along.

Hazel left me by the riverbank. Like me, she was host to her own emotional parasites, but she'd allowed the hostile microbes to gnaw her thin. I refused to waste away like that. I was managing my illness, or attempting to.

I departed my paltry square of grass and drove to my parents' house, where I returned the box I'd taken from Justin's room so many months before. Then I turned my Sube toward the highway. I had pulled out of the UMass entomology project and instead was going to see my parents in the Cook Islands. They wanted to know how long I'd be visiting, and I told them the trip was not a visit, but a next step.

"A next step toward what?" my mother wanted to know. I had no answer.

I wasn't sure I'd miss teaching. I'd resigned in May as one of Mariana's most well-respected teachers. But I'd also failed in numerous ways. I'd returned to prove my own hypothesis — that given the right support, students would learn to think for themselves. But one cannot teach according to the scientific method. A lab experiment is centered on a control; in teaching there are only variables.

Exposing Prisom's Party didn't change or even improve the school's culture. As far as I could tell, most of the kids remained as stressed out, misguided, and socially stratified as ever. Iris had become dangerously attached to me — way beyond what the odd experience we'd shared in December would account for. All through second semester, Hazel's warning plagued me: *Young girls get carried away. You need to watch yourself.* I feared that Iris had turned me into a symbol of something — I couldn't imagine what — when I was only a teacher, and a flawed one at that. The only way I knew how to address the problem with Iris was my special approach of tough no-love.

But like so many of the tactics I'd tried with my students, this one didn't work. The look of sadness on her face as she took the exam from me was too painful. It was wrenching. She deserved *something* from me, a small gift as she continued her journey and fought her battles. What I finally offered was inadequate. It was, simply, an admission of my gratitude. But it was real, and I hope she saw that.

Only after the school year ended did I start to understand how extraordinary Iris was. The difference between her and almost everyone else at Mariana was that she understood the paradox of preparatory school: that preparing and doing are mutually exclusive states. She knew that a student who spent his time getting ready to live and to learn wasn't doing either. In a way, the idea of prep school flouts evolution itself. From single-cell organisms to human beings, each stage of life is an active and living moment. Nature in a state of preparation makes no sense.

Of course, in some distant future, the high-powered prep school will become obsolete. Centuries from now, students will spend their days in isolated pods having lessons transmitted into their brains via satellite. Until that time, kids will have to learn how to survive in the teeming culture that is a high school. We all desire immunity, the ability to deflect pain the way some microorganisms do. We want to shrug off radiation like a halophile or survive crushing pressure like a piezophile. But we are only human beings. My brother was not the weakling I once thought him to be. In his few years on this earth, he represented the very best of his species: someone who failed often and continued to strive. Moving forward, I aspire to be more like him.

Iris

AROUND THE TIME that Peter was expelled from school, a girl from my bio class said, "You've got to hand it to him: he has integrity." In the strictest sense of the word, she was right. When it came to Prisom's Party, Peter showed total unity. He refused to give up the names of his Party co-conspirators; not even the police could break him. Unlike me, Peter put his morals (as screwed up as they may have been) before his fear of punishment. A small part of me admired him for that.

The remaining members of Prisom's Party remained anonymous. Second semester, I couldn't walk through the halls of school without scrutinizing the faces streaming by and wondering if I was looking at Julia, or O'Brien, or Syme. Getting through the day was like slogging through four-foot snowdrifts. I waited anxiously for my confession video to appear online or in the news. I had nightmares in which Hazel's freckles were billions of mites swarming over her body and mine. In other dreams, Dalia sat naked in a tub of bright red water, the stitches on her wrists matching those across my face. *Come join me in the bath*, Dalia said. *The water's fine.*

My parents grew worried. They took me to a new shrink. They whisked me off to Florida for spring break, hoping a vacation might relieve my symptoms. It didn't. I'd misjudged all of the people who were supposed to care about me, but Mr. Kaplan hurt the most. Maybe

I really was a naïve kid, dumb to believe that adults would ever treat me as one of their own. But I'd learned my lesson. Grief is personal; you can't share it with anyone.

The end of school was a tremendous relief. When the weather warmed up, I spent my afternoons reading on the Morgans' front porch and, after dinner, watching the fireflies glow and fade in the dusk. When you live in a big city, where the summers are all scorching pavement and rippling heat, you forget what it's like to have a million green leaves breathing overhead. But I wasn't sad to be leaving Nye. I couldn't wait to be alone in the middle of Boston, making my way around town. The *Globe* news desk was giving me a press pass, and when I called a source, I'd be able to say, "Iris Dupont calling from the *Boston Globe.*" Just thinking about this conjured up thrilling images of cover stories and full-page spreads adorned with the hottest accessory of all — my byline.

A few days before my internship began, I was sitting on the Morgans' porch swing when a familiar car pulled up. Peter. I hadn't seen him or heard from him since first semester. I'd tried not to think about him. My feelings about what had happened between us were a maze of arguments that circled back on themselves and generally made my brain hurt.

It was dark, and Peter didn't see me until he'd made it halfway up the walk. He stopped and we looked at each other. Then he came to stand at the steps below the porch. He hadn't changed at all in five months. I imagined us lying together on that ratty Outpost mattress. I felt his fingertips sweeping along my arm. I wished I didn't want him to be here. I started rocking in the swing, just enough to hear the chains creak overhead.

"Did you really believe all that stuff about Edmond Dantes and Thelonius Rex?" I said.

"Didn't you? Isn't that why you went along with us?"

I didn't want to answer this question.

"We wanted Mr. Kaplan to leave us alone, Iris. We didn't know Hazel had personal motives. When she brought us into Prisom's Party two years ago, all of our activities concerned current events. We never dealt with the past at all. And then . . ."

"And then cue Iris Dupont, the unwitting ingénue."

"Come on, Iris. Give yourself some credit."

"Why?" I snorted. "I trusted Hazel and she funneled everything I told her in confidence straight to all of you."

Peter nodded, and I clenched my teeth to keep the tears from spilling out.

"But you were so much worse than me," I said, my mouth quivering. "You gave Hazel the documents I found in Mr. Kaplan's car. You *published* the *Devil's Advocate* about Justin Kaplan's death. That story was so punishing, Peter. Imagine if you'd lost someone so close to you. Imagine how reading a story like that would feel!" I was crying now, but I didn't care. Peter hadn't lost anybody, so he couldn't understand.

"That paper was supposed to be about Jimmy Cardozi's money. I swear to you, Iris. O'Brien was in the middle of writing copy about the theft when Hazel came in with her own article. She said we had to switch up the stories."

"And you let her do it."

His face glowed with an emotion that resembled shame. But I didn't believe Peter felt any of that.

"What were we supposed to do? We trusted her. She changed our lives, pulled us out of our pitiful, weak existences, and—"

"Stop it. Just stop it!" I shook my head, hoping I could deflect the words from my ears. It hurt too much, hearing him talk about how Hazel used him. Knowing how she'd used me.

"You know your conscience isn't clear either," Peter said. "I hardly think Murrow would have found you innocent beyond a reasonable doubt."

These days when I thought about Murrow, I imagined us as adults living at the same historical moment, sitting side by side in some journalists' watering hole, our sleeves rolled up, laughing about the characters we'd interviewed that day. Our conversations were never serious or heavy; we knew we were doing the valuable work of democracy, and that was enough.

I was smiling through my tears, and Peter was clearly confused by the emotional mash-up. He frowned and said, "Look, I just came over to give you this." He thrust a small plastic case through the porch railings. "This is the only copy, so you don't need to worry about any surprise attacks."

I turned the case over in my hands. It was unlikely that Lily had sat on this same swing with her copy of *Sacrificial Lamb* when she decided not to destroy the video, but I liked to entertain the possibility. I'd despised her after watching that movie. I'd believed many horrible things about her. But after my confessional against Mr. Kaplan, I knew I'd pegged Lily wrong. I, too, had become lost in a moral maze where the opposite of up was wrong and the reverse of down was right. Because the girl reading the Party's script resembled me, and sounded like me, and might actually have *been* me in spurts and flashes. But she wasn't the flesh-and-blood me. The consistent Iris Dupont. I guessed it was much the same with Lily.

I looked up to ask Peter why he'd decided not to release my confessional, but he was already heading back to his car. I watched him get in, and after he drove away I watched the place where his car had been. Then I went into Lily's room and slipped my confessional in beside *Sacrificial Lamb*.

Later that night, I was in the middle of packing for Boston when my mother called me downstairs. I slumped over the suitcase and pretended I hadn't heard. In the lead-up to my departure she'd instituted a regimen of daily heart-to-hearts, and now, after Peter's visit, I didn't feel like talking to anybody.

"Sit down," my mom said when I finally dragged myself into the living room. She and my dad were on opposite ends of the couch, looking serious.

"We've been talking," my father said, "and we'd like to know how you'd feel about attending Blessed Sacrament in the fall." I watched my parents shrink back just a little, as though afraid I'd throw a lamp at them.

"BS? You mean of the hideous tartans and diabolical nuns?"

"It's just a suggestion," my mother said.

A suggestion, as opposed to a dictum? This was an unexpected play from the Dupont duo. "Can I think about it?"

"Absolutely," they said in unison, their faces slack with the relief of people who have just watched the tornado slam into somebody else's house.

I returned to my suitcases. *Blessed Sacrament,* I thought, sitting on Lily's antacid carpet. *Now there's a challenge.* BS wouldn't be thrilled to enroll a girl like me, mired as I was in scandal. From what I could tell, they didn't like their young ladies ballsy or ambitious. They certainly wouldn't like a fifteen-year-old who looked as though her face had picked a fight with a scimitar. Just wait until their paper, the *Blessed Sacrament Confessional,* learned about me. Headline: MARIANA'S MAGDALENE! Subhead: IRIS TO DEFLOWER OUR HOLY HALLS.

Iris

JULY 2013

THE T RUMBLED up and out of its minelike tunnel and into the afternoon sun. I'd been riding underground for thirty minutes, since I boarded at Harvard Square, and the world wavered obliquely through the train windows. I squinted against the glare and, feeling suddenly vulnerable, pressed *Marvelous Species* against my chest. I'd wrapped the book in tissue paper, but now the crinkling stuff seemed horribly insufficient as protection. I ordered myself to relax. I'd schlepped this book all around Mariana Academy, practically waving it in people's faces — I was almost as bad as Chris Coon, who'd gone an entire year with the *Fountainhead* fused to his back pocket. But Mariana was tiny, like one of those miniature self-sustaining ecosystems that Mr. Kaplan once disparaged as "expensive windowsill knickknacks, for science dilettantes." I was in a real city now, and this trip marked the book's last hour in my care.

I was traveling on the B Line toward Boston College. In the month I'd been here, I'd been terrified that a *Globe* assignment or personal mission would send me back to Beacon Hill and, worse, to Dalia's old street. I'd fled death like everyone else: Dalia's parents, who'd sold their house in the weeks after her funeral; my parents, who'd whisked me off to the mountains; and Lily, who'd vanished from Nye after Justin's accident. Of course, these migrations accomplished very little; when you left dead people behind, their ghosts simply packed up and followed you out the door.

The car emptied considerably when it surfaced to street level, and I watched the streets slide by: the monochromatic apartment buildings, rows of parked cars, and occasionally a train moving in the opposite direction. We entered the suburbs, and gray brick gave way to leafy green, thick foliage that presented the illusion of wilderness. Almost exactly a year before, my mother and I had left Boston for Nye, our new home on the nameless mountain. I'd been so many things then that I wasn't now: frightened, overconfident, dependent, grief-stricken. Well, maybe the grief was still lurking inside of me, but I felt differently about it now. Grief never really goes away. It becomes part of you, takes up permanent residence inside your heart. This doesn't mean you can't ever be happy again. It just means the space allotted for feeling happy is smaller. *Isn't that right, Murrow?* I thought, now more out of habit than conversation. Before coming to Boston for the summer, I'd taken his picture down from Lily's wall and stowed it away. Its presence had begun to embarrass me, a constant reminder of Hazel's conviction that a person alone was a person unseen. But Hazel was wrong. To be visible, I didn't need her, or Mr. Kaplan, or Edward Murrow, or even Dalia.

My train reached the end of the line and I climbed down, still holding tightly to *Marvelous Species.* I didn't want to give it up, but it wasn't mine to keep. Less than a week before, my parents informed me that Lily and her husband were back from Africa, and that she'd be teaching public health at Boston College in the fall. They suggested it would be "fun" for me to meet the woman whose room I'd been inhabiting, though I suspect they were really looking for an adult in the area to check up on me. They gave me her email, courtesy of Elliott Morgan. I had an awful time composing the message. I felt oddly compelled to present myself as witty and sophisticated, but every draft read like bad high school poetry, which is to say like high school poetry. After an hour of revising, I deleted the pretentious copy and simply told Lily that I would very much like to meet her — and that I had something of hers that I thought she'd want in her new home.

Her response was prompt, if terse. *You're welcome to visit. I'll be home this Sunday.* So now here I was, walking down Lily's street, approaching her front door. I pressed the doorbell and swallowed hard, my fingers trembling around the spine of *Marvelous Species*. I thought I'd extracted myself from Lily's world, but now, on the verge of meeting her face to face, I realized that Lily—and her complicated past—was also embedded in *me*. Once she opened that door, we'd become even more closely entwined.

I heard footsteps and the door before me seemed to shiver, like it, too, was waiting, expectant.

I hoped that returning *Marvelous Species* would be more than a painful reminder to Lily of what she'd lost and left behind, so perfectly preserved, in Nye. I hoped it would allow me to share the events of this year and Lily's inadvertent role in them. One day, I hoped she'd be open to hearing Mr. Kaplan's side of the story. But not today. Mr. Kaplan was halfway across the world and silent. So I would have to speak up instead. I would report the truths that he could not, tell the facts as *I* knew them. The story that I clutched to myself, more tightly than the book in my hands, was ugly and strange. But it was also marvelous. It was mine.

Acknowledgments

I am indebted to my incredible agent, Mollie Glick, who gave me the confidence to pursue fiction seriously and who pushed me to write the best second and third drafts of this novel that I possibly could write. I am also in awe of my equally talented editor, Jenna Johnson, whose energy and commitment toward this book have been unfailing. Mollie and Jenna, you are amazing ladies.

Thanks to the team at Houghton Mifflin Harcourt, especially Summer Smith and Hannah Harlow, for getting so firmly behind *Gadfly*. Katya Rice, you are a copyeditor extraordinare. Thank you to my colleagues at the School of the Arts for bringing so much thoughtfulness to our workshops and to my friends and professors at the J-School, without whom there would be no Iris. I owe great thanks to *The Outer Reaches of Life* by John Postgate, *Murrow: His Life and Times* by A. M. Sperber, and *Edward R. Murrow and the Birth of Broadcast Journalism* by Bob Edwards. Politics and Prose Bookstore, thank you for existing.

Risa Berkower and Marian Makins, your endless support and brainstorming sessions proved invaluable. Emily Day and Laura Jean Moore, I can't thank you enough for your constant motivation. David Goldberg, Megan Palmer, Dan Sharfman, Jon Cooper, and Jen Last, your memories and insights helped bring Justin Kaplan to life. Danny Miller, if you hadn't been such a bad-ass in high school, this book would not have existed. Rich Cooper and Judy Areen, I am grateful to have you in my life. This book is especially a tribute to you.

Of course, I am indebted to my parents for their unquestioning love and support. You stood by me even though I treated this manuscript like a classified government document.

And, finally, to Jason, my husband, who never suspected that he'd be applying his editing talents to fiction. Working on this book together has been amazing. I am so lucky to have you as my co-scribbler.